THE GYPSY MORPH

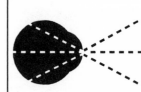

This Large Print Book carries the
Seal of Approval of N.A.V.H.

THE GYPSY MORPH

TERRY BROOKS

THORNDIKE PRESS
A part of Gale, Cengage Learning

Detroit • New York • San Francisco • New Haven, Conn • Waterville, Maine • London

GALE
CENGAGE Learning

LIBRARY OF CONGRESS CATALOGING-IN-PUBLICATION DATA

Brooks, Terry.
   The gypsy morph / by Terry Brooks.
     p. cm. — (Genesis of Shannara) (Thorndike Press large print core)
   ISBN-13: 978-1-4104-1125-9 (alk. paper)
   ISBN-10: 1-4104-1125-7 (alk. paper)
   1. Shannara (Imaginary place)—Fiction. 2. Twenty-first century—Fiction 3. Regression (Civilization)—Fiction. 4. Imaginary wars and battles—Fiction 5. Good and evil—Fiction. 6. Magic—Fiction. 7. Elves—Fiction. 8. Large type books. I. Title.
PS3552.R6596G97 2008
813'.54—dc22   2008036831

Published in 2008 by arrangement with The Ballantine Publishing Group, a division of Random House, Inc.

FOR ANNE SIBBALD

Agent and friend, the Queen of the Silver River

ONE

Wills walked the empty corridors of Hell, looking for the code. He walked these same corridors every day, all day, searching, thinking that there had to be someplace he had overlooked and that on this day he would find it. But he never did. And knew in his heart that he never would.

It was over. For all of them. In more ways than one. The others were already a long time dead. The entire command, wiped out by whatever virus had wormed its way in, sliding down through the air vents past the filters and cleaners and medico screens and whatever other safeguards the builders had installed all those years ago. They hadn't all died at once, of course. Eight of them had, and that was now more than two years ago. At least, that's how long he thought it had been. Time was uncertain. The rest had died one by one, some sickening right away, others staying healthy and providing false hope that a few might survive.

7

But none of them had. Only him. He had no idea why. He had no sense of being different from the others, but obviously he was. Some small genetic trait. Some antibody peculiar to him. Or maybe he was mistaken and it was just plain old luck. He was alive; they were dead. No sense to any of it. No prize awarded to the last man standing. Just a mystery without a solution.

Abramson and Perlo had been the last to go. If you didn't count Major whatever-her-name-was. Anders, Andrews, something like that. He couldn't remember anymore. Anyway, there was never much hope for her. She got sick and stayed sick. By the time she died, she had already been dead for weeks in every way that mattered, her brain fried, memory emptied, mouth drooling. Just lying on the floor making weird sounds and staring at them. Just gibbering about nothing, her eyes wide and rolling, her face all twisted. He would have put a stop to it if he could have made himself do so. But he couldn't. It took Perlo to do that. Perlo hadn't harbored the same reservations he had. He hadn't liked her anyway, he told them. Even when she hadn't been sick, when she was normal, she was irritating. So it was easy, putting the gun to her head and pulling the trigger. She probably would have thanked him if she could have, he said afterward.

Two weeks later, Perlo was dead, too, shot

8

with the same gun. He'd decided he couldn't stand the waiting and pulled the trigger a second time. Left the gun with an almost full clip for the other two, an unspoken suggestion that they might be wise to follow him.

They hadn't taken the hint. Abramson had lasted almost seven months longer, and he and Wills made a good pair in that short time. They were both midwestern boys married young, gone into the service of their country, officer training, fast track to promotion, full of patriotic duty and a sense of pride in wearing the uniform. Both had been pilots before assuming command positions. All that was dead and gone, but they liked talking about how it had been when things were better. They liked remembering because it made them feel that even though things had turned out the way they had, there had been a reason for sticking with it, a purpose to their lives.

It was hard for Wills to remember what that purpose was, now. Once Abramson was gone there had been no one to discuss it with, and over time the nature of the reason had eroded in the silence of the complex. Sometimes he sang or talked to himself, but that wasn't the same as having someone else there. Rather, it made him think of all the stories of prisoners who went slowly mad in solitary confinement, left alone with themselves and the sound of their own voice for too many months. Or too many years. It would be years for him if nothing changed, if he didn't find anyone, if no one came.

Major Adam Wills. That was who he had been, who the military would say he still was, serving his country deep in the bowels of the earth, a quarter mile underground beneath tons of rock and steel-reinforced concrete, somewhere in the middle of the Rocky Mountains. Where he had been now for five long years, waiting.

He thought about that word. *Waiting.* He stopped walking and stood in the center of one of the endless corridors and thought about it. *Waiting.* For what? It seemed to change with the passing of time. At first, he had been *waiting* for the wars to be over. Then he had been *waiting* for someone to come to relieve those on duty in the missile command center who were left alive. Then he had been *waiting* to be let out because he couldn't get out if someone in authority, someone who could tell him it was time to leave, didn't key the locks to the elevators from the surface.

For a long time after he knew that there might be no one left in authority, he had simply been waiting for his transmitter signals to raise a response from any source. He no longer used a secure code. He simply opened all channels and broadcast *mayday.* He knew what was happening aboveground. The cameras told him much of the story. A bleak, barren countryside, a few wandering bands of what appeared to be raiders, a handful of creatures he had never seen before and hoped never to see again, and endless days of sunshine and no rain. Colorado had always been dry, but never like this. It had to rain sooner or later, he kept telling himself.

Didn't it?

Waiting for it to rain.

The government had been all but obliterated even before he had been sent to Deep Rock, the nickname given to the missile command complex. He was still on the surface then, stationed at a base in North Dakota, living in military housing with his family. Washington had been taken out in the first strike, and most of the East Coast cities shortly after. The environment was already in upheaval, huge portions of the country all but uninhabitable. Terrorists were at work. Plague had begun to spread. His last orders had sent him here, joining the others who had been dispatched to the bunkers and the redoubts and the protected complexes that honeycombed the country. A general from the National Command Authority was issuing the orders by then and not just to them but to the whole country. The orders had been grim and everyone had known that things were bad, but they had also known that they would get through it. There had been camaraderie, a sense of sharing a disaster where everyone would have to help everyone else. No one had doubted that they would survive, that they could withstand the worst.

After all, Americans always had. No matter how bad it had gotten, they had managed to find a way. They would this time, too. They were infused with pride and confidence, the certainty that they had the training, the skills, and the determination that were needed. They had even accepted without question that they would have to leave their families behind.

Wills smiled despite himself. What blind fools they had been.

He had quit believing when he heard the last radio broadcasts, heard the descriptions of mass hysteria, and listened to the final pleas and desperate prayers of the few reporters and announcers still on the air. The destruction was complete and total and worldwide. No one had been spared. Armed strikes, chemical warfare, plague infestation, environmental collapse, terrorist attacks — a checklist of assorted forms of madness that proved overwhelming. Millions were dead and millions more dying. Hundreds of millions worldwide. Entire cities had been obliterated. Governments were gone, armies were gone, everything even faintly resembling order was gone. He had tried to reach his family at the base in North Dakota, but there had been no response. After a while, he accepted that there never would be. They were gone, too — his wife, his two boys, his parents, all of his aunts and uncles and cousins and maybe everyone else he had ever known.

It began to feel like everyone was gone except for those few hunkered down in Deep Rock, waiting their turn to go, too.

Which, of course, had arrived all too soon.

Wills walked on, walked on, walked on. He had no destination, no particular route, and no plan. He walked to have something to do. Even though the complex had only eight rooms, not counting storage lockers and the cold room. Even though there were only three short corridors that, when added together, measured no more than a hundred yards. He carried his handheld receiver, which was linked to the communications center, which in turn was linked to the satellite system. It was a waste of time, but he carried it out of habit. Someone might call. You never knew.

At the cold room, he stopped and stared at the heavy iron doors. He imagined what lay behind them, but only for a moment, because that was all he could bear. Seventeen men and women, stacked like cordwood in an eight-by-ten space. Stacked with the perishable food, which had long since perished. He couldn't bear thinking about what was happening to the bodies, even at the freezing temperatures the cooling system maintained.

He hadn't gone in there since he had added Abramson to the pile, and he was pretty sure he would never go in there again. What was the point?

Still, he stood at the doors and stared at them for a long time, his mind conjuring dark images. In the old days, this wouldn't have happened; they wouldn't have all been grouped together where a virus could wipe them out. They would have been assigned to a dozen different command centers. You wouldn't have found more than two or three staffing any one, each center responsible for only a handful of silos. But near the end, when it became clear to someone in authority that an enemy strike was imminent, they had established this base, believing a central command center necessary. It had become home to dozens of teams moving in and out over a twenty-year period, each waiting for the call. His group of nine had been the last, but the team before his, the one on which Abramson served, had been unable to leave. The National Command Authority had decided to seal them in as a precaution. Rotation of personnel was temporarily suspended.

Just until conditions improved.

When he walked on again, he did so with less purpose, his head lowered. He should do something, but he couldn't think what. He wanted out of there badly, but he couldn't manage it by himself. Not unless he found the code he was searching for, the code that would activate the elevators and open the outer doors. That was the way the complex was constructed, a safeguard against infiltration by unauthorized personnel. The military thought of everything. He grinned. Sure, they did. They just overlooked the possibility that those inside might not be able to get out if the code was lost.

Or maybe they hadn't overlooked it. Maybe they just didn't care.

As commanding officer, Aroñez had carried the code coming in. He was the one who knew it, no one else. After gaining them entrance he had put it away, and everyone had forgotten about it. Except that when he caught the virus, he didn't think to pass it on. Or maybe he did think and decided against it. Cold and calculating Aroñez — it was possible. He might have. In any case he was dead within twenty-four hours, and the secret of the code's whereabouts had died with him.

Except that Wills knew that it had to be written down somewhere, a safeguard that Aroñez would not have disregarded.

So he searched. Each day, all day. Endlessly.

He wasn't sure why. Even if he could get out, what would he do? He was miles from anything and had no direct knowledge of where anyone was. His family? His home? His superiors at the National Command

Authority? Gone. Oh, there might be someone left somewhere, but it was unlikely to be anyone who could issue orders, who could take his place, who would know what needed doing.

It was unlikely to be anyone who could lift from his shoulders the burden he bore, anyone to whom he could pass the pair of red keys he wore on a chain about his neck.

He reached down to finger their irregular shapes through the fabric of his shirt. His and Abramson's. Well, not really Abramson's. Abramson had taken his from Reacher after he died, because someone needed to have it, just in case it was required. When Abramson was gone, Wills had taken that one, too.

Just in case.

Yeah, just in case.

As he fingered the keys, he thought about what was once the unthinkable. Even though he knew he shouldn't. Even though thinking about it was dark and terrifying.

He thought about the missiles.

He thought about launching them.

He could do so. Had done so, back in the beginning when the general was running the country. The general had the code and had authorized the launches. A handful of surgical strikes against countries and bases that, in turn, were targeting them. Wills had used the key together with another man he couldn't remember. What was his name — Graham or

16

Graves, a captain maybe? They had turned their keys together to open the switches and activate the triggers. They had waited as the trajectories had been punched in and the release mechanisms activated. Armed and ready, the warheads had been dispatched from miles away in a silence that within their underground command center was deafening.

But that was the end of it. There had been nothing since. The general had never contacted them again. No one had. The communications board had gone silent and stayed silent. The cameras had shown them snatches of life moving on the surface, much of it strange and frightening, but communications had ceased. They were left to wait, cocooned in a vacuum of fear and doubt, of non-information and empty hope.

But there were dozens of missiles still active and available. Dozens, all armed with nuclear warheads, some here in their mountain silos, some as far away as what remained of the coasts. The navy was gone and the air force with it. No ships sailed and no planes flew — at least not those of a military nature. Everything that was left that was usable was in the silos. But that was enough to take out anything.

Or everything.

He could launch a missile, just to see. He could choose his own target, something that needed taking out, obliterating. He had that power. He had the red keys and the knowledge. The retinal scans had been modified long ago to accept a single key holder using both keys for just this sort of doomsday situation. All it required was activating a remote device situated at the National Command Authority, and that had been done long ago. The machinery here no longer responded to other command centers, if there were any. It was autonomous and functionally independent. It did what its users told it to do with no need for anything but the knowledge and the keys, and he had both.

But what would he blow up?

And why?

He closed his eyes against the darkness of the suggestion. Sending more nuclear warheads only fed the madness. He would not be a part of it. Even though it was tempting at times and he had the means, he would not.

He was better than that.

He walked back to the command complex's nerve center and sat in his chair and stared at the monitors and readouts. Even though the people were gone, the machines worked on, powered by the solar collectors that functioned aboveground, doing what they had been created to do. He watched the monitors sweeping the empty vista of the rocks, and the readouts reporting that the weather and climate were unchanged. He fiddled for a time with the communications board, sweeping the signal range for a contact, finding nothing.

He looked at the framed picture of his wife and boys where it sat on the narrow shelf in front of him, always visible from any part of his workstation.

Then suddenly he bent forward, lowered his head, squeezed his eyes tightly shut, clasped his hands in front of him, and began to pray, mouthing the words softly.

The Lord is my shepherd; I shall not want.
He maketh me to lie down in green pastures;
He leadeth me beside the still waters.
He restoreth my soul.
He leadeth me in the path of righteousness for His name's sake.
Yea, though I walk through the shadow of the valley of death,
I will fear no evil . . .

He stopped abruptly, the words catching in his throat, lodging there and refusing to emerge. He could not finish.

"Please," he whispered into the darkness behind his closed eyes. "Please, don't let me die here."

Two

Angel Perez walks the hot, dusty streets of her barrio in East LA, her small hand clutching Johnny's. She hovers beneath the reassuring mantle of his protective shadow, feeling safe and warm. She does not look up at him, because holding his hand is enough to let her know that he is there, looking after her, staying close. The world around her is peaceful and quiet, a reflection of her sense of security, a testament to what being with Johnny means. People are sitting on their stoops and leaning out their windows. Their haggard, worried faces brighten at Johnny's appearance. Hands wave and voices call out. Johnny's presence is welcomed by everyone.

She glances up at the sky. It is cloudless and blue, free of the smoke and ash that have plagued it for days. Months. Years. There have been gang activities all through the region, much of it ending in fighting and looting. But Johnny keeps all that away from this neighborhood, and today there is no evidence of it anywhere. The clear sky and the silent air are proof of a fresh cleansing. She smiles, thinking of it. She wonders if perhaps something good is coming their way. She feels that it might be possible, that a turning of the wheel of fortune is about to occur.

"I am so happy," she says to Johnny.

He says nothing in response, but words are not necessary when she feels the gentle squeeze of his hand over hers. He understands. He is happy, too.

They walk for a long time, content just to be with each other, like father and daughter, like family. She thinks of them this way, of herself as his daughter, him as her father. There is more to family than shared blood. There is trust and friendship and commitment. She is only eight years old, but she already knows this.

They pass out of the wider streets and into some that are narrower, moving toward the edge of the neighborhood. She is not allowed to go beyond the boundaries that mark their barrio, but he takes her to those boundaries often so that she will know where she is allowed to go in his absence. He travels outside the barrio, but he does not talk of where he goes or what he does. When she asks, he only smiles and says it is necessary. He is her father in all but blood, her best friend and her protector, but there is much about him that is a mystery.

At a corner marked by houses with broken-out windows and crumbling walls, they encounter members of a gang. She knows what they are from their markings, but she does not know their names. Johnny stops at once, confronting them. There are five in all. Their clothes are ragged and dirty, their faces hard and dangerous. They do not have weapons in their hands, but she knows they have them hidden in their clothes. They stare at Johnny for a long time, barely sparing her a glance. Then they turn aside and disappear into the ruins of the buildings.

Johnny does that to people. She has seen it over and over. If they are like these sad creatures, they back away. There is something in his eyes that tells them what will happen if they don't. There is a presence about him that warns of offering challenge. Johnny never needs to say anything much to those who pose a threat. They instinctively know what they risk and are likely to lose.

The barrio ends at a forest of half walls, steel beams, and rubble piles, all that remains of what was once a warehouse district. The sun beats down on blocks and blocks of silent, empty ruins. Nothing lives here. Nothing will sustain life.

"Walk with me, *pococito*," Johnny whispers to her.

He has never taken her beyond this point, so she is surprised at his request. But she does not refuse. She will go anywhere he wants to take her. Her trust in him is complete and unequivocal. She is not afraid.

They thread their way into the maze, winding down narrow passageways that are more alleyways than streets and in some cases not even that. The air is heavy and thick with dust, and it is difficult to breathe. But she does not complain. She ignores her discomfort and walks with him as if everything were as it should be.

Indeed, with Johnny, how could it ever be anything else?

But as their journey through the surreal landscape continues, she becomes aware of a slow darkening of the sky. It happens gradually and for no apparent reason. There are no clouds, no storms approaching. The sun simply begins to fade until their surroundings are wrapped in twilight. If Johnny notices, he is not telling her. He walks steadily ahead, her hand in his, his stride even and unchanged. She keeps pace, but she is looking around now, wondering. It is midday. How can the light be so dim?

Then suddenly Johnny stops, and his hand releases hers. For a moment, she cannot believe he has let go of her. She stands quietly, motionless in the fading light, waiting for him to join hands again. When he does not and when he says nothing, she looks up at him.

He is no longer there.

He has disappeared.

She catches her breath and shudders. How has this happened? How can he have vanished so completely?

Ahead, a shadow figure appears, cloaked and hooded, its features hidden. It does not move, but stands facing her. She does not know what it is, but it makes her feel cold and alone.

"*¿Quién es?*" she calls out, her voice breaking.

The figure says nothing, but starts toward her, moving woodenly through the rubble, cloak billowing out behind it in dark folds. She knows suddenly what it is and what it wants. She knows why Johnny has brought her here and why he has left her.

She waits, already anticipating the inconceivable.

Angel woke suddenly to biting cold and darkness. She lay half buried in a snowdrift, her damaged body stiff and drained of warmth. Her wounds were frozen beneath her clothing and in some places to her clothing, but she could feel almost nothing of the pain. The wind blew in sharp gusts, causing the snow to swirl across the empty landscape in intricate patterns. Particles of ice stung her face where there was still feeling, dancing at the edges of her vision like tiny creatures. Overhead the stars were bright and clear in the cloudless night sky.

She was on the mountain the Elves called Syrring Rise, collapsed in the snow that layered the upper slopes. She had crawled this far after her battle with the demon, seeking to reach the ice caves into which Kirisin and his sister had gone earlier. She had used up the last of her strength to get to where she was, but she already knew that it wasn't enough to save her.

She was dying.

She was amazed at how readily she embraced the fact, how clearly she recognized it. She should have been fighting against it, struggling to break free of its grip. She knew that the Elves might be in terrible danger from the second demon and have need of her. She knew that if she continued to lie there, to fail to rise and go on, she would be unable to help them. But a deep and pervasive lethargy gripped her, discouraging resistance to its immense weight, leaving her content merely to lie there and accept the dark hands reaching out to gather her in.

She saw the cloaked figure in her dream anew, the one the ghost of Johnny had taken her to meet. Death was waiting patiently for her to come, and now she was almost there. She thought again of the four-legged horror that had brought her to this, a thing of chameleon shapes, first a woman with spiky blond hair and finally a monstrous cat, but always a demon with an insatiable need to destroy her.

Which now, it seemed, it had.

She was tired. She was so tired.

25

She could feel the tears gather at the corners of her eyes, then trickle down and freeze on her face.

Her hand gripped the carved surface of her black staff, but she could feel no life in it. The warmth that marked its magic was gone and the runes that signaled its readiness, dark and unresponsive.

What should she do? She could continue to crawl forward through the snow, searching for the ice caves and shelter. But she had no idea where they were, and in the darkness there was nothing to show her the way. Her wounds from the battle had drained her of energy and strength, of willpower and purpose. It all felt so hopeless. She knew it was wrong to feel this way, but she couldn't seem to help herself.

The dream, she thought suddenly, had been a premonition of what was coming. She was going to meet Johnny. She was going to where he waited for her, away from this world, away from the madness.

¿Tienes frío, Angel? she heard him asking from the darkness. Are you cold? *¿Tienes miedo de morirte?* Are you afraid of dying?

"Estoy muy cansado," she whispered. So tired.

She would go to him. She would let go of what held her tethered to this world, to her hopes and plans and sense of obligation to the Word and its order. She had done what

26

she could, and she could do no more.

She closed her eyes and began to drift, the sensation both freeing and welcoming. She floated on the promise of a long, deep sleep that would end with her waking in a better place. With Johnny, once more. Her child's world had been so good with him. That was why he was in her dreams. It was the best of what she remembered of a shattered childhood, of her dead parents, of her world destroyed. Johnny.

Then suddenly he was coming for her, surrounded in a blue light that blazed out of the darkness like a star. She opened her eyes in surprise, the brightness reaching for her, bathing her in warmth. It approached from across the broad expanse of the snowy slope, a steady beam that stretched from far away to draw her in. She lifted her hand in recognition, reaching out to grasp it.

"Angel!" he called to her.

She watched him materialize out of the blowing snow and dark night, shrouded in a heavy-weather cloak, the blue light shining out of his extended hand. She tried to call back to him, but her mouth was dry and the words came out a thin, hoarse whisper.

"Angel!" he repeated.

"Johnny," she managed to respond.

He knelt in front of her. The blue light went out. "Angel, it's Kirisin," he said, bending close, his young face pinched against the cold.

27

She stared at him, trying to find Johnny's face in his young features, failing to do so, and then realizing who it was. Not Johnny. Kirisin. She blinked against her tears. She was back in the real world in an instant, lying cold and exposed on the frozen slopes of Syrring Rise, still alive, but not by much. "Kirisin," she answered.

He brushed snow from her crumpled body, his eyes scanning her bloodstained clothing. "Can you get up?" he asked.

She shook her head. "No."

"I'm going to help you," he told her at once. "You're freezing to death. We have to get you inside, out of the cold."

He worked himself into position that allowed for decent leverage and put an arm under her body to pull her upright. The pain returned to her in a sharp flood as he did so, the wounds opening anew. But he got her into a sitting position, put both arms around her, and heaved her to her feet. She stood leaning into him, unable to move.

"If you can't walk, I will carry you," he told her, his mouth against her ear so that she could hear him through the howl of the wind. "Do you understand me?"

She almost laughed aloud; she knew he was too small for such a task. Nevertheless, she let him try. She brought the black staff around and used it for leverage, putting her weight on it. She found she could take a step by doing so. Then take another step, move the staff, take another step, and so on, while he moved along with her, taking her weight on his shoulders, guiding her with his arms.

"It isn't far," he said, breathing hard.

She nodded. Couldn't speak.

"Is the demon dead?" he asked a moment later. The powdery snow had already formed a layer of white on his hunched body, a cloak of sorts, blown in from the Void. He looked to be a ghost. As she must, too.

She nodded. Dead and gone. "The other one?" she managed to gasp out.

"Dead, too. I'll explain everything, once we're inside."

They labored ahead a few more steps, and then a few more. The snow swirled viciously about them, attacking with tiny, stinging bites. Angel had never been so cold, but at least she was feeling something again. Not everywhere — much of her body was numb and unresponsive — but enough that she could tell herself she was still alive. She thought fleetingly of the dream and of Johnny, leading her from life to death, from this world to the next. It had seemed so real, so close. She had wanted to go with him, to be with him. But now she understood that it was the hurt and the cold that had seduced her. The dream was a trick, a way to steal away her willpower and make her a slave.

She wasn't ready yet for death. Death

29

would have to wait.

But maybe not for long, she added. She had pushed it away, but it lingered at the edges of her vision and in the corners of her ruined body. It would come to claim her quickly enough if she faltered even a little. Kirisin had saved her for the moment, but only that. If she were to survive this, it would take an immense effort on her part.

An effort that only a Knight of the Word could summon.

She stumbled and nearly went down. Kirisin tightened his grip to hold her upright, pausing in his efforts to guide her until she had regained her balance. She straightened, and her gaze locked on the darkness ahead where the side of the mountain was a black wall rising to meet the stars.

"I almost didn't find you," the boy said suddenly, his voice nearly lost in a sudden howling gust of wind. He was struggling for breath, his own strength depleted from his efforts to help her. "I didn't think of it at first. Too new, I guess. But the Elfstones can find anything. Even you."

The blue light, she thought. It was the magic of the Elfstones seeking her out in the shroud of darkness. Kirisin had come looking for her using the Elfstones. Clever boy. She wouldn't have found him on her own, wouldn't have made it out of the snow and cold. He must have realized this.

30

"I had given up," she admitted, her voice a whisper.

He didn't reply, but his grip tightened about her waist. *Don't give up now,* he was saying wordlessly. *I'm here for you.*

Locked together, they staggered ahead into the night.

THREE

Kirisin tied off the last of the stitches closing Angel's many wounds, put aside the needle and thread, and rocked back on his heels, looking down at her still form. She was sleeping, the medicine he had given her to take away the pain and render her unconscious working as it should. Numbed to the point of senselessness, she would have felt almost nothing of the work he had done, which was a good thing, given the extent of her injuries. But when she awoke the pain would be back, and he would have to give her another dose.

He was aware suddenly that he was staring at her nearly naked body, the tatters of her clothing removed to give him better access. He hadn't even thought of it at the time, thinking only about how much blood there was on her body and clothing, how much more she must have lost back on the slopes, and how close to death she probably was.

He pulled the blanket over her and tucked

it in carefully. She would forgive him if she lived.

"Finished?" Simralin asked from one side. She was sitting up now, leaning her back against a rock outcropping.

He glanced over and gave a quick nod. "I've done what I can, Sim. I just hope it's enough."

They were settled well back in the ice caves where the wind and the blowing snow couldn't penetrate. Only the cold refused to be kept at bay, and there was nothing they could do about that. They were dressed in their all-weather gear, and Simralin and Angel were wrapped in their blankets, as well. A pair of the solar lamps had been placed at the perimeter of their little campsite, lighting the dark interior of the caves. A fire would have been better, but there was nothing to burn except for their gear. Simralin had given Kirisin a sun tab, an artificial heat generator, to place under Angel's makeshift bedding, but it wouldn't last for more than three hours and she didn't have any more.

He smiled at his sister. "You seem better."

She grimaced and touched her head experimentally. "Don't be fooled. My head feels like it's been split open. But the bleeding's stopped." She cocked one eyebrow. "Mostly, it's my ego that's injured. It never occurred to me to wonder what Culph was doing here, how he had survived his supposed death, or

33

how he had found us. I just accepted it. I thought it was a miracle of some sort, turned my back on him, and gave him a chance to whack me on the head. Stupid."

"I wasn't any smarter," Kirisin admitted. "When I saw you lying there, bleeding all over everything, I thought you were dead. Even after he said you weren't, I thought you were. I thought he had killed you."

He was still speaking of Culph as if he really had been an Elf and not a demon, still not quite able to banish the image of the old man who had pretended to be their friend. Culph had fooled them all, manipulating them every step of the way on their journey to these caves. From the moment he had caught out Kirisin and Erisha in the basement archives of the Belloruus family home, he had used them. The memory burned like fire, and Kirisin knew it would be a long time before he could lay it to rest.

"He would have killed us both," his sister declared, "if he'd gotten his way with the Loden. Me first, you whenever you had finished whatever it was he was trying to get you to do."

Kirisin shuddered at the memory of how it had felt to be under the demon's control, hypnotized by the movement of the silver cord and rings the latter had dangled in front of him. He had been deep under the other's strange spell, unable to help himself, when

34

Simralin, her consciousness regained after the blow to her head, had stabbed the demon through the leg with her long knife, breaking its concentration and allowing her brother to use the Elfstones to destroy it.

To burn it to ash.

Had he known somehow that the Stones could do this? He thought about it for the first time since it had happened. Subconsciously, perhaps. He couldn't ever be sure, but his instincts had told him that the demon was afraid of the magic, that it had needed him from the beginning in order to control it. Once the boy had broken free of the hypnotic effect of the rings and cord, the magic had been his to summon, and the demon had no defense. That was its undoing.

Old Culph, dead for real this time.

"What was it that it had intended you to do exactly?" his sister pressed.

They had spoken of it only sparingly while he worked to close Angel's wounds after he had gotten her inside the ice caves. Before that, there had been no time for anything. The demon was dead, his sister was unconscious, and their friend and protector was out there alone in the cold and the night, possibly doing battle with the second demon, the four-legged one that had killed Erisha, possibly injured or dying. He didn't stop for more than a few seconds once he had regained his senses. He had wrapped himself in his cloak and rushed back through the tunnels, headed for the slopes of Syrring Rise.

It was odd in retrospect that he had known instantly what he needed to do to find Angel. Having discovered the power of the Elfstones to destroy the demon, he had remembered quickly enough that they were seeking-Stones, as well, capable of finding anything hidden from the user. It didn't have to be a thing; it could be a person. In this case, it could be Angel. He had stood at the mouth of the caves, staring out into the blackness of the mountain's sweep beneath the star-strewn skies, picturing her face and summoning the magic. It was still hot and alive within him, not yet settled back from his battle with the demon, and it had flared to life instantly. At the crest of its bluish glow, he had seen Angel's snow-covered form collapsed on the slope not a hundred yards below where he stood and had gone to her instantly.

After that, after finding her and bringing her back inside, he had found Simralin awake, bloody and groggy but alive. Seeing the condition of the Knight of the Word, she had urged him to go to work on Angel at once. While he did so, his sister had cleaned away the blood from her own injury and bound it with a crude bandage, saying little to him while he labored over Angel, not wanting to distract him. Only once had she spoken to him, and that was to ask about the silver cord and rings. Kirisin had explained what they were intended to do, how they were meant to bind him to the demon and would have done so if she hadn't stabbed it and given Kirisin a chance to use the Elfstones to incinerate it.

"I wish I could have done it myself," she had muttered before settling back and dozing off.

He had worried about her falling asleep with a head injury, but had been too preoccupied with treating Angel to do anything about it until after he had finished. Now and then he had paused in his healing work to call over to her, waking her from her sleep long enough to force her to grunt angrily and mutter something about leaving her alone. But at least he could be certain each time that she was still alive.

Even so, he had been relieved when she finally woke up for good and began speaking with him again.

"He planned to take me back to the Cintra and use the Loden to imprison Arborlon, the Ellcrys, and the Elves," he explained. "Once he had all of the Elves in one place, the demons could take them out at their leisure and do what they wanted with them. He would use me as his tool for accomplishing this, and I don't think anyone would have stopped him. No one would even have known what was happening."

He glanced down at the bulge in his pocket — the bag that contained the Elfstones. "You know something, Sim. I hadn't thought about it before, but the Stones are as dangerous to the Elves as to anyone else. The magic doesn't recognize race or measure intent; it treats everyone the same. All Culph had to figure out was how to find an Elf who could be persuaded to use it."

Simralin's smile was tight and bitter. "Don't be too quick to blame yourself, Little K. None of us understood the rules of the game being played. Not until now. None of us even understood the nature of the magic being put to use. That ghost in the Ashenell, Pancea Rolt Gotrin, she knew. She understood. That was why you were given those warnings. If Angel had died on the slopes and Culph had killed me, you would have been left on your own and not been master of your own behavior. And we almost let this happen. All of us."

"Well, it won't happen again," Kirisin declared softly. "I promise you that."

"I'll hold you to your word. We still have a ways to go before this is over. First we've got to get back to Arborlon."

"Wait a minute!" Kirisin exclaimed suddenly, his eyes widening. "I just remembered something. Culph said that he — the demon said that it had summoned an army to Arborlon to make sure no one escaped before it returned with me to imprison the city in the

Loden! It bragged about it while it was busy using that cord and those rings to hypnotize me! An army of demons and once-men, Sim! It's probably already there, waiting!"

Simralin straightened, winced from the resulting pain, and quickly lay back again. "All right. Then we need to warn Arissen Belloruus and the High Council. We need to tell them to get everyone out of there."

"How are we going to do that?" Kirisin demanded. "The King and probably the entire Council think that we killed Erisha! They think we're some sort of traitors! They won't believe us!"

His sister stared at him a moment, then said, "We'll make them believe us."

"Oh, that shouldn't be too difficult."

"Wait a minute, Little K. Maybe we don't have to tell anyone. Think about it. An entire army moving on the Cintra? The Elves probably know about it already. Their scouts and sentries will have told them. They'll have seen something that big coming from miles away."

Kirisin shook his head. "Maybe, maybe not. I don't know how they planned to do this. Maybe the army isn't supposed to get close until the Elves are trapped in the Loden."

His sister nodded. "Maybe. Maybe nothing is supposed to happen until you get back. The other demons can't know that Culph is dead. Or his four-legged companion, either. They have to wait to see what happens. That gives us a chance."

"A chance to get ourselves thrown into the cells by the King," Kirisin said. "I still don't know how we'll ever convince him that we're speaking the truth. Even if he sees the army coming, he'll probably think we had something to do with it. I bet he's already made up his mind about that, too."

Neither said anything for a moment, looking at each other across the silence of the cavern chamber, the darkness and cold pressing in around them. Kirisin was thinking that they were all alone in this; there was no one they could turn to, no one who would help them. He was thinking that it wasn't likely anything would change this.

"We'll be all right," his sister said softly.

Sure we will, Kirisin thought. *Assuming we can learn to fly and disappear into thin air.*

"I know," he said instead. He yawned. "I'm exhausted, Sim. I'm going to get some sleep. Maybe you should, too."

Simralin didn't say anything. She just sat there, staring at him. After a moment, she said, "You'll see, Little K. We'll be fine."

She was still sitting there, staring, when he fell asleep.

He awoke to shards of daylight spilling down the cavern passageway through ice-frozen cracks in the ceiling. Simralin was moving quietly about the chamber, gathering up their gear and redistributing it into two packs. She looked pale but steady as the light caught the planes and lines of her bruised, ravaged face.

"Sleep well?" she asked without irony. She still had her makeshift bandage wrapped about her forehead and her all-weather cloak wrapped about her shoulders. She looked like a wraith. She caught him staring at her and said, "What's wrong?"

"Well, *you* are, for starters. You look like you've been blood-drained. Are you all right?"

"Right as can be under the circumstances. Better get yourself up. We leave as soon as I'm finished."

He pushed himself up on one elbow, and the residual effects of yesterday's struggle recalled themselves painfully. "Leave for where?"

She nodded toward the passageway. "Back outside and down the mountain. You did the best you could with Angel, but she's in need of someone better trained in the art of healing."

Kirisin glanced over to where the Knight of the Word was still sleeping. Except for her face and hands, she was buried in the folds of the coverings in which they had wrapped her the night before, and he couldn't tell if she was breathing or not. She was wearing fresh clothing; his sister must have dressed her while he slept. He studied her a moment, then said to Simralin, "Is she still alive?"

41

"She was half an hour ago. Why don't you have a look?"

Kirisin pulled himself to his feet, fighting off the stiffness and the pain that ratcheted through his muscles and joints and made him feel as if he had been hammered with rocks. Dropping his cloak, he stumbled over to Angel and knelt down. He could just discern the slow rise and fall of her chest. Her face was purpled with bruises, and the knuckles of her hands were scraped raw. That was just the surface damage. The damage beneath the coverings was far worse.

"How do we get her back down the mountain?" he said.

"We make a sling and carry her. We can't afford to try to slide her down. The terrain is too rough for that. She's damaged internally — ribs broken, maybe more. We can't risk knocking her around by dragging her along the ground. We have to keep her elevated and still. We'll use her staff as a support for the sling. Why don't you see if you can pry it loose from her fingers so I can get to work?"

Kirisin glanced down. Angel gripped the black staff tightly with both hands and didn't look ready to let go. Nevertheless, he reached down carefully and tried to slide the staff free.

Instantly the Knight's eyes snapped open. "Kirisin," she whispered in a voice dark with warning. "Don't."

He pulled back quickly. "Sorry. But we

need your staff to make a sling to carry you back down the mountain so that we can . . . we can find help for you . . ."

He trailed off, realizing suddenly that he didn't know how that was supposed to happen. He looked over at Simralin, who had stopped what she was doing and was watching them. "I guess I don't know what happens when we get back down the mountain."

His sister rose and came over to them, kneeling next to her brother. "Once we reach the meadows, we'll use the hot-air balloon to fly ourselves out of here." She bent close to Angel. "Here's the truth of things. Kirisin has done what he can for you, but his training is in healing plants, not people. I don't know how bad your injuries are, and neither does he. We need someone more skilled than we are to determine that. How bad do they feel to you?"

Angel shook her head. "Broken ribs, maybe my arm. Or maybe they're only cracked. Hard to tell. Everything hurts, even when I don't move." She wet her lips and shifted her gaze to Kirisin. "Did you find the Loden?"

He nodded. "I have it."

"Tell me what happened."

He glanced at Simralin, who nodded. Quickly he sketched out the events that had led to the unexpected appearance of the demon Culph and the discovery of its complex deception. He told of entering the ice dragon's maw and gaining possession of the Loden, then emerging to find the old man waiting. He related how the demon had tried to hypnotize him using the silver cord and rings, intending afterward to transport him back to the Cintra and there use him to summon the Loden's magic and imprison the Elves and their city. Simralin had saved him by stabbing the demon in the leg with her knife, disrupting his concentration and allowing Kirisin to break free of the spell that bound him and use the magic of the blue Elfstones.

He quite deliberately said nothing of the strange euphoria he had experienced when he summoned and gained command of the Elfstone magic, not yet certain how he felt about it, keeping it a secret even from Simralin. He wasn't ready to talk about it yet, wasn't ready to admit what it might mean.

"You were incredibly brave," she told them. "Both of you. I thought that if I didn't reach you, the demon would finish you both. But I was the one who needed saving."

"Tell us what happened after we left you," Simralin urged her.

So Angel related the details of her battle with Culph's companion, the four-legged demon that had tracked her all the way from Los Angeles, first as the spiky-haired blond female and later as a wolfish beast. How much farther it might have evolved was a

matter of speculation, but it had been dangerous enough at the end to almost finish her.
As it was, she had been unable to do more
than crawl uphill in the general direction of
the entrance to the ice caves before she
passed out.

For her part, she said nothing of her dream
of Johnny and the sense that he had led her
to a waiting death to which she had been willing to give herself over.

She took a deep breath against the inevitable pain and tried to raise herself to a sitting position. She failed and lay back again.
"You'll have to help me up," she told them.

"We'll have to carry you, is what we'll have
to do," Simralin observed. "Don't try to rush
this."

"I'm trying not to. But I know what's at
stake. Kirisin has to get back to the Cintra.
He has to use the Loden to save the Elves.
Otherwise, this has all been for nothing."

Simralin nodded. "Kirisin will get his
chance. But first we have to do something
about you."

"You have to take me with you."

Simralin actually laughed. "Now there's a
good plan. Why didn't I think of it?"

"I mean it, Simralin. You have to take me
with you. It is the mission I was given — to
be your protector. I can't let you go alone."

"Well, I don't think this is your decision."
The Tracker bent close again. "I've seen dead

people in better shape than you are. If you try to go with us, you'll be more hindrance than help. I can't protect you and him. And you can't protect either of us until you're healed. I'm taking you to someone who can make you well again. Then I'm taking Little K back into the Cintra where he can do what he is supposed to do."

Angel shook her head stubbornly. "Not without me."

Simralin sighed. "I thought you promised not to make this so hard on us."

"I don't care what I said. I'm going."

"I'm afraid not, Angel."

She reached down, pressed her fingers into the other's exposed neck at the base of her skull, and held them in place. Angel's eyes fluttered momentarily and closed.

Simralin stood up. "She's unconscious. I'll give her something in a little while to keep her that way. Stubborn, isn't she? Determined. No wonder she's still alive." She motioned to Kirisin. "Take the staff from her hands, Little K. Be gentle."

Together they made up the sling using the staff and one of the cloaks, tying and looping the sleeves and the loose ends of the flaps to form the cradle. Then they fitted Angel inside, shouldered their packs, and picked up the sling. It felt to Kirisin as if Angel weighed three hundred pounds.

"Don't worry," Simralin grunted from the

46

other end of the staff. "We'll stop and rest on the way. Just let me know when it gets to be too much."

It was already too much, Kirisin thought. But he didn't say so. He just nodded. He would do what it took to get Angel down the mountain. She would have done the same for them.

She would have given up her life.

Half an hour later, they were back outside the caves and making their way across the ice fields toward the snow line and the meadows that lay below.

FOUR

It took Kirisin and Simralin almost four hours of hiking interspersed with frequent rest stops to carry Angel Perez back down the slopes of Syrring Rise to the meadow where they had left the hot-air balloon. Their trek was lengthened by the need to take a circuitous route in order to avoid the rougher terrain. By the time they reached the edge of the ice fields and stepped off the glacier onto visible ground, it was already midmorning. When they came in sight of the balloon, the sun was directly overhead and midday was approaching.

The day started out bright and clear, but as the hours wore on it turned hazy and the sky began to fill with clouds. A storm was forming over the mountain, and they had to get away before it struck or they would be trapped another night. Simralin pushed hard to keep Kirisin moving, even after he told her that he didn't think he could go any farther. He surprised himself by putting aside any thought for his own discomfort and responding to his sister's urgings and his own sense of duty to the injured Knight of the Word.

If Erisha were there, he comforted himself, she might even tell him he was finally growing up.

Angel, for her part, slept the entire way, drugged by the sleeping potion Simralin had prepared and trickled through her lips and down her throat, a powerful medicine meant to keep her unconscious until well into the following day. It might have been dangerous to give her such a strong potion, but Kirisin understood that it would be more dangerous still to have her awake and struggling to change their minds about not taking her with them. However determined she was, however well intentioned, she was not capable of helping them in what they had to do. He understood how she felt about carrying out the mission given to her by the Word, of fulfilling her duty as one of its Knights, but that alone was not enough to see her through what lay ahead. Simralin was right: Angel had to stay behind.

Once they arrived at the meadow, they lay Angel down on a soft patch of grass and went to work on enabling the balloon. No one had disturbed its various parts, and within a short time they had the blower operating and the bag filling with hot air. Simralin worked to secure all the stays and ties while Kirisin

49

monitored the blower. The meadow and its surroundings remained otherwise empty and quiet, but the sky overhead continued to darken. It seemed odd to watch a storm develop; it had been years since weather this threatening had come to the mountains of the Cintra. A little rain now and then, but nothing like this. Still, Syrring Rise was special, and the work of the Elven caretakers on the forests and plants had created a climate peculiar to the mountain. Kirisin found himself wondering what it would be like to live and work here, to be one of the caretakers rather than a Chosen. Here the challenges were greater and the skills needed to keep the mountain free of disease and poison more demanding. Kirisin knew he was good at healing and possessed both learned and innate understanding of the ways in which he could protect the native vegetation. Working here on the slopes of Syrring Rise would be a thoroughly satisfying experience.

Though now, it seemed, he would never have a chance to find out, since the Elves would be leaving the mountain and the world of Syrring Rise was ending.

How much of that world, he wondered, would survive in the aftermath of the predicted destruction?

He thought about that as he worked, about how it would be for the Elves once they were no longer living in the Cintra — or perhaps anywhere else that they knew about or could even imagine. The new world might be entirely foreign to them. He wondered how life would change when the disaster foretold by the Ellcrys came to pass. He didn't bother using the word *if* in reference to the prediction. He accepted the inevitability of the world's passing in the same way he had come to accept everything else the tree had told him. The presence of demons among the Elves had convinced him that a new way of looking at things was necessary. The deaths of Ailie and Erisha had only reinforced that conviction, providing sharp reminders that the life he had once taken for granted was coming to a close. This period in the history of the Elves was over, as much so as that long-ago time when magic had ceased to be a part of their lives and humans had become the dominant species. No Elf wanted to think this way, least of all Kirisin, who still wanted to believe that the Elves, as the first people, would one day regain their elevated position in the order of things.

But in the world of the present, the world of demons and once-men and things so terrible that they belonged in the darkest of nightmares, no one species or race or civilization mattered more than another. What happened to one would ultimately happen to all, and no amount of healing skill or Elfstone magic or wishful thinking would change this.

"Little K," Simralin snapped, interrupting his ruminations. "The storm is coming. We need to leave. Help me with Angel."

Together they lifted the unconscious Knight of the Word into the basket and settled her comfortably, her body braced with packing, strapped in place, and wrapped in several cloaks so that she would be stable and warm for the flight. Loading their packs and what remained of their supplies, they released the anchors that secured the balloon and lifted off.

This time, Simralin took them east over the mountains, tacking on the prevailing winds that blew through the craggy peaks, angling the balloon this way and that to carry them across. Kirisin stayed out of the way and watched Syrring Rise slowly shrink against the darkening horizon. The storm clouds were coming down from the north in heavy banks, more weather than he had seen in a long time, and soon the entire peak was enveloped.

Gone, as if it had never existed. As if it were lost to all of them forever.

He didn't like thinking that way, didn't like imagining anything gone forever. Yet that was what was going to happen. That was the future.

He turned away and watched his sister maneuver the balloon, directing bursts of hot air into the bag and vents, opening and closing flaps to change direction, pausing every so often to study their movement and gauge the thrust of the wind. It was tricky business, but she seemed at ease with it. He was struck by how steady and assured she was in her handling of the balloon, how confident in the making of her choices. He admired Sim greatly, his big sister, beautiful and clever and skilled at so many things. He wished he were that way, but he knew he wasn't. He was a Chosen, and that gave him what status he enjoyed among the Elves, but he would never be as accomplished as Simralin.

The best he could do with his life was to see that he did not fail the Ellcrys in the charge she had given him. He thought for the first time since gaining possession of the Loden what that meant. By using the Elfstone magic, he would be taking responsibility for the tree, his city, and the Elven people. Their safety and security would become his responsibility until they got to wherever it was they were supposed to go. Others would help him, his sister included. But in the end, as both the Ellcrys and the shade of Pancea Rolt Gotrin had warned, he would be alone in this. The burden and the consequences of how well he bore it were his. His measure would be taken in the days ahead, and he was terrified — thinking of it here and now, suspended in a basket hundreds of feet in the air — that like the air filling this balloon, his own efforts might leak away and he would fall short.

They flew on through the afternoon, riding on the back of the leeward winds down the spine of the mountain chain, sailing over the canyons and flats, the land beneath them becoming stark and barren once more. Gone were the green meadows of Syrring Rise, gone the fresh smell and taste of the air. Here the air was bitter and fouled, and the earth a lifeless landscape of dirt and rocks. Now and then Kirisin caught sight of movement, but it was always brief and he could never identify its source.

They ate midway through their flight, consuming a little of their dwindling supplies and water as they monitored the balloon's progress, Kirisin taking his turn at helping when Simralin needed a rest. He found that he could understand a little of why the balloon responded as it did and what was needed to keep it on course.

At one point, Simralin reached out and squeezed his arm. "I think you'll make a balloon pilot yet, Little K. You've got the nose for it."

He grinned his appreciation of her compliment, but could not help thinking that flying hot-air balloons would not matter to either of them much longer.

Wondering, at the same time, what would.

■ ■ ■ ■

It was late in the afternoon when they reached
the banks of Redonnelin Deep and began
tacking upriver toward their destination.

"Is that a good idea, Sim?" Kirisin asked
when he heard what she had planned for
Angel.

"Taking her to Larkin Quill? Of course it's
a good idea." She waved him off dismissively;
her eyes were fixed on the landscape below,
watching the slow passing of the river and its
confining banks. She took a moment to
glance northward in the direction from which
they had come. "Storm looks to be coming
down this way. It's not staying on the mountains like it should. Odd."

"But he's blind!" Kirisin persisted. "You
said yourself that she needed someone with
special healing skills if she was to be helped!"

His sister gave him a sharp look. "You don't
think Larkin knows something about healing?
After living out here on his own all these
years? He knows more than most about how
to cure your ills and mend your wounds. He
will know just what Angel needs and he will
be able to provide it. Don't underestimate
him, Little K."

Kirisin nodded. "I just don't want anything
to happen to her."

"It won't. Larkin is a skilled healer, but he

55

is also one of the few people we can trust. If we take Angel back to the Cintra, we risk giving her over to the King. Here she'll be safe from whatever happens back there. Larkin will tell her where we've gone and what we're doing. If we succeed, we can come back for her. If we don't, maybe she can come for us. Take hold of this line. I don't like what these winds are doing to us. We have to set down."

They worked together to land the balloon on flats not too far upriver but on the opposite bank from where Larkin Quill kept his cottage. It took both of them to navigate the tricky winds that blew down the river channel, but in the end they succeeded in landing the basket safely and with only a slight bump as it tipped sideways. Simralin leapt out at once and began gathering in the deflated balloon while Kirisin struggled to anchor the basket so that it would not drag farther.

It was almost dark by the time they finished. After they had hauled the basket and the equipment back into a stand of trees and carried Angel to an overhang of rocks that jutted out from the cliff face, Simralin extracted a strange flute-like object, placed it to her lips, and blew hard. The sound was high and piercing, and Kirisin winced despite himself.

"Larkin will come at dawn and take Angel back with him," she told him, returning to sit beside him in the gathering dark. "It would have been better to put down on the south bank, but too risky with the storm coming in and the winds blowing so hard."

In the distance, thunder rumbled and lightning flashed against the northern horizon. The storm was gathering strength and moving closer, clouds rolling out of the darkness in massive banks.

"I can't remember the last time we had a storm with thunder and lightning," Kirisin said quietly. "Do you think it will rain hard?"

His sister nodded. "I do."

"Maybe it means something," he murmured.

"Maybe it means we will be getting wet before this night's over. Better keep your cloak close at hand, Little K."

They were silent for a time, listening to the peals of thunder, blinking against the sharp flashes of lightning, waiting for the storm to reach them. Kirisin realized all at once how sleepy he was and then remembered that there hadn't been much time for sleep in almost two days.

"Angel will be furious when she finds out we've left her behind," he said.

"Angel might be furious, but she will also be alive." His sister gave a small sigh. "I don't like leaving her, either. She's a lot better equipped than we are to fight off what we are likely to come up against. But not like she is. She has to be well enough to stand on her own first. And we can't wait on that. We can't wait on anything if we're going to help our people. We just don't have a choice."

"I know," he said.

The rain began to fall, a steady downpour that quickly turned into a deluge. They huddled back against the cliff, doing what they could to stay dry. Everything more than ten feet away disappeared in shimmering wet curtains of water, swallowed as if it had vanished entirely. It was an unsettling feeling. Kirisin wondered what would happen if the river rose another foot or two, but decided the chances of that were small. Even a storm as strong as this one shouldn't be able to swell the river that much. Redonnelin Deep had been ten feet higher twenty years ago, he had been told. But the weather patterns had changed, and rain was a rarity these days, even here in the northwest part of the country, where it had always rained regularly in the past.

"How are we going to do this, Sim?" Kirisin asked her suddenly.

For a moment, she didn't say anything. It was so dark by now that he could barely make out her face. "I don't know," she said finally.

"Will they even give us a chance to tell them what might happen? Will they listen to anything we have to say?"

"Kirisin, I don't know," she repeated. She glanced over, and in a sudden flash of lightning he saw anger on her bruised face. "You have to find a way to make them listen, Little K. That's what's expected of you. That's what you've been given to do. You have to figure out a way to do it!"

He was surprised at her vehemence, and he went silent immediately in response, hunkering down farther into his cloak to ward off the harshness of her words as much as the chill and the damp. He wished he hadn't asked the question, that he had kept quiet about the whole business. She was right, after all. It was his charge to fulfill and his responsibility to figure how to carry it out. She had come with him on this journey out of love and loyalty, his big sister looking out for him. She had nearly died because of him back in the ice caves on Syrring Rise. Ultimately, she had saved his life. He had no right to expect anything more from her, no right to ask it.

He was embarrassed and ashamed that he had.

Nevertheless, after a long silence, she said, "I'm sorry. I shouldn't have said those things. This isn't your charge alone anymore. It's mine, too. I accepted that when I decided to go with you in search of the Loden. I just get so frustrated about things. I know I don't show it much. My Tracker training, I guess. I keep everything inside. I let it get away from me this time, and I shouldn't have."

"I shouldn't be asking you to solve my problems," he responded quickly. "You were right. I am the one who has to figure out how to make everyone believe. I am the one asking for their trust. So I have to demonstrate that I deserve it. You can't do that for me."

She reached over and squeezed his shoulder. "But I don't have to make a big point of it, do I? What you need to hear is that I intend to stand with you no matter what."

He grinned. "I never thought you would do anything else."

He reached out to her and hugged her through the rain, feeling the reassuring comfort in her strong arms as they embraced him back. For just a moment, he could believe that no matter what obstacles they might face, they would be able to overcome them.

"Go to sleep," she told him, breaking away. "I'll keep watch."

He was too tired to argue the matter, his eyes already drooping, his body stiff and aching. "Wake me so you can sleep, too," he said.

But even as he hunkered down to shield himself against the weather, he knew that she wouldn't.

He woke to find Larkin Quill standing over him. Even from the back — for he was turned away — the cloaked form of the ex-Tracker was instantly recognizable. He was facing toward Simralin, who was busy strapping a still-unconscious Angel to a wooden frame that cradled her body on a broad piece of tightly stretched canvas. Kirisin raised himself to a sitting position, noting as he did so that the day was bright and sunny and all but devoid of evidence of the previous night's storm. Save for a few puddles and damp spots on the otherwise dry ground, there was nothing to indicate the deluge had ever happened.

"Wake up, wake up, Kirisin Belloruus," Larkin Quill intoned. He turned his head slightly. "Awake, maybe you can be of some use."

Kirisin rubbed his eyes and stretched. "Sim was supposed to wake me. She let me sleep."

"Yes, it is all her fault, no question. She's like that, Simralin is, always thinking only of herself. So selfish." He was grinning as he gestured toward the river, swift flowing and choppy in the wake of the downpour. "But now that you've made it back from the land of dreams all on your own, I need to be going my way, as well. Would you help me carry our wounded Angel down to the boat so I can ferry her back across?"

Kirisin rose, and together they bore Angel Perez along the banks of Redonnelin Deep to where the ex-Tracker's boat was beached and tied off. As before, Larkin Quill was surefooted and steady, seemingly able to see as well as the boy. Simralin came, too, lending an extra hand while they loaded Angel aboard and settled her on a long bench at the stern where the stretcher could be secured.

61

"I have a ramp at my dock that will allow me to drag off the stretcher when we get to where we're going. I've had to do this before when I wasn't ready for it, so this time I came prepared."

"Can you help her?" Kirisin asked.

The older man grinned. "Oh, I think so. She's banged up pretty good, but she's already healing at the breaks and cracks. Some of that Knight of the Word magic, I imagine. I'll be able to help her mend faster still with a little magic of my own, the kind that relies on potions and poultices and sleep. A week or so, she'll be back to fighting form."

"That's awfully fast," Kirisin said doubtfully.

Larkin said nothing.

"She won't be easy to keep down even that long," Simralin declared. "She'll want to be up and on her way."

Larkin Quill shrugged. "I wouldn't worry about that. I can manage her. You have the harder task, I'd guess."

"We'll do what we have to," Kirisin declared bravely. "We won't let anything stop us."

Larkin grinned anew. "Well said, young man. Still, be careful how you go. Especially with the King. He's not to be trusted, whether he is Elf or demon. You'll need the Council's support to keep him in line. A few are worth enlisting to your cause. Ordanna Frae's a good man; he will see that you have your say.

Maybe more than that, if you're lucky. You can trust Maurin Ortish, too, even if he isn't a member of the Council. The Home Guard lives for him as much as for the King, though I would never say it to his face. The rest you should not put your faith in."

He walked over to Simralin and embraced her. "You were always the best of the lot, you know. The best of the Trackers I knew. The others were good — skilled and brave. But you were the smart one, the clever one, the one who always knew how to make the right decision." He turned toward Kirisin. "If anyone can see you through this, your sister will. Pay attention to her."

"I know enough to do that," the boy answered. "I won't take foolish chances."

"I think that might be so." Larkin Quill's smile dropped away. "One last thing. The King's Hunters. They haven't come here yet, which is troublesome. They should be looking for you everywhere by now, and especially here. They know we were friends, Simralin, and a handful, at least, know how to find me. But no one has come. It may be that they know something none of us does. So watch yourselves. Keep your presence hidden from them for as long as you can and then choose wisely a time and place to reveal yourselves."

He turned away, put one hand on the gunwale of his boat, and vaulted aboard effortlessly. "Not so old, you see?" he offered, turning back to them. "But I could use a push off the rocks."

Simralin obliged, putting her shoulder against the bow and shoving until the boat slid free. Larkin Quill was already at the helm, the sails raised and billowing with the fresh breeze. "I'll see you on the new wind," he called back to them as he leaned into the rudder and the boat began to turn away.

"Good-bye, Larkin," Simralin shouted.

Kirisin called out to him, as well, something about seeing him again soon. But he could not shake the feeling that they were all wishing for something that would never happen.

FIVE

Simralin waited until the boat carrying Larkin Quill and Angel Perez was well out on the water and heading for the far shore before turning to the task of reinflating the hot-air balloon so that Kirisin and she could set out for the Cintra. Kirisin, who had been cleaning up the campsite, packing away their foodstuffs and supplies, was glad to begin preparations for setting out. Movement helped ease his discomfort with leaving Angel behind, focusing his thoughts to the particulars of what was needed to get under way.

It took them less than an hour to set up the balloon, fill the bag, load their supplies, and cast off. The day remained bright and welcoming as they lifted into the sky, empty of clouds and filled with sunshine. Kirisin glanced down several times to see if he could spy Larkin Quill's boat, but it had disappeared somewhere along the far bank, back in the heavy trees and the inlets, safely out of sight.

Good luck, Angel, he mouthed silently.

He glanced over to see Simralin watching him, and he blushed despite himself.

They sailed across Redonnelin Deep and the beginning of the Cintra Mountains, reaching the northern edge of the chain by midday. Kirisin expected them to continue on immediately, but Simralin told him they were taking the balloon down again and anchoring where they were until dark.

"Can't risk traveling farther south in the daylight," she said as they worked together to leak the air from the bag and land the balloon in a meadow at the foot of the mountains. "We're too easy to spot up there against the sky. They might not know who we are, but they will be quick to want to find out. They can track our silhouette and be waiting when we land. At night, we won't be so visible."

Kirisin had to agree, even though he wanted to set off right away. Delays of any sort at this point were frustrating. But he didn't argue. Instead, he helped her land the balloon, pull in the deflated bag, and anchor the basket. Then he offered to keep watch so that she could sleep for a few hours.

"Much appreciated, Little K," she told him, yawned, stretched out, and went right to sleep.

He watched her for a time, smiling inwardly at how quickly she could make the transition.

Then his attention wandered to the countryside surrounding them, bleak and withered and dominated by the barren craggy peaks of the mountains. Having just left a mountain so different from these, a mountain on which trees and grasses and flowers still grew in lush profusion, green and fresh and thriving, he was dismayed anew at the devastation that had taken hold of his world. No number of Elves could change this, he thought darkly. The sickness and rot were too pervasive and deep-seeded. It made him angry all over again at the humans who had been so careless with their caretaking, at their failure to act more quickly and reasonably when they still had a chance to stem the tide. But he guessed they hadn't been any more successful at saving themselves, and the price exacted for their foolish inattention was far greater than he would have wished on them.

Except that the Elves were paying the same price. Every living thing was paying it. When a massive failure to preserve the integrity of an ecosystem occurred, no one escaped the consequences.

The hours slipped by. Simralin slept, her breathing deep and even. Kirisin pondered the world's destiny along with his own, and after a time drifted into memories of Erisha. He found himself wishing he could see her once more, to tell her how much knowing her had meant to him and how sorry he was that he couldn't have done more to protect her. He thought about how they had played together growing up, in a time when everything happening now would have seemed impossible. It still seemed impossible. Erisha dead. Simralin and himself fugitives. Culph a demon that had betrayed them all.

He was particularly bitter about the old man. He could see his face, smiling and reassuring. He could hear his voice, could feel it make him want to shake his head in blind agreement. He hated that he had thought Culph was his friend, but he hated even more that he had liked him. Nothing would ever change the sense of outrage he felt at knowing how badly he had been deceived. He would live with that memory until he died. It might even go with him to wherever he went afterward.

The recognition burned like fire, and he tamped it down and shoved it away. In the aftermath of its fading, he found himself staring off into middle space, seeing nothing but the past, and then seeing nothing at all. His thoughts wandered like children lost, seeking peace and comfort in the presence of the familiar.

His thoughts strayed, and without thinking about it or even wanting it he followed after.

Who told you that?
The voice whispered through the darkness,

sharp and accusatory. He looked around and found himself in the stone gardens of the Ashenell. Massive sepulchres and blocky vaults cast their shadows over a forest of smaller markers. The night was quiet, a shroud over the graves of the dead. Yet a voice had spoken to him.

He saw Erisha then, standing less than ten feet away, her clothing torn and bloodied, her slender white throat sliced open to the bone. She stood solitary and ethereal in death, cast out into the Void by the loss of her life.

She looked at him and tried to speak, but no words came.

Erisha, he said. *I'm sorry.*

She tried again to speak, and again she failed.

Who told you that?

The voice again. Not her voice, but another's. He searched for the speaker and found him standing close to the girl. Old Culph, his grizzled face and gnarled body unchanged from life. Yet he was a ghost, too. The boy could see it in the translucence that radiated from him, in the way the starlight shone through him.

He could see it in the silhouette of his bones through his skin.

The old man was grinning, his lips curled in disdain, his sharp old eyes fixed and staring.

Who told you that?

Kirisin did not understand. Told him what? What was the old man talking about? The demon, he corrected. What was the demon saying?

He looked again at Erisha, who did not seem to see the demon. She was speaking once more, but still no words would come. Her mouth opened and closed, and there were tears in her eyes.

Then a third figure appeared, cloaked and hooded, dark and forbidding, hovering back in the deep shadows at the edge of his vision. A wraith, perhaps. But no, not this one. This one was alive, was of flesh and blood. It stared at him from out of the folds of the hood, and while he could not make out its features, he could feel its gaze.

Kirisin started toward it, and the ground seemed to give way beneath his feet. Suddenly he was falling, pitching forward into blackness, leaving Erisha and Culph and the Ashenell behind.

Only the dark figure stayed with him, one hand reaching. Its voice hissed in warning.

Who told you that?

Kirisin's eyes snapped open, and his slumped body jerked upright. He had been dreaming. Daydreaming perhaps, but maybe something more, something deeper. A vision? He couldn't be sure. He wet his lips and stared out into the sun-drenched day. How much time had passed? Only moments, it seemed. But then he looked at the sky and saw that the sun had moved far to the west. He had been sleeping or daydreaming or whatever it was for hours.

And what had the dream been about?

Who told you that?

The words echoed faintly in his memory, vaguely recognizable, and for a moment he almost had a grip on their origin. But then the link faltered, and his grip was gone. He tried to regain it and failed. For the moment, it was lost to him.

But not forgotten. At some point, he would remember.

He sat quiet and unmoving for a long time, coming back to himself in bits and pieces. The dream had disturbed him in a way that transcended his memory of the images or even the words. It was the feel of it, the way it pressed down on him like an oppressive weight. It was also in his recognition that it meant something that he could not decipher.

What had prompted the dream?

Simralin woke. Her eyes blinked at him, and she smiled. "Time to set out again, Little K. Are you ready?"

He smiled back, cold inside. "Ready as I'll ever be."

They drew out the air bag and refastened its lines to the basket. Then Simralin engaged the blower and began filling the bag anew. As she did so, she glanced over to where her brother sat staring into space. "What's wrong?"

He shook his head. "Nothing. Well, maybe nothing. I dozed off and had a dream of sorts. About the Ashenell and Erisha and Culph. It was disturbing. Still is, thinking about it."

"Well, try not to think about it, then. Dreams have a way of mirroring our doubts and fears. They suggest things that might be true, but usually aren't." She waited a moment for his response. When he failed to give it, she said, "Want something to eat?"

Leaving him to direct hot air from the blower nozzle into the slowly inflating bag, she reached into their supplies and pulled out some bread and cheese. Together they ate their meal and marked time. Kirisin tried hard not to think of the dream and ended up thinking about it all the more. Telling him not to think about something was tantamount to ensuring that he did. He didn't blame Sim, though. She was just trying to be helpful.

Once they were airborne, he was able to shift his attention to the sweep of the countryside below, from the high desert to the mountain peaks, whiling away time searching out their route. The sun had moved farther to the west and south, and daylight was fading fast. The loss of light cast the shadow of the mountains far out across the high desert, layering it in dark, uneven stains. The moon was rising on the eastern horizon, a white crescent against the blackening sky. Kirisin gazed out over the landscape for a long time, saying nothing.

"Don't worry, Little K," his sister said suddenly, giving the air bag a fresh burst of heat from the blower. "We won't get lost. The moon and stars will guide us, and I know this part of the country well enough to stay clear of trouble."

"Will we reach Arborlon tonight?" he asked.

She nodded. "Early tomorrow morning, while it is still dark. Then we will have to decide where to land and what to do after that."

Kirisin looked away. He had no plan to offer. It seemed that their only chance was to change minds already made up against them, and he had no idea of how to do that. For a long moment, he considered a radical approach. Upon reaching the Elven home city, he could put the magic of the Loden to use without telling anyone what he was doing. Just trap the Elves and their city and the Ellcrys inside and take them away to where they needed to go to be safe. But in doing so, he would be condemning an entire city and its population to indefinite imprisonment without giving a single one of them a chance to walk away. He would be using the magic of the Loden in an arrogant and cowardly manner. If his efforts to save them failed, he would have killed them all with his precipitous decision. No, he would need to tell them first, would need to seek the support of the King and the High Council. No matter where that led.

They flew on through the twilight into night, the darkness deepening steadily, the stars and crescent moon brightening overhead. Kirisin's thoughts drifted and the hours slipped away. He was conscious of their general progress, but did not have enough flying experience to be able to judge how far they had come. After a long time, Simralin turned them into the mountains, tacking back and forth along the wind riffs between the peaks, angling the balloon through gaps and up and down valleys and defiles. At times, they were so close to cliff faces that the boy was certain they were going to collide. But Simralin kept them clear, always steering them away just when it seemed she might not be able to, staying on course.

Finally, they were deep in the mountains on the western side, the forests of the Cintra a dark spiky carpet below. The silver ribbons and bright splashes of the rivers and lakes caught the moonlight and reflected it back from out of black folds. The air was cool and sweet, free on this night, at least, of the smell of the poisons and rot that infected so much of the earth below.

"That's Arborlon ahead," Simralin called over to him, pointing.

He peered downward and caught sight of

the flicker of tiny lights. They seemed a long way off still, but already he was feeling a sense of dread seep through him.

"What do we do?" he asked her.

She shook her head. "I can't tell what's down there in the darkness. If there are demons present, they could be anywhere. All I can think to do is land high enough up on the mountainside that they won't notice us coming down. The backdrop of the peaks will hide our descent."

Kirisin peered groundside some more, the balloon slowly descending toward the upper slopes. If they just had some way of making sure what was down there . . .

"Wait, Simralin!" he called out sharply.

He was so excited that he grabbed her arm to make sure he had her attention. She turned at once, and he could feel her body tense in expectation of trouble, her face ribbed with worry lines beneath the bandages. "No, it's all right," he said hastily. "I've got an idea. What if I use the Elfstones to find out if demons are hiding in the forests! Wouldn't the Stones tell us where they are? Wouldn't that give us a better idea of where to land?"

She studied him a moment. "I don't know. I've been thinking since that last night on Syrring Rise what using the Elfstones means. Remember how we wondered how Culph and that four-legged monster managed to track

75

us? How did they know where we were going? Even we didn't know until we used the Elfstones. Yet they were always right behind us. At the end, they even managed to get ahead. I'm guessing, but I think it's possible they had the ability to detect any use of magic. I think that's how they knew where to find us, and I'm worried that the same thing might happen here."

Kirisin hadn't thought of that. If the demons could sense his use of the Elfstones, they would be quick enough to pick up on where he was. It was a possibility he couldn't ignore. On the other hand, it was his best chance of finding out if they were down there waiting.

"What should I do, Sim?" he asked.

She shrugged. "I don't know. Take a chance, I guess. Go ahead. Use the Elfstones. But be quick about it. Even if it alerts them to our presence, we're moving and they might not be able to figure out exactly where we are. We just don't want to give them any better chance than we have to."

He nodded his understanding, wondering at the same time what that meant in practical terms. How long was too long? How closely could he afford to look at what was down there before he gave them away completely? There was no way of knowing, of course. He would just have to do the best he could.

He brushed back his wind-tangled dark hair

and reached deep into his pocket. He found the blue Elfstones easily enough and pulled them out past the larger bulk of the Loden. Then he leaned over the side of the basket. Arborlon was just ahead, the number of visible lights increasing steadily as they neared.

"Hurry up, Little K!" his sister urged. She was working the vents and flaps with quick, rushed movements. "Much closer and we won't have any option but to land farther down the slope!"

Which was where the greater number of demons was likely to be concentrated, she was suggesting. He tightened his fingers about the Elfstones and extended his arm in the general direction of the city. He kept his eyes open this time, concentrating his attention on the middle space between the balloon and the earth, in the vast sprawl of the night's darkness, envisioning the demons and their followers, spying out an army hidden from view. He pictured that army as he thought it might be, an army of creatures of the sort Culph and the four-legged demon had been, humans become monsters. He imagined their dark intention of hunting down and destroying the Elves. He reached out as he had on the slopes of Syrring Rise when searching for the ice caves.

The response was instantaneous and completely unexpected. Whatever he had been prepared for, it wasn't this. The blue light blazed from his closed fist in a brilliant ball and then exploded in a swath so wide and all-encompassing that it seemed to flood the landscape for miles. When it settled, the light had formed a wide, jagged curve that wrapped the lower slopes of the Cintra. The magic heightened and clarified the faces and bodies of myriad creatures, each a point of light within the band, allowing them to take shape, giving them form and identity.

Kirisin caught his breath. It was the demon army they had feared, and it was gathered just below the Elven home city. It was thousands strong. The numbers seemed endless.

"Sim," he whispered.

"I see," she replied in a high, tight voice. "Call back the magic, Little K. Quickly!"

He did so, and the light of the revealing magic died at once. They were left wrapped in darkness and star glow and in disbelief.

"So many," he murmured.

"Too many not to be noticed." Simralin was already working the ropes, bringing the balloon slowly downward. "Something's wrong. How can the Elves not know about them? There's no sign of anything happening anywhere. No defensive preparations, nothing."

"Is it possible that we've come too late?"

She glanced at him. "There wouldn't be any lights if we were too late. There would be fires and screams and much worse."

"But what are they doing?" he asked. "What

are they waiting for? Why haven't they attacked?"

She handed him one of the ropes to help her steady the basket. "Only one possible answer, Little K. Culph told you he had summoned an army that would be waiting for his return because he would have you in tow. So they're waiting on you. They want the Elves inside the Loden and the Loden under a demon's control."

Kirisin felt a chill run down the back of his neck all the way to his heels, the sort you have when you've encountered the freakishly impossible. He stiffened momentarily, then shook his head.

"They'll wait a long time for that to happen," he muttered. "I can promise you that!"

Simralin gave him a doubtful glance, but didn't say anything more.

Deep in the forests of the Cintra, in the midst of his army, the demon that called itself Findo Gask blinked twice as he caught the first whiff of the magic's use. At first he thought he had been mistaken, that his senses were deceiving him, but as the magic steadied and sharpened, he could feel its proximity and recognize it for what it was. The sharp old eyes fixed on a point in space, and his senses drank in the full extent of what they were experiencing. He shut out everything happening around him — the noise, smell, and movement, and the creatures that generated them — and he began to search.

Quickly, quickly . . .

But he wasn't quick enough. There wasn't enough time. The magic was there for a few seconds, tight and strong and recognizable, and then it was gone. He was unable to determine its source.

Still, a smile crossed his lips, deepening the lines of his face.

Someone was being very careful.

He rose and stood looking off into the darkness of the trees. It didn't matter, really. He knew what was happening. He knew why and he knew how. In the end, it would all turn out the way he had planned. The boy was back, and he had found the Elfstones. The nature of the magic he had sensed was unmistakable. Elfstone magic was distinct from any other kind of magic, different from that of the gypsy morph or the Knights of the Word. Magic was not of a single kind; if you knew it was there, you could teach yourself to identify its nature.

And this was unquestionably Elven.

So the demon that called itself Culph had succeeded in tracking the boy to the Elfstones, gaining control over the magic, and bringing both back to serve the demon cause. He wondered briefly if Delloreen had played any part in this, if she had somehow tracked the young female Knight of the Word to the

Elves and dispatched her. That would have made her very happy, and he would never begrudge her happiness of that sort. On the other hand, it would be convenient for him if she had failed and was dead. Increasingly dangerous, she needed to be eliminated in any case. If the Knight hadn't done so, he would have to.

He banished Delloreen to the back corners of his mind and pondered momentarily what the use of the Elfstones meant beyond the obvious. Why had the magic been summoned now? There didn't appear to be any point in it.

But then it occurred to him that perhaps it was a way of letting him know how matters stood — that the boy was back and the Elfstones recovered. The message might be that it was time to prepare for the jaws of his trap to close. Once the Loden was employed and the city and the bulk of its population imprisoned, it would be time for his army to complete the eradication process.

Still, it seemed an unnecessary use of the magic. He would know that it was time to act, after all, when the city and its population disappeared. And there were other ways for his ally to inform him of his return.

Why allow the boy to invoke the magic and risk its detection?

Vaguely dissatisfied, he stood alone without moving for a long time, carefully avoided by his followers as he pondered the matter, his ancient visage dark and troubled.

Six

"Well, don't just sit there! Tell us what happened!"

Panther was agitated, impatient. His hands gestured to emphasize the urgency of his request; his dark face was flushed. "Why aren't you dead, Bird-Man? We thought you went over the wall and into the light and you was dead! Now you just walk out of nowhere and look like nothing ever happened! Talk to us, damn it!"

Owl, seated in her wheelchair with Candle in her lap, smiled despite herself. It took something to get Panther this worked up and then to let it show. But the others were anxious, too. It reflected on their faces, bright and eager in anticipation of hearing a new story, this time one that Hawk was going to tell.

They were gathered in a circle in a field not far from the side of the freeway, the AV and the wagon drawn up next to them. Twilight had departed and night had settled in, a dark blanket of still air and quiet expectation. They had not started a fire or eaten a meal. There was no time for that when there was so much catching up to do. Moonlight brightened the faces of those gathered — the Ghosts and Cat on the one hand and Hawk and Tessa on the other. Cheney lay off to one side, his shaggy bulk just visible in the pale light. He had greeted them all in his typically aloof way, sniffing momentarily at Cat to make sure of her, glancing at Rabbit — which was more than enough to send the terrified feline scrambling for safety — and then slouching over to where he was settled now. As far as the big wolf dog was concerned, nothing much had changed.

But everything had changed for the rest of them, she thought. Hawk was back. The boy with the vision was back to lead his children to the Promised Land.

"Tell us, Hawk," she urged gently.

He looked at her, a flicker of uncertainty in his green eyes, an unmistakable hesitation in his effort to respond. "I'm not sure where to start," he said. "I'm not even sure *how* to start."

"Start with what happened at the compound," Sparrow suggested. "I saw that strange light flash from where I was standing on the rooftop just before I went down the ladder and found Panther and we had to run from the Croaks to . . ."

She stopped, smiling sheepishly. "Start there," she finished.

"Where did you go?" asked River, dark eyes already wide with wonder.

"I went into these gardens," Hawk said. "Tessa and I were thrown from the wall and everything was suddenly blinding and I must have lost consciousness. Then I woke up in these gardens and there was this old man. Real old. He said he was a Faerie creature." He caught a glimpse of Panther's smirk. "I know, Panther. It sounds crazy. I thought so, too. But that's what he said, that he was a Faerie creature. He called himself the King of the Silver River. He said the gardens were his and that he had brought me there to learn about myself. He saved me because he said I had something I needed to do."

"You went into the light, is where you went," Panther insisted. "I heard about people doing that. You died and came back, is what you did."

"Yeah, maybe," Hawk replied, shaking his head. "I don't know for sure where I was. But the old man didn't seem to think it was anything big. He told me the same thing Logan Tom told me in the compound cells — that I was a gypsy morph, that I was made out of a kind of magic. But I was a boy, too. Just like everyone else," he added hastily. "Except that I had to do this thing. I had to come back and find you and all these other

85

kids, and then I had to take you to this place where you would be safe."

"Safe from what?" Panther wanted to know at once.

Hawk hesitated. "From the end of the world."

"The end of the world," Fixit repeated.

"Oh, man," whispered Chalk.

The others muttered similar pronouncements, glancing uneasily at one another and then back at Hawk. This caught even Owl off guard. "Are you sure about what he told you?" she asked him.

Hawk nodded. "It gets stranger. He told me that others would be coming with us. I mean, besides the children. He said there would be Elves."

For a moment, no one spoke.

"Sure there will," Panther declared, nodding soberly. "Probably trolls and pixies, too. Maybe some dragons. Just like in that book Owl read once, the one with all those magic things."

"He knows what he was told," Tessa insisted, coming to Hawk's defense. "This isn't what you think. He's serious about this."

"You saw all this?" Panther pressed.

She shook her head. "No, I was asleep. When I woke up, we weren't in the gardens anymore. We were on the banks of the river south of here — Hawk and Cheney and me. But if Hawk isn't telling the truth, how did we get there? How did Cheney end up with us, for that matter?"

"How did you get *here?*" Owl asked, steering the conversation in a different direction while everyone was still calm enough to listen.

"We just started walking," Tessa answered. Her dusky face lifted into the moonlight and her eyes shone. "Then we found this camp with all these children and their protectors. Hundreds of them, come up from somewhere south, fleeing an army that had killed everyone else. Hawk took them across the river, over a bridge." She hesitated, as if she might say something more about this, but then decided against it. "After we were across, he told the others to wait for him there until he returned with his own family. Then we came looking for you."

"You knew where we would be?" Owl said.

Tessa nodded. "Hawk knew."

Owl and the others looked at the boy. Hawk shrugged. "I just did. I can't explain it. It has something to do with the magic."

Panther looked off into the night. "I'm not calling you Bird-Man anymore. I'm calling you Magic Man. Or maybe Crazy Man."

"Panther." Tessa spoke his name firmly and waited until he looked at her. "Don't call him names. You haven't seen what I've seen. He isn't the same as you remember. He's something else now, something special."

"Tessa, don't," Hawk said. "I'd say the

same thing as Panther if he were telling me all this."

"So tell us more about the world ending," Chalk urged, brushing past the rest of it. "Is this for real?"

"The old man said so. He said it was all ending, and we had to get to someplace safe until everything got better and we could go out into it again." Hawk shook his head. "I asked him if he was serious, if he was sure about this, and he said he was. He said it's all gone too far and everything's ending. I guess I believe him."

"Look around you," Cat said suddenly from one side, the scaly patches of her mottled face reflecting the moonlight. They all turned to look at her. "I don't know about this old man, but I know enough to believe what he says about the world. It's already ruined. Anyone with half a brain can tell that. Why should it be so hard to think it's going to end?"

"She's right," agreed Sparrow. "Giant centipedes and armies killing off the compound people. Croaks and Lizards and all the rest. I think it's ending. What do we do, Hawk?"

"We go back and join the children I left behind, and then we head east to wherever it is we have to go to be safe."

"But you'll know where that is?" Sparrow asked.

"The old man said I would." He paused.

"I've been thinking about what that means. I think it has something to do with the gardens. He said that was where I was conceived. It was where he kept me until it was time for me to come out into the world and become who I am. Maybe there is a connection. Maybe I am supposed to find my way back again."

"How you gonna do that? You couldn't do it before! Didn't even know they existed!" Panther threw up his hands. "You better be Magic Man or we're gonna be lost out here forever!"

"I think it makes a difference that I didn't know about the gardens. I don't think I was meant to find them before this. I think that's what the old man intended all along."

"Oh, sure. Now you know, so nothing to worry about." Panther shook his head. "Listen to yourself. Then look at who we are. Kids! A bunch of kids! With more kids waiting to join us? Hundreds of them? So this bunch of kids and some Elves and some other people are supposed to hike off into the wilderness to somewhere that no one but you know, and even *you* don't know it yet! We're gonna hike to someplace we'll be safe, even though the rest of the world is gonna buy the farm? Does anyone but me find this a little weird?"

"How many times have you listened to the story of the boy and his children, Panther?"

Owl gave him a warm, reassuring smile. "Didn't you believe in that story? Isn't that why you stayed with us? You knew about Hawk's dream. His vision. That was his story, the same as now. We all understood that. We were all waiting for it to happen, ever since we were together. We all believed in it then and I think we all have to believe in it now."

"Yeah, Panther," Sparrow agreed. "Where's your faith?"

"Where's your brain?" Panther snapped back. "A story's a story. It ain't necessarily the truth. What's real is what counts. What's real is what's out there waiting to chew us all to bits!"

"You think we might be better off if we didn't believe Hawk?" River asked quietly. Her dark eyes fixed on him. "Are you saying we should turn around and go back? That we should find some other city where we could make a home? What are you saying? If you tell us that Hawk's vision isn't true, what's left for us?"

Panther stared at her. "I don't know. I'm just saying we have to be careful of things. We have to watch out."

"How is that different now than it was yesterday?" River pressed. She pointed at him. "You do what you want. But what matters to me is that Hawk is back, and I'm going wherever he takes me."

Owl was surprised and pleased. River

90

hadn't said more than two words since her grandfather's death and her recovery from her bout with the plague. To hear her speak like this, sounding strong and self-assured again, was a small miracle.

"River's right," Sparrow echoed.

"How are we gonna protect ourselves?" Panther demanded, unwilling to give it up. His face was dark with anger. "Tell me that!"

"Where's Logan Tom?" Hawk asked. "He was sent to protect us. He can help."

"He can't protect no one!" Panther sneered. He brushed angrily at the air in front of him. "Why do you think he's not sitting in on this, O mighty one who sees and knows all?"

"Watch your mouth, Panther Pee!" Sparrow snapped at him. She was on her feet, her fists clenched.

"Watch your own mouth, birdbrain!" Panther rose, as well.

"Oh, sit down and grow up!" Cat growled from back in the shadows. Rabbit hopped out of her lap and hissed. "Go on, little children! Sit down!"

She said it without shouting, but there was an edge to her words that stopped both where they were. Glowering at each other, they sat.

"Logan is in a coma," Owl interjected before Panther and Sparrow could start up again. "He was in a terrible fight, and he was almost killed. Panther and Catalya rescued him, but he's been unconscious ever since.

We've done what we can to help him, but he won't come awake."

"Might not *ever* come awake," Panther muttered, giving Sparrow a hard look.

Quickly Owl said, "Why don't all of you tell Hawk and Tessa what happened to us after they disappeared?"

The others were eager to do so, and for a time the conversation turned away from the end of the world and the journey ahead to a recounting of the escape from the city and the trek south in the wake of the invasion off the harbor. They told about the attack on the compound; about the boy with the ruined face and the death of Squirrel; about the encounter with the "Creepers," as Panther had named them; and about the attack on the camp by Croaks that had led to Candle's kidnapping. Everyone shared a piece of the story. Even Catalya took part, relating how she had encountered Logan and taken him to the Senator and what had happened afterward.

Owl let the others talk without joining in, content to watch how they interacted, paying particular attention to Hawk. She was still getting used to the idea that he was alive. It wasn't that she had believed he was dead. It was mostly that she had lived for so long with the possibility of it. Having him back was such an enormous relief that she was overwhelmed by it.

She found herself thinking about how much the members of her little family had changed since they had left their city home. They had grown, some differently than others, but all in one way or another. She was pleased that River had come back from the loss of her grandfather, her dark despondency and apathy faded into the past. Fixit was better, too. He no longer talked about his failures and his shortcomings. He no longer agonized over his part in the death of the Weatherman. Even Cat was beginning to feel like one of the family. Slowly but surely, the others had accepted her, in small ways first, then in large measure. Panther was especially attentive, as if what they had shared in rescuing Logan Tom had forged a bond between them.

Maybe we can't make this journey Hawk wants us to make, she thought. *But it doesn't feel that way. Not to me.*

"So we got out from under the stands," Panther was saying. "All these Krilka Koos stump heads start running for their lives. Logan, he was throwing fire at them with that black staff, yards of it, everything burning. It was something! But we got to him, me and Cat — he didn't burn us — and we got him out of there and back up to the freeway. That's where the Ghosts found us."

"I brought the AV back to get them," Fixit said proudly. "I told Owl we couldn't wait anymore to see what was going to happen, that we had to come back for them. We would have gone right into that camp if we'd had to! Wouldn't we, Owl?"

He stopped suddenly, staring at her. "What's wrong?"

They were all looking at her, and she realized that she was crying. She wiped at her eyes, knowing she couldn't explain why. "I was just thinking about Squirrel," she lied. "Go ahead, keep talking."

They hesitated for a moment, not sure what they should do, then gave in to their excitement and went back to their story. Owl took a deep, steadying breath. Fixit had been so unexpectedly brave, telling her he had to go, wheeling the AV around with only Chalk and Sparrow for company, leaving the rest of them to wait. Had to be quick and mobile, he had told her, so the wagon and the other Ghosts had to stay behind. She was afraid for him, but she knew that he was determined and that what he was doing was the right thing. Chalk was his reluctant companion; he went because Fixit was his best friend and they did everything together, even the things that one of them didn't want to do. Sparrow went because she knew how to use the Parkhan Spray.

"We been heading south ever since," Panther finished up. "That's how you found us, coming down the freeway to find you."

"Logan Tom is still unconscious?" Hawk

94

asked him.

"Ain't said a word or moved a muscle since we got him out." The other boy gave him a dark look. "So what's to keep us from being sliced and diced out there on the trail once you take us to wherever, Bird-Man? We ain't got Mister Knight of the Word anymore. We ain't got anyone with real skill in the staying-alive way. We got some firepower with the flechettes and the sprays, but nothing like that black staff."

"Maybe we do," Hawk said quietly.

They all looked at him, Owl hardest of all.

"Hawk, don't . . . ," Tessa started to say.

He held up one hand quickly, like he knew what she was going to say and didn't want her to, Owl thought. Tessa, in turn, it seemed, was afraid he was going to reveal something that he shouldn't. Owl didn't know what it was, but she was pretty sure it had something to do with the way he had changed on finding out the truth about who and what he was. She could sense that change, but not yet define it. She watched him closely to see what he would do next, searching for the answer.

Then all at once Hawk was staring right at her.

"Can I have a look at Logan Tom?" he asked.

Owl led the way, wheeling herself with help from Candle, who climbed down off her lap and walked beside her. The others trailed along behind, whispering among themselves. The night had gone deeper and darker, and while the stars continued to fill the sky with their pinpricks of light, the moon had disappeared. In the distance, lost in the blackness, a dog howled.

Cheney, who had risen from his repose to follow Hawk, never even so much as glanced in the direction of the sound, his dark muzzle swinging from side to side in that familiar way. Hawk was watching Owl again, thinking that she recognized that something was different about him and was wondering what it was. She was too smart not to pick up on it, too connected to him. She knew it was real; she just didn't know yet what form it had taken because it wasn't something she could see.

Eventually, she would figure it out. They all would. Or events would force him to reveal it.

That the magic that had formed him had surfaced from its dormant state and was now a full-blown presence.

He was a boy, same as always. But he was a gypsy morph, too. It was odd to think like this. He didn't feel any different than he had before the King of the Silver River had saved him and brought him into the gardens. But where before he had lacked knowledge of his origins, had accepted his memories of his

96

childhood as real, now he knew the truth. Not only knew it, but had seen the extent of it demonstrated at that militia-controlled bridge where he had used his magic — almost without knowing what he was doing — to turn everything into a tangled green jungle.

But that didn't mean he was ready to talk to the others about it. Tessa knew because she had seen what he could do. But the others were still getting used to the idea that the Hawk they knew was only a small piece of the Hawk he had become. They needed time to come to terms with this, and telling them too much at once risked an unpleasant response. They were his family, but even your family could be alienated by discoveries they were not prepared for.

Hawk did not want that to happen. On the other hand, he had no idea what to do to prevent it once the whole truth came out.

Logan Tom lay atop the hay wagon, wrapped in blankets and asleep on one of the collapsible stretchers. Beneath bruises and scratches, his face was bloodless in the pale wash of the starlight; his skin felt damp and cold to the touch. He was breathing in uneven, shallow gulps, and now and then he twitched as if plagued by troublesome dreams.

Hawk climbed up beside him and knelt close. The others stayed where they were, standing next to the wagon, peering upward like supplicants. Even Tessa did not try to join him, sensing perhaps that he needed to do this alone and without the possibility of distraction. He glanced at her and smiled. She smiled back, her beautiful face brightening in a way that left him weak with need. He loved her so much, and it made him suddenly afraid. All he wanted was to be with her, but he knew in that instant — in a way that defied argument — he might be wishing for something that could never happen.

He put the thought aside, unable to accept it, even to consider that it might be true. His eyes left her face, and he turned his attention to the man lying on the stretcher. Logan Tom, Knight of the Word and his protector. Now it was Hawk's turn to protect him. He wondered momentarily if he could do it. Then he thought of Cheney as the dog had lain dying in their home in Pioneer Square, and he knew that he could.

He reached out to Logan, placed his hands on the other's body, and felt the other twitch slightly in response. He was awake inside his damaged mind, but he couldn't find his way out. Or perhaps he didn't want to; Hawk couldn't tell which. What mattered was that he needed to know that someone was out here who cared about him and would welcome him back from the darkness into which he was submerged.

"Logan," the boy said softly, and moved his

hands from the other's body to his head, palms pressing gently against either side of the wan face.

Logan, he repeated in his mind.

Then he reached down and enfolded the sleeping man in his arms, closing his eyes as he did so, hugging the limp body close. He felt Logan twitch again — once, twice. Then he was still. Hawk pressed the other close, held him as he had Cheney, and willed him to come back.

Wake up, Logan.

He said it several times, each time pressing his palms into the other's back. He felt the warmth growing inside him, just as it had with Cheney, and he knew the magic was working. He let the feeling build and did not try to rush what was happening. He knew from before — with Cheney and again with the foliage on the bridge — that it was a response he could not control, a response that surfaced from deep within and took the course of action that was called for. It was like watching the birds for which he'd named himself take flight. He could not determine where they would go; he could only soar with them in his mind and imagine their freedom.

The warm feeling peaked and then exited his body through his hands in short bursts. He could feel the familiar bitter taste on the tip of his tongue, widening to fill his mouth. It lasted only a few moments. Then the

99

warmth faded and the bitterness disappeared. He released his grip on Logan Tom and gently laid him down again.

When he straightened, the Knight of the Word was looking up at him. "You're back," the other whispered.

"So are you," Hawk answered, smiling.

Gathered close around the hay wagon the Ghosts stared wordlessly, eyes wide, except for Catalya, who was standing well back from the others where they couldn't see that she was crying.

SEVEN

Logan Tom could not remember all the details. Whether it was the intensity of his battle with Krilka Koos or his shock at being stabbed with a viper-prick or something else entirely, he had lost bits and pieces of what had happened just before he lapsed into his coma. Hawk's gypsy morph magic had been enough to bring him back to consciousness, but not enough to restore his memory.

Given what he could recollect, he decided it might be just as well.

Because what he did remember haunted him in a way that nothing had since the death of Michael. It had taken him years to come to terms with that experience, and in truth it was just weeks ago, while on his way west to find the gypsy morph, that he had finally done so. There in that mountain pass amid the spirits of the dead, he had put the ghosts of his old life to rest and banished at last the terrible sense of guilt and failure they had fostered in him.

Now it seemed he might have awakened to an entirely new form of haunting.

It wasn't the events themselves that were troubling. He understood that he couldn't expect to control events any more than he could control the rising and setting of the sun. He had responded to them in the best way he knew how, and by doing so had saved his life. He did not regret any part of that. Nor did he feel any particular regret for what he had done to Krilka Koos, a dangerous and messianic madman who would have killed others if he had not been defeated and disabled. Krilka Koos had courted his fate and had found it.

No, it wasn't in the events themselves. It was in his response to them. Not in how he had reacted to them physically, but in how he had responded emotionally. The former was over and done with in moments, but the latter lingered on. Emotional response was an aftereffect of every battle, every violent encounter, and over the years he had learned to recognize it and live with it. Every time he attacked and destroyed a slave camp and the children on which the demons had experimented, he lived with the pain and the sense of horror and guilt for weeks afterward. Sometimes months. If he was brutally honest, he would admit to himself that he was living with it still.

It was so here, but in a different way. Doing

battle with Krilka Koos had awakened something new. He didn't feel pain or horror or guilt about what he had done to the rogue Knight of the Word. But in the course of his struggle he had lost control of himself. This wasn't new; it had happened before. In the bloodlust of battle, losing control was almost a given. If you weren't madder and more reckless than those you fought to defeat, you were probably going to die. Michael had taught him that, and Michael had been right.

But this time something new had happened. This time he had enjoyed it. He had reveled in it. And now, in the aftermath, he was eager for a return of the feelings it had generated.

How much worse, he wondered, could it be than this? His unwanted fascination with and desire for a resurgence of those feelings of power and freedom was terrifying. It suggested the onset of a steady disregard of the moral compass that had guided him all these years. He had always worried that someday the power of the black staff of his office, the magic that defined the Knights of the Word, would prove too much for him. The simple fact that there seemed to be almost no boundaries to its limits save those placed on it by the strength of commitment and sense of right and wrong of the user had troubled him from the beginning. But he had been confident that he could handle it, still a young man who believed in himself completely. He understood the risks, but he was more than willing to accept them for a chance to strike back at the demons and once-men responsible for the loss of his family and his childhood. Revenge was a powerful motivator, and it gave him a reason to embrace a power he might otherwise have shunned.

But that power had now peaked in him, had overwhelmed and claimed him, and he was no longer its master. Not that he couldn't control it; he could. Not that he still wasn't able to wield it effectively in his efforts to do what needed doing; he was. But he knew, at the same time, that any use of the magic of his staff was tainted by his freshly discovered craving for it. Rather than think of the magic as a necessary evil, he thought of it as an unsatisfied need. He wanted more of it — its taste and feel, its wild surge through his body, and the sense of freedom it generated within him.

He kept this to himself. He could not discuss this with the Ghosts. They were only kids, and they might not even understand what he was talking about. But more than that, they depended on him. He couldn't very well saddle them with the knowledge that he might not be as dependable as they wanted him to be, that he might not be master of the magic in all the ways he should. He could not give them reason to doubt him.

He tried to take comfort from the fact that he was still alive. It was no small accomplishment to have done battle with a rogue Knight of the Word and been able to walk away. Damaged perhaps, but in one piece. He had survived the other's madness and dark purpose. He had put an end to a dangerous enemy. Even the poison of the viper-prick, plunged into his body in a last-ditch effort to finish him, had failed to kill him. He owed Catalya for that; he owed her his life. Panther, of all people, had been quick to let him know. She might have kept it to herself; she likely would have. But Panther had formed an unexpected bond with her, and he was eager to share his feelings. Telling Logan what she had done to save him when it seemed that saving him was impossible was one way of doing that.

All these thoughts roiled through Logan Tom as he rode in the front passenger's seat of the Lightning S-150 AV the following day. Fixit drove, his experience behind the wheel giving him fresh confidence in his ability to master the vehicle's sometimes complicated handling. He smiled frequently, an indication of the pleasure he was taking in his work. The final vestiges of the sickness that had claimed him following the death of the Weatherman had vanished.

River, too, was almost back to normal. She sat with Owl and Candle in the backseat. The others rode in the hay wagon, even Panther and Catalya, who were deep in conversation at the wagon's very rear, heads bent close. Rabbit had climbed onto Panther's lap and curled up. The boy seemed unaware of the cat's presence, his entire attention riveted on the girl. A strange pairing by any measure, yet it seemed to be working. It made Logan smile.

They were traveling south again, following the cracked and weed-grown ribbon of the freeway through country that was hilly and forested with the skeletal remains of dead or dying trees turned silvery and black and barren, limbs stripped of foliage and rendered as stark and lifeless as bleached bones. The plan was to continue on the more accessible paved roadway until they found an intersecting road that would take them east to where Hawk had left the camp of children and caregivers on the banks of the Columbia River. Traveling cross-country as the boy and Tessa and Cheney had done in coming west was impossible with the hay wagon, and abandoning the wagon meant that most of them would have to walk. Walking would slow progress considerably, and everyone agreed that speed was important.

Travel gave Logan time to consider his response to the magic, the feelings it generated, and what he must do to live with it. He knew he had to find a way to control it, if he could not banish it. Rash use of the staff's terrible power could be as addictive as any drug. He had been so grateful to leave behind the days of ferreting out and destroying the slave camps to come in search of the gypsy morph. He'd needed to find something new so that he could rebuild his emotional shield. But he had jumped from the frying pan into the fire. He had traded one form of madness for another.

It was nearing dusk when they found the road they were searching for, a two-lane highway angling east off the freeway into the foothills that fronted the distant bulk of the Cascade Mountains. They were almost to the Columbia River by now, as reckoned by Hawk, and would sight it by morning. They pulled the AV and the wagon it was towing into a paved roadside rest area built for travelers in better days and set up their camp. They ate from their dwindling supplies — reminding Logan once again that they needed to forage for food — and when dinner was finished drifted into smaller groups to talk until they grew sleepy.

Logan let the others gather without him, moving over to a rusting picnic table to take a seat alone. He was surprised when Candle came over to sit across from him. The little girl didn't say anything for a long time. She just sat there, staring down at her feet and off into the leafless trees, her red hair catching the last rays of the fading sun as the night closed in.

Finally, she looked up at him. "Thank you for everything," she said.

He grinned despite himself. "That's a lot to be thanked for."

"Well, for keeping us safe." When he didn't say anything in response right away, she quickly added, "Not just the other night, but all the other times, too. We wouldn't have gotten this far if you hadn't come with us."

He nodded, vaguely uneasy that a ten-year-old child could make him feel so embarrassed. "I'm just doing what I was sent here to do," he said, the reply sounding lame, even to him.

"No," she said, her somber face lifting, her eyes fixing on his. "You were sent to help Hawk. Not us."

She was so smart, he thought. She understood so much. "I know that," he said. "But I have to do what's right, too. Helping all of you feels right to me."

"Even though we aren't magic?"

"Even though. Anyway, Hawk wouldn't be very happy with me if I told him we were leaving you behind."

"Hawk would never leave us," she said. She studied him a moment. "Hawk is our father."

He nodded. "I know that. I know that Owl is your mother. Maybe I'm your uncle. Or something like it."

"You're our friend," she said.

He smiled. "Yeah, I guess I am."

She didn't smile back. "I just wanted you to know."

She got up and walked away. He stared after her, wondering at her grasp of things. She knew better than anyone about keeping those she cared about from danger. Except she hadn't done so lately, he realized suddenly. Owl had told him about her gift, a gift that had saved the Ghosts from harm any number of times. But Candle hadn't warned them of danger even once since he had arrived, he realized.

What did that mean?

He watched Owl while she finished putting away their dishes and supplies with help from River and Sparrow and then as she gathered the Ghosts around her and read them a story. He sat back in the shadows, listening to the sound of her voice in the darkness.

When she was done and the kids were drifting off to sleep, he walked over to where she was sitting in her wheelchair and knelt down beside her. "I enjoyed that," he said.

"That story?" She laughed softly. "Everyone likes being read to. Reading and storytelling before bed has become a tradition with this family."

"It's a good one to have." He looked off into the darkness. "I was talking with Candle earlier, and it got me to thinking. You told me she senses trouble, danger. She has a gift. But she hasn't used it the whole time I've been with you. Not even when we walked into that trap set by Krilka Koos. What do you make of that?"

Owl shook her head. Her brow furrowed and her plain, warm features tightened. "I don't know. She's always had the gift. This is the first time it hasn't worked for her. Maybe it has something to do with you being here to help us. Maybe she thought that was enough and wasn't paying attention."

"Maybe." He hesitated. "I was thinking it might have something to do with Hawk."

"Why Hawk?"

"Because he wasn't with us. Hasn't been since we left Seattle. Maybe she can't use her gift if he isn't present. Maybe it doesn't work then."

"But that doesn't make sense. It was working before she ever came to us." Owl studied him intently. "Unless something has changed."

They looked at each other without speaking for a moment, each waiting for the other to provide the answer to the riddle.

"Maybe you could ask her," Logan suggested.

"She doesn't like talking about it. In fact, she never talks about it anymore. I don't know. I think we have to let it be."

"We can't rely on her then. We can't risk

it." He held her gaze. "Sooner or later, someone is going to ask her if she senses anything. What happens then? We won't be able to trust what she tells us if we don't know the truth."

Owl didn't answer, her eyes troubled. "I'll see what I can do," she told him finally.

After she was gone, he walked over to the AV, retrieved a blanket from the storage compartment, and stretched out on a patch of dry earth. Slipping off his boots, he rolled himself into the blanket and lay back, staring up at the stars. He thought about what he had asked Owl to do. It amounted to asking her to question the value of one of her children. Who was he to ask that of her? He was less trustworthy and dependable than they were.

What right did he have to question anyone else?

He pictured Candle's young face, and he wished suddenly that he could take back what he had said to Owl. But words spoken can never be taken back. They can only be measured for and judged on the strength of their sincerity and need.

Because here there were lives at stake, perhaps that would be enough.

Logan Tom.

He wakes on hearing his name spoken, but when he rises he cannot find the speaker. The

111

night is deep and still, the darkness complete. There is no moon. The stars seem diminished and faint; they seem much farther away than they should, tiny and unreachable. He feels isolated by their distance, a feeling he cannot trace the source of. His lack of understanding disappears when he realizes that he is alone. The Ghosts are gone. The AV and the hay wagon are gone. The camp and its meager supplies are all gone.

He looks around, taking in his surroundings. He is on a barren plain, a flatland stripped of anything even remotely suggesting life. No trees, scrub, brush, animals, insects, or birds. No sounds. No movement. Dirt and rocks and the vast, broad ocean of the night sky — that's all there is. Nothing looks familiar. This is not where he went to sleep. Somehow he has awakened in a different place. He does not think he has come to this place of his own accord. He has been brought here, and his companions have allowed it to happen. He does not like to think that he has been abandoned, but he feels as if he has.

"Logan Tom."

This time there is no mistake. The voice is high and sweet and clear, and he recognizes it at once. It is the Lady who speaks. He stands where he is, unmoving, searching for her in the dark. It seems impossible that she is there; he can see for miles and miles in all directions, the land flat and bare and empty, and there is no one. Nevertheless, he knows she will appear. She always does. He must be patient until she shows herself, allowing her space and time to do so.

The seconds tick away. She does not come. She does not speak. He is still alone, and he grows anxious.

Then all at once she appears right in front of him, a vision of white in the darkness. She hovers in the air, her feet not touching the earth, her gown trailing out behind her like white smoke. Her face radiates peace and comfort, and it brings him instantly to tears. He tries to move closer to her, but he cannot make his legs obey.

"Lady," he whispers.

"You are needed elsewhere, Logan Tom," she responds softly. "Your skills and talent and experience are required by others. Even though you are responsible for the safety of the gypsy morph, you must leave him now and travel south to the city of the Elves."

Elves, he thinks in disbelief. *She said, Elves.*

"They are threatened by the one you seek, the one promised to you if you complete your charge. Demons and once-men close in on them, and if you do not reach them in time, they will disappear from the earth. The future we seek to preserve will not come to pass."

He says nothing, taking it all in and thinking how crazy it sounds.

Elves.

"Another Knight of the Word has helped secure a talisman for the Elves, but she is injured and cannot aid them further. So it is given to you to go in her place. The talisman must be put to use and those who use it protected and guided to where the boy who will lead you all will be waiting to take you to the safehold. To the old man of whom the boy has spoken. To the King of the Silver River."

Logan has no idea what talisman she is talking about. But he knows there is no point in asking for explanations. "How am I to find the Elves?" he asks instead.

"Trim will guide you." Her slender arm lifts and points into the distance. "Go south. He will meet you on the road. Go afoot. Go alone."

"Trim?" he repeats.

"He is small but very durable. Trust in him to lead you."

He wants to know more. "Who am I looking for among the Elves? Is it someone in particular? Who possesses this talisman?"

Her smile dazzles him. "You will know when you have found who you are looking for. You will know it in your heart."

Another enigmatic answer, but one that she seems to feel says everything. He shakes his head. "What of these children I am leaving? Who will protect them?"

"As before, Logan Tom, they will protect themselves."

She is shimmering now, a sign that she is getting ready to leave him. He wants to hold her back, to preserve the feeling of comfort and peace he always finds in her presence. But he knows he can do nothing to stay her, that he has no hold on her. He watches her begin to fade.

"Brave Knight," she whispers to him.

He cannot speak. Then she is gone, and he is alone again, emptied out inside, bereft of something important. He clenches his fists and teeth and by doing so manages to keep himself from crying out his dismay.

The sun had barely risen, its golden orb hazy behind a screen of pollution and dust at the crest of the mountains east. Owl stared into the murky film and thought about what lay ahead. "Are you certain about this?" she asked him again.

Logan nodded. He was packing food and water into a backpack, enough for a week if he was careful with his usage. He knew how to provision for a trek like this, even if he hadn't been on one for more than a year. He thought he was fit enough, though, and ready.

"But why would you be sent to us and then asked to leave before doing what you came to do? Especially if Hawk is so important to everything. I don't understand it."

He looked over at her. "I don't understand it, either. But it isn't my place to refuse. If the Lady asks it of me, I am required to comply. It is in the nature of my oath as a Knight of the Word."

She could tell that his mind was made up, that there was no arguing the point. His sense of duty was too strong to be swayed by anything she might say.

"Hey, Owl, we'll be all right. We can manage without Mister Knight of His Broken Word." Panther sounded angry. He practically sneered. "Come and go as he pleases, that's him. No matter who saved his life, he's gonna do what he wants to do. We can be damned, for all it matters."

"Shut up, Panther," Catalya snapped.

"Yeah, shut up!" Sparrow echoed.

Panther stared at them, then shrugged and walked away. "Do whatever you ladies say," he called over his shoulder. "You just ask."

"I'm leaving the AV," Logan told Owl. He looked around, found Fixit, and tossed him the keys. "You're in charge. You know best how she works. Take good care of her until I get back."

Fixit nodded but said nothing.

Hawk walked over. "We know you have to go," he said. He waited for Logan to look at him. "It's all right. Don't worry about us. We can take care of ourselves. We're together now, and we have Cheney. We'll be careful."

"Yeah, don't be worrying about us!" Panther echoed from twenty feet away.

Logan shoved the last of his supplies into

the pack and stood up. "I know I don't have to worry. But I will anyway." He glanced again at Owl. "Listen to her advice. She's the one who will do the best to take care of all of you. Do what she says."

Hawk gave him a faint grin. "We know that."

"I'll be back as quick as I can manage it."

"Quicker, if it's possible," Owl called to him.

She watched him sling the backpack over one shoulder and pick up his black staff. She saw him start to say something and then stop. He shook his head.

All at once Candle came running over to him and threw her arms around his waist. "Come back to us," she said, her voice so soft that only Owl and Logan heard clearly.

The Knight of the Word put a hand on the little girl's head and pressed her against him. "I will, Candle."

He met Owl's eyes briefly and looked away. Then he disengaged himself from Candle and began walking down the freeway. He took long, steady strides, the tip of his staff clacking softly against the pavement.

Owl and the others watched after him until he was out of sight.

EIGHT

The day improved with the passing of the
hours as the sun brightened, the haze lifted,
and the sky cleared. Logan Tom made good
progress following the highway south through
the foothills, the slopes he was forced to
climb gentle enough that they did not wear
him down. He knew he hadn't recovered
from the aftereffects of his battle with Krilka
Koos; he could feel it in the ache of his
muscles and stiffness of his joints. But whatever Hawk had done to bring him out of his
coma had also healed the worst of his injuries.
Walking helped loosen him up, the blood and
adrenaline pumping through him working
like a restorative.

He kept a sharp eye out for any sign of
danger, but saw nothing. Now and then a
bird would wing its way overhead, sometimes
more than one, and once he saw what might
have been a fox. He couldn't be sure; he was
too far away to make it out clearly. He passed
abandoned, rusted-out vehicles and piles of

debris. He passed downed trees and limbs, pieces of fence wiring, and old tires and axles, all reminders of what was past, all of it useless. Even after so many years, it made him sad.

In the welter of his sadness, he found himself mulling over what he knew about the direction of things. The world's destruction was imminent, its end a certainty. All the terrible things that had happened before were just a prelude to this finishing off, this endgame. When it was over, everything would be changed. What would the world be like then? What shape would it take in the aftermath? Would the people and creatures led to safety by Hawk be all that were left? Would anything else survive, anything outside the protection of the safehold? How long would it be before they could reemerge from hiding?

So many questions, and no answers to be had. He wondered if even the Lady knew how things would turn out. He thought that maybe she knew better than he did, but perhaps not so well as he imagined.

He wondered suddenly if he would live to see any of it, or if he was fated to go the way of the other Knights of the Word. Whatever the case, he had been promised a chance to settle matters with that old man, that demon that had destroyed his family. It would be enough if he were given that. He had always known it would be enough.

Morning crawled toward noon. He was on the freeway bypass, a broader, less cluttered stretch of pavement. Buildings began appearing on either side of him, clusters of residences and businesses, some collapsing, some shuttered and barred, all abandoned. He kept looking for someone who might be his guide, kept looking for Trim, but no one appeared. He assumed that whichever way he went, whatever road he chose, he would be found. Nonetheless, he found himself wondering how long he would have to walk before that happened. He guessed he shouldn't worry, but he didn't like the uncertainty of traveling toward an unknown destination.

Toward a city of Elves.

Elves, he thought again, still astonished by the idea.

He shook his head. What would they look like? He remembered fairy creatures from his childhood from stories read to him by his mother. But he couldn't picture them. They were little people, weren't they? Tiny and argumentative? But magical, too? He thought about it, trying to remember something more, but couldn't. It would have to be a surprise.

Like almost everything else in his life.

Just after midday, he crossed a bridge over the Columbia River and entered Oregon. More hills awaited him, and in the distance to the east a huge peak loomed over everything. He kept walking, eyeing fresh clusters of buildings separated by broad stretches of grass and fields withered almost to dust. The landscape spread away like a still life.

A shadow passed over him, causing him to flinch. He looked up in time to see an owl swoop down out of the sunlight and glide into the trees ahead. He stared, surprised. What was an owl doing out in the daylight? What was an owl doing out at all? He hadn't seen one in years. He had thought them all extinct.

He walked on a little farther and then stepped off the side of the road to sit and eat something before continuing on. There were buildings all around him by now, flat-sided, weather-beaten, and crumbling, but there was no sign of life. The air was heavy and still, and the smells of oil and decay permeated everything. He tried to ignore them as he ate, but it was impossible to do.

He was midway through his meal when he heard a sound behind him and turned to find a girl standing ten feet away. She was maybe fifteen, ragged and dirty, thin to the point of emaciation, her brown hair lank and un-combed. She wore an old coat that hung open over a dress. Both were of indeterminate color, the leavings of some better time and place, the discards of a better world.

"Got any food to spare, mister?" she asked him. She did not look at him as she spoke, her eyes lowered as if she had no expectation that he would even respond. "I'm awful hungry."

He looked past her for others, for the ones who might have sent her out here to distract him, predators seeking to take anything he had on him. But he saw no one.

"Where is your family?" he said.

She glanced up briefly, shrugged. "Dead. Mama died last week. I'm the only one left."

"It's dangerous, being out here alone like this."

Another shrug. "The compounds won't have me. They wouldn't have any of us, when I still had my family. Street people, they called us. Trash. Sometimes worse."

He studied her for a moment. Then he sighed. "Come over here and sit down with me."

She did so cautiously, suspicious of his motives. When she sat, she was careful to keep out of arm's reach. He supposed she understood the dangers better than he did. Wordlessly, he passed her food and water in their prepackaged containers. "Here. Take these."

She ate and drank as if she hadn't done so in a very long time. He watched her devour everything, barely pausing to look up. "Tastes good" was all she said.

He finished his own meal, and by then she was done with hers. She wiped her mouth on the sleeve of her coat. She was sullen-faced and not very pretty, but her smile was nice. She inclined her head in his direction. "Thanks."

He nodded. "You don't have anyone you can go live with?"

She shook her head. "No one close. Wouldn't know if the ones farther off are even alive." She hesitated. "I could come with you."

He furrowed his brow. "That's not a good idea."

"I can keep up. I'm a good walker. I could help carry stuff." She licked her lips, looked back down at her feet. "I could keep you warm at night. I could do things for you."

"I'm going somewhere dangerous. You wouldn't be safe."

She curled her lip disdainfully. "Safe? What are you talking about? I'm not safe here! I'm not safe anywhere! You know what happens to girls like me out here alone? You know what's already happened, not two days after Mama died? Safe? Hey, mister, what world are you living in?"

He shook his head. "It doesn't matter. You can't come with me."

She stared at him a moment, then let her shoulders sag. "I thought you would say that, but I had to ask. You don't look like someone who needs me or anybody." She eyed him furtively. "Can you spare me a little more food? Just a little?"

He gave her half of what he had brought. He couldn't seem to help himself. When he looked at her he saw Meike, the freckle-faced girl he had left behind at the Safeco Field compound in the aftermath of Hawk's disappearance. He had told her to run away, but had she? If she had, had she ended up like this girl — ragged and starving and alone? He didn't like thinking about it, but there it was. All these abandoned children, tossed into a world of predators and poisons, bereft and hopeless waifs. He wanted to save them, just as Michael had saved him all those years ago. But he knew it was impossible. He couldn't save them. Probably no one could.

"You sure you won't take me with you?" she asked him again. "I won't be any bother. I'll do whatever you tell me to."

He shook his head. "Tell you what you should do," he said to her. "Go back up the road, cross the bridge into Washington, and keep going north on the freeway. First two-lane road you come to — only one you'll pass that's a real highway — you take it east toward the mountains. Some other kids are going that way. There are even more kids waiting for them, and some adults, too. They're all heading for a place that really is safe. If you can catch up to them, you'll be all right."

She looked at him doubtfully. "For real?"

"Better than staying here, isn't it?"

She nodded slowly, flicking back loose strands of her long hair. "Okay. I guess I can try. I can walk all right. I can find my way. Some other kids would be good company."

"If you leave now, you can get to the crossroad by nightfall. Just keep traveling east after that until you catch up to them. Be careful."

She grinned crookedly. "You don't need to tell me that." She paused. "Is it really all that dangerous where you're going?"

"Worse."

She studied him a moment. "Okay, I believe you. Good luck. Thanks."

He set out alone a short time afterward, waving good-bye to her as she began walking in the opposite direction. She didn't appear to have any supplies or clothes or anything beyond what he had given her or what she was wearing. She was a skinny, ragged figure as she disappeared from view, and he wondered, as he had about Meike, if he would ever see her again.

A short time after that, the owl reappeared, swooping down right in front of him, nearly taking off his head. He drew up short and stared at it as it circled away and then back again. He peered upward at the bird in disbelief, shading his eyes against the glare of the sun. *What in the world?* The owl soared overhead, spiraled down, and landed on a split-rail fence not a dozen yards from where he stood.

"What's the matter with you?" he yelled at the bird.

The owl stared at him, its yellow saucer eyes unblinking. It was a small bird but strikingly marked with a speckled white breast and black bands on its wings and rings about its eyes. It had a decidedly durable look about it, he thought, even though it was sort of small for a . . .

He paused in midthought, remembering suddenly where he had heard those words before, realizing as he did so what he was looking at.

"Trim?" he asked the bird.

The owl blinked in response, spread his wings briefly, and settled back again.

A bird, he thought. *She's sent me a bird for a guide.* At first he found it ridiculous. The owl was an oddity that didn't seem right for what he needed. But the more he thought about it, the more sense it made. He had expected Trim to be a two-legged companion, one he could converse with and ask questions of. But that wasn't what he needed. What he needed was a creature who could go anywhere and could find the least dangerous path to where he must go. What better place to do that than from the air? If Trim could make known to Logan what he must do, he might prove to be exactly the guide he required.

"All right," he said. "What do I do now?"

He had no idea if the bird understood him, no reason to think he did other than it seemed sort of necessary. In any case, he had to try something to find out if they could communicate.

To his surprise, Trim gave a short screech, lifted off from the fence, and winged away. Giving a mental shrug, Logan Tom set out after him.

Less than five miles farther on, Trim flew off the freeway and down a smaller road leading east toward the huge mountain he had seen earlier. He disappeared for a minute and then flew back again, circling overhead. Clearly, he intended for Logan to follow, so Logan did.

This new road traveled in a straight line through residential neighborhoods and strip malls, shops and schools, a community of thousands in better days, but mostly deserted now. If there were people, they were staying out of sight. All Logan saw as he passed were packs of dogs and stray cats, and these didn't look particularly friendly. He kept to the middle of the road and stayed watchful for any signs of danger, but nothing approached.

He passed through the heart of the community, buildings standing silent and empty, and entered a new stretch of countryside. Here the trees grew thick and skeletal about structures that were on the verge of collapse.

Dark interiors were visible through missing doors and windows, and shadows draped everything in pools of black. There was an unpleasant feel to everything, as if the destructive forces that had claimed the people who once lived here were still hungry.

He had reached the far edge of the community when Trim veered off the road and landed on the roof of a garage set back in a tangle of collapsed fencing and rusted-out vehicles. Logan left the road and walked over to where the bird roosted. By now he was beginning to understand better Trim's method of communication and knew what was expected of him. Even so, he was cautious. He hadn't missed seeing the clutch of lantern eyes peering out at him from inside one of the buildings he had passed earlier.

Behind the garage, hidden from the road, was a metal-sided shed with locks closing off a heavily reinforced door. The metal was rusted and weather-stained by now, but still solidly in place. Trim left the garage roof and settled atop the shed. Logan stood looking up at him for a moment, and then walked over and tested the locks. There was no give at all. He looked up again at the bird, who looked down at him. He sighed heavily. Then he brought up the staff and burned the locks away.

The door to the shed swung open.

Inside sat a bulky, four-wheeled vehicle of

considerable size. It was covered with a fitted tarp, but he could make out what it was through rips and holes in the worn fabric draped over it. An AV of some sort, similar to the Lightning but much bigger. He walked over, pulled off the cloth, and stepped back in surprise.

He was looking at a Ventra 5000, a huge, muscular machine that was in near-mint condition. There were a few dings and scratches on the paint, and there was dust and bits of debris coating the finish, but aside from that it was untouched. He smiled despite himself. He had seen only one of these machines in his entire life, and that one hadn't been working. Ventras were famous, attack vehicles that surpassed even the Lightning in firepower and strength. The Lightning was quick and mobile, but the Ventra could take a direct hit from a shoulder rocket and keep going. In his days with Michael, stories of Ventras were legion. But all of them supposedly were destroyed during the militia wars, appropriated by the governments and sacrificed in battles that no one won. He had never thought to see another in his lifetime.

He walked over to the driver's door and pulled the release. The door opened with a soft hiss of pistons relaxing, and lights came on in the interior. The solar cells that powered the beast weren't dead, which meant that the Ventra might still run. He couldn't believe

129

his good fortune. With a machine like this, his journey would take only a fraction of the time of walking. Not to mention the protection he would enjoy on his way.

He glanced back outside and found Trim sitting on an old barrel, staring at him with his saucer eyes. Guess luck wasn't a part of the equation, he thought. But how in the world did an owl know that a Ventra 5000 was inside this shed? Maybe Trim was something more than he appeared. Maybe the Lady, in sending the owl, had known what Logan needed better than he did.

He found the hood release and pulled it, lifted the hood, and peered inside. Eight huge cells rested in their cradles, their power indicators pulsing with a soft green light. All charged and ready to go. He walked to the rear of the vehicle, found the storage compartments for the additional cells, opened the lids, and discovered that these cells were not only fully charged but attached to charging terminals, as well. He stared for a moment, and then climbed up to peer at the Ventra's broad roof. Solar collectors were built into the armor in narrow strips.

He climbed down again, shaking his head in amazement. Of all the things in the world he expected to find, a Ventra was among the last.

"Nice work, Trim," he called out to the owl, who ignored him.

He climbed into the driver's seat, feeling the air-infused cushioning wrap solidly about him. He found the belting mechanism, triggered it, and was locked in place. He looked down at the dash. No key. Just a numbered pad. You had to know the code. He thought about it a moment, and then felt under the gear locks. Sure enough, the code was engraved on the underside of the column. That was the way the owners did it with these machines, Michael had told him. If they were amateurs.

He traced the numbers with his fingers, reading them. Another trick Michael had taught him. It was sometimes better to start a vehicle in the dark, avoid using a light that would alert an enemy. He repeated the numbers to himself and then punched them in.

The Ventra's engine came to life, a soft velvety purr that barely registered inside the cab. Logan smiled some more. He glanced at the rear seating — room enough for seven or eight — and then farther back at the storage and weapons compartments. There were two, long and wide enough for Parkhan Sprays and Tyson Flechettes. Equipped, he would wager.

He glanced down at the weapons panel and its array of blinking green lights. Rockets, sprays, lasers . . . He stopped, catching sight of something new and unexpected. The black lettering leapt out at him from the panel. Carbon Seekers. He hadn't ever seen those, only heard about them. They weren't installed on anything that wasn't government-issue, in the days when there were still governments. But he knew how they worked. They targeted carbon-based life-forms — everything human, for starters — dispatched a dissolver, and the target simply ceased to exist. Very dangerous. Very effective. The thought that he had possession of not one, but two, gave him pause.

Who was the owner of this vehicle, and what had happened to him? Was this his escape transport when things got too bad, a transport he hadn't had time to reach?

An instant later he heard Trim screech, and he looked up in time to see the owl lift off and disappear skyward. Something had disturbed the bird. Logan climbed from the Ventra without turning off the engine and hurried through the shed doors.

Outside, a huge Lizard was lumbering toward him, moaning and growling and raising its massive arms threateningly. The Lizard was covered in thick, jagged scales and was wearing the ragged remains of what had once been some sort of military uniform, now reduced to tatters.

The Lizard saw him and pointed as if seeking to freeze him in place. It stopped and began gesturing; then it pointed at the shed and shook its head as if to admonish Logan, waving its arms some more. For a moment, Logan thought it was simply crazed from its transformation.

Then all of a sudden he realized what was happening. The Lizard was trying to drive him away from the shed and its contents.

He had found the Ventra's owner.

Which explained everything. The owner had been keeping his precious AV hidden away, waiting for who-knew-what. Whatever he was waiting for didn't happen soon enough, and the owner exposed himself to radiation and began to change into a Lizard. He couldn't stop the change, but he couldn't make himself give up the vehicle, either.

Now he was too huge and too clumsy to operate the Ventra, which was why it was still locked away in the shed. All the owner could do was look at it.

"I'm sorry," he told the Lizard. "I'm going to have to take it. I need it to help others who are in trouble."

The Lizard tried to say something, but the words came out as gibberish that Logan couldn't decipher. Apparently the mutation had affected its ability to speak. But there was no mistaking its intent. The Lizard did not want him to take the Ventra.

"I can't let you keep it," Logan answered. "I wish I could, but you don't need it and there are others who do."

The Lizard made a threatening movement, but Logan brought the black staff up at once. "Don't do that," he advised quickly. "I know how strong you are, but the staff makes me much stronger. You can't stop this from happening. Even if you try, you can't."

A long few moments passed. The Lizard stood there, staring at him, not moving, no longer speaking. It didn't seem to know what to do.

"I'm leaving now," Logan told him. "If I can, I'll come back for you when I'm done." He tried to think of what else to say. "Look, I'll take good care of it. The best I can."

He realized how foolish that sounded, but it was all he could come up with. He hesitated a moment; then he went back into the shed, climbed into the AV, closed its heavy doors, and engaged the belting locks. He put the Ventra in gear and eased it through the shed doors out into the yard.

The Lizard was waiting. It stood directly in his path, intending to stop him. Logan kept the vehicle rolling toward it, not rushing his approach, taking his time. The Ventra would turn the Lizard to mush if he floored it, notwithstanding all that scaly armor.

Step aside, he thought, staring out at the Lizard, holding its gaze through the AV's windshield. *Just let me pass.*

The Lizard put out its massive hands and braced itself against the Ventra, trying to stop

134

its forward motion. Logan kept the machine moving ahead, slowly, steadily, inexorably. The Lizard bunched its muscles and dug in, but the AV forced it to give ground.

At last, seeing it could not stop the AV, the Lizard stepped aside. As Logan rolled past, it slammed its huge fists against the hood, a futile, ineffective expression of rage.

It stood looking after the Ventra as Logan drove it away. Then it covered its face with its hands and began to cry.

NINE

The night was deep and still, its darkness a layer of cottony impenetrability that cocooned Kirisin and Simralin as they crept through the trees toward the sleeping city of Arborlon. They moved like cats, their footsteps soundless, their presence invisible. No talking was allowed, Simralin had instructed before they set out. No communication of any sort if it could be helped. She would lead, and Kirisin would follow. What she did, he was to do. If they were lucky, they would not be detected.

They had left the balloon behind, its bag deflated and tucked away with all stays and equipment stowed for ready access and a quick escape. The time for such an escape would come, and speed and efficiency at preparing the balloon for another liftoff might be the difference between life and death. If the demons were waiting for the Elves and their city to be encapsulated within the Loden, they would be quick to act the moment it was done.

Kirisin imagined all those points of light, each representing a demon or its creature, converging on him. The image made him shiver.

They had landed the balloon above the sleeping city, choosing a meadow just beyond the tree line and below the bare rock of the upper slopes. It was a considerable distance from where they had to go, but there was no safe or suitable landing sites closer. Whatever else happened, they could not risk damaging their only means of escape.

"Remember, Little K," his sister had said to him as they prepared to set out. "Follow in my footsteps and stay close. I will keep us safe."

He trusted her to do so. Hadn't she done so on their journey to Syrring Rise? Hadn't she always done so when danger threatened? And when it came to a Tracker's skills, hers were the best. Larkin Quill had told him on that very first night on Redonnelin Deep that he had watched her pass right through the center of a large camping expedition of humans, and not one of them had caught even a glimpse of her. Anyone who could do that was something special, he'd said.

On this night, he depended on her to be so again. She did not tell him where they were going. She did not say what she intended to do. That was all right with him. He didn't

137

have any suggestions in any case. She knew what was needed, and she would have that firmly in mind, wherever she took them.

The minutes slipped past as they worked their way down the mountain slope and into the heavy forests that concealed Arborlon. Overhead, the stars speckled the dark sky, thousands upon thousands. Their brilliant light filtered through the canopy of the old growth and let the Belloruus siblings find their way more easily. It also revealed them. Twice Simralin stopped where she was, holding up her hand, listening to the silence, her head turning first one way and then the other. Both times she altered course slightly. Both times Kirisin saw and heard nothing.

I would be lost without her, he thought.

Nevertheless, he concentrated on keeping eyes and ears sharp for movement and sound. He would help as much as he could, although he did not think his sister required it. Now and then, his hand would stray to where the Elfstones nestled in his pocket, touching them, finding reassurance in their presence. He thought of how much his sister and he and the Knight of the Word, Angel Perez, had gone through to retrieve them from the ice caves on Syrring Rise. He thought of the hardships they had endured during their search for the Stones and of the lives that had been sacrificed. Barely a month had passed, but it felt like so much more. It all seemed as if it had happened in an earlier life.

He shook his head. What had begun as a group effort had ended as a responsibility given solely to him to fulfill. He understood and accepted this charge, but at the same time he wished that it could be over. He wanted things to go back to the way they were when he had been just another of this year's Chosen and the boundaries of his life were defined by nothing more than his obligation to care for the Ellcrys and her gardens.

But he knew the truth of things. However this turned out, nothing would ever be the same.

Their progress through the forests of the Cintra was slow and cautious, and by the time the first houses of the city came into view the eastern sky was beginning to lighten. They moved more quickly then, passing out of the trees and onto the small pathways that skirted the buildings and the edges of Arborlon. A few distant figures passed through the shadowy predawn. But mostly the Elves slept still, not yet ready to rise for the new day. They were through the sentry lines, Kirisin knew, so those they encountered now would be average citizens on their way to their work rather than Elven Hunters or Home Guard. The danger lay mostly in coming face-to-face with someone who might recognize them.

They avoided this, and in another thirty

minutes they had reached Tragen's cottage. Without hesitating Simralin took them up on the porch and into the shadows of the overhang. She knocked softly and, when there was no response, retrieved a key from a space above the lintel and unlocked the door.

Once inside, she closed and locked the door behind her, and then moved quickly through the rooms to make certain they were alone.

"He must be on duty," she told Kirisin when she returned. "We'll stay here for now. I don't think we can risk going out in the daylight. We have to wait until dark."

"Wait?" he repeated in disbelief.

She took hold of his shoulders and brought her face close to his own. "Think about it. The demons aren't attacking or even in position to attack. They're hanging back, waiting. On you, I expect. They want you to use the Loden. They think Culph is bringing you back to them. They will wait a reasonable time to hear from him before attacking. But if Arissen Belloruus gets his hands on us, he might decide to make us disappear with no one the wiser. He'll be furious enough to do that. Then you'll never get a chance to use the Loden and the demons will attack anyway and everything we've done will turn out to have been for nothing."

Kirisin frowned. "You're probably right. So what happens when it gets dark?"

"We go before the High Council and de-

140

mand to be heard. We have to make certain they know what is happening and are taking steps to prepare for it. If nothing else, we can tell them about the nature of their enemy. If we can reach the Council chambers without being seen, we have at least a small chance of gaining an audience before the King can stop us."

"You really think that will be enough to persuade them to let me use the Loden?"

She gave him a look. "Well, you better hope it is because that's the only chance we have. If we can't convince them we're telling the truth and that any failure to act on what they've heard means the end of the Elves, we're finished."

They stared at each other in the gray dawn light for a moment, the silence deepening.

"Maybe I better practice up on what I'm going to say," Kirisin said finally.

His sister cocked her eyebrow. "Maybe you better get some sleep first."

He started to protest, but she shoved him toward the bedroom. "Use Tragen's bed. I'll wake you in six hours. Go on, don't argue. I'll keep watch."

"Whoever chooses you for a life partner deserves what he gets," the boy called back to her just before falling across the bed.

He was asleep instantly.

When he woke again, it was still daylight. But

on looking out the window, he could see the shadows lengthening and the light fading. He was groggy and heavy-eyed, and wanted nothing more than to go right back to sleep. But he resisted the impulse, knowing that sleep was an escape from reality at this point. He had to clear his head and get ready for his meeting with the High Council. He walked into the other room and found Simralin asleep in one of the chairs. He stared at her a moment, and she opened her eyes.

"Why are you so noisy?" she asked him.

He grinned, shaking his head. Only Sim could look like she was asleep and not be. He walked over to the sink and pumped some water to wash his face. The water was cool and refreshing, and he lingered for a moment. "I'm sorry I got you involved in all this," he told her.

"I think I got myself involved."

"Well, I'm sorry, anyway. I wish you hadn't."

She rose and stretched her lanky frame, loosening her head scarf to let her long blond hair fall free. She ran her fingers through the thick mass, then tossed her head back to get the hair out of her face and retied the scarf. "That would have been too bad for you, Little K. You have the heart for this, but I have the skills. Anyway, it's good that we can look out for each other."

She came over to the sink to join him,

washed her own face, and pumped water for them to drink, as well. She looked out into the yard and the trees beyond. "I wonder why Tragen isn't back."

"Do you think something might have happened to him?"

She shook her head. "I think he might be out tracking close to where the demons mass. They would have sent a handful of Trackers just to keep watch. He would have been a logical choice. He's as good at it as I am."

Kirisin dried his face. "No one is as good as you are."

She laughed. "Let's have something to eat while we wait for it to get dark. Maybe there's some food in the pantry."

They sat at a little table by the front window and ate a meal of bread and cheese washed down by glasses of ale, all food and drink they found in Tragen's small larder and stone cooler. Kirisin didn't miss that Simralin was so familiar with the house and seemed to know where everything was. He wondered how often she came here, but left the matter alone. They didn't say much while they ate. Kirisin thought about Erisha, remembering how committed she had been at the end of things to saving the Ellcrys. He would tell that to the King. He would make Arissen Belloruus understand how much his daughter had believed in what she was doing. He would find a way to make the King believe, too.

"It's dark enough," Sim said finally, glancing out the window. "Time to go."

Kirisin started for the door. "Wait," his sister called after him. He turned. "Leave your weapons behind." When he looked doubtful, she added, "The guards don't allow weapons in the chambers. Besides, weapons won't help us anyway if we can't do what's needed with words."

They stripped away their long knives and Simralin's bow and arrows and adzl, leaving them on Tragen's small table. Then they wrapped themselves in their cloaks and went out the door of the cottage and into the trees. It was only a short distance to the High Council chambers, but Simralin was taking no chances. She chose a little-traveled path for them to follow, keeping away from the main roads to minimize the possibility of unexpected encounters. It took twice as long for them to get where they were going, and by the time they had reached their destination Kirisin was so anxious and tense that everything he had rehearsed so carefully had flown right out of his head.

There were guards at the entrance to the building, but Simralin never hesitated. She marched right up to them, not bothering to try to disguise who she was. When they recognized her, she held up her hand to stay theirs and said quickly, "It's all right. The King is expecting us. Is Maurin Ortish inside?"

The guards looked at each other and nodded. "We've orders to take you directly to the King if we find you," one said doubtfully.

She smiled. "Now you don't have to bother, Rish. We've found you instead, and we're on our way to see the King. Why don't you come with us?"

Without waiting for a response, she moved past them and through the doors. Kirisin followed close behind, not daring to look at the guards. There were many more guards inside, and a low murmur quickly built as they realized who had appeared. Still, no one tried to interfere, perhaps uncertain as to what they should do. All of them simply stared in a mix of surprise and disbelief as Simralin cheerfully offered greetings, not once suggesting that she and Kirisin were in any sort of trouble.

Then Maurin Ortish appeared through the Council chamber doors, alerted by the sounds without that something was happening. His appearance immediately calmed everyone around him, all heads turning toward him to see what he would do. He took one look at Kirisin and his sister and limped over to them, beckoning to the Home Guards who were still rooted in place.

"Make certain they are unarmed." He stood

in front of Simralin. "I don't know why you came back. You were safely away from here. You should have stayed so."

"Do you really not know why we are here?" Simralin asked him, holding his gaze with her own. "It's because the Knight of the Word told the High Council the truth. Demons and their creatures mass within the forests of the Cintra. They threaten the city. But they do not attack. Kirisin and I know why. We also know who really killed Erisha."

He stared at her, assessing her words. "My orders — direct from the King — are to put you somewhere no one can find you and leave you there until he can question you personally." He paused. "Those are not orders I can question, let alone disobey."

"Do I lie about the danger to the city and our people?" Simralin asked him quickly.

"No," he said, his soft voice almost a whisper.

"Does anyone here know why there has been no attack?"

"There is speculation that the enemy does not know for certain we are here, that they mass for another reason entirely."

"Yes, and cows fly," she snapped at him. "You know better than to believe such nonsense, Maurin. Give us a chance to tell the Council what is happening. What is *really* happening."

"As I said, Simralin, my orders —"

"The King is not thinking clearly," she cut in. "He is enraged over the death of his daughter, and rightly so. But he wrongly blames us. The real killer is an enemy from without, a demon who was disguised as an Elf. Let us reveal all this. Give us a chance!"

"If you don't," Kirisin added quickly, "the enemy attack will come all too quickly and you won't be able to save anyone. You must have seen their numbers. We saw them from the air. There are thousands. Far too many for the Elves to defend against."

"Maurin, please," Simralin begged, lowering her voice, leaning close. "You have known me my whole life. You have known Kirisin. We would not lie about something like this. We would not turn traitor to our own people. Do you really think we are capable of such a thing?"

"People are capable of anything," he replied. "Even Elves. Even good Elves, like you."

"If you take us away, if you do what the King has ordered, you will never know the truth."

"The King will extract the truth from you."

"What the King is looking to extract is revenge. He will not listen to the truth. He has already made up his mind, and you know it. He is half mad with grief. In there, in the Council chambers, he might be made to listen. Alone with us, he won't bother. He will simply find a way to kill us and call the matter closed."

They stared at each other silently, desperation mingling with uncertainty. Maurin Ortish shook his head, and Kirisin thought, *We failed.* "You realize what you are asking of me?" the captain of the Home Guard said softly.

"I am asking you to do what you have always done before," Simralin replied. "I am asking you to do what is right."

He said nothing in response, but instead looked off into the distance. There was a hushed silence in the hall as everyone waited to see what he would do. One way or the other, Kirisin sensed, this was the turning point. He decided to try to tip the balance.

"Can you move everyone away from us for a moment?" he asked the captain of the Home Guard.

Ortish glanced over at him, hesitating. Then he motioned the guards to move back.

"You were there in the Council chambers when the Knight of the Word and the tatterdemalion told the King that the Ellcrys had spoken to me," Kirisin said quietly, keeping his voice too low for anyone but Ortish to hear. "So you remember what they said. That I was to go in search of the Loden Elfstone. That when I found it, I was to use it to place the tree and the city and the Elven population inside so that they could be taken to another, safer place. No one believed this. No one even thought an Elfstone existed after all this time. There was no record of an Elfstone, nothing to support what any of us were saying."

"I remember."

Kirisin reached into his pocket and pulled out the Loden. He cupped it in the palm of his hand so that only Maurin Ortish could see it. "This is it. The Loden Elfstone. We found it on Syrring Rise. This is what will save us all. If you doubt my sister, if you don't believe her, this should change your mind."

The captain of the Home Guard stared at the Elfstone, and then he looked up at the boy. "How could you have found something like this, Kirisin?" he asked. "Are you sure of what it is?"

But before the boy could answer him, a familiar figure appeared in front of them, big and looming. "So there you are, Little K."

Kirisin looked up to find Tragen standing next to them, his dark features lined with a mix of worry and confusion. And something else. Despair? Desperation? Kirisin wasn't sure.

The big man tried a quick smile. "Hello, Sim."

"What is it, Tragen," Maurin Ortish asked, clearly irritated by the interruption.

Tragen looked exhausted. His clothes were torn and dirtied, and his face was scratched.

"I need to speak with the King at once. Things are much worse than we thought."

"Give your report to me."

Tragen shook his head. "If I give it in the presence of the King and the members of the High Council, maybe I can say something that will help Kirisin and Simralin. About what they are telling you. About the Loden Elfstone. Please, Captain, let me come inside with you."

Kirisin blinked. How long had Tragen been standing there? How much of what was said had he heard? Where had he come from, for that matter? He hadn't been there before, had he?

Ortish glanced past the big Tracker. "Where are the others?"

"Dead. We were discovered, attacked, and then chased. The enemy caught up to us all, one by one. I was lucky. I fell down a ravine, and they lost sight of me in the dark. I hid until they had wandered away and I was able to crawl out again. Captain, please."

Kirisin suddenly realized that he was standing there holding the Loden in his hand for anyone to see who happened to walk up to him. He closed his fingers around it and dropped it back into his pocket.

"Maurin, I think we all need a chance to speak before the High Council," Simralin repeated. "Please give it to us."

Maurin Ortish nodded. "I won't promise

that you'll get two words out before the King has you hauled away. But I will take you into the chambers and let you do your best. Tragen, you might as well come with them if you've got something to say that bears on this."

He signaled over to four of the guards. "But you'll have company, so please don't do anything to make me regret this decision."

Leaving the remainder of the Home Guard without, he led the way over to the chamber doors and pushed them open.

TEN

As Kirisin entered the chambers of the High Council, following close on the heels of Maurin Ortish and flanked by Simralin and Tragen, a heated debate was taking place. Various members of the Council were trying to talk over one another, and the King was shifting his dark gaze from one to the next, looking as if he would like to see all of them dropped into a deep hole and covered over. He didn't notice the newcomers right away, his attention on something that Basselin was saying to a tall, sharp-featured woman whose name Kirisin could not remember.

The Council chambers were layered in shadows, the light reduced to a few wall lamps and a series of glow sticks hung from the rafters. It appeared that the meeting had begun in daylight and no one had bothered to do anything about the failing light when it had gotten dark. There was an air of desperation and distraction to the proceedings, reflected on the faces of the Council members and in the intensity of their words. No one seemed to have the attention of anyone else. No one looked the least bit happy.

Ordanna Frae glanced over and saw them, and he brought up one arm in a gesture that appeared to reflect a futile effort to ward them off rather than point them out. He tried to say something, but the arguments raging around him drowned out whatever words he spoke.

"My King! Ministers! Your attention, if you please!" Maurin Ortish was shouting in a way Kirisin had not thought possible given his normally soft manner of speaking. Heads turned. "I'm sorry to interrupt, but I think you need to hear what these three have to say about the threat we are facing." He paused as the King turned to look, and then he bowed deeply. "High Lord, your pardon."

Arissen Belloruus was on his feet. His voice, when he spoke, was just barely under control. "You had best beg for my mercy, Captain. You have disobeyed me! *Deliberately* disobeyed me, Captain! What sort of madness has taken hold of you? Do you think yourself above me and therefore able to countermand my orders?"

The arguing ceased abruptly as the remaining members of the Council turned to look at what was happening.

The King wasn't finished. His hand shook as he pointed at Ortish. "There is no excuse for what you have done. None, Captain. I am shocked and disappointed in you. Have these traitors taken out of my sight and locked up until I can deal with them! When that is done, you are relieved of your command and confined to your rooms!"

Maurin Ortish straightened. "My lord, I understand your anger. But young Kirisin has found the Loden Elfstone, and he and his sister claim to be able to shed light on the truth about your daughter's death —"

"Enough!" the King shouted, fists clenched, face contorted. "Don't say another word, Captain Ortish, or by everything the Elves believe in I'll have you —"

"My lord, we are in need of knowing more! Look at what threatens us! Tragen returns to give us his report on the size and intentions of the enemy. His entire command was killed, all five of them. If you will just listen to what young Kirisin . . ."

He kept talking, but his words were drowned out by the King's roar of fury as he charged down off the dais. He might have reached his captain of the Home Guard and attacked him, but Ordanna Frae stepped directly into his path and took hold of his arms.

"My King, please." He blocked the other physically, smaller and older than the King, but determined. The King tried to shove him aside, but other members of the Council had risen to their feet to block his way, as well. He slowed, and then stopped, breathing hard, glaring at Ortish.

"My King," Ordanna Frae repeated. He waited for the other man to look at him, flinching at the rage mirrored in his eyes. "No one here blames you for your anger over Erisha's death. But our city and our people are threatened, and we must find a way to save them. To do that, we need to hear anything — *anything* — that might bear on the subject. If young Kirisin has something to tell us, we should hear him out. It cannot hurt us at this point. It cannot hurt you."

There was a general murmur of agreement from the rest, save for Basselin, who was looking at Maurin Ortish as if he would welcome the chance to find out exactly what form the King's wrath might take.

For another instant Arissen Belloruus looked as if he might try to break free. Then the tension fled his body and he stepped back. "We cannot trust anything they say, Minister Frae. You should know that as well as I do. What is the point in listening?"

"We can measure truth and falsehood, my King. Even in lies there are sometimes truths revealed. Let us listen to what the boy has to say and judge the matter when he is finished." Ordanna Frae released his grip. "If our captain of the Home Guard was convinced that he should bring them before us — knowing full well your likely reaction — then I think we must accept that he saw something of importance in what they said to him. We need to hear what that was."

"We need to hear nothing!" Basselin interjected, moving over to insert himself between the King and Frae. "The King is right. We are wasting our time. We already know the truth of things. The boy was seen bending over Erisha Belloruus with a knife. They fled the city afterward rather than stay to explain. They allied themselves with a human, a treacherous Knight of the Word who aided them in their efforts to undermine Elven authority. We know enough to make up our minds about them without hearing more."

"But they returned voluntarily to speak to this Council," Maurin Ortish declared. "They were safely away from us, and they came back. Why would they do that if they were guilty of the crimes with which they have been charged? If we want to be sure of what we think is true, we need to hear their explanation."

"Lies, all of it!" shouted Basselin.

There was renewed arguing as the ministers took sides for and against the idea of listening to anything Kirisin and Simralin wanted to tell them. The boy shrank from the heat and fury of their words. He was the youngest person in the room, but he wasn't so young that he didn't realize what was happening.

Somebody had to do something right away or this would get too far out of hand.

"Wait!" he shouted suddenly. "Wait! Listen to me!"

Surprisingly, they did. The arguing died away, and they all turned toward him, their faces mirroring their feelings about what they believed to be true. He did his best not to read what was there, but instead reached into his pocket and brought out the Loden. "This is what the Ellcrys sent me to find. This is what will save the Elves. The army that waits in the trees waits only for me to use it. Listen to me. Listen to the truth about what happened to us."

Without waiting for them to grant him permission, he began to speak. He described the real traitor, the demon who had posed as Culph, watching and waiting for its chance. He explained the reason for Erisha's and Ailie's deaths. He told of their flight afterward, of racing to reach the Loden in time to save the Elves, of the battles with the demons on Syrring Rise, of how both Angel and Simralin had very nearly died — the former so badly injured that she could not return with them to the Cintra to support their cause. He skipped through the details of how he had nearly been subverted by the power of the silver cord and rings, moving quickly to an explanation of what the demons intended once Culph brought him back.

"They know everything of what the Ellcrys means to us. They know what it means if she is destroyed. But what they really seek is to encapsulate the Elves within the Loden, choose a place and time, and then release them to be destroyed. All of them. A massacre of our people — Culph revealed it all to me before Sim and I killed him."

"This is the worst load of nonsense I have ever listened to!" Basselin interrupted, almost screaming the words he was so outraged. "Do you expect us to believe any of this? Your lies are transparent!"

"But what is the purpose of offering them up for your consideration if they are lies?" Simralin asked him. "What is the point in our coming back if all we intended to do is tell you lies? What do you think we hope to accomplish?"

"Culph has disappeared," Ordanna Frae offered. "No one has seen him since Kirisin and Simralin disappeared from the city. Nor have we heard any better reason for why the demonkind do not attack us than the one offered by the boy."

"You speak like an old fool!" Basselin snapped. "You seem intent on believing these two!"

"Maybe there is reason to do so," another minister ventured guardedly.

Basselin wheeled back toward the King. "My lord, think what this boy is asking of us!

158

Placing our city and our people inside the Elfstone — if indeed that is even possible — is too dangerous. Entrusting the Elfstone to the boy is suicide! Even if he didn't betray us — something of which I am not at all convinced — he is still only a boy. How can we even think of doing what he suggests?"

"We had better at least consider it, Basselin," said the tall, sharp-featured woman the first minister had been talking to earlier. "Our only other choice is to flee this army that surrounds us. Thousands of Elves would perish in any escape attempt. There is no chance that all of us can hope to elude an army of the size and swiftness of the one that threatens."

"Some would die, yes," Basselin conceded. "Better some than all. We must make that sacrifice."

"Basselin is making a hard choice, but it may be the right one," another of the Council declared.

There were murmurs of assent from some of the others. The discussion went on, and Kirisin found himself studying the faces of the men and women speaking, trying to read what was behind their words. As they talked, the King sat stone-faced atop the dais, and although he had said little since his initial outburst, he was clearly unconvinced of what needed doing.

Simralin stepped close. "I don't like how

this sounds," she whispered, as if reading his thoughts.

"They don't trust me," he whispered back. "I don't blame them."

"Maybe. But they have no choice. If they want to save the Elven people — all of them, not just some — they must trust you." She paused. "Besides, not everyone has to be put inside. Elven Hunters can be kept out to help protect you."

"Maybe no one's thought of that yet."

"Maybe we better say something."

But before they could do so, Maurin Ortish moved in front of them, dragging a reluctant Tragen with him. "My King, this is the Tracker who was in the enemy camp and has returned with his report. Perhaps it would help to hear it now."

The King glared at him, but then he gestured for Tragen to step forward. "Tracker, what have you to say?"

Tragen's face flushed deeply at the sudden attention. "My lord." He bowed, looking uncertain. "As the captain said, I was sent to see what I could learn of the enemy's intentions," he began. "With five others, who are now all dead."

As he continued speaking, Kirisin found himself recalling how much Tragen had helped Angel, Sim, and himself when it seemed as if there was no one left to turn to. He had risked himself more than once for them, probably out of love for his sister, but surely out of a sense of doing what was right, as well. Kirisin had never thought much of Tragen before, but he was revising his thinking now.

The Tracker was explaining how he had tried to get close enough to learn something of the enemy's plans. Elves were good at becoming invisible even when it might seem impossible. Because he knew both Kirisin and Simralin well, he had already decided that they were not responsible for the deaths of Erisha and Culph. He had hoped he might overhear something that would tell him who was.

He was careful not to say anything about his involvement with the escape of the Belloruus siblings from the city, which Kirisin thought was a wise decision. It was still uncertain how the King and the High Council would react to such a revelation. Nor did Tragen say anything of his efforts to shelter them or of how, at their behest, he had gone in search of Culph to warn him that he was in danger and then found him dead . . .

And suddenly, in that way the mind has of jumping of its own accord from one thought to another, of making connections unasked, he heard himself in the ice caves of Syrring Rise, speaking with what had seemed at the time a ghost:

"I thought you were dead!"

161

"Well now, what led you to believe that, Kirisin?"

"Tragen found your body!"

"Is that what he told you?"

As if he were surprised. As if he were amused. The tone of voice had been unmistakable, but Kirisin, caught up in the moment, had paid no attention. *Tragen found your body.* But apparently he hadn't. So whose body had he found?

Had he found any body at all?

Then he remembered his dream of the dark cloaked form standing in the Ashenell and asking, over and over again, *Who told you that?*

He found himself staring at Tragen as if seeing him for the first time, newly revealed, finding something odd about him, something strange. He could not quite bring himself to embrace fully what he was thinking because it was too terrifying.

"Sim," he said quietly.

She glanced at him. "Shhhh."

Tragen had finishing giving his report and was answering questions from the members of the High Council. Kirisin didn't listen. He didn't do anything but stare, and then he repeated everything he remembered, and then he again tried unsuccessfully to get Simralin to listen to him.

You can't be right about this, he told himself. *Don't be stupid. You're imagining things.*

He hugged himself, ran his fingers through

162

his tousled hair, and then jammed his hand deep into his pocket where the Elfstones nestled, seeking reassurance from their presence.

Tragen found your body!
Is that what he told you?

"Tragen!" he called out suddenly, not really meaning to do so, acting impulsively and without thought. The Tracker turned. "Whose body did you find if it wasn't Culph's?"

Everyone was staring. "What are you talking about?" an irritated Arissen Belloruus asked him.

Kirisin ignored him, watching Tragen. "You said you found Culph's body. But he wasn't dead. So whose body did you find?"

The big man shook his head. "You're mistaken. I said I found evidence of a struggle. I said it looked like someone had been killed in Culph's house. Just remains. No complete body."

"No," Simralin said quietly. "You told us you found Culph's body. You said that he was dead."

There was a hushed silence as the members of the High Council, not quite sure what was happening, looked at one another in confusion. The King was leaning forward, dark gaze intense. "What body do you mean? What is this all about?"

"Whose body did you find?" Kirisin pressed, his eyes locked with Tragen's. "There

163

wasn't one, was there?"

Tragen sighed. His smile could not quite hide the trapped look reflected in his eyes. "You always were a bright boy, Little K."

Then he produced a long knife as if it had been conjured by magic and drove it into Maurin Ortish. The captain of the Home Guard gasped in shock and dropped to his knees, hands reaching futilely for the killing blade. Tragen was already leaping toward Kirisin and his sister. He was much quicker than either had expected and was on top of them before they could react. He backhanded Simralin so hard she was sent sprawling, her head snapping back as she crashed into the far wall. A moment later the Tracker had Kirisin in an iron grip, his arm about the boy's neck as he yanked him off his feet and pinned him to his chest.

The Home Guards were rushing forward by now, weapons drawn. But Tragen produced a handgun, an automatic weapon hidden within his clothing, black and short-barreled and wicked-looking, and shot all four in a span of as many seconds. Kirisin had a second or two to recognize that having a weapon of this sort confirmed his worst fears — that Tragen wasn't what he appeared to be, wasn't Elven, likely wasn't even human. Then the Tracker was dragging him over to the Council chamber doors and throwing the locking bar that kept anyone else from entering. As the members of the High Council rose, yelling for help, Tragen leveled his weapon and sprayed them indiscriminately. Kirisin watched Basselin and the sharp-featured woman and several others collapse. The King was hit and knocked backward. Blood splattered on the walls and dais and chairs in a red mist. Bodies tumbled in heaps and lay unmoving.

Kirisin fought to break free, but the arm that pinned him was like a band of iron across his neck, and he couldn't begin to loosen it.

"Stop struggling, Little K," his captor hissed in his ear. "You have a duty to fulfill, and you're going to fulfill it! You mustn't disappoint all those who depend on you!"

Kirisin screamed at him, calling him something unmentionable, something he had never called anyone, furious and almost in tears. Across from him, not ten feet away, Maurin Ortish knelt with his hands locked on the knife handle where it protruded from his chest, his body limp. In front of the dais, one of the Council members moaned softly. Fists pounded on the locked chamber doors, and voices yelled in fear and frustration.

"Enough of this foolish pretense," Tragen muttered, eyes on the door. "Time for you and me to be going, Kirisin."

In the next instant Simralin slammed into him, all three of them sprawling across the floor. Tragen, caught off guard by the attack,

165

lost his grip on the handgun and on Kirisin, as well. While he didn't let go completely, he did release the boy enough that he almost twisted free. Almost. One hand clung to him by its fingertips — a hand that had shed its skin and become scaly and clawed — fighting to retain its grip as the three combatants tumbled across the stone floor of the chambers and rolled to a stop. But Simralin landed on top and began tearing at the Tracker's face and eyes. Roaring in fury, Tragen let go of the boy and struck out at Simralin, missing her head but landing a blow to her shoulder that was more than sufficient to dislodge her.

Rolling free, he came to his feet with a second long knife in his hand and scrambled toward her.

But Kirisin was quicker. Freed of Tragen's grip, he reached into his pocket and snatched free the blue Elfstones. Having discovered what they could do in the ice caves of Syrring Rise, he knew they were his only hope. Tragen wasn't an Elf and he wasn't human. He was a demon, and only magic was going to be enough to stop him.

"Tragen!" he screamed.

The Tracker half turned, slowing only marginally, but it was enough. He caught sight of the blue fire that exploded out of the boy's hand just before it struck him full on. The impact knocked him backward, off his feet and onto the stone flooring. Then it followed him down in a blazing arc, burning into him. Tragen screamed, thrashing to break free. But the magic enfolded him, directed by Kirisin's rage and determination, set upon its course and unalterable. It burned through skin and scales. It burned down to the bones and then through the bones themselves. Tragen became a fiery stick man, a blackened husk, and finally a pile of steaming ashes.

When it was finished, Kirisin stood looking down at the remains, the Elfstones gone dark and cool in his hand. His face reflected the mix of horror and excitement that using the magic had wrought. Feelings he could only barely recognize as his own coursed through his body, hotter than his lifeblood.

Simralin climbed back to her feet and hobbled over to stand next to him, staring at his twisted features. "Shades, Little K," she whispered.

Arissen Belloruus sat silently atop the dais as healers worked on his injuries. He had been struck twice by handgun bullets, once in the shoulder and once in the side. Neither wound was life threatening. Neither would do more than cause him pain in the days ahead. Four other members of the High Council were not nearly so fortunate. Three were dead, including First Minister Basselin, and the fourth was likely to be so before the day was out.

Maurin Ortish was dead, as well.

Kirisin and Simralin sat nearby, watching as Elven healers bandaged the King's wounds, their backs to the wall, their arms wrapped about their drawn-up legs.

"He doesn't look good," Kirisin observed quietly.

"He's in shock," his sister said. "No different from you or me."

No arguing that, Kirisin thought. Who would have believed that an attack of the sort they had just witnessed could ever have taken place in these chambers? Such things didn't happen. Tragen had gone berserk. Or the demon had, he corrected. Gone mad. Determined to do what Culph had failed to do, to convey him to the demons and make him use the Loden to imprison the Elves. Was there ever any chance of him doing that? Any chance of making an escape from these rooms with Kirisin in tow? Clearly the demon had thought so. It would have killed everyone to make it happen.

"I should have waited," he said. "I should have kept quiet."

His sister looked over. Her face was bruised, and there was blood smeared on her forehead. She looked a wreck. "Let's not revisit what you or I should have done. I probably have more regrets on that subject than you do."

He thought about her involvement with

Tragen, thinking that she must feel violated in a way he could never understand. In any case, she was right. It was a waste of time to wish that things had happened differently. It was easy in retrospect to think that he should have held off exposing Tragen until it was safer to do so.

"What do you think will happen now?" he asked.

Simralin shook her head. "What we want to happen, I hope."

The boy nodded. His gaze wandered over the blood-drenched room. The bodies had been removed, but the evidence of their fate was still there for everyone to see. The cleanup would begin when the King gave his permission. For the moment, it seemed, Arissen Belloruus seemed intent on burning the image into his memory.

Ordanna Frae reappeared, still shaken but otherwise unhurt. He stopped in front of them. "That was very brave of you, Kirisin. To fight back like you did. Very brave. You saved our lives. I think we all believe now that you are more than capable of protecting the Elves, should it come to that."

He moved away, joining the King on the dais, bending close to speak with him. "You *were* brave, Little K," Simralin agreed.

The King was on his feet now, his healers moving away. With Ordanna Frae trailing, he walked over to where they sat, looking angry and determined. He shouted to his attendants to clean up the room, and they moved quickly to comply.

Kirisin and Simralin got to their feet at once. The King faced them, his strong features set.

"Erisha loved you," he began, speaking directly to Kirisin. "She believed in you, and she trusted you. I know you fought from time to time, but you played together as children and have been each other's friend since birth. You were — you are — a member of our family. I never wanted to think that you could harm Erisha. Even now, when I saw you again, come back to Arborlon, I didn't want to believe it."

For a moment, he couldn't continue. It took everything he had to compose himself, but he managed to subdue his grief. "I have not been thinking clearly on this. Not for some time. I realize that now. I have been a fool. What I've witnessed here has convinced me of that."

He paused, his eyes still locked on Kirisin. "When my daughter came to me about the Ellcrys and the Loden Elfstone, I turned to Culph for help. I asked him to look into the Elven histories to see what was recorded. He did so and told me that he had researched the histories front-to-back, as well as all the notes that might possibly bear on the matter of the missing Elfstones, and had found nothing. He lied, of course, but I did not realize it. He insisted there was nothing, even when I pressed him to look harder. But he said there were rumors he had heard as a child from other, wiser heads. Rumors warning that using a Loden Elfstone was dangerous. The user of such a magic, he had heard, was bound to it. What that meant, he warned, was that if this Elfstone were recovered and the Ellcrys placed within, the user must carry the Stone until the tree could be released. He cautioned that the weight of such responsibility was too much for my daughter to bear, too much for any child of Erisha's temperament, and that I must do what I could to protect her. He suggested that it would be best if I discouraged her from being involved and left the matter to you."

He shook his head. "I did as he suggested. I chose to sacrifice you in order to protect my daughter. I didn't see it that way at the time. I convinced myself that it didn't matter, that none of this would ever come to pass. I convinced myself that the danger to the Ellcrys was exaggerated. I convinced myself that you were on a hopeless mission to find something that didn't exist. I persuaded myself that I could not risk my only daughter." He took a deep breath and exhaled. "I am ashamed for this, and I apologize."

Kirisin nodded his understanding, even though he wasn't sure he understood at all.

But the anger he might have felt before did not surface now. Instead, he felt only sadness for the King.

"I am going to do what you have asked of me," the King declared, his voice firm and steady once again. "We have to protect the Elven people and the city. I'm convinced that you are capable of that. Your use of the Elfstone magic to stop Tragen tells me so. Erisha saw that, as well, I think. Are you still willing to use the Loden and to act as our protector?"

The boy nodded at once.

"Then this is what you will do. As soon as dawn breaks, you will place the Ellcrys, Arborlon, and the Elven people within the Loden. I will remain outside with our Elven Hunters to protect you. We will do whatever is needed to see that you get safely away from the demon army to where it is that you are supposed to go. You have some sense of where this is, don't you?"

Again, the boy nodded. In truth, he wasn't sure. But he wasn't about to admit to it. "I will need to speak with the Ellcrys," he said.

"You will have that opportunity. She has guided you well so far. Much better than I have." He glanced quickly at the room behind him, as if making sure it was secure. "Ordanna Frae is now first minister. He will go into the Loden with the rest of the Elves to form a new High Council and advise the El-

172

ven population of my decision. He will be responsible for preventing panic and for preparing our people for whatever awaits them."

He paused. "A lot depends on you, Kirisin."

"I know."

"If anything happens to you, the Elves will be trapped within the Loden. Perhaps forever. Basselin was right about that much."

"He knows," Simralin answered for Kirisin.

The King glanced sharply at Simralin, but did not rebuke her. "I suppose he does." He looked back at the boy. "If you find yourself in real danger or are injured badly, you must release the Elves. If you are trapped and cannot escape, you must release them. If I order you to do so, you must release them. They are not to be abandoned, no matter what. Promise me."

"I promise."

The King nodded. His strong face tightened with determination, and he straightened his big frame. "Do you think there might be other demons among us?"

Kirisin had no idea. He hadn't even considered the possibility, still shaken from discovering that Tragen was one. The suggestion that there might be others still was terrifying.

"I don't think we can discount the possibility." Arissen Belloruus paused, seeing the look on his face. "So I am asking your sister to take personal responsibility for your safety.

She will choose a handful of others to help her." He looked at Simralin. "After Tragen, it will be difficult to know whom you can trust. You couldn't even trust me until now. I realize that. I gave you every reason not to. But we have to start somewhere."

"I'll take care of him," Simralin promised.

The King gave her a fleeting smile. "I know you will. You will take care of each other. Better than I was able to take care of Erisha." He shook his head. "I still can't quite make myself believe that she's gone. I keep waiting for her to come home." He rubbed at his face, hiding his eyes. Then he straightened abruptly, exhaling. "I have difficulty imagining what is happening. To leave the Cintra, after all these years. After decades. Centuries. To be threatened like this. To know what lies ahead. Or, more correctly perhaps, not to know, but to be able only to speculate."

He trailed off. Then he took Ordanna Frae's arm. "Come with me, First Minister. There are preparations to make."

Kirisin and his sister watched them go. For a moment, neither spoke. Then Simralin took her brother's arm. "Come on. Let's go. Dawn is six hours away. We need to get some sleep."

Together they stumbled lead-footed from the room.

ELEVEN

Logan Tom drove the Ventra 5000 southeast into the mountains for what remained of the day after leaving the Portland area, following the two-lane road upon which Trim had set him. There were opportunities to take other roads, but the owl kept to the one they had started out on. He flew ahead, frequently cutting cross-country over fields and through forests, leaving Logan to assume that he would be met again somewhere down the road, which he always was. His hesitation about following Trim, so pronounced when he had first discovered that the owl was to be his guide, had given way to a grudging reliance. He supposed he would have been uneasy about following anyone, owl or human; his natural instinct after all these years on his own was to trust no one. But there was no one with whom to argue the matter, and Trim seemed set upon their course, so Logan quickly accepted the inevitable and went where he was led.

When darkness began to set in, they were at the foot of the big mountain he had spied earlier while crossing into Oregon over the Columbia. His maps identified it as Mount Hood. It was a massive rock, and the road led right up one side and into mountains that stretched beyond it to the south, so Logan knew he was going to face some rough traveling before the night was over. Stopping for sleep didn't seem to be in the owl's plans; he kept flying ahead, taking Logan higher and deeper into the chain, past Mount Hood and into the tangle of peaks beyond. Progress was slow, the roads narrow and winding and frequently littered with debris of one sort or another. In some places, the pavement was so badly split by crevices or collapsed beneath sinkholes that Logan had to drive the Ventra off road to continue. But the Ventra was such a beast that it surmounted obstacles almost effortlessly, its big wheels, high chassis, and powerful engine giving it the ability to do everything but climb trees. And Logan wouldn't have bet against that.

When it finally got too dark to go farther safely, Trim winged his way back to Logan and settled on the Ventra's roof. Logan pulled over, climbed out, and checked to be certain of the owl's intent. Trim regarded him from the roof with saucer eyes, and then took flight. Logan watched him fly off a short distance and roost in a nearby tree. When the bird showed no signs of doing anything more, Logan climbed back inside the Ventra, shut down the AV's engine, locked the doors, set the security alarms, settled back in his seat, and drifted off to sleep.

He woke to the sound of the owl's soft hoot and a scrabbling of its talons on the Ventra's metal roof. Sunlight was pouring down out of a cloudless sky, the day bright and clear. From the position of the sun, he guessed it was nearing midday. He rubbed the sleep from his eyes, ate and drank a little something, turned the Ventra's engine back on, and set out once more.

This day's journey was rougher and more protracted. They left Mount Hood behind early and moved into high desert country where the landscape was bleak and empty and the road frequently disappeared beneath sand and scrub. Flat stretches were interspersed with hummocks and ravines, with dry washes and ridges so rocky that they looked like dragon spines. The country was volcanic, dotted with cinder cones and awash in cinder dust and lava rock. Cactus littered the terrain in vast clumps; everything else that grew was stunted and wintry and edged with thorns or razor-sharp bark. He drove the AV around and over and through it all, letting Trim show him the way, keeping clear of places where the sand and grit looked uncertain, as if covering sinkholes and crevasses that might drop him into a black pit.

Sometimes, he found himself navigating through ravines so deep that he could not see beyond the rims save for where the sky domed overhead. He had to trust to Trim in those situations, unable to determine with any accuracy even which direction he was going. Everything took a long time, and the hours rolled by without any noticeable progress. One section of the land looked pretty much like another. Off to the west, distant and remote, the chain of the mountains stretched parallel to his drive, their dark barren peaks cutting sharply against the sky, their rock a wall that locked away whatever lay beyond. There was an alien quality to those mountains that reminded him of his encounter with the spirits of the dead in the Rockies, and he found himself hoping that he would not have to go into them in order to find the Elves.

Elves. He thought about them the way he thought about the spirits of the dead — as insubstantial as smoke, as ephemeral as mist. He could not put faces to them, could not give them features, could not imagine their place in the world. Memory of the dead faded with time; of Elves, there were no memories at all. He might try to believe in them, but it would take an encounter with one to make them come alive.

He stopped and ate once during the day's

long drive, pulling off into a barren flat where the horizon stretched away into tomorrow. The emptiness was depressing, a warning of the world's future. He tried not to think about that future, about what the Lady had told him, but he might as well have been trying not to think about eating and drinking. It was an unavoidable presence in his life, a reality that rode on his shoulders like a weight.

He switched his thinking over to Hawk and the Ghosts, wondering how they were managing without him, left to make their way east to where the boy would become leader of a tribe of children and caregivers, of strays and castoffs, and of creatures once human but no longer so. The boy and his children, Owl would say. He couldn't quite picture this, either. But he knew it would happen because that was the task that the gypsy morph had been given to do.

And he would go with them.

To someplace new and different, to a fresh beginning.

He shook his head. He was twenty-eight years old, and he had lived almost his entire life traveling a single path, engaged in a single struggle. He could not imagine the sort of change that lay ahead. He could not imagine his place in it.

Sunset came and went, and still Trim led him on. Stars brightened the night sky, and because there was no competing light from anywhere on ground level he was able to keep track of the owl's flight and find his way. The terrain had flattened out in the last hour or so, the road winding through low hills, closing on the mountains west. Within an hour of darkness pushing the last of the light below the horizon, he had left the highway and was driving along a singletrack road that was rutted and grown thick with weeds and scrub. He was in the mountain chain by now, the peaks dark pinnacles against the night sky. The Ventra worked its way steadily ahead, climbing and descending by equal turns, following the road he had set it upon, an old logging road, he guessed. Complete concentration was required in order to avoid the larger obstacles that might cause trouble even for the Ventra, so he was unaware of time passing as he drove.

Eventually, he gained the far side of the mountains and found himself deep in forests thick with foliage and glistening with life. He stared around, not quite believing what he was seeing. He had never seen trees as lush and full as these; he didn't think they existed. It was the way the old world might have been, before the poisons and the changes in climate ruined it. The road wound through its center for a long time, navigating streams not yet dried out and ravines in which ferns grew, undulating in a soft wind like waves on open water.

Unable to help himself, he stopped the AV and climbed out. Motionless, he stood looking out into the darkness, into the forest that surrounded him. He smelled the air, breathing it in. Fresh and clean. He tasted it and found it free of bitterness, of any metallic edge. He listened. Night birds called to each other or maybe just to be heard, their cries echoing through the trees.

Where was he? What place was this?

Trim flew back into view and settled on the roof of the Ventra, round eyes regarding him intently. Logan stared at the bird. "Why don't you tell me what else you know that I don't?" he said.

He got into the AV and prepared to set off again, but the owl didn't move from the vehicle roof. Apparently, this was it for the day. He climbed out again, asked aloud if they were done, waited for an answer — as if there might be one — and finally climbed back into the cab, secured the locks, and went to sleep.

When he woke next, it was not yet dawn. Trim was perched on the hood of the Ventra staring at him through the windshield, saucer eyes glowing like lamps. It was the stare that had brought him awake, he decided, pushing himself upright. He was stiff and groggy, but he made himself get out and walk around until both conditions had disappeared. The forest was a lush damp curtain, filled with new smells and muted colors. There were wildflowers growing all around him, an impossibility, a miracle. He stared at them as if they were something born of an alien world. He stared at the huge trees surrounding him, some with trunks so massive they dwarfed the stone columns of the abandoned government buildings he had seen in Chicago as a boy. The trunks were twisted and gnarly and had the look of something that had been tall and straight once but had been melted by the sun. They were all different, each one a sculpture carved by an artist of endless imagination.

He walked over to one, a giant with limbs that stretched so wide they brushed up against the other trees surrounding it, and he touched its rough bark with his fingers. He looked up into its center where shadows and leaves intermingled and everything felt hushed and hidden. He could see shards of starlight slanting through its multilayered canopy, dappling its limbs. He moved to one side and let a slender ray fall across his face. He smiled in the softness of its glow.

When he stepped away again, there were tears in his eyes. He couldn't explain what had caused them, couldn't understand how they had surfaced so quickly. Maybe they had been triggered by a memory from his boyhood or a dream he had forgotten. He brushed them away with the back of his hand. It was too much, he thought. This forest, with its smells and tastes and look and feel — it was too much. Everything was so overwhelming. No wonder he was crying.

Then Trim gave a small screech, and he glanced over to find the owl perched on the roof of the AV. Trim was ready to go. Logan sighed, turned away from the trees, and walked over to the bird. Immediately it flew away into the forest. Logan watched it go, waited for it to circle back in the way it did when telling him he needed to follow, saw it reappear higher up in the trees, and started to get into the AV. But then he realized that the road that had brought him in ended at this clearing. He scanned the landscape for signs of another road, then a trail, and finally a pathway or anything that resembled one. Nothing. Moreover, the trees were too thickly massed for the Ventra to pass. Wherever he was going, he was going to have to get there on foot.

Stuffing food and water containers into a backpack he slung over his shoulder, he picked up his black staff and set out.

He walked for about an hour, wending his way through the dark mass of the trees, climbing over fallen logs and in and out of shallow ravines, fording streams and skirting thorny brush, all the while following his winged guide. Trailers of mist curled through the forest like ethereal snakes. Starlight shone down through the screen of the leafy canopy, made pale and diffuse. Shadows layered the earth, climbed the trunks of the trees, crawled out on limbs, and disappeared into the ether. Birdsong followed after him, rose ahead of him, spread out around him in lilting welcome, brought to life by dawn's approach. He found himself smiling. Where would he rather be than here, whatever the reason for coming?

Nowhere, he answered himself. *Nowhere else.*

He came upon the clearing unexpectedly, his eyes following Trim's flight through the trees, only half paying attention to what until now had been an unchanging forest. But all at once he was standing in an open space on the high slopes of the mountainside, looking down on a forestland that stretched away for miles.

He was also staring at a hot-air balloon.

He recognized it for what it was immediately. The basket was sitting upright in the clearing with the air bag lying uphill on the ground in front of it, all of its stays attached, a compressor motor situated with a hose end funneling into the bag's mouth, everything ready to fill the bag and take flight. He walked over to the balloon and stood looking down at it, wondering what it was doing here, who had flown it in, and why it was set out this way.

Trim had flown back again and was roosting on one edge of the basket, round eyes fixed on him.

"Another Knight of the Word," a voice said from behind him. "What's your name?"

He turned quickly, bringing up his staff. A young woman had emerged from the trees behind him. Mist wrapped her legs and spread away before her in a heavy carpet, giving her the appearance of having somehow been formed of it. He hadn't heard her approach, hadn't heard her at all. That didn't happen often. She was tall and lithe with long blond hair tied back from her face with a headband. Her loose clothing blended perfectly with her surroundings, and the way she carried herself suggested that this was her country.

"Who are you?" she repeated.

When she spoke this time, he could see her perfectly, her features revealed by pale silver light that striped her body from head to foot and gave her an exotic, alien look. He felt something shift inside. The shift was small, but intense. He could not define what it was, but he knew instinctively what it meant. Nothing would ever be the same for him again.

He tightened his grip on the black staff out

185

of a sudden need for reassurance. "I'm Logan Tom."

She inclined her head, a cross between a greeting and an acknowledgment. "Are you friends with Angel Perez?"

He started to answer, to tell her he didn't know anyone named Angel Perez, and then suddenly he noticed her ears, slightly pointed at the tips, and her eyebrows, which were slanted upward across her forehead. He stared at her just long enough that there was no mistaking what he was looking at.

He flushed, embarrassed. "Sorry. It's just that . . ." He trailed off. "You're an Elf, aren't you?"

She nodded. "Did Angel tell you about us?"

"I don't know Angel. I was sent by the Lady to find you. To find the Elves, I mean."

She shook her head. "The Lady?"

"The voice of the Word."

"I know of the Word. Of her Knights. Angel was one. She came to us earlier. To help us. Is that why you were sent?"

"That's pretty much it. I was told there was a talisman you must use and that after you had done so, I was to guide you to where you were supposed to go." He paused. "I was told that Angel was hurt, and I needed to take her place."

"She was hurt keeping us safe, protecting us from demons that tracked us to where we found the talisman."

They stared at each other for a moment, not speaking. Then Logan shook his head. "I don't know what to say. I can't stop looking at you. I didn't know there were Elves before I was told to come here. Even after I was told, I didn't believe it. Maybe I still don't."

The corner of her mouth twitched. "I think maybe you do. Now. At any rate, we need you to believe if you are to help us."

"I know that. I think what's bothering me is that I didn't know what to expect. I was looking for . . . something else."

"And you found me."

He nodded. "I guess that's it."

"No one is supposed to know about us, Logan. No one is supposed to believe we exist. That's how we stay safe."

"But now the demons know, don't they? They've found you?"

She nodded.

"Are they here?"

She walked over and stood before him, so close she could have reached out and touched him if she had chosen to do so. She was too close, Logan thought. He stared at her. He had never met anyone like her, seen anyone like her, imagined anyone could make him feel like this. He didn't care that she was an Elf. He didn't care what she was. He barely knew her, and already he was thinking about things that he had never thought about anyone.

You will know who you are looking for, the Lady had told him when he asked, *because your heart will tell you.* He hadn't understood until now what that meant.

He stared at her, and she stared right back at him. The connection was so strong it was palpable. He was suddenly confused and embarrassed. She shouldn't have been able to tell what he was thinking, but she smiled as if she could.

"I'm Simralin Belloruus," she said, taking his arm. "Walk back with me. It might take me a while, but I'll explain everything."

In the cool of the predawn, Kirisin walked from his sleeping quarters to the gardens that housed the Ellcrys. Ostensibly, he went alone, having been awakened by his sister before she left to assemble and make ready the hot-air balloon that would spirit them away after he had used the Loden. But he knew that in the shadows were Elven Hunters chosen by her to make certain he stayed safe. He didn't see them, but he knew they were there. Sim wouldn't have had it otherwise.

The path he followed was familiar, a path he had traveled hundreds of times in the company of the other Chosen on their way to offer morning greetings to the tree they were all sworn to protect. Biat, his best friend, Raya, Giln, and Jarn — how many times they had walked it. Erisha, as well, although it was

188

hard to think about her now. He would have gone to the others last night and told them everything that had happened since his flight from the city. He would have assured them that he had not killed Erisha, that he had tried to save her, that he would try to save them. He would have told them everything. He would have stayed with them and slept in his old bed. But Simralin said no. It wasn't a good idea. No one must be told what was going to happen. The danger of panic was too great. She didn't even mention the possibility of word slipping out and reaching the demonkind if too many people found out what was planned. But he understood it anyway. Any reunions or explanations would have to wait until this was over.

So in a small act of rebellion, he had chosen to take this more circuitous route from the sleeping quarters she had selected for him. At least he could walk the path he had shared with his friends. They would be sleeping and would not wake before he had done so, and his visit to the Ellcrys would be finished by the time they rose. Not long after that, they would be enclosed in the Loden and explanations and reunions wouldn't matter.

He thought about the consequences of his actions for a moment. So much could go wrong, and almost all of it had to do with him. If he faltered, if he misjudged, if he rushed or hesitated at the wrong moment, he would fail. If he failed, everything would be lost.

In the moments before rising, lying silently in his bed, just coming awake, he had considered the possibility of keeping another of the Chosen out with him, a safeguard against his death before the city and its people could be restored. Biat, perhaps. Steady, reliable, the perfect choice. But did he have the right to ask such a thing? The burden, after all, had been given to him. Whoever stayed behind with him would share that burden, no matter how hard he tried to argue otherwise. Biat or another of the Chosen would stand at his shoulder and by doing so face the same dangers he did.

It was Simralin who had put it in perspective when asked her opinion earlier this morning. She was crouched next to him in the darkness, dressed and ready, her weapons strapped about her waist and over her shoulders, preparing to leave.

"You could do that, Little K. But if the demons manage to harm you, even to get close enough to do so, everyone around you, myself included, will already be dead. The presence of another Chosen wouldn't make a difference."

"But what if I am killed accidentally, even though you have expended your best efforts to keep that from happening?"

"What if you lose the Loden?" she replied.

"What if you break it? What if it gets stolen? You can speculate all you want, Little K." She paused. "Why don't you just ask the Ellcrys what she wishes you to do?"

Ask the Ellcrys. Yes, he had thought afterward, that was what he would do.

So now he was on his way to speak to her. Or, more to the point, on his way to the gardens so that she could speak to him. But his uncertainties had not faded as he had hoped. Instead, they had intensified. He was awash in doubts. Not about the wisdom of keeping out another Chosen to aid him, but about his own abilities. He was being asked to do so much. Without skills, experience, or even much in the way of wisdom, he was being given a responsibility no one should have to bear. How was he to carry it out? How did he invoke the Loden's power? What was needed to persuade it to enclose the Elves and their city along with the Ellcrys? How would he know afterward where he was to go and what he was to do once he got there? Thinking about it, about all of it, was so overwhelming that he almost turned back from his meeting. Someone else should be doing this, he kept thinking. He was not the right choice.

When he reached the gardens, he stood at their edge for several moments, looking at the tree and gathering his courage. He wasn't sure what he would hear or even that he wanted to hear it. He wasn't sure he wanted to go any farther.

In the end, he did, of course. He stepped out into the starlit brightness of the clearing, out from the trees into the open, flinching as the light fell across his face and revealed him. As if, somehow, she could see that he was there. He came forward slowly, drinking in her impossible beauty, discovering anew aspects he had forgotten. He stood before her, just out of reach, staring into her scarlet canopy, blinking at the reflection of light from her silver limbs, awestruck in her presence.

She chose me, he thought suddenly. *She could have chosen someone else, but she chose me.* To his surprise, the words comforted him.

He walked into the dark pool of her shadow and dropped to his knees, head lowered, eyes closed, motionless and silent, waiting.

Waiting.

What if she does not speak to me?

He felt the spidery touch of a slender branch brush against his slumped shoulders.

–My beloved–

He almost cried, so grateful was he, so relieved. "I have done what you asked of me," he whispered aloud.

–Use the magic of the Loden and place me within, still rooted in my earth. Use the magic to place the Elves and their city within, as well. All of us belong within your safekeep-

192

ing. Take us to where we will be made safe from what is to happen. You will know where that is and how you are to go. Others will show you the way. Others will go with you and protect you–

"But I don't know how . . . ," he started, then stopped instantly as he felt the tip of the branch move to his neck.

–The path lies before you. The journey is set. You are my Chosen. You are my beloved. You will know. You need no instruction or help to find your way. You need only your courage and your determination. Do you believe me–

"Yes," he said at once. "I believe you."

–Then do what you must, Kirisin Belloruus. Do what I have given you to do–

He might have said more. He might have asked her more. He might have tried to discover the answers to questions that remained unanswered. But her limbs withdrew, and she was gone. He knelt before her, staring up into her branches, searching for movement, for recognition, for something further. But nothing revealed itself. She had said all she would.

He rose after a moment, waited a moment longer, still hoping, and then took a deep breath, turned, and walked away.

Logan Tom walked next to Simralin Belloruus, head lowered in thought. She had just finished telling him everything that had happened to the Elves over the past few weeks leading up to the moment of his arrival, and he was trying to digest it. *Trying to make it seem real* might be a better way of putting it. He had seen and heard of some strange things in his time as a Knight of the Word, but never anything like this. That an entire city and its people could be saved from demons and once-men by being placed inside a gemstone was almost too much to accept.

Almost.

"You don't believe me, do you?" she asked him, apparently able to read his mind.

She didn't sound angry or disappointed. She sounded mostly curious to hear how he would respond. She looked over at him, and for what must have been the fiftieth time in the past hour he found himself wishing she would never look away.

"I believe you," he said. "I would believe you if your story sounded three times this crazy."

He had never been in love. He had not known what it would feel like. He understood what the term meant, but his life had not allowed for exploring its possibilities. There had been few he had really loved. His parents; Michael. That was it. And that was love of a different kind. Less intense, less hungry. What he felt for Simralin went so far beyond anything manageable that it shocked him. He could tell himself it was because he found her beautiful in a way that transcended anything he had ever known. But his attraction to her was a response to so much more. To her self-confidence and her way of speaking. To her smile and the quirky way she lifted one eyebrow when she was amused. To the way she carried herself. To the way she looked at him.

Feeling like this, being suddenly, impulsively in love, was so ridiculous and so reckless and wrongheaded that he could hardly come to grips with it. There was no space in his life for this. There was no time for it. He was engaged in the most important struggle of his life, entrusted with carrying out a mission that would ensure the survival of an entire nation — a race of people he hadn't even believed existed before he found them. He needed to be cool and detached from everything but the responsibility he had been given. Yet here he was, imagining what it would be like if this woman were to love him back.

"Your brother," he said, needing to break the silence between them. "So much depends on him. Is he up to that sort of pressure?"

She was looking away now, off into the trees. "Little K is a lot stronger than people give him credit for. He's tough and he's smart. He saved my life in the ice caves on Syrring Rise. He saved Angel's life, too.

Someone else — maybe almost anyone else — would have collapsed under the weight of the responsibility he was given. Fleeing his home and his city and his people when he had never been away for more than a few days and then just a short distance, using the Elf-stones when he didn't know what that would do to him, that took courage. I can't even imagine what standing up to Culph and then to Tragen required."

Logan nodded. "It might get worse."

"It will get worse. That's why you're here, isn't it?"

He smiled despite himself. "Kirisin was doing pretty well with you as his protector. I don't want you to think I'm trying to replace you."

She gave him a look. "Does what I think worry you?"

He shrugged.

"You don't seem like someone who cares what others think," she pressed, making it sound like she was very sure. "You seem pretty self-sufficient."

"That's how it is with Knights of the Word. They work alone. They live alone." He paused. "Worrying about what others think can get you killed."

She was quiet for a moment, and then she said, "Tell me something about yourself."

He looked over at her. "Tell you something?"

She nodded. "I told you everything about what happened to me. Tell me about what's happened to you. About what you've been doing that brought you here."

He was surprised at how eager he was to do so. He started at the very beginning, with his meeting with Two Bears, and then carried forward to his last visit from the Lady. He skipped some of it, the things that she didn't need to know, the details of his battles, of his private struggles. He kept it simple and straightforward, telling her of the Ghosts and the gypsy morph and what was going to happen. She listened without interrupting him, watching his face, the look so intense he could feel its heat.

When he was finished, she gave him a smile. "If you weren't standing here, if someone else told me this story, I would think it was just a story and nothing more."

He smiled back. "I would think the same. If I hadn't lived it."

"Do you know where we're supposed to go, even if Kirisin isn't sure? Do you know where we will find this boy and all the other children? Angel's children?"

He thought about it a moment. He didn't know exactly, but somehow he thought he could find it anyway. Maybe Trim would know the way. But Trim had disappeared. There hadn't been a sign of him since Logan had first encountered Simralin.

"I can get us to where we need to go. Then it's up to the boy Hawk."

Ahead, cottages appeared through the trees. The sun had risen behind them, a hazy orb hanging low in the east, still screened by the forest, its light diffuse and silvery. The predawn silence had given way to a steady rise of birdsong. From somewhere not too far ahead, a dog barked and voices could be heard.

"We'll be there in a few minutes," she said. "Arissen Belloruus will need to hear what brought you to us. But he will be happy you've come."

They passed through the trees and found a pathway leading to the cluster of houses. The scent of flowers filled the morning air. Logan breathed it in.

"I'm happy you've come, too," Simralin said suddenly.

She said it in a bold, challenging way, as if speaking the words cemented something between them that she understood better than he did. He looked over at her, but she was already striding ahead of him.

"This way," she called back.

He had an odd thought at that moment, one he hadn't had since Michael's death.

He would follow her anywhere.

TWELVE

It was three hours after sunrise, the sky a brilliant blue sweep through the tangle of the forest branches, the sun a bright orb hanging low on the eastern horizon, the day smelling of new life and fresh possibilities. Kirisin Belloruus stood on a rise east of the city, just at its edge and deep within the concealment of the forest. He carried the three blue Elfstones and the Loden, all tucked within his pockets, and he was dressed in the clothing he would wear when they made their escape into the mountains. A handful of Elven Hunters stood nearby, armed and ready to leave with him. Another handful of Elven Hunters, all Trackers, had spread out in a screening movement that would detect any enemy approach.

The King and more than a thousand of his Hunters were gathered at the west end of the city, forming a screen between the demonled army and Arborlon. When the city and its people were encapsulated within the Loden, the Hunters and their King would shift their defenses to protect Kirisin. Retaliation would be quick once the demon leaders got over their initial shock. They might not realize right away that Culph and Tragen were dead and that Kirisin was acting not at their behest but on his own . . . though it wouldn't take long for them to figure it out. No word had been received of his return, of his capture and subjugation, or of a time or place that the Loden would be used. When the Elves and their city disappeared, there would be an immediate response.

Kirisin knew that he'd better not be anywhere close when that happened. The plan was to make sure he wasn't.

The boy looked up at the sky and then off into the distance. It was all so surreal that he was having trouble believing it. He still didn't know for certain that he could use the Loden. He certainly didn't know how. The Ellcrys had told him nothing, only left him with the impression that when the time came, he would know instinctively. He supposed this was possible. After all, hadn't he known instinctively how to use the blue Elfstones? Well, after the first time, anyway. Would he need a first time with the Loden? How much time *would* he need? How much would he *get?*

He squeezed his eyes shut and gritted his teeth in response to his uncertainty. *Trust in yourself!* He mouthed the words silently, took a deep, steadying breath, and opened his eyes again. He wished this waiting were over. He wished he were doing something. But he had been told to wait for the King to signal that all was in readiness, that the army was in place and able to protect him.

As if anyone could really protect him. Even Sim.

He peered downward through the trees to the city. Arborlon's people were awake, but almost none of them understood the enormity of what lay ahead. They had heard about the attack on the High Council and the resulting deaths. They had been told that a meeting of the new members of the High Council had been set for midday today. They knew that no one was to leave the city for any reason until permission had been given. Home Guards were blocking all routes, a protective measure to assure that no one would be caught outside the city and left behind. Almost no one understood what that meant. Aside from new First Minister Ordanna Frae and two other ministers who had survived Tragen's attack, no one understood much.

They would know soon enough, of course. An announcement of what had been done would be made at a general gathering of the populace, once they were encapsulated inside the Loden. Home Guards would be everywhere when that happened. There would be hysteria. There would be anger and disbelief. There might even be insurrection. No one knew. No one had lived through this. Only a handful had ever even heard of the Loden Elfstone before today, and no one at all knew what life inside the city would be like after it was put to use.

It was new country for all of them.

He thought momentarily of his parents, who would be among those discovering the truth for the first time tonight. They had returned to the city in his absence, unaware of what had happened. Upon their return, Arissen Belloruus immediately placed them under house arrest. It was only last night that Simralin had gone to them, had told them they were free again, that the arrest had been a mistake, that she and Kirisin were well and would see them soon. A small lie? He shook his head. No, a rather large lie. He might never see them again.

But Simralin could not tell their parents the truth any more than he could tell the other Chosen. Secrecy must be maintained. Caution dictated what was permitted and what was forbidden. Mistakes could not be afforded.

Even so, he wished he could have seen his parents one more time before the closing away. He wished he could have explained things for himself instead of relying on Simralin. But he guessed it wasn't the first or last wish he wouldn't be granted in this business.

Simralin walked over from where she had been talking with the Knight of the Word and put a strong arm around his shoulder. "Are you all right, Little K?"

He nodded and gave her a smile. She hugged him and stood next to him for a moment, leaving her arm draped over his shoulders possessively. She was trying to reassure him, he knew. He was grateful to her for that, but reassurance came hard just now. There were so many uncertainties, so many doubts that beset him. She would do her best for him; she always did. But in the end, he suspected, it would come down to what he could do for himself.

His eyes shifted to where Logan Tom stood by himself off to one side, leaning on his black staff. There was something about him that bothered Kirisin. He was a lot scarier than Angel, who had always seemed a friend despite her service as a Knight of the Word. Logan Tom didn't seem like a friend to anyone. Although he didn't seem like an enemy, either. He just seemed . . . apart. As if he might disappear in a heartbeat, gone back to wherever he had come from.

But the boy knew that this impression was faulty, that Logan Tom would stand and fight. You could see it in his eyes. You could tell from the way he moved and talked — steady, confident, determined. Driven. Simralin had told him a few things about the Knight, things she had somehow discovered while bringing him back to Arborlon after he had come upon her at the site of the hot-air balloon. It was a great deal more than what he suspected Logan Tom would normally have given up to someone little more than a stranger. Stories of how he had gotten to them, of how he had found and rescued the boy who was actually a Faerie creature, a gypsy morph who would save them all from the demons. It was scary stuff, but kind of reassuring, too. Because buried in the details was the unmistakable promise that safety for all of them was not just a dream.

"He's awfully dark, isn't he?" he said softly to his sister.

She followed his gaze over to Logan Tom. "He's a lot of things," she murmured.

"You think we can trust him?"

"I think maybe we can." She smiled ruefully. "But I thought that about Tragen, too."

"That was different."

"This might be different, too."

"He looks dangerous."

"No more so than Angel."

"Much more so, I think. The kind of dangerous that means he won't let anything get in his way. I wouldn't want to get on his bad side. But maybe he can do what he says he's come to do."

She nodded. "Maybe."

She left him a few moments later and walked back over to Logan Tom. The Knight of the Word straightened and turned immediately, his entire demeanor changing. Something about his reaction to his sister reminded Kirisin of Tragen. But that was ridiculous. The two had just met, and besides, Tragen had been pretending. It was just the way men responded to Simralin.

Even so, he watched them for a moment, pondering the idea that men found his sister irresistible. He didn't. Mostly, he found her smarter than he was. But she was his sister, after all. She was just Sim.

He jammed his hands into the pockets of his pants and grasped the Elfstones between his fingers, impatient with the wait, looking for something to do. He was still looking when an Elven Hunter burst into the clearing and hurried over to Simralin. She listened for a moment, and then turned to look at her brother. Kirisin felt his breath catch in his throat. He knew at once what she'd been told. He didn't wait for her to approach. He simply nodded.

It was time.

He took a deep breath and exhaled, trying to relax himself. Then he brought out the Loden Elfstone and stood looking at it as it rested in the palm of his hand. Would it do what he wanted? What would using it feel like? Was he up to this?

He brushed the questions and doubts aside, knowing they did him no good, that they only served to distract him. What he needed was to concentrate. What he needed was to believe. He could do this, he told himself. He could do whatever it took. The Ellcrys had confidence in him, and he must have confidence in himself. He had gone through a trial by fire to get to this moment. Two precious lives had been lost in the process, one belonging to a Faerie creature and one to his cousin. They must not have been lost in vain.

He was aware that everyone was looking at him. No one was saying anything. No one was moving. They were simply watching and waiting. A silence had settled over the surrounding forest, a deep hush that refused to be broken. He could hear himself breathe in that hush, could hear the beating of his heart in his ears.

Do it now.

He closed his fingers over the Loden, feeling his skin mold itself against the Elfstone's faceted shape. He could feel every knife-edge ridge, every smooth surface, the details forming a picture in his mind. He closed his eyes. He knew what was needed — to imagine what he wanted to see happen, to visualize it as clearly as he could and by doing so bring it to life. That was how the seeking-Elfstones worked. That was how the Loden would work, as well.

He pictured the forest, the city, its people and animals, the Ellcrys and her gardens, everything that stretched around them in a sylvan cradle of life save for the defenders, who were crouched well back in the trees, away from where he would attempt to direct the magic. He envisioned it all, took hold of it, and drew it in. By doing so, he drew himself in, as well. He went down inside, carrying everything he had pictured with him, taking it deeper than he had thought it possible to go. He felt himself sinking, but even though it frightened him at first, his fear quickly gave way to recognition.

He no longer needed to worry if he could find a way to summon the power of the Loden.

Its magic was coming awake.

He could feel it unfold like a flower and then work its way through him, an entwining of heat and light, a twisting of something alive. It was magic born of the Loden, but of himself, too. He could not explain how he knew this or why it should be so, but he could sense it as surely as he could sense the change happening. He opened his eyes, a quick peek. In the palm of his hand, the Loden was a glowing orb. Heat was rising and light spreading, the former filling him up, the latter encapsulating him. He experienced a moment of panic, but fought back against it and locked it away.

He closed his eyes once more. There was no point in watching. Watching only frightened him, a window on possibilities he would rather not consider. Whatever was going to happen, it was too late to stop it. The heat flooded through him, its temperature steady now. The light was all around him and still spreading. He could feel it, even without looking. It was stretching and reaching and gathering in the city, the Elves, the Ellcrys, everything that was fitted around and under and above them. He could see it happening in his mind, the whole of it, a miracle.

He was taking in deep gulps of air, panting hard with the effort. He couldn't seem to stop. He tried to steady himself and failed. His body was responding to the magic's invasion, adjusting perhaps. Or fighting back. He let it happen, but kept himself still. Until the wind started, howling around him like a winter storm, harsh and raw, blowing with a ferocity that backed him up a step, unprepared. He squinted, but there was nothing to see. The light had closed him away, and everything beyond was gone. He hunched his shoulders and gritted his teeth against the force of the wind, wondering what would happen if it picked him up and blew him away. He shifted into a half crouch, again wishing he knew more, knew what else to expect. But his ignorance was complete, and he thought in a moment of lucidity that perhaps it was better so.

The wind rose to a shriek, mind-numbing and bitter. Then its fury spiked, diminished, and was gone. All that remained was the deep silence of before, when he had first called up magic. He waited, uncertain. He could no longer sense the presence of the Elfstone's light or feel its warmth. It sat within the palm of his hand, cool and still.

In the ensuing silence, he heard a series of gasps and sharp intakes of breath. He could feel the tension and shock radiating from all quarters.

He opened his eyes in response.

He stood at the edge of a massive crater, shallow but so broad it stretched away down the slope of the mountain farther than his eyes could see. Everything that had occupied that space had vanished — the whole of the Elven community. Gone, every last vestige. As if a giant's hand had reached down into the earth beneath it and scooped it away. He stared in disbelief at the scar that remained. At the emptiness. Even knowing what had happened, he could not bring himself to believe what he was looking at.

Nothing remained. His friends, his family, his home — virtually everything he knew from the whole of his life had vanished.

In the palm of his hand, the Loden Elfstone glimmered faintly. He could see traces of movement in its depths. Life.

His sense of loss collided with his sense of responsibility, and for a moment he was so overwhelmed he could not move.

Then Simralin was next to him, the Elven Hunters had closed about, and the Knight of the Word, Logan Tom, was saying, "We have to go. Quickly!"

Even so, even though they started away almost as soon as Logan Tom urged them to, they lingered long enough to look back on the beginnings of the battle between the Elves and the demons. The enemy hordes appeared almost instantly, flooding out of the woods below the crater, thousands strong, a river no dam could hold back. *Once-men,* Logan Tom had called them. They were wild, unkempt things, humans turned into dark imitations of themselves, more animal than man or woman. Ragged, dirty, brandishing everything from lengths of pipe and jagged sticks to automatic weapons, they shouted and screamed their incoherent words of rage and frustration. They never slowed as they reached the crater's rim, but simply kept coming, sometimes stumbling over its edge. Those that fell either rose quickly or were trampled by those that followed. A surging mass, they spilled into the bowl of the crater in a flood.

When they were halfway across, the Elves, concealed in the trees on one side, counterattacked. Hundreds of arrows tore through the demon ranks, a deadly rain out of the sky. They died by the scores, screaming as they fell, slowing those that followed and making them better targets for the hidden archers. At first the enemy could not understand what was happening. Even when they did, they could not determine the source of the attack. Hundreds more died as they slowed within the killing bowl of the crater, turning first this way and then that, easy targets for the Elven archers. Some fired their automatic weapons blindly into the trees. Some fired them into their fellows. The chaos and slaughter were indescribable.

But they kept coming anyway, and because there were so many the living finally surmounted the mounds of dead and reached the far side of the crater. There, within the shelter of the trees, they posed a flanking danger for the lines of Elven Hunters positioned farther down the slope, and so Arissen Belloruus was forced to pull back.

By now Kirisin and his companions were rushing up the slope toward the hot-air balloon, intent on getting away before the enemy got any closer. But even as they did so, they heard fresh shouts and cries from the trees to their right. The once-men had gone not just into the crater but around it, as well. In doing so, they had encountered the Trackers set to screen against any enemy approach, and the two forces were engaged in battle. Logan Tom, in the lead, called back to Kirisin and the others, urging them to hurry, to shift left, away from the fighting. Even as he did so, the boy saw movement in the trees ahead, shadowy forms scrambling to cut them off.

Simralin, trailing him by several steps, saw them, too. "Logan!" she called ahead, and at the sound of her voice the Knight of the Word immediately wheeled back.

In the next instant a small owl swooped down out of the trees, nearly colliding with Logan Tom, who flinched and then turned to watch the owl wheel away. Again, he started forward, and again the owl intercepted him, cutting him off.

He turned back this time and waited for the others to catch up before saying, "We have to change direction. The once-men are ahead of us. They must have begun encircling the city during the night. We can't go forward. Take everyone left, Simralin, through those trees."

He pointed to a towering stand of old growth that layered the earth beneath in shadows and climbed through an outcropping of rocks to the wall of the mountains.

"But the balloon is the other way!" Simralin insisted.

Logan shook his head, eyes shifting quickly, scanning the trees behind them. "We'll have to leave it. They've probably found it. In any case, we can't fill the air bag in time to make an escape. Do what I say."

For just a second, Kirisin thought his sister was going to argue. She didn't take orders easily. But Logan Tom was a Knight of the Word, and perhaps that proved the difference.

"Let's go, Little K," she called to him.

They charged ahead once more. Behind them, Logan Tom was hanging back, protecting their rear. A scattering of figures burst from the trees. Elves. Trackers. Kirisin recognized Praxia and Ruslan. Then Que'rue and several more he knew appeared, as well.

Seconds later a wave of once-men charged into view, brandishing their weapons. One dropped to his knee and leveled a gun. Kirisin gave a short cry of warning, but Logan Tom was already bringing up the black staff. A blue bolt exploded from one end and sent the once-men flying backward. They landed in crumpled heaps and did not rise.

"Run!" he called up to the Elves, seeing them hesitate.

They did so, gaining the forest of old growth and rushing into its shadowy maze. They were not more than twenty strong, a small force against what appeared to be hundreds. Kirisin could see the movement of their shadows and hear the sounds of their approach. Farther down the slope, the battle between the Elven Hunters and the larger portion of the demon army had shifted from the crater into the trees and was moving their way, as well. The Elven lines were clearly broken, the weight of enemy numbers forcing the defenders to give way. How much longer they could stand against such a huge force was anybody's guess, but Kirisin did not think there was much hope.

"Faster, Little K!" Simralin shouted in his ear, coming up on him all at once and giving him a hard shove.

He thought he was moving fast enough, but when Sim told him to go faster, he knew enough to do so. He redoubled his efforts, flying through the last of the trees. Behind him, he could hear the sounds of battle drawing nearer. When he risked a quick look over his shoulder, he caught a glimpse of combatants flooding the forest, fighting on the run, the Elves falling back as quickly as they could, the once-men trying to bring them down. The gap between them was narrowing, and the Elves' forward progress had slowed as they struggled through the forest debris. The way ahead, beyond the tangle, seemed open, but it was impossible to be certain. Dozens of hiding places lined their passage — fallen logs, clusters of boulders and heavy scrub. The Elven Trackers saw the danger. They closed about Kirisin protectively, carefully warding him on all sides as they tried to look everywhere at once.

An explosion from behind caused all of them to slow and turn. Blue fire flooded through gaps in the huge trees, a wall of flames that momentarily blocked the enemy pursuit. Logan Tom was creating a protective screen for the fleeing Elven Hunters, providing them a measure of relief from the enemy pursuit. He stood against the rush as long as he could, then turned and ran toward them, his black staff dotted with brightly glowing runes that pulsed like white-hot coals. The Knight's face was dark with purpose, and his eyes were dangerous. Kirisin looked away as he swept by and took back the lead from the Elves.

"Just ahead!" he called out to them.

Moments later they reached a clearing in which an armored vehicle sat waiting. Logan Tom released the locks and opened the doors, beckoning for Kirisin to climb inside. "Belt yourself in tightly, Kirisin," he told the boy. "This won't be easy."

Then he was holding Simralin by the shoulders, a gesture so familiar and protective that Kirisin gasped. "Remember the plan, Simralin. Bring the King and rest of the Elves to Redonnelin Deep, down by the bridge. Everyone who's left, bring them there. We'll be waiting."

Simralin reached up suddenly and touched his cheek. Then she was calling to Praxia, Ruslan, and Que'rue to climb into the vehicle

215

with Kirisin. A pair of Elven Hunters joined them. Kirisin sat frozen in place a moment longer, and then he was out of the AV and running to his sister.

"What are you doing?" he demanded, seizing her arm. "You have to come with us!"

"I can't do that, Little K."

"What are you talking about? We have to stay together!"

"Not this time. Arissen Belloruus is risking a great deal for you. I have to stay to help him." She reached down and removed his hand from her arm. Then she embraced him. "I love you, Kirisin. Now go!"

She shoved him away. "Keep my little brother safe!" she shouted over to Praxia and the others.

"But, Sim —"

"Go, I said!" she snapped, turning away.

"Wait!" he cried. Impulsively, he reached into his pocket and pulled out the blue Elfstones. "Take these." He thrust them into her hand. "That way you'll be sure to find me."

"I can't do that!" She tried to give them back. "They belong to you! They were given to you!"

"Well, now I'm giving them to you!" His hand closed over hers. "You can give them back when you find me again."

"Kirisin, no!"

He was already moving away. "That's how

it is, Sim. You stay, the Elfstones stay with you."

She started to say something more, then decided against it. She gave him a final look, a quick wave of her hand, and turned away, moving off into the trees where the bulk of the Elven Hunters were just appearing. She didn't look back.

Kirisin rushed to the AV and climbed inside, still not quite believing he was going without Sim. Logan Tom scrambled in after him, closed his door, threw the locks, and started the engine. Kirisin shivered, not quite certain why. The Knight of the Word looked over at him, dark face set, unreadable. His gaze shifted almost immediately to the Elves in the back and then ahead to the road leading out.

"Hold on," he said softly, and threw the levers on the dash all the way forward.

THIRTEEN

The Ventra 5000 lurched ahead through the trees at breakneck speed, bouncing wildly over ruts and holes, hummocks and fallen branches, its broad frame shaking and groaning, its big engine whining in protest. Trees whizzed past the vehicle occupants in a blur of dark vertical shadows, and the rising sun burned through the canopy of the forest in fiery flashes. Kirisin was gripping the armrests in preparation for an inevitable collision with something, but Logan Tom seemed to know what he was doing, even when there was every reason to doubt it. His dark face was angry and set as he drove, his eyes fixed on the road, his hands moving over the control levers and wheel with quick, sure movements.

"First time in one of these?" he asked the boy.

He never looked over, never changed expression, never showed the slightest interest in Kirisin's answer. He just asked the question and kept driving.

"*Last* time," the boy answered finally.

He gave the Knight of the Word a quick glance. Logan Tom was stone-faced. "Maybe. Maybe not."

They struck a deep hole that caused the AV to pitch forward, jump up sharply, grind as if metal was tearing loose, and then gain fresh purchase and rumble on. The straps securing Kirisin had been wrenched loose, and he tightened them at once. He risked a quick glance over his shoulder and found Praxia staring at him from out of the Elves clustered in the rear seats. The young woman's face was pale, her lips set in a tight line, her hands clenched in fists. But she gave him a wry smile.

"Scared, Little K?" she asked.

He shook his head and looked away again. He didn't like Praxia, mostly because Sim didn't like her, and he wasn't about to give her the satisfaction of hearing him admit to something like that. Even if it meant lying. Besides, she looked more scared than he did. They all did. None of them had ridden in one of these machines before. Probably none of them ever would again.

Kirisin hunkered down in his seat, riding out both the rough passage and his growing fears. He wanted to look out at the forest to see if he could detect any pursuit, but he was afraid doing so would make him sick. Already his stomach felt more than a little queasy. He settled for keeping his eyes fixed on the rutted road they were careening down, willing the AV to stay centered and not go crashing off into the forest and overturning. Let Logan Tom worry about any pursuit.

After a time the trees thinned, the road smoothed, and the wildness of the ride subsided. Soon after that, they turned onto a road with a smooth surface, one made by humans in better times, and they followed its winding stretch through the high desert heading north. The mountain peaks receded behind them, their jagged tips distant and stark in the midday sunlight. Kirisin glanced back and then away, thinking that like those peaks his Elven past was already a long way behind him.

He looked over at the Knight of the Word, studying his still-angry face, hard and intense and filled with hints of thoughts too dark to reveal. He looked more dangerous than ever, a man who might do anything.

Logan caught him looking and glanced over. "What is it?"

Kirisin shook his head. "Nothing." He was silent for a moment, and then suddenly, impulsively, he said, "You shouldn't have left Sim behind."

"I shouldn't have, huh?"

"You could have said something to her. It looked to me like she was paying an awful lot of attention to you. Why didn't you tell her she had to come with us?"

The dark gaze shifted away, fixing once more on the road. "Ask yourself this. Does she always do what you tell her to do?"

"No."

"So what makes you think it would be any different with me?" He sounded really angry now. "I just met her yesterday. I'm not the one who could change her mind, even if I wanted to. Anyway, she's not my responsibility. You are."

Kirisin felt a sudden surge of anger. "It probably helps that you're a Knight of the Word and don't have to answer to anyone for your decisions!" he snapped.

Logan Tom glared at him. "Is that what you think? That I don't have to answer to anyone? You don't know anything."

"I know that you left my sister behind!" Kirisin was furious. "I know that there wasn't any good reason she couldn't have come with us! I know I didn't see you try to change her mind! You just left her!"

They sat in silence after that, the AV bouncing and sliding along the weather-damaged road, the sounds of their passage cocooning them away with their anger. Kirisin was furious, but he was also afraid. He knew next to nothing about Logan Tom, and now he was in the Knight of the Word's care. He might have been smarter to keep his thoughts to himself. But he could hardly stand it that they had abandoned Sim.

"She insisted on staying," Logan Tom said suddenly, his voice unexpectedly calm. "We talked about it last night. I asked her to come. I told her you needed her. But she refused. She said you would be all right with me. She said she was the only one who would know how to guide those Elves who stayed outside the Loden to where they need to go. She refused to leave them on their own."

Kirisin was quiet for a moment, his own anger dissipating. "That sounds like Sim."

"You would know."

"I still think you should have insisted she come."

Logan Tom gave him a look. "Would that have worked?"

Kirisin hesitated. "Maybe." Then he sighed. "All right, no. Probably not."

"Then stop talking about it. It's over and done. She made her choice, even if it was the wrong one. She stayed behind and she has to catch up on her own. Maybe she can do it, I don't know. She seems to think she can."

All at once Kirisin realized that Logan Tom was afraid for Simralin. For reasons that the boy could scarcely fathom, the Knight of the Word cared a whole lot about what happened to her. Why that should be was hard to figure out. He supposed it had something to do with Sim's effect on men, the same thing he had thought earlier when he watched them standing together before he used the Loden. But his reaction this time seemed so intense, so much stronger than it should have been.

They were silent again as the AV rolled on, the road noise from the big tires a steady rumble. Kirisin squirmed in his seat, glanced over his shoulder. Those sitting in the back of the AV couldn't have heard what he and Logan Tom were saying even if they had wanted to. Still, talking about Simralin like this made him decidedly uncomfortable.

"How do you feel?" Logan Tom asked suddenly.

He was so surprised by the question that for a moment he didn't answer.

"After what happened," the other said. "After using that . . . what do you call it, a Loden?"

Kirisin almost didn't answer the question, unsure of the other's motives in asking it. But then he decided that not answering was pointless. "I don't know. It happened so fast." He shrugged. "Maybe I'll know better later. Right now, I just feel relieved that it worked."

"Did you know you could do that? Your sister didn't seem to think so."

He didn't like hearing that: that Sim had talked about him with Logan Tom. But he let it pass. "She was right," he admitted. "I didn't. I didn't know what would happen. I'd never used the Loden before. No one had."

"What if you hadn't been able to summon

223

the magic? What would you have done then?"

Kirisin looked at him. "What would you do if you couldn't make your magic work?"

That produced a tight smile. "Die, probably. It's what keeps me alive. Same with you, I gather. So Simralin says." He paused. "I was just wondering if using magic feels the same to you as it does to me. Call it professional curiosity. I think it must. I think magic works the same, no matter if it's a human or an Elf using it."

"I suppose."

Kirisin leaned back in his seat. He was wondering how much Sim had told Logan Tom about what had happened to them on Syrring Rise. A lot, it seemed. For some reason, that made him uncomfortable. Why would she tell him so much? She barely knew him.

He was aware suddenly that the other was looking at him. He shrugged. "Using the magic makes me feel like something is coming alive inside me, something that generates heat and light, but something else, too. It's hard to explain. It consumed me when it surfaced. It filled me up." He shook his head at the memory, then added softly. "It took me over."

The Knight of the Word nodded. "It's the same with me. Tell me some more."

To his surprise, Kirisin did, happy all at once to be talking about it, to be sharing what he knew. Logan Tom already knew so much that telling him this probably didn't matter. Besides, he hadn't talked about it with anyone else who understood magic, and while he would not have believed earlier that he would ever talk about it so freely, he found it easy to do so. That they shared a common experience and responsibility where magic was concerned certainly helped. Angel had never wanted to talk about herself, only about him. For all his brooding and intensity, Logan Tom seemed less constrained.

They were in the middle of exchanging thoughts on the matter when the Ventra's engine suddenly died and the AV slowed to a stop.

"What's happened?" Praxia wanted to know at once, leaning forward from the backseat.

Logan shook his head, released his seat belt, and climbed out of the cab. He moved to the front of the AV, opened a metal covering, and leaned in for a look at the engine. Kirisin got out, as well, and walked around to stand next to him. Logan was peering at a cluster of tiny dials protected by thick pieces of round glass recessed into narrow metal cylinders.

"The connectors have failed," he said quietly. "The solar cells are dead. There's no power." He walked to the rear of the vehicle, with Kirisin following, and opened a storage compartment where several more of the cylinders were resting in slots obviously constructed to hold them. "These, too. All dead."

He straightened and looked at the boy. "I'll have to find out what's gone wrong or we'll have to walk. A long way. Back to where you traveled before, the Columbia River, what you call Redonnelin Deep." He glanced back the way they had come. "Too risky. They'll be coming. Skrails. Perhaps some others."

His dark face studied the horizon for a moment longer; then he ordered everyone out of the AV and began pulling open metal plates covering machine compartments and nests of wire. Kirisin watched him for a time, and then he walked over and sat down on a log by the roadside. Maybe he should have asked about skrails. But maybe he was better off if he didn't.

Seconds later Praxia appeared and sat down beside him. She didn't say anything for a moment, just stared off into the distance, her dark features expressionless. Finally she looked over. "Why do you think the Ellcrys chose you?"

Kirisin shook his head, not looking at her. "I really don't know. I guess because I was there."

"So were the others. She didn't choose one of them."

He didn't know what to say. He didn't want to tell her about Erisha. That was private, not

226

something she needed to know. "I can't explain."

"You must have been surprised when it happened." She was still looking at him, her eyes locked on his face. "What did you think? Did you think you were losing your mind?"

"No, I didn't think that."

"What did you think, then?"

"Why do you want to know, Praxia?" He looked at her now, growing suddenly irritated. "Why should I tell you?"

She didn't answer for a moment. Then she said, "I wish it could have been me. I wish she would have asked me. I know she wouldn't; I'm not even a Chosen. But I wish it anyway."

He stared at her in surprise. "Why?"

"Because what you did back there, that was the most wonderful thing I have ever seen. That was . . . I don't have the words for it. How the magic came to life. How it gathered in our city and all our people, scooped them up like toys and drew them inside. Like a mother with an unborn baby, keeping it safe and alive inside her body." She shook her head, her eyes filled with wonder. "I wish I could have done that. I would give anything."

The way she said it made him look at her with new eyes. She wasn't teasing or making fun. She meant what she was saying. Even if he didn't like her all that well, her words moved him.

"I know this might seem like an odd thing to say," she continued, looking away now, "but even though your sister and I don't always see things the same way, I've always admired her. She's what everyone says she is. The best at what we do as Trackers."

Kirisin cocked an eyebrow. "You should tell her."

Praxia grimaced. "I don't think so. I'd rather just tell you. That's difficult enough. You tell her, if you want." She bit her lip. "Can I ask a favor? Can I see the Elfstone for a moment? Just take a quick look at it?"

Kirisin was instantly wary. But he tamped down his immediate response and nodded. He had placed the Loden in a small pouch that hung about his neck on a cord. He reached down his neck, found the pouch, and brought the Elfstone out into the light. Praxia didn't try to take it from him. Instead, she leaned forward to peer at it, her brow furrowing in concentration.

"Kirisin," she whispered. "I can see movement inside. I can see a little of the city and the Elves!" Her voice was filled with excitement. "I can see them, right there, inside!"

"I could see it, too," he said. "After the magic drew everything in, I looked. I could see movement, too."

He gave her another few moments, then put the Loden away. Praxia smiled. "Thanks for letting me see. It makes what we're doing real. It makes it have meaning. Saving our city and our people." She paused. "You're very lucky."

"Is that what I am?"

She nodded. "I know you must be scared. I would be. I know you must have all kinds of doubts about what you are doing. But I meant it. I wish it were me. No matter what that means. I wish it were me. I would die for that to happen."

Her words were so intense that for a moment Kirisin just stared at her, unable to say anything.

She brushed stray strands of her dark hair from her eyes. "I would, Kirisin. I would."

The afternoon wore on, the sun passing west toward the mountains and finally dipping below the jagged peaks. Twilight settled in, a slow fading of the light toward darkness, a gradual emergence of stars and moon, a cooling of the air. Even though the landscape was stark and barren and seemingly empty of life, the gathering darkness softened and smoothed the rougher edges. Kirisin sat with Praxia and the other Elves and watched it slowly disappear into blackness.

All the while, Logan Tom continued to work on the Ventra 5000, tinkering with its parts, laboring over the solar collectors that powered its engine.

He was still working on it when Kirisin, who had stretched out on the ground close by to watch him, fell asleep.

His sleep was deep and untroubled, a blanket of silence and darkness wrapped tightly about him. He was unaware of time's passage, of anything having to do with the waking world.

Kirisin.

His mother was calling his name.

Kirisin.

Her face appeared from out of the darkness, familiar and welcoming, and he smiled with joy.

"Kirisin!"

His eyes snapped open. Praxia was bending over him, her small, wiry frame taut, her face dark with misgiving and fear. She put a hand over his mouth when he tried to speak, silencing his effort.

She bent so close he could feel her breath in his ear. "Get up. No talking. Walk over to the transport and get inside. The skrails have found us."

He flinched at her words, even without knowing yet what skrails were. She released her hand and straightened, turning away from him and staring off into the darkness. Looking past her, he could see Logan Tom still working on the Ventra, hunched over the open hood, hands buried somewhere in the engine workings. His black staff rested against one fender, its runes glowing as if they were on fire. The other Elves were spread out in a loose circle, weapons drawn, dark shadows in the pale glow of the starlight.

He listened for a moment. He could hear nothing.

He climbed to his feet carefully, making no noise at all. Praxia was standing right next to him, a long knife in each hand, crouched and ready.

"How long was I asleep?" he whispered.

She shook her head. "Not long. Get inside the transport."

From somewhere off in the distance, back the way they had come, a series of high-pitched screeching sounds broke the silence. It reminded Kirisin of the cries of hunting birds, large and fierce predators, and it sent a chill up his spine.

"Go!" Praxia hissed at him, gesturing urgently with her long knife.

He had only moved a couple of steps when he was struck from behind, a hard blow to his head and shoulders that sent him sprawling. Fire lanced across his back where claws had raked through his clothing to tear into the skin, and he could feel the blood running freely from his wounds. As he struggled to his feet, he saw dark forms swooping down out of the night, a gathering of shadows that completely surrounded the Elves and the Knight of the Word. Sharp, piercing cries filled the night, mingling with shouts and cries of warning.

"Kirisin! Run!"

Praxia dodged and weaved as the night fliers came at her — one, two, three of them, claws ripping at her head. But she was small and quick, and they missed their target, catching only air. Her knives flicked out at them as they passed, and two shrieked in pain and anger, one rising only momentarily before falling back, wings beating uselessly. Kirisin saw it clearly as it landed, a human-shaped form with leathery wings and a reptilian spine and tail.

Human once, he thought, scrambling away. Reptile now. Changed into something monstrous.

A flock of them had fallen on the two Elven Hunters and both had gone down, buried in a mass of beating wings and ripping claws. The boy heard them scream as their lives were torn out, their efforts at defending themselves too little, too late. Others were coming at Ruslan and Que'rue, but both had backed themselves against the AV and were using short swords and long knives to keep their attackers at bay. Three of the skrails died right in front of the boy, cut to pieces. Others escaped with deep cuts and slashes. Blood flew everywhere from the injuries, some of it spattering his face.

Logan Tom had turned away from his work to summon the magic of his black staff, had called it up and sent it arcing across the night

232

sky. It illuminated the darkness and revealed dozens of skrails. The Knight of the Word spun the magic out across the flats, into the darkness, and more of the skrails, revealed in its blue blaze, were caught up in its sweep and incinerated. Shifting his stance, Logan Tom raked the skies overhead, and another knot of attackers was beaten back.

"Get into the AV!" he shouted at the Elves.

Kirisin was already trying to do just that, but the path was blocked by skrails and Trackers locked in combat. The battle was raging back and forth in front of the Ventra's doors, and the boy could not find a way past.

Then Praxia was next to him, grabbing his arm, hauling him ahead, into the teeth of the fighting. She cut their way through, shouting at Que'rue and Ruslan to let them past. In desperation, she threw herself into the battle ahead of him, and the three Trackers fought to clear a path through the knot of skrails. From farther out on the flats, Logan Tom was struggling to keep others that were still in the sky from joining those on the ground, his magic flaring into the darkness in sharp bursts. But the skrails were coming at him from everywhere, recklessly flying into the magic's fire, almost as if eager to sacrifice themselves.

Kirisin hesitated, uncertain which way to go.

"Get down!" he heard Logan Tom yell at him.

He dropped to one knee, searching wildly. Dark bodies surged toward him, flew at him. He hunched his shoulders and tried to think which way to go.

"Kirisin!" Praxia screamed.

An instant later four sets of talons locked onto his shoulders. He had been seized by not one but two of the skrails, huge creatures with reptilian faces that were beaked and horn-encrusted. Their leathery wings beat madly as they hoisted him aloft, and although he twisted and thrashed in their grip he could not break free. The ground fell away beneath him, and his companions began to diminish in size.

He experienced an overwhelming terror as he realized what was happening. He screamed for help, but it was already too late. Even if he were freed from the skrails, the fall would kill him. His companions were not going to be able to save him. Already he could barely see them. Only Praxia was giving chase, shouting up at him futilely.

A cold certainty flooded through him. He knew where he was being taken and the fate that awaited him when he got there. Demons would be waiting for him, and he would be made to use the Loden exactly as Culph had intended.

In desperation he yanked the pouch that

contained the Loden Elfstone from within his shirt, broke it free from its cord, and cast it away. He watched it fall to earth. At least they wouldn't get that, he thought.

But would his companions find it? Had they seen him drop it? Would they even know to look for it?

Then he was too high to see anything more, and he quit looking.

FOURTEEN

Angel Perez sat in an old rocker on the cottage porch and stared out into the screen of trees that masked the sluggish flow of the Columbia River. It was midday, the heat penetrating even the thick canopy of the forest. Only the breezes off the river kept it cool, but today they were sporadic and slight. She was tired of the heat, the cottage, the inactivity, and the long days and longer nights. Mostly, though, she was tired of not knowing what was happening to those who had left her behind.

She exhaled wearily, thinking of it. Her recovery had been slow, if steady. She had been with Larkin Quill for more than a week now, sleeping most of the time at first, and then dozing frequently after that until she'd had enough of sleep and healing and the corner on her recovery had been turned. Her pain from her wounds had been harsh but bearable. Her magic had helped her to mend as an ordinary person could not have, restoring her health so quickly that even Larkin Quill, who had seen much of injuries and recoveries in his time, was surprised.

"You would be laid up for another month, were you a normal young lady," he had declared that very morning. "I thought I knew something about healing, but you could teach me a few things."

Well, she could if she understood how it worked, but she didn't. She had always healed quickly since becoming a Knight of the Word, the process enhanced and quickened by her magic, by her being who and what she was. There was no mystery to it. It was necessary that she heal swiftly if she was to survive. It was required of those who were constantly in danger.

Or all Knights of the Word.

She wondered how badly you had to be damaged before even the magic couldn't save you. She thought she had reached that point on the slopes of Syrring Rise, that the combination of blood loss and cold was enough to finish her. She had crawled through inky darkness and howling wind in search of a cavern entrance she could not see, and she was certain she was going to die. She had come close, she thought. She had come as close as she could without crossing over.

But here she was, still alive, her wounds healed, her strength mostly back. A miracle.

There was movement in the cottage, and

Larkin Quill stepped onto the porch beside her, his milky gaze fixed and unresponsive, but his smile warm.

"You seem much better," he said.

How he could tell she would never know. She was constantly amazed at how he was able to discern so much of what would normally require sight. He was better at it than she was, she believed. He had that gift or skill or whatever it was that enabled him to sort things out with his other senses. She had seen him do it over and over since she had arrived, in small but no less incredible ways.

"I am better," she agreed. "Thanks to you."

His lean, sharp features crinkled with the appearance of his self-deprecating smile. "I supplied the small kindnesses and little medicines, but mostly you did this yourself. You and your magic, Mistress Knight of the Word."

She shrugged. "Some of each played a part, I imagine. What matters is that I am better."

"Indeed. Now we need to think about getting on with things. It's been a week, and Sim and Kirisin aren't back. I don't know if that means anything, but we should assume the worst for purposes of your own situation. What do you want to do?"

Angel didn't hesitate. "Go after them."

"Go after them?" Larkin shook his head. "No, that's a bad idea. You aren't strong enough for that yet. Even if you think so, you aren't. You'd have to go afoot. It's a long way to another balloon, even if you could get there, and neither you nor I can fly it." He smiled. "We have to be patient, Angel. We have to wait on them."

"What if waiting on them is not what's needed?"

He shrugged. "Give me your second choice. What else would you do with yourself while waiting?"

She thought a minute. "I would find Helen Rice and the children I left in her keeping when I came in search of the Elves. They are supposed to be somewhere on the Columbia . . . sorry, somewhere on Redonnelin Deep."

"And so they are," he said. His quirky smile was back. "They are a dozen miles upriver and have been for as long as three weeks. More than two thousand of them, by my count." He didn't explain how he had managed that; he just shrugged. "I can take you there, then come back and wait."

"If I agree to that," she said carefully, locking eyes with him as if he could see — and perhaps, in a way, he could — the intensity mirrored there, even in that blank gaze, "then you must promise you will bring Sim and Kirisin to me at the camp or come to get me if you discover they cannot reach us without help."

239

He nodded. "Very well, I give you my word. You should be strong enough by then." His brow furrowed. "Now, however, I have my doubts even about the short hike you propose. We might need to see how far you can walk before we set out. You haven't tested yourself yet." He gestured toward the river. "Want to give it a try?"

They set out along the riverbank, picking their way over fallen logs and roots, following the flow downstream with the sunlight arcing over their shoulders. Angel had taken short walks, but only close by the cabin and not too far out of sight. This day, it seemed, Larkin Quill intended to go a good deal farther. She took her time following him, noting how smoothly and easily he made his way through the tangle of vegetation, how effortless he made it seem. She carried water and drank from the skin often, measuring her pace, gauging her strength, careful with everything. She carried, as well, the black, rune-carved staff of her office, its smooth wood comforting, its presence reassuring. The day was hot, but the breezes that blew off the water kept them cool as they walked.

"I think you saved them," he said suddenly at one point. "Simralin and her brother, up there on Syrring Rise. They didn't say it, but that was the impression I got."

"They saved me," she said.

"A good partnership, then." He kept walking steadily ahead and didn't look back at her. "Between humans and Elves. A good sign of what might lie ahead, don't you think?"

"I hope so. If there's no cooperation, there's no survival. We'll all be destroyed by whatever's coming."

"Or by whatever comes after," he added. "It never ends, really, does it? You overcome one obstacle, one evil, one enemy, and another steps into the unoccupied space. I think about that. We persevere, but it isn't ever really over for us. Not even for those who don't want any part of it. The Elves are a perfect example. They want no part of the human world, no part of its evils, of the demons and once-men and all the rest. They just want to be left alone, and so they isolate themselves and stick their heads in the ground so they won't be seen." He made a vague gesture. "You can see where it's gotten them."

"They seem to be doing something now," she observed.

"That's so," he agreed. He glanced back. "Too little, too late, perhaps? Time will tell."

They had gone about three miles when he stopped, looked around, and moved into the shadow of a small cluster of conifers that fringed the mudflats they had passed onto. He found what was left of the trunk of a fallen tree and sat down.

She moved over and sat beside him. "I'm

winded."

"You've done well. I didn't think you would get this far without resting." He reached over and patted her leg affectionately. "I think you're ready to make the trip upriver to your friends. We'll go in the morning."

"I would like that, Larkin." She gave him a genuinely warm smile, not caring that he couldn't see it. "You've done a lot for me, *mi amigo.* You took risks for me when you didn't have to. You've been a good friend."

Larkin laughed. "Did I? What was I thinking?"

She laughed with him, and then she rose and stood looking off into the distance, across the river to the cliffs beyond. "I need to try something," she said quietly. She glanced back at him. "I need to see if I can summon the magic."

He looked puzzled. "Why wouldn't you be able to?"

"I don't know. I just know I have to be sure." She hesitated. "I lost something back on the mountain. My life, almost, but something more, too. Something of myself. It's hard to explain, but I won't feel complete until I know I have the magic to command. I won't feel whole."

He brushed idly at his shock of wild black hair. "And how will you test it?"

"I only need to make certain I can summon it. It won't take a moment."

He didn't say anything further, so she stepped away from him and faced off into the distance, holding the staff before her, both hands gripping its smooth surface, her fingers working slowly over the indentations of the runes. The staff was her life, the verification of who she was and what she did. She needed to know that her close brush with death hadn't robbed her of its power, hadn't leached it away. She knew she was probably being foolish, that such a thing couldn't happen. But her confidence was diminished, and she needed to strengthen it anew.

She reached down inside herself and called the magic to her, joining with the staff, feeling it become a part of her.

The runes began to glow instantly, bright red beneath her fingers, and the magic flared from the staff in a soft, white glow that widened against the dappled shadows cast by the branches of the trees. She felt a surge of relief, vindication of her need. The magic was there and it was hers. She was still a Knight of the Word.

She let it fade quickly, exhaled sharply, and turned back to Larkin Quill.

"Are you reassured?" the Elf asked with a wry smile. "Doubts chased back into the dark corners, everything sunny and bright?"

"Everything sunny and bright," she replied.

Not five miles distant, close by the waters of

the Columbia, the Klee stiffened in recognition. It stood where it was for a long moment, as if become a stone carving, its huge, shaggy bulk blocking the way forward on the narrow trail it followed, bits of debris broken off by its cumbersome passage littering the ground behind it. A deep quiet settled in all around it, a widening arc of silence that reached well beyond what it could see with its weakened eyes, a caution that reflected both the nature and extent of the danger its presence posed.

When the moment ended, it turned slightly in the direction of the magic that had attracted its attention, magic generated by a creature that it sensed instinctively was not a demon. Its instincts told it that the magic was of a foreign nature, of a different form. The Klee was not overly bright, but it was deeply attuned to and capable of differentiating among forms of magic. It could not see well, but it could hear and taste and smell what other creatures would simply overlook. It tested the air now, and, even as far away as it was, it caught a whiff of what had distracted it from its search.

A whiff, it concluded, of what it might be searching for.

It shambled down to the riverbank and began plodding upstream toward the magic's source. It advanced steadily for the better part of an hour, a bulky, almost featureless form passing through a mix of sunlight and shadows, a monster set loose. It was neither fast nor supple, but steady and dogged. Once it began a search, it would not quit. That was its value. The old man in the gray cloak and slouch hat relied on it to do what no other demon could — to track a scent from a scrap of cloth or a single footprint or even a momentary vision. A peculiar mix of blood-lust and hunger drove it, guided it, and infused it with purpose. The Klee was a special breed of demon, one that came along only now and then. Its makeup was unusual enough that a demon less astute than the old man might not recognize its talent. Repulsive and terrifying, a monster in both appearance and behavior, it did not invite close examination.

To make any use of it, you had to be able to embrace an unspeakable evil, and the old man had.

The Klee didn't care what others thought of it. It only cared that its urges and needs were given an outlet. On this occasion, the old man had given it what it craved most — an uncomplicated directive to kill everything it encountered. The Klee did not understand the reasons for this or even care to discover them. It understood instinctively that the old man was worried, something that rarely happened, and required of the Klee that it do whatever was necessary to make that worry disappear. There would be no restraints, no limits, and no recriminations for what happened. It was the Klee's favorite kind of work. The Klee was to kill the magic user and everything and everyone that stood in the way of its doing so.

Easy enough when you were the most dangerous creature alive. Easy enough when you knew you had never failed.

The Klee walked until it reached the spot where the magic had been expended. The taste and smell of it were still present, stronger here, pungent with power, a shadowy residue that hung on the air like smoke. The Klee stood where it was for a long time, drinking it in, as if it were a creature parched with thirst and the residue fresh, clean water. Its huge bulk shifted slightly as it tested the air over and over.

Then it saw the footprints embedded in the soft mud of the riverbank.

Without a second thought, it began to follow.

Nightfall brought a cooling in the air and fresh solitude to the forest bordering the Columbia. The walk back had tired Angel sufficiently that she had fallen asleep almost immediately on her return and not awakened again until Larkin told her that dinner was waiting. Sitting on his porch, looking out into the failing light cast across the surface of the river by the setting sun, she worked her way slowly through her meal, washing it down with cold springwater, and thinking ahead to the trip upriver to where the children were encamped. She ate in silence, and Larkin let her be. Maybe he sensed that she preferred it that way. Maybe he just wasn't feeling talkative himself. He sat across from her, his blank gaze fixed, his face expressionless.

When her dinner was finished, she went out back of the cottage to where the waterfall provided a makeshift shower and washed the day's grime and sweat from her body. She closed her eyes and let the water splash over her, leaving her skin alive and so cold that it tingled.

Alive, she thought, speaking the word silently. One word. A word that could mean so much.

She had finished washing and drying and was wrapped in her towel and standing in the tiny room Larkin had provided for her when the Elven Tracker appeared suddenly beside her, materialized as silently as a wraith returned from the dead.

He touched his finger to his lips, warning her not to speak. He touched his clothes, telling her to dress. She stared at him, and then dropped the towel and quickly slipped into the pants and tunic and boots he had provided her. All the while, Larkin stood as if poised to flee at a moment's notice, his body still, but his head turning this way and that. His black hair, spiky and stiff, seemed a conduit for his fear. Angel felt it radiating off him and taking up residence in her, sharp-edged and roiling.

He stepped forward cautiously as she pulled on the second boot and straightened. "Something is out there," he whispered, his words so soft that Angel could barely make them out. "A very dangerous something that . . ."

In that same instant, she saw the feeders, crowding through the doorway behind him, lithe and shadowy.

"Larkin!" she hissed.

The floor exploded beneath him, and a huge, mud-clotted arm fastened on his ankle and pulled his entire leg into the hole. He went down in a heap, arms flying out from his sides, head thrown back. A second arm, as massive and encrusted as the first, reached up, tearing apart more of the already splintered floorboards. Angel barely had time to grasp what was happening before she heard Larkin Quill's neck snap and watched his lifeless body cast aside as the feeders, pouring through the doorway now, swarmed over him in a blanket of darkness.

It happened so fast that for an instant she couldn't quite believe it had happened at all. One moment Larkin had been standing there, poised to run, mouth open to speak, and in the next the life was ripped from him with less thought than might have been given to brushing aside a scattering of leaves.

Dead, just like that.

She stared in disbelief. It shouldn't have happened. Perhaps it was the familiarity of its smell that had prevented Larkin, who otherwise sensed so much, from detecting it — a raw earthen stench that permeated his surroundings, blending with the ground itself, infused with the damp and decay of plants sinking back into the mire. Perhaps it was something in the creature's makeup, a composition the likes of which Larkin had not encountered before and could not identify.

She felt a wave of recrimination wash over her. *It shouldn't have happened.* If she'd been holding on to her staff, it wouldn't have. Its runes would have flared up in warning, and she would have known to act, would have had time to do something. If she hadn't set the staff down to wash, if she'd been paying better attention . . .

Her mind spun with a litany of missed opportunities, of possibilities lost, of regrets and self-accusation, all in the passing of a few horrific seconds as she stood rooted in place.

Then the feeders, done with Larkin, turned toward her.

Just in time, she broke free of her shock. She was leaping for her staff when the monster that had killed the Elven Tracker heaved

249

up through the damaged floorboards, shattering them completely, opening a gaping hole into the crawl space it had used to creep up on them undetected. She avoided its attempt to grab her legs and drag her down, vaulting past it to snatch up her staff and wheel back in response to the attack. Summoning the magic in a blur of white fire, she sent it exploding into the monster. But her attacker shrugged off the blow as if it were nothing and began tearing at the floorboards with its huge hands. The boards split and heaved upward, knocking Angel back against the cottage wall. She stayed on her feet, desperate to keep the thing at bay. She attacked again, the magic lancing out in a sharp thrust. Again the monster shrugged it off. But this time it came up out of the hole, eight feet tall and massive, and started toward her.

She backed quickly from the room, through the door and into the grounds and the trees beyond, her staff held protectively before her. She wheeled left and right, searching for it, trying to catch the sound of its movement, readying for the next attack. Her breathing was harsh and raw, and tears stung her eyes. She felt the world tilt beneath her feet, and she grew light-headed.

But the monster had disappeared, taking the feeders with it.

She took a deep breath, steadying herself. She didn't understand, but she couldn't afford to take time to try to do so. She backed up against a massive old tree. When it came for her, she would see it or hear it. She waited, staff poised, magic at her fingertips, body tensed to lunge in whatever direction the circumstances required.

But nothing happened.

She waited as long as she could stand, and then she worked her way around to the front of the cottage. The monster's trail was clearly marked from where it had emerged from the crawl space, a series of deep prints and scattered debris. She followed it with her eyes until she lost sight of it at the water's edge. She tracked it then, moving slowly, cautiously to the riverbank.

Far out in the water, a dark shapeless bulk surged through the waters of the Columbia, heaving its way north toward the far bank.

She stood looking after it. Had it really been a demon? She couldn't be sure, but she thought so. If that's what it was, it would know she was a Knight of the Word. So why hadn't it come after her? Why had it killed Larkin, but let her be? Why had it chosen to leave?

Had she frightened it? Had her magic been more effective than it seemed?

The unanswered questions floated through her mind like the ghosts of the dead.

When she had determined for certain that

the monster was gone and not coming back, she went into the cabin, hoisted Larkin Quill over her shoulder, and carried him out into the open air, back into the woods below the cliffs. When she found a patch of high ground, she laid him down and went back for a shovel. It took less than an hour to dig the hole and bury him, and when she was done she stood over him for a long time, remembering how much she had liked and admired him. She tried to think good thoughts and not bad, tried to think of him alive and not dead. She wished Simralin, who had been so close to him, could have been there to share the moment. Simralin would never have a chance to grieve over his body. She would never have a chance to say good-bye. Angel was sorry for this, but it couldn't be helped.

She said a few words in Spanish, soft words that she remembered Johnny saying over the body of a boy he had liked and lost. Life was uncertain. Death was forever.

When she was finished, she packed a sack with water and food, closed up the cottage for the last time, and set out upriver to find the children and Helen Rice.

FIFTEEN

The sun was barely up, and the Ghosts had already been on the road for an hour, inching their way down the two-lane highway. The choice of pace wasn't theirs to make; Mother Nature had made it for them. Weather, war, and neglect had combined to both erode and bury the concrete surface in more places than not. The damage had been minimal at first — barely noticeable the previous day, when they had set out. But today, on reaching the foothills below the Cascades and the first of the passes edging along the banks of the Columbia River, conditions had changed dramatically. Slides blocked whole sections of the road, potholes and fissures left huge gaps, and limbs and debris littered what remained. None of it would have deterred the Lightning, but the hay wagon was another matter. Unsteady and difficult to maneuver under the best of circumstances, it was virtually unmanageable now.

"This is like riding the rooftops in Pioneer

Square during one of the quakes!" Chalk declared, giving Fixit a worried look as the wagon swayed and bounced beneath them, a platform threatening to overturn with every new obstacle encountered.

Fixit didn't like the way the wagon rode, either, but he was more confident than his friend that they were safe enough if they avoided dropping a wheel into one of the holes in the road surface. Still, he hung on to the bedding stakes just as tightly as the other boy, gritting his teeth against the rough ride.

By midday, the road had worsened sufficiently that they were forced to stop and clear the way repeatedly in order to get through. Hawk walked point with Panther, the two of them choosing the path of least resistance when conditions demanded it, which was increasingly more often. The others still rode, save Catalya, who seemed uncomfortable with anything that didn't involve walking. With Rabbit hopping along next to her, she strayed from one side to the other, studying the countryside, looking this way and that as if searching for something hidden in the landscape that only she would be able to see. Which was probably a good way of putting it, Fixit thought more than once, watching her from atop the wagon. She seemed more attuned to the larger world, to all that was out there, much of it concealed, much of it dangerous. She was always on guard, always keeping watch, never taking anything at face value.

He liked it that she was that way. You could never keep watch too carefully, take your safety for granted. You could never afford to relax.

He was thinking about that when they stopped for the night, close within the shadow of the mountains but still miles away from the larger peaks and the destination that Hawk had told them lay beyond.

"I'm glad we've got Cat with us," he declared, sitting next to Chalk as they ate their dinner. "I think she's pretty good at seeing the things we need to avoid. She's got good eyes, good instincts." He paused. "I like her a lot better now than I did at first."

Chalk glanced up at him. "She's a Freak."

"Well, she's *our* Freak. Anyway, I don't care what she is. You notice Panther doesn't seem to care anymore, either, for all his big talk. He's with her all the time now. Like she's his girlfriend or something."

Chalk grimaced. "Not while I'm eating, please."

They were sitting apart from the others, something they often did. They were comfortable by themselves, sharing conversations that belonged just to them. No one bothered them when they separated themselves like this, either because they all knew that was the way the two liked it or because they didn't care anyway or some of both.

Chalk finished his meal and hunched down, pulling his knees up against his chest and hugging them. His pale skin looked even paler, reflecting starlight against the night's deep blackness. "I wish we were back in the city. Back in our home. I don't like it out here."

"You'd like it less back in Seattle just about now," Fixit declared drily.

"Sure, I know that. But I felt better in the city, in the home we built for ourselves. I felt safer."

Fixit nodded. He didn't feel particularly safe out here, either. He didn't like change. He liked things to stay the way they were, and now nothing was the same.

"At least Hawk's back with us," he said.

"Hawk's not Hawk anymore."

Fixit stared at him. "Sure he is. What are you talking about?"

"Haven't you been paying attention? Hawk's changed. He's not like us anymore. He's some sort of fairy creature or something now. He's the savior of mankind. He fell off a wall and nothing happened to him. He was taken to some gardens in a ball of light and brought back again. He touches dying people and animals and makes them well again. How's that like the Hawk we knew?"

Fixit scowled. "Sometimes you sound like your brain isn't working."

256

Chalk shrugged. "Look in a mirror if you want to see what's not working."

Fixit ignored him. "You're twisting things around. Hawk is the boy and we are his children; that's the way it's always been. So what does it matter if now we know he's something more than what we thought. Is that so bad? Does it seem bad to you? He's leading us to a safe place, something we always knew would happen. How many times has Owl told us the story? Now we're going, along with some other kids and some adults and maybe some Freaks, too. So what? Just so we get there in one piece!"

Chalk threw up his hands. "Jeez, Fix! You should listen to yourself! You sound like someone who thinks that if he wishes hard enough for something, it will happen. *Hawk's going to save us. Hawk's the boy who will lead his children.* It's just a story, dummo. Even I know that much. A good story, and we want it to happen, but think about it! Logan Tom says it's all over, the world's coming to an end, and you think a boy who's not really a boy, but a fairy creature, is gonna save us? How's he gonna do that? He couldn't even save himself when he was thrown off the compound wall. He had to be saved by someone else!"

"That doesn't change anything," Fixit insisted stubbornly. "He's still Hawk, and he's still leading us."

257

"Yeah, I know, I know. He's leading and we're following. So what are we arguing about?" Chalk seemed unwilling to pursue the matter further. He brushed at his shaggy white-blond hair with one hand. "I just wish we were back in the city. I just wish none of this was happening."

Fixit studied him a moment, then nodded. "Me, too."

"Yeah? Really?"

"Sure. You think I like being out here any better than you do? I miss my equipment, all the good stuff I built to protect us and help keep us alive. I miss my manuals. I couldn't bring most of them with me. Too much weight and stuff. I had to pick a few and leave the rest." He paused. "I haven't even looked at them since we left. Too much happening."

They were silent then, keeping their thoughts private as they stared off into the dark. Off to one side, Panther was arguing with Bear and Cat. His voice was strident. Fixit watched them for a moment, and then glanced over at Candle, who was sitting next to Cheney. The big dog was asleep, but she was petting his head gently, looking down at him. Then she looked up suddenly and caught Fixit staring at her. The boy blushed for no reason and waved awkwardly. She waved back, but she didn't look happy.

"What's happened to Candle, do you think?" he asked Chalk.

"Something's happened?"

"Well, she doesn't seem to get those, you know, 'premonitions' anymore. Since we left the city, she hasn't warned us once about being in danger, not even when we really were." He paused, thinking. "Not since that kid with the burned face took her away."

Chalk thought about it. "Guess that's right. What do you think happened to her?"

"I don't know. I'm just saying."

"Maybe he did something to her."

"No, Owl would know. Candle would tell her. I think it's something else, but I don't know what. I know I don't like it. We could always count on Candle to keep us safe. Now we can't. I don't think we can, anyway. I don't think she's getting those warnings anymore." He pursed his lips. "That's another reason I think it's a good thing we have Cat with us. She's almost as good at sensing danger as Candle."

Chalk sniffed. "Yeah, she was great back there when Krilka Koos and his militia found us and took Logan Tom away. She sensed that one right away."

Fixit did a slow burn but managed to keep himself from taking the bait. "I'm just saying," he repeated, and went silent again.

Sparrow had been watching Candle, too, and was harboring many of the same thoughts as Fixit. She was sitting with Owl and River, but they were busy talking about what to do to replenish their diminishing supplies and paying no attention to her. So she got up and walked over to where Candle was petting Cheney and sat down beside her. She didn't say anything right away, just reached over and joined the little girl in stroking the wolf dog's shaggy head. Cheney, who looked asleep but wasn't — same as always — was ignoring both of them. But with Cheney, you couldn't always tell. He might actually be enjoying the attention.

It was Candle who spoke first. "I'm glad Cheney's back," she said quietly. "Aren't you?"

"I'm glad all three of them are back," Sparrow answered. "It didn't feel right when they were gone."

Candle nodded. "Do you think Cheney missed us?"

"I don't know. Maybe."

"I think he did. I think he knows we're his family, and when he isn't with us, he misses us."

She spoke in short, breathy bursts, as if struggling to get it all out. She didn't sound at all like the Candle that Sparrow knew. "I think you're probably right, peanut," she said.

Candle didn't look happy with this. "I just wish he'd do something to let me know for sure."

Sparrow ran her fingers through her spiky

blond hair. She had cut it short a day earlier, tired of dealing with longer hair. But it needed a wash. She needed a wash. For that to happen, of course, she needed water, and there wasn't any for baths. There was barely enough for drinking.

"Why don't you try to go to sleep now?" she suggested.

Candle looked at her, her gaze intense. "Sparrow, do you think the other kids still like me?"

Sparrow stared at her in shock. "Of course they like you."

"Don't say it just because you think I want to hear it. Tell me the truth. Do they?"

"Candle, why wouldn't they like you?"

The little girl didn't say. She just ducked her head, looked at her feet, at Cheney, and then off into the darkness as if the answer was out there somewhere. "Just because."

"Has someone said something?"

Candle shook her head.

"Done something?"

Another shake of the moppet head.

"Then I don't understand. Why would you think that, all of a sudden, for no reason, they don't like you?"

"What if there was a reason?"

Sparrow thought she knew what was coming, but she didn't want to be the one to say it. Candle needed to do that. Speaking the words was the first step toward coming to terms with what they meant.

"What sort of reason?" she asked.

Candle shrugged. "No one needs me any-more." She was still looking at her feet as she paused, not finished, but not ready to con-tinue, either. "You know."

Sparrow reached over and put a hand on her chin and lifted her face so that they were looking right at each other. "No, I don't know. You have to tell me."

Another long pause. Then, "I can't sense when we're in danger anymore."

There it was. Out in the open. Sparrow breathed a sigh of relief. Now maybe she could do something about it. She reached out for Candle and hugged her close. "Oh, Candle," she whispered.

Then she backed away so that they were looking at each other again. "My mother told me something once. I was just about your age. I thought my mother was the most wonderful person in the world. I loved her, but I admired her even more than I loved her. I wanted to be her."

She smiled. "You know this. I've told you before. Anyway, I was worried that it wasn't going to happen, that it didn't matter what I wanted. I was small and not very good at anything. I told her this. I said I didn't think I would ever be like her, not even a little bit. This is what she told me. She told me that we don't know who we're going to be or what we're going to do when we're still children. She told me we don't find that out until after we've grown up. So you can't ever know what's supposed to happen until you get there."

She squeezed Candle's thin shoulders. "My mother was right. I had to be a lot older before I found out that maybe I would be like her."

"You are like her," Candle said quietly. "You are brave and strong. You killed that centipede."

"That's right. But I couldn't have done that even a year ago. I couldn't have fought like that, like my mother. But look at you, Candle. You already know you have a special gift. And even if it isn't working right now, that doesn't mean it won't work sometime later. Maybe it's resting. Maybe you are trying too hard. But even if it never comes back, even if it's gone forever, your family will still love you. The Ghosts will always love you and want you to be with them."

"Are you sure?" The little girl looked doubtful.

"They don't love you and want you in the family because of your gift, Candle. They love you for who you are inside."

She leaned over and kissed Candle's forehead and cheek, smoothed the thick red hair. She could barely keep the tears from her eyes. "We would never not want you in the family," she whispered.

"Okay," the little girl replied, her voice so small it was barely audible.

"Your family needs you, Candle. We always will."

She gave Candle a reassuring smile, but the little girl didn't smile back.

Some distance away from the others, concealed by the night's darkness, Hawk was talking quietly with Tessa. They were crouched within the shadow of a grove of withered ash, their heads bent close so that they could see each other's faces clearly in the starlight, their hands clasped together. It was their time alone, something they knew would be a rarity in the days ahead.

"It's nice when it's like this," he told her, giving her hands a squeeze. "Just you and me. Just the dark and the silence."

He could hear the others talking, their words soft and indistinct, but it was almost like silence. He was tired and more than a little worried, not only about their present situation, out here on the road, slowed to a crawl, but also about their future. He hadn't said anything, but he was already wondering how much more he could do to fulfill the charge he had been given by the King of the Silver River. His doubts and fears mounted every time he thought about how poorly prepared and ill equipped he was to help anyone.

"You're awfully quiet," she told him.

"Just thinking."

She bent forward and kissed him. Her face glowed in the starlight, and her eyes were so bright and clear and revealing that he could read the love mirrored there. It was welcome reassurance that at least one person believed in him.

"You can do this, Hawk," she told him. "I know you're worried. I know you think you have been given too much. But I know how you are. You're different from other people. Not just because you have Faerie blood or magic you can use. But because you have an inner strength that makes it possible for you to do things other people couldn't even begin to think of doing."

He smiled despite himself. "That sounds pretty good."

"Don't laugh at me," she said at once, her expression changing from soft to hard. "I'm not telling you this just to make you feel better about yourself. I'm telling you this because it's true and you need to remember it."

The smile faded. "Okay, I didn't mean to make fun. I know how you feel about me. It's the same way I feel about you. I know how you are, too. I saw how strong you were in the compound at our trial. Even when the judges didn't want you to speak up for me.

Even when your mother wouldn't stand up for you. Even after they said they would throw us from the walls."

He paused. "Even when they did."

She kissed him again, harder this time, her seal of confidence. "Then you should believe me when I tell you that you can do the things you've been asked to do. It doesn't matter how impossible they sound. You can do them. You can find a way."

She leaned back from him. "There's something else I need to say, and I need you to listen carefully and not interrupt. And not judge me."

He gave her a look. "I don't have the right to judge you."

"You haven't heard what I have to say yet."

"It doesn't matter," he insisted. "You can say anything."

"All right." She gripped his hands again, held them tight. "When we stood before the judges at our trial in the compound and it seemed that everything was against us and we had no hope, I told the judges that I was bonded to you and carrying your child. I did so to save us, to persuade the judges not to have us thrown from the walls. But the judges didn't care. They wouldn't recognize the marriage or the child. They made that clear."

Hawk started to speak, but she quickly put her finger to his lips to silence him. "You promised not to interrupt," she reminded him. She took her finger away. "When we were on the walls afterward, you asked me if I had told the truth, if there was a child. I said that there wasn't, that I had told the judges this just to try to save us."

She paused. "I lied to you. There is a child. Our child. But I couldn't tell you. I couldn't watch you die knowing that we had a child and that our child was dying with us. So I lied."

She gave him a small smile. "That was why I couldn't jump when you asked me to do so. I couldn't make myself kill our child even if there seemed to be no hope left. I couldn't do that."

She looked at him, studied his face carefully. "Okay, it's your turn. Now you can say anything."

He shook his head in wonder. "Can I say how happy I am?"

She nodded, tears in her eyes. "That would be nice."

"Can I tell you that I don't care about anything — *anything!* — as much as I care about this? When you told those judges we would have a baby, when I heard you say that, I couldn't believe it. But later, back in my cell, I thought about it. I thought it was sad and terrible and wonderful, and I wanted it so badly I could hardly stand to think about it because I didn't believe it could happen. We were sentenced to die. We would never have a child. So I asked you on the wall, and I *was* relieved when you said there was no child."

He exhaled sharply. "But now. Now, Tessa, I am so happy. I don't care that you lied. I know you did it for me. I know that. But I want this child. No matter what else happens, I want it. The newest member of our family. Of the Ghosts. But not another Ghost that will haunt the ruins that our parents destroyed. Not that. This will be a child who will help rebuild the world. This child will be the beginning of something wonderful."

"I'm glad you're not mad at me," she said.

"Mad at you? I could never be mad at you. I understand why you lied. I would have done the same. That's in the past. We can forget all that. We have a new beginning." He shook his head, still smiling. "I can't believe it. A child. Our child."

She leaned close. "A special child," she whispered. "Born of you and me, of our two worlds, of our two bloods. A child who'll be a leader, like you. I know it. I can feel it."

He drew her against him and hugged her fiercely. He had never loved her so much as he did in that moment. He thought maybe he would never love her so much again.

A child.

Sparrow stood in the shadows, her heart racing. She had heard everything. She had heard

268

it all. There was to be a child. Hawk and Tessa were going to have a baby, and it would be the first of a new generation of children.

She had come looking for Hawk to ask him to speak with Candle, to reassure the little girl about her place in the family, knowing that it would mean more coming from him than from her. She had not meant to overhear but she had not been able to help herself. She had found them just as Tessa was telling him about the baby, and she could not help listening to everything.

She stood rooted in place, undecided about what to do next. Should she reveal herself to them? She felt like a spy, hiding in the shadows, hearing secrets not meant for her ears. How would they feel if she stepped out now and let them know?

Perhaps it was better to wait. If she said nothing, she could wait until they told the others, and then she could pretend she was hearing it for the first time. That might be better. More comfortable for everyone.

She backed away noiselessly, leaving Hawk and Tessa alone, wrapped in their joy and their love. She would like to have that someday, she thought. She would like to have someone to share her life.

The secret of the baby was hers to keep, but halfway back to rejoin the others she had already decided she was going to tell Owl.

SIXTEEN

The sunrise was blood red. Hawk had never seen one like it, and it disturbed him for reasons he could not explain. It was more than the strangeness of it. It wasn't even that it felt ominous. It was that it signaled something, a shift in the order of things perhaps, that wasn't apparent on the surface but that he could feel somewhere deep down inside where such things wedge themselves and refuse to be dislodged.

Still flushed with the news of Tessa's pregnancy, he had risen in the best and most hopeful of moods. No matter the odds, no matter the obstacles, no matter anything that might lie ahead, he and Tessa would overcome it because they had a child to nurture and protect. He knew little of babies, but everything of children, and he was ready to see that his was given every chance at growing up strong and healthy. Even in a world that was all but destroyed. Even in a world he was trying to leave. Hawk wanted this as he had wanted little else in his life. His child, his and Tessa's. Its birth would be the most beautiful thing that had ever happened to him. It gave him hope; it made him feel that everything he had gone through or might go through in the days ahead was worth it.

His euphoria was dimmed but not overwhelmed by the odd sunrise, and when they set out that morning he was still smiling inwardly at the thought of his secret. A baby. What could be more wonderful than that?

He went to Tessa while she was still sleeping and woke her, hugging her close, kissing her and telling her how much he loved her, how pleased and excited he was. She hugged him back, and for a few moments the oppressiveness of the sunrise faded behind the bright veil of their happiness.

"We'll tell the others at breakfast," he whispered to her.

"Not until tonight," she urged. "I want to tell Owl first. I want her to know before anyone else."

He was quick to agree, and he went about the business of rousting the others and preparing for them to set out with such enthusiasm that more than a few looked at him as if he had lost his mind. He ignored the looks and the mumbled comments and all the rest, caught up in his own celebration.

"Try to get a grip, Bird-Man," Panther grumbled at one point, his minimal patience with such euphoria quickly exhausted. "You look possessed or something. Real scary-like."

Owl, wheeling herself over to the AV, overheard the comment. She stopped long enough to tug on Hawk's sleeve. "Don't listen to him."

Hawk glanced down and shrugged. "Don't worry. He's just being Panther."

"I know. But nevertheless." She grinned. "What you look like is someone who has a secret that he ought to share."

He gave her a sharp look, caught the satisfaction reflected in her eyes. "You know, don't you?"

"I might."

"Tessa told you?"

"Sparrow. She overheard you talking last night."

He shook his head. "Jeez. Why don't we just post a big sign for everyone to read?"

"Why don't you just tell everybody and get it over with?"

"Tessa wanted to wait until tonight."

Owl nodded. "It might not keep that long. You know how this bunch is with secrets."

He wheeled her over to the AV and helped her inside, where Candle and River were already waiting. He called Tessa over and tried to put her in the vehicle, too, but she waved him off. "You ride for a while," she told him. "You never ride."

"Yeah, you must be exhausted, what with

272

all that baby-making and stuff," Panther sniffed, walking by.

Just like that. He didn't slow as he said it, didn't even look back as he strolled on. Hawk stared after him, openmouthed.

River leaned forward from the backseat. "What are you going to name the baby, Hawk?"

"Is it going to be a little boy or a little girl?" Candle wanted to know. Her blue eyes were bright and eager. "I'm going to have a little brother or sister. Sort of. Almost. I can pretend, I think."

"As I was saying," Owl declared softly.

Hawk rolled his eyes and walked away, calling for Fixit to take the wheel of the Lightning and Chalk to keep him company. So much for secrets and surprise announcements.

They rolled east into the mountains, winding through a pass that took them away from the banks of the Columbia and up into the higher elevations. For a time, it looked as if they were going to cross quickly and be back on the flats beyond. But by midday, they had encountered a section of roadway riddled with rockslides and sinkholes too wide to be avoided, and they were forced to abandon the hay wagon, pack what supplies they could atop the AV, and continue with half their number afoot. Progress slowed, and the day seeped away like water through cupped hands.

By nightfall, they were still only midway across, still high in the passes and forced to sleep on ground virtually empty of grasses and littered with rocks. Owl, River, and Candle slept in the AV, but Sparrow turned up her nose at the idea, declaring she was as tough as any boy, and Tessa slept with Hawk, curled up against him, sharing her warmth and the promise of their future.

Hawk did make the baby announcement that night at dinner, but by then it was old news to almost everyone but Fixit and Chalk, who were always the last to know everything. Cheers and smiles greeted the news anyway, even by those who had known all day, and only Cat kept pointedly aloof from the celebration.

"Sort of silly, all this celebrating about a baby not even born yet," Panther sneered quietly, sitting down next to her when things had quieted down.

"I don't think it's silly," she replied.

He looked at her. "Well, your face says something else."

"My face, huh?"

"Sure." He sounded less certain. "Says different."

She looked him full on, her mottled face set in a hard glare. "Says different, you think?"

He didn't say anything this time, just nodded.

274

"You're awful quick with that mouth of yours."

He dropped his eyes. "Sometimes."

"Here's the thing, Panther. When you look like me, you don't want to hear about other people's babies. That kind of happiness isn't ever going to be yours. You don't want to even think about it. You just want to hurry up and get on with your life."

He stared back at her, his dark face flushed. Then he shrugged away his discomfort and said, "Sorry. I didn't mean nuthin' bad. I was just talking."

"Well, don't," she snapped. She stared at him a moment longer, anger reflected in her green eyes. Then she reached up suddenly with her hand and stroked his cheek. Her voice softened. "Just don't."

The next day was another slog through the passes under skies turned dark with clouds and the air grown thick with dust and ash. Where this weather had come from was anybody's guess, but it wasn't friendly and it wasn't conducive to good thoughts. The Ghosts walked all day, navigating a roadway littered with rocks and debris, some of which had to be removed by hand on numerous occasions to permit passage for the AV. It rained at one point, a thick spattering of heavy droplets that barely dampened the concrete of the highway and the earth of the surrounding countryside before being absorbed. The air turned hot and cold by turns, and the haze came and went.

Hawk, walking point with Bear, had never seen anything like it. He wasn't sure if it was a quirk in the weather pattern or a reaction to all the pollution, poisonings, and chemical warfare. Or if it was generated by a deeper, more pervasive climatic change that had been building for much longer than he had been alive. What he did know was that it made him uneasy. It made him want to gather up everyone whom he was supposed to lead to safety and get to where they were supposed to go.

When the earth rumbled later in the day, a violent shake that sent those walking to their knees and caused the AV to skid sideways so far it almost went off the road, he thought maybe this was a prelude to something much bigger. He glanced at Bear, down on his knees beside him, and shook his head.

"Smell the air," the other boy said quietly.

Hawk did, taking a deep sniff. "Sulfur," he said quietly.

Bear nodded. "Bad stuff, sulfur. We had a pool of it back on the farm, down by the south pasture. The smell was so bad that no one went near it. It could knock you out, make you real sick."

Hawk glanced at the sky. "Maybe it will blow away by dark."

It did, but the haze remained, thick and

clingy, a visceral feeling to it. The Ghosts hunkered down in their coats and tried to breathe through parts of their clothing. The twilight was raw with its presence, the sky colored metallic and the surrounding countryside flat black and gray, as if there were no depth to anything.

They were passing through the hill country below the peaks, expectations of reaching their destination beginning to crowd in on their discomfort, when they saw what appeared at first as a soft glow against the horizon. But as the little company drew closer, the light became a glare, one that all of them instantly recognized.

"Watch fires." Bear said it first. "All across the roadway ahead."

Hawk nodded. "Someone's blocking the way."

"Militia," Catalya declared, coming up beside him. "Wait here while I have a look."

Without waiting for his permission, she bounded off into the darkness. Panther was slow coming up or he would have gone with her, Hawk thought, hearing the other boy mumble a low curse as he realized what had happened.

"You should've stopped her," he snapped.

Hawk glanced over. "Don't think that was possible."

"Shut up, Panther Puss," Sparrow muttered, shoving him aside as she shouldered her Parkhan Spray and stood braced and ready, facing out toward the fires. "Save it for those who need it."

They waited impatiently, silently, a clutch of dark figures slowly disappearing into the deepening night's shroud. Time slipped away on wings that flew swift and sure, and Catalya did not return. Hawk began to grow uneasy. The girl was smart and experienced, but one mistake among adults with weapons would undo all that in a moment's time. If she had been seen, they would have already seized her and made her their prisoner. In that case, he would have to go in after her. Not Panther, who couldn't be trusted with that sort of task. Not the way he felt about this girl. No, Hawk knew that he would have to do it.

Then all of a sudden she was back, appearing out of the night as if born of it, her slight figure materializing right in front of them.

"Frickin' hell!" Panther snapped at her. "You shouldn't of done that, going off by your own self! Who do you think you are, girl? You couldn't wait for me?"

She gave him a glance. Then her eyes were back on Hawk. "It's a militia of some sort, several hundred, maybe more. Planted right across the roadway and for some ways to either side. I couldn't be sure. They almost had me. They've got some good ears and eyes in that bunch. I don't know what they're doing, but they're set on holding this road. You can tell."

Hawk nodded. "Then we have to go around." He glanced at the others. "I don't like trying this at night, but we have a better chance of not being seen if we do it now. What do you think?"

"I think we do it like you say," Bear answered for the others, who just nodded. Except for Panther, who spit and walked away in disgust. With Panther, you never knew.

Hawk split them into two groups. He put Fixit at the wheel and Chalk beside him in the AV, with Owl, Candle, River, and Tessa in back. He put Sparrow on the AV's roof with her Parkhan Spray. He took Panther, Bear, and Cheney with him, and put Catalya on point, her sharp senses their best defense against hidden dangers now that Candle no longer seemed reliable. He was sorry about that loss — sorry for Candle and for them. He had talked with Owl about it, tried to come up with a reason for it, but neither of them could solve the puzzle of the little girl's problem. In any case, they could not rely on her. They would have to do the best they could with the new girl.

He glanced down at Cheney, and the big dog's head lifted slightly, the dangerous eyes meeting his own. Cheney would help them if he could.

Catalya deposited Rabbit in Owl's lap, and they set out. They moved off the highway and into a long rolling stretch of hills that were lightly wooded. Catalya took them northward on a course parallel to the fires, staying well back from where the militia would be keeping watch on the countryside. The AV rolled like a big, sluggish beast over the rough terrain, the engine a soft growl, but still audible from some distance away. Hawk wished they could muffle the sound further, but there was nothing he could do about it. A wind was blowing down out of the mountains, and sudden gusts cut into the low rumble and might fool anyone who didn't know better. But Hawk didn't think they could depend on that.

It took an hour before Catalya turned them east again, down a ravine and then up again along the windward side of a high berm. Suddenly they were moving through a blackness sheltered from the distant firelight, a landscape illuminated solely by moon and stars. The sky remained overcast, so there was little light by which to navigate, only enough so that the Ghosts were able to make their way. The north wind had died away, leaving the night still and empty-feeling about them.

They emerged from behind the berm into rolling grasslands. A heavy mist had moved in, settling in pools in the low places, in the ravines and depressions, like standing water concealing hidden depths. Hawk didn't like it. It was becoming increasingly difficult to see anything or to judge accurately the nature of the terrain they were trying to cross. He caught up with Catalya and warned her in a hushed voice to be careful of sinkholes and rifts. She nodded without speaking, her eyes intense as she scanned the landscape ahead.

They continued, and the fog increased, growing heavier and thicker about them, rising slowly until they were wading through it. Catalya signaled for a halt and came back to huddle with Hawk.

"Can't see anything now," she admitted. "I don't like it."

Hawk glanced toward the watch fires south. They were almost clear of them now, some distance off, but still too close. "It can't be any better for them," he told her. "Maybe we should just wait this out, give it time to thin. Wait here. I'll talk it over with the others."

He was starting back, his mind made up, when he heard Cheney's low growl. He looked left and then right, just in time to see a scattering of figures appear through the gloom, still far off, but coming closer. He heard shouts and saw several of the figures pointing, and then the mist rose in a sudden swell and swallowed everything.

"Run!" he shouted to the others, waving for the AV to follow.

They charged ahead, angling away from the shadowy figures. Militia scouts, Hawk decided. Not that many, but they would be armed. Whether they had heard the Ghosts or just stumbled on them was difficult to say, but the result was the same.

Panther caught up to him, his Parkhan Spray held ready. "Can we take them?" he asked, breathing hard. "You and me?"

"No fighting!" Hawk hissed at him. "We don't fight unless we have to!"

Panther grinned wickedly and sprinted ahead, as if looking for an excuse. Catalya went after him, giving Hawk a look of disgust as she went by. For him or for Panther, he couldn't tell. Bear was lumbering just behind, and the AV was lurching through the fields, bouncing wildly across the rough spots.

He heard shots then, somewhere off to his right where they had first spied the militia scouts. The shots were sporadic and didn't seem directed at anything in particular. Meant to scare them, he thought. He glanced around as he ran, trying to count heads. All he could see was Bear. The murkiness was growing thicker and heavier, more difficult to penetrate. Already the AV was gone, although he could still hear it. They were in danger of becoming separated, he realized. He peered ahead for Panther and Catalya, but he couldn't see them.

"Bear!" he shouted. "Stay close!"

But Bear was swallowed in the haze. He couldn't see Cheney, either.

He couldn't see anyone.

Inside the Lightning S-150 AV, there was complete chaos. Everyone was yelling at once, mostly at Fixit because he was the one driving. They were shouting at him not to lose sight of the others, not to turn this way or that, not to run over anyone, not to hit any big holes, you name it. Even Owl couldn't make herself heard above the shouting. Fixit was doing his best to stay focused on the task at hand, regardless of the wildness of the other kids, but he was having a hard time of it. He couldn't see any of the Ghosts outside the vehicle; he could barely see to drive, the mist a thick blanket surrounding them on all sides. He could hear gunfire somewhere off in the distance, but he had no idea which direction it was coming from.

Chalk grabbed his arm, nearly causing him to lose control. "What's happened to everyone?" the other boy yelled.

"Let go of me!" Fixit yelled back, jerking his arm free.

The wheel spun through his fingers, and he grabbed hard to steady it, but the AV skidded sideways, bounced, and then lurched ahead once more. By now Fixit had no idea where he was, let alone where the others were or the people firing weapons. He reached down hurriedly and switched on the loran. The landscape came into sharp focus, the AV a green dot against the flat, empty background, and he had his direction back again.

"Shut up!" he shouted at everyone yelling around him.

To his surprise, they quieted down instantly. He glanced angrily at them as he drove, eyes searching. "If you want to do something helpful, look for the others," he ordered. "See if you can spot anyone in this muck!"

He slowed the vehicle, crawling ahead cautiously, and they all began searching the haze. Fixit rolled down their windows so they could hear better, maybe catch a hint of what was happening outside. Nothing. No weapons fire, no shouts, no sounds at all. Just the low rumble of the AV. He tried to think what else he could do.

"Over there," River said suddenly, pointing left.

Fixit saw two shadowy figures making their way through the haze at a rapid pace, not quite running, but almost. They were slight of build, kids like himself. He swung the AV toward them, reaching down to snap the safety off the stun charges. He wanted to be ready, just in case.

"That's Panther," Owl said quickly.

The two figures heard them coming and stopped to wait. It was indeed Panther and, with him, Catalya. They were breathing hard as the AV rolled up to them, and they came over to peer inside.

"What's happened to the others?" Panther demanded. "Where's Bird-Man and Bear and Cheney?"

Fixit shook his head. "We got lost. We don't know where they are. We were lucky to find you!"

"Well, you have to find them, too. Stump-head militia's looking for them, somewhere back there." He pointed in the direction from which they had come. His dark face glowered. "Don't know where, exactly. Can't see anything in this stuff."

Catalya looked worried, unusual for her. "I thought I saw something else back there. Something big."

The others stared at her. "Something big?" Panther repeated. "I didn't see nuthin'."

"If they're behind us, maybe they can catch up if we just wait," River suggested.

"Don't think waiting around is a good idea," Panther said at once. He glanced in at the control panel. "Hey, Fixit, you got a way of tracking movement on that thing? You know, finding anything else that's moving around out there?"

Fixit frowned. "I don't know. That wasn't something Logan Tom taught me to do. He didn't trust the loran. So I just use it to find directions. I haven't tried using it to track anyone."

"Well, try now."

Fixit bent to the loran, fiddling with the

switches and buttons, attempting to decipher what they would do. There were menus and choices of all sorts, and many of the words were unfamiliar to the boy.

"Wait," Owl said suddenly from the backseat. "Ask Sparrow if she's seen anything!"

"Sparrow?" Panther asked in confusion.

"She's on the roof," Owl explained, thinking even as she said so, *Why is she so quiet?* "Sparrow!" she called.

Panther and Catalya glanced quickly at each other, then at the AV roof and then back at Owl. "Forget it," Panther said. "Ain't no one there."

Everyone stared at him in silence.

SEVENTEEN

It was a particularly sharp jolt that threw Sparrow from the roof of the Lightning AV. The sudden lurch of the vehicle as it ripped across the mist-shrouded terrain was so severe that even though she was holding on with everything she had, it still wasn't enough. In truth, at the moment her hold on the roof railing failed, she was looking at something else and might have lost a fraction of the concentration she needed to stay aboard. It was easy to second-guess herself afterward, when it was over and done with and she was lying in the dirt, the wind knocked from her, the Parkhan Spray lost, and the AV rumbling off into the haze. She was so disoriented that for a moment she just lay there, badly shaken, staring up at the impenetrable fog and waiting for her head to clear.

When she regained her senses she scrambled to her feet, thinking she might still catch up with the AV. But her legs were wobbly, and a fresh dizziness overwhelmed her so completely that she dropped back to her knees and retched. By the time she had gotten past that, the Lightning had disappeared and she knew she couldn't have caught it if she'd tried. She wasn't even sure by then which way it had gone. The best she could hope for now was that someone would notice she was missing. But she didn't hold out much hope.

Still, her luck hadn't deserted her entirely. She spotted the Parkhan Spray lying not six feet from where she knelt, its barrel a dull gleam against the dusty soil. She climbed to her feet, walked over, and picked it up. Undamaged, she decided, testing the weapon's mechanisms to be certain they still worked, hearing all the familiar clicks and scrapes from the loading and firing chambers. At least she was armed.

She was also lost.

She looked around at the haze, a thick blanket that spread away in all directions. She had only a general idea of where her companions had gone, and they might change direction at any time. She could no longer hear the AV's engine, no longer hear anything but the silence. Even the sounds of pursuit from the militia had disappeared. Or at least become muffled. It felt as if she were completely alone in the world.

She experienced a moment of panic, but

fought back against it and forced it down. She was her mother's child, she reminded herself. Her warrior mother's child. Panic was not allowed.

She ran her fingers through her short-cropped blond hair, slung the Parkhan Spray over one shoulder, and started searching the ground for tire tracks. She found them almost at once. *There,* she thought, *no need to worry.* She ran through a litany of responses to possible threats that would keep her safe. If she saw fires, she would move away from them. If she heard noises, the same thing. Unless she decided they were from the Ghosts. If she saw movement, freeze. Stay clear of everything until it got light again, and then she could orient herself and find her way. She knew in general where she was going and what she was looking for. She had been lost before in places much more dangerous than this, and she had been much younger when it had happened. This was just another variation on a familiar experience. She would be all right.

But a small voice warned her to be careful. Just before she had fallen off the roof of the AV, she had spotted something strange. A huge, misshapen thing had appeared out of the fog, something vaguely human-shaped. It had shambled into view momentarily, walking upright like a man, but much larger, and then it was gone again. She had lost her concentration and in the next moment she had fallen. She still didn't know if what she had seen was real or not. But it had felt real, and that was enough to trouble her now.

She had no idea at this point where it was, and she did not think she wanted to find out.

A sudden boom sounded off to her right, too far away to be a threat or even to be identified. She glanced in the general direction of the sound, but didn't see anything. She kept walking, doing her best to keep a straight line, following the tracks of the AV, which were plain enough to see in the soft earth, even in the mist and darkness. She gained back a measure of lost confidence as she progressed, her uneasiness over her situation steadying, her determination hardening. It would take worse than this to throw her off stride, she told herself. A lot worse.

She found herself thinking back to the conversation she had overheard the night before between Hawk and Tessa. A baby. They were going to have a baby. It made her smile. To her way of thinking, it was the giving back of a life for the loss of Squirrel. She would have a new child, a new little boy or girl to care for. Tessa would let her help; she was sure of it. She would read to this baby in the same way she had read to Squirrel and Candle. She would look after it when Tessa was too busy. She would make sure it was kept safe.

"I wonder what they will name it," she muttered absently.

She stopped, conscious suddenly that she had broken the silence without meaning to. She stood quietly, looking out into the haze and listening. Nothing. *You are so stupid!* she chided herself angrily. She knew not to speak aloud. Her mother had taught her better than that. She must be more careful.

A hint of movement spied from the corner of her eye caught her attention and brought her about, the Parkhan Spray leveled. She already had the safety off, her fingers working smoothly and quickly, anticipating that she would need to fire without pausing. She stood peering into the murk, listening and watching. She held herself rigid. She stopped breathing. Nothing moved. No sounds broke the silence. She waited as long as she could, and then she waited some more.

Off in the distance, she heard cries, sharp and riddled with terror. Cries that turned to screams and begged for release. She wanted to block out the sounds, but couldn't. Their raw edges tore at her defenses and turned them to water.

Mama, she said to herself, a terrified whisper in her mind.

She began walking once more, keeping the Spray ready, the safety off, the clip lock released. She had gone cold inside, her blood turned to ice. She had heard such screams

291

before, and they always meant the same thing. Someone was dying. But it wouldn't be anyone she knew, she told herself. It wouldn't be people she cared about.

It wouldn't be the Ghosts.

She heard her mother's voice, singing to her.

Hush little baby, don't say a word.
Mama's gonna buy you a mockingbird.
If that mockingbird don't sing.
Mama's gonna buy you a diamond ring.

She repeated the words to herself, mouthing them silently. She didn't stop to think about her training or being cautious or anything else. All she could think about was putting one foot in front of the other. She just wanted to open as much distance as she could between herself and the sound of the screams. She just wanted to make the screams go away.

Then suddenly they did, and she was alone again with the silence. She kept walking, moving steadily, deliberately across the empty, gloomy terrain. The chill inside lessened. The fear subsided. She was okay, she told herself. She was all right. Her mother's ghost was with her, and her mother would never let anything happen to her.

All around her, the world was a vast cauldron of darkness and roiling haze, a thick impenetrable soup. But this would end, too. Come morning, the light would brighten, the mist would dissipate, and the world would return. She just needed to be patient. Just needed to stay strong.

Then sudden movement broke the slow swirl of the murk off to one side, and she felt her strength drain away.

Hawk stood staring off into the mist the other Ghosts had disappeared into, wondering what he should do. He wasn't even sure which way anyone had gone, save Panther and Cat, so he started walking after them. He could still hear sounds of pursuit behind and off to his right, but they were faint and scattered, and he thought that the militia might have given up, discouraged by the lack of visibility. Nevertheless, he kept alert for any indication that they were renewing their efforts, moving as quietly as he could. He caught glimpses of AV tracks in patches of soft earth and followed them into the gloom. Somewhere ahead, the Ghosts would be stopping to wait for him. He wasn't worried so much about those in the AV as he was about those afoot. Bear, in particular, because it was likely the big kid was still somewhere behind him.

A pair of huge lantern eyes appeared, gleaming wickedly, and his throat constricted in shock. Then the eyes blinked, and Cheney materialized, huge bristly head swinging from side to side, tongue lolling. The big dog ambled up to him as if everything were just as it should be, looking unconcerned and aloof.

Hawk exhaled. "Where's Panther?" he whispered to the dog, kneeling in front of him. "Where's Bear?"

He couldn't tell if Cheney understood him — probably he didn't — but it made him feel better to think he might. Cheney looked at him as he spoke, intelligence reflected in his bright smoky eyes, and to Hawk's surprise he started off at once, moving back the way the boy had come but angling off to the left. It was the wrong direction, but Hawk hesitated only a moment before following. He had learned to trust Cheney. He would not stop doing so now.

His faith was quickly rewarded. They came on Bear almost immediately, the boy lumbering out of the mist carrying the big Tyson Flechette, looking remarkably calm. He saw Hawk and waved, and Hawk hurried over to him.

"Guess I got lost," Bear admitted sheepishly.

"Nothing's changed," Hawk told him. "You're still lost. You just have company now. Have you seen anything of the others? Panther or Catalya?"

The other boy shook his head. "All I've seen is a whole bunch of nothing. Heard a lot of things, though. But not for a while. I think they gave up the chase, but I can't be sure. This stuff is awful." He gestured at the mist, shrugged. Then he glanced at Cheney. "Maybe Cheney knows where we should go."

Hawk nodded. "Maybe." He knelt in front of the dog for the second time. "Where's Panther, Cheney? Can you find him?"

Cheney turned away and started off. Hawk and Bear followed wordlessly, moving across the rough terrain, wading through the haze. Hawk found himself somewhat reassured now that he had found Bear, a reasonable start to his efforts to get everyone back together again. With luck, Cheney would lead them to Panther and Catalya, and from there they would eventually catch up to the Lightning and the others. If the militia actually had given up pursuit, they might manage to reach the camp with the children and Helen Rice without further trouble.

He smirked at his own optimism. Unwarranted, unjustified, and totally unrealistic. Life did not work out like that in his world.

They walked for a long time — or what seemed to him a long time — before Bear spoke.

"Do you think you can really do it?" the big kid said quietly.

Hawk didn't need to ask what he meant. He knew. "What do *you* think? Do you think I can?"

Bear shrugged. "I don't know. You can do a lot of things no one thought you could. I think you can probably do some more. We all think that. But this? I don't know."

Hawk nodded. Fair enough. He found himself tired all of a sudden, as if the long journey from the walls of Safeco compound to the gardens of the King of the Silver River to the banks of the Columbia and finally to here had sapped him of his energy. He really didn't know the answer to Bear's question. He didn't know if he could do it. How could he? He didn't know where he was going or how far it actually was to the haven promised by the old man, the place where the coming destruction of everything could not touch them. He wondered if it even existed. He hated himself for thinking this way, but he couldn't help it. He wondered how there could be anywhere safe in a world that was coming apart all around them. How could anyone survive such a thing?

Nevertheless, he knew he had to believe they could. He had to believe that his child would have a chance at life and not end up like so many others. His child and Tessa's — he had to believe. He had to believe for the Ghosts, too. And for the children in the camp, waiting for him to lead them to safety. And for the others who would be joining them along the way. And maybe for the world's future, as well. He had to believe.

But it was hard when there was so little reason to do so.

"When I was younger," Bear said suddenly, "still living on the farm with my family, no one believed in much of anything. That was the problem. They only believed in what they could see. They believed in the present, but not the future. They were just hanging on, living day to day."

"That's what most do," Hawk said.

"Not us. Not the Ghosts. We have something more. We have a future we believe in. That's what's different about us. We're not just hanging on. We're going toward something. Even if we can't see it and don't know exactly what it is. It doesn't matter. Your vision feels real to me."

He paused, head lowered. "So I guess maybe I do think you can do it." Hawk looked over at him, and he shrugged. "You're not like the rest of us. Even before I knew about this gypsy morph thing, I knew that. That's why we all follow you."

"Maybe my vision isn't going to work out," Hawk said.

Bear shook his head. "You don't believe that."

"No, I don't guess I do. I think it's real. I just wish I knew more about it than I do."

"Maybe you know all you need to know."

Hawk smiled despite himself. Such faith. "Maybe I do," he agreed.

Ahead several paces, Cheney suddenly gave a low growl, and the thick hair on the back of his neck bristled. He stopped moving, freezing in place. Hawk stopped, too, listening. He heard Bear release the safety on the Tyson Flechette. Then nothing. He waited a moment. Cheney growled again and started forward. Hawk and Bear reluctantly followed. Neither liked it that they could see so little. Neither liked the idea of encountering a danger they couldn't measure in advance. But there was nothing they could do about it; they had to keep moving and find out what was waiting. Better to find it than to let it find them.

They walked in silence, eyes and ears trained on the dark and mist, searching for some indication of what Cheney had sensed. The big dog walked point, head lowered and swinging side to side. He had stopped growling, but Hawk couldn't be sure if that meant the danger had passed or if Cheney was just masking his presence. The silence was unnerving, but he held himself steady and waited it out.

When the screams started, not long after that, they drew up short instantly. Cheney cast about, eyes narrowed and teeth bared. Bear's stoic face turned pale and then empty of expression. Hawk listened to the screams rise and fall and then disappear. He could not be sure where they had come from. He couldn't tell who had uttered them. The haze distorted both vision and sound and lent a feeling of disorientation to everything. Hawk tried to sort out what he was hearing and couldn't.

When the screams stopped, they stood where they were for a long moment, waiting for more. When nothing happened, Bear said, "Should we take a look?"

Hawk shook his head. "Not in that direction." He took a deep breath, reached down to touch the tire tracks of the AV in the loose soil, and said, "Cheney, track."

They set off a second time, decidedly uneasy now, less certain of themselves. Hawk, carrying only a prod, reached into his pocket and extracted a viper-prick. If something was going to happen, he thought, it was going to happen soon. He glanced skyward and wished for what must have been the hundredth time that the mist and clouds would clear. But he knew his wish was futile, that there would be no clearing before dawn and perhaps not even then. Finding their way would depend on luck and Cheney's instincts. Finding the others might depend on more than that.

The minutes dragged on. The silence and the night deepened. Cheney kept moving at a steady pace. Nothing appeared. Hawk had almost decided that nothing would when Cheney gave a deeper, more threatening growl.

Ahead, masked by the haze, something moved.

A bright pair of eyes appeared from out of nowhere as Sparrow swung the barrel of the Parkhan Spray about, her finger tightening on the trigger. The safety was already off, the clip locked and loaded, and the weapon ready for firing. She almost went the whole way, so startled by the movement that she was ready to shoot anything. She held up just in time, even though the glint of those big eyes caused everything inside to tighten from her throat to her knees. Something about those eyes, some small detail, made her pause, and a second later Cheney's grizzled head swung into view, clearing the curtain of the mist.

The big dog moved toward her, and a second later Hawk and Bear appeared right behind him.

"Hawk!" she called, lowering her weapon and rushing over to him. "Jeez, am I glad to see you!"

He stared at her in disbelief. "Sparrow, what are you doing out here? I thought you were in the AV. What happened to the others?"

She hugged him impulsively. "I don't know," she said into his shoulder, refusing to let go. Clinging to him as if he were a lifeline. Very unlike Sparrow.

As if sensing what he was thinking, she

stepped back and abruptly released him. "I was thrown off the roof of the Lightning after we got separated, and they didn't know I was gone. I've been wandering . . ." She gestured toward the wall of mist. "All over." She took a deep breath and exhaled. "Hawk, I think there's something out there, tracking me."

"There's something out there, all right," he agreed. "But I don't know that it's tracking you. I think it's just mist and night and some militia people running into each other. Look, we have to get moving, follow the tire tracks of the AV until we find them. It's not safe to stay here."

Bear ambled over. "You look spooked, Sparrow," he said quietly.

She glared at him. "You think? Didn't you hear those screams?"

He nodded slowly. "I heard."

"Didn't they spook you?"

He nodded uncertainly. "Sure."

"Then shut up." She turned back to Hawk, her eyes dark and angry. "Can we go now?"

He was about to say yes when the Klee stepped out of the fog.

EIGHTEEN

For a few endless moments, no one moved. Not even Cheney, who must have sensed the danger instinctively. None of them had ever seen anything like the Klee — had not even imagined such a thing could exist. They stared at it as people always stare at things so foreign and so unlikely, they seem a trick of the mind. They stared at it, as well, with the cold realization that they had come up against something much more terrifying than anything they had encountered before.

The Klee stared back at them, immobile against the screen of the dark and the mist.

No, not at them, Hawk corrected, catching the glint of its tiny eyes beneath the heavy brow. Not at *them*.

It was looking right at *him*.

Perhaps the others didn't know this, but he was certain of it. He didn't know why he had been singled out, but he knew he had. Perhaps something about him had caught its attention. Perhaps it had been looking for him all along. For reasons he couldn't fathom, he was the one it was focused on, the one it wanted.

"What is it?" he heard Sparrow whisper.

He had no idea. It was of monstrous size and appearance for something that walked upright and was vaguely human. It stood well over eight feet, its massive body coated with a mix of scales and tufts of long hair and clots of debris that seemed to have grown into its leathery hide. Huge, bowed legs supported its tree-trunk body; its overlong arms hung loose from its shoulders, ridged with muscle. Wicked green eyes peered out from beneath a brow formed of bone grown thick with scars, and there was an intent in those eyes that left Hawk chilled all the way through.

Cheney growled deep in his throat and took a cautious step forward, muzzle drawn back, teeth gleaming.

"No, Cheney," Hawk said at once.

He reached down and touched the dog's thick ruff to reinforce his command, and he felt Cheney shiver in response.

"What do we do?" Bear asked.

"Back away," Hawk ordered.

He took one step and then another. Sparrow and Bear went with him, their movements slow and cautious. Both leveled the barrels of their weapons and pointed them at the monster. Hawk took a third step, and his companions did the same.

Cheney had not moved.

"Cheney," Hawk whispered. "Back."

Still the dog did not move. He remained frozen in place, his eyes fixed on the monstrosity confronting them, head lowered, ruff bristling, muscles gathered. The mist drifted in curtains across the barren terrain, ceaselessly changing the look of things, conspiring with the darkness to trick and deceive, to cause the eyes to question.

"Back, Cheney," Hawk repeated, a sinking feeling blooming in the pit of his stomach.

Then the mist swept in out of the night, a suffocating blanket that enveloped everything, and the creature facing them was gone.

For a second, no one moved, staring into the hazy darkness, waiting for it to clear and for the monster to reappear. But when the dissipation finally took place, the monster was nowhere to be seen.

Cheney remained in his defensive crouch.

"Can we go now?" Sparrow asked in a small voice.

Hawk nodded without answering.

They set out anew, moving away from the place where the monster had appeared and then vanished, following the tracks of the AV, still trying to make their way toward their destination. They walked in a tight cluster, Bear and Sparrow with their weapons held ready, Hawk with his eyes on the darkness, and Cheney, who was again on the move in front of them, leading the way. Cheney didn't seem entirely satisfied with the decision not to stand their ground, a reluctant participant in their efforts to get away. He slouched guardedly some half a dozen paces ahead, muzzle lowered, head swinging, the hair ridging his spine bristling like spikes.

No one said anything.

The minutes passed, a slow progression that measured their efforts at putting as much distance as possible between themselves and the creature, efforts that did nothing to reassure them. There was something about the encounter that left Hawk wondering if what they had seen was even real. It felt as if what they had witnessed was the emergence of an apparition, a specter not subject to natural laws. Nothing about it felt right. Its abrupt appearance and disappearance suggested that their encounter had been with a ghost come out of the ether rather than a creature of flesh and blood.

And yet he could not shake the feeling that there was substance to it, that the weight of it, should it be felt, would be crushing.

Like the weight of its gaze as it stared at him, he thought. Immense, implacable, and overpowering.

More time passed, and they kept moving, passing in and out of chambers formed of mist and darkness. Distance lost meaning, the terrain unchanging beneath their feet, a swampy combination of sucking mud, sand, and withered scrub. The horizon was a low, jagged line fading into the night's gray emptiness. There was no sound and no movement. They might have been alone in the world, the last of its creatures.

"Maybe we lost it," Sparrow ventured finally, a hopeful whisper in the deep silence.

"I don't know," Bear whispered back. He glanced about, looking decidedly uneasy. "It doesn't feel that way to me."

"You're just spooked," Sparrow continued. She gave him a quick grin and glanced at Hawk. "What do you think?"

The boy shook his head. "I don't like it that we can't see anything. I wish it was daylight."

Bear shook his head. "I wish we hadn't left the city. These mountains don't feel right. All this open space feels dangerous. It reminds me of the farm when I was a kid."

"What do you mean?"

Bear shrugged. "No protection from anything. I like walls with doors, and doors that lock." He paused. "That thing back there. We used to see things like that now and then, roaming the fields. Mutants, changed by the chemicals and radiation from the bombs. Lizards and Croaks and such, but other things, too. Some of them were big and mean. Some of them didn't even seem to have a reason for being. You had to watch out when you were out in the open. You had to be real careful all the time. We learned that the hard way. My little brother . . ." He trailed off and shook his head. "We lost him because of one of those things. We didn't go out much at night after that."

No one spoke for a moment, and then Sparrow said, "In the mountains where I lived with my mother, we never saw anything like you described. Or like that thing back there." She shivered. "Maybe there were monsters, but they didn't come around. The only monsters we saw were members of the militias that were hunting us. That was bad enough."

"Everything's hunting us," Bear said quietly.

True enough, Hawk thought. Street kids were at the bottom of the food chain. All kids, for that matter. He tightened his grip on the prod and peered ahead into the darkness where the mist was beginning to thicken again. Bear was right. It was harder to defend yourself out in the open, away from the protection of walls and doors, from the safety of barricades that would keep the bad things out. He remembered how safe it had felt inside their home in Pioneer Square, the rest of the world locked out by Fixit's inventions and the sense of security that being part of a family created. He wondered if they would find that again where they were going, if the sense of always being hunted would finally end, if the shelter that was promised really would be waiting when they arrived.

He shook his head. He couldn't imagine it, but he wanted badly to believe that it could happen — an escape from the madness of the world, a retreat from their fear that everything could end at a moment's notice. It didn't seem too much to ask, he thought. Not if the vision he had been shown so often was true.

The fog was growing heavier about them, an ebb and flow of shadow movements that could have been anything. Their vision was down to less than a dozen feet and still diminishing. Hawk kept his eyes on Cheney, a few steps ahead of them, watchful for any signs of danger. The big dog kept moving at a steady pace, head swinging, muzzle lowered. Maybe he knew where he was going. At this point, none of the rest of them did. It was impossible even to determine direction.

"Morning can't be far away," he said quietly. "It can't be long now."

"Hope so," Bear mumbled.

The ground dropped away into a shallow ravine, and the mist that had collected there stole the last of their vision. They moved through it blindly, fearfully, anxious to get past. "Damn," Bear muttered.

When they climbed out again on the far bank, they were back on level ground. But the mist was even thicker here.

Bear grunted. "Hope this isn't going to continue all the way to . . ."

He gasped sharply. The Klee had materialized right in front of him. He had just enough time to bring up the barrel of the Tyson Flechette before a backhand blow sent him tumbling head-over-heels into the ravine and out of sight. Hawk and Sparrow were already falling back, scrambling away like frightened cats, when Cheney burst out of the darkness and flung himself on the Klee. His body weight and the ferocity of his attack staggered the monster but did not knock it over. The Klee straightened as Cheney tore at one arm, and then shook free of the big dog. When Cheney came at it again, it was waiting. Cheney was airborne when the Klee braced itself, stopped the dog's momentum with one arm, and delivered a devastating blow to the shaggy head with the other. Cheney went down and did not move.

Sparrow screamed in horror and fury, leveled the Parkhan Spray, and pulled the trigger.

Nothing happened. The weapon was jammed.

The Klee brushed her aside as if she were not even there and came for Hawk.

He is just a boy and not much of one at that. Eleven or twelve years old, scrawny and awkward. Uncomfortable in his own skin and never

309

certain that he is where he should be, he is stumbling toward his teenage years with uncertain steps. He spends most of his time with his parents, who are still alive, their presence a constant reassurance in a world where little else is. He is living on the Oregon coast somewhere remote and wild, away from other families, but away, as well, from the things that hunt those families. He knows about these predatory things because his parents have told him about them. Incessantly. He must be cautious. He must think before doing anything. He must never go out alone unless he is in sight of his house. He must carry a weapon everywhere he goes. He hates that part; weapons frighten him. Yet he must remember that danger is never very far away.

"Even here," his mother tells him, her voice firm and insistent, "you are not safe. There are terrible things hunting you, and you must keep watch for them."

He does not know what these terrible things are, and his parents are vague when he asks what they look like. They look like lots of things, they tell him. They take many forms. They can be anything and everything. You must not trust your eyes.

He doesn't know what that means. If he doesn't trust his eyes, what is he supposed to trust? How is he supposed to tell what these monsters look like if no one can describe them? How is he supposed to protect himself from something so unknowable?

He is very young when his parents first warn him and the dreams begin. The dreams do not come every night, but they come often. Far too often. They are always the same. He is in his house or just outside. He is alone. He is doing something that pleases him — he can never remember what — when he hears an unexpected noise. He turns toward the source, but sees nothing. The noise comes again, from another direction this time. He looks around guardedly, remembering his parents' warning to be careful. It has been daylight until now, but suddenly it begins to get dark. He calls for his parents, but they do not come. He is no longer in his home or even near it. When he tries to find it, he cannot. When he tries to make his way to safety, he cannot. He cannot move. His lack of confidence in himself paralyzes his muscles. Nothing he does seems to help.

And nothing ever changes what happens next.

As he struggles to find shelter, to find help of any sort, he becomes aware of a hidden presence. He searches for it frantically, trying to protect himself, but he can never quite manage to discover where it is hiding. Even when he is standing out in the open, he can feel it right next to him, but he can never see it. Finally, he breaks free of his immobility. He starts to run — through the rooms of his house, suddenly numerous and enormous, or through trees of a forest if he is outside — seeking escape from the thing he senses shadowing him. He runs until he is exhausted, until he has run as far as he can. But the presence is still there, dark and malevolent and implacable in its efforts to hunt him down. He knows what it is. It is the thing his parents have warned him about. It is the thing he has been told to avoid. But he has failed in his efforts to heed and obey, and now it has found him.

He tries closing his eyes against what he knows is coming, but somehow he cannot manage to do even that. He cannot help himself — he must look. He must see what it is that has hunted him for so long. He must see what it is that his parents have warned him about. He must know the identity of his hunter.

He can feel it looming over him. He can feel it reaching for him.

He opens his eyes and looks around wildly, but there is nothing there. He is more terrified than ever. Sometimes, he cries. Sometimes, he screams. Nothing helps. There is never anything there.

And then his hunter falls on him like a massive black weight, still invisible, still unknown, and he is crushed.

As the Klee lumbered toward him, Hawk's childhood nightmares returned in a flood of dark images. Because he no longer knew how much of his childhood was real and how much the creation of the King of the Silver River, he could not be certain if his memories were real. But they felt real, which was enough to give them the substance of reality. Enough, too, to remind him of a truth he had always known, a truth so terrible and so inexorable that he had lived in dread of it his entire life.

If the dreams crossed over from sleeping into waking, his life was over.

He had only an instant to remember all this, come face-to-face with the something he had thought he had left behind — only a moment to come to terms with what it meant. He was backing away, trying to think of what to do, how to escape. The creature was almost on top of him, moving more quickly than should have been possible given its size.

Its massive arms reached for him.

Hawk reacted instinctively. He thrust his prod at it in a futile effort to slow its advance. He jammed the weapon into its spongy chest, amid hair, scales, and debris, and gave it a full charge. But the creature never even flinched. It simply snatched the prod from his hands and tossed it aside.

Hawk had nothing left with which to defend himself save one of the viper-pricks. He had no faith in a tiny needle, no matter how venomous. He knew instinctively that the creature's mottled, debris-coated body would resist such a weapon, might even prevent it

313

from penetrating.

He backed away some more. The creature was still coming, but its advance was unhurried. Its gimlet eyes were fixed on Hawk, studying him, and something reflected in those eyes revealed what it was thinking. That the boy was trapped. That he could not escape. That it could do whatever it wanted with him.

It was toying with him. It was enjoying this.

His nightmares had found him in the form of this monster, and the monster was taking its time.

Hawk backed up another step and bumped into something. He reached back without taking his eyes off the monster and touched the rough surface of a narrow tree trunk, its barked surface dry and peeling. A cluster of scrawny trees blocked his way. He backed into them, guiding himself between the tangled trunks using his hands, thinking that maybe he could hide if there were enough of them, eyes locked on the monster, telling himself, *I can't let it touch me!*

Then a strange thing happened. The monster suddenly stopped where it was, a puzzled look in its mean little eyes. Hawk froze, not daring to move. Even though it was staring right at him, it didn't seem to be seeing him. It looked left and right, searching. Something was confusing it. It was almost as if Hawk had disappeared.

An instant later the Tyson Flechette boomed out, the muzzle flashes bright against the darkness — once, twice — the charges slamming into the monster with enough force to stagger it. Bear had climbed from the ravine and was coming to Hawk's rescue, shouting and screaming all at once, making more noise than Hawk had ever heard him make in the entire time he had known him. Bear fired the flechette a third time, but an instant later the monster was gone, vanished back into the mist as if it had never existed.

Hawk stayed where he was, holding his breath. He could feel his hands shaking as he clutched the trunks of the slender trees.

"Hawk!" Bear called out to him. "Where are you?"

Sparrow had reappeared, as well, limping badly. Cheney was only steps behind, fur matted and dust-covered, his big head streaked with blood.

"Hawk!" Bear called again.

"Hawk, where are you?" Sparrow echoed.

Hawk was standing right in front of them, not twenty feet away. The mist was thick, but not so thick that he shouldn't have been visible to his friends. Yet neither of them could see him. He was so astonished that for a moment he just stayed where he was and watched them cast about for him, searching the haze and the darkness.

He tried to wrap his mind around it. *They*

can't see me!

Then Cheney pushed past them and came right up to him, shoving at his legs with his dark muzzle. Hawk took his hands away from the trees and reached down to ruffle the big dog's head.

"There he is," Bear said at once, as if Hawk had just reappeared.

"Hawk, are you all right?" Sparrow cried.

He stepped out from between the trees as they rushed up to him, their clothes filthy and torn, their faces scratched. Sparrow looked furious, Bear simply relieved. He hugged both of them in turn, still caught up in what had happened, unsure of which was the more astonishing — the appearance of the monster from his childhood dreams or his unexplained invisibility.

He looked around quickly, half fearing what he would find. "Let's get moving," he urged.

They began walking again, wrapped anew in the mist and the silence and their fears, what weapons they could salvage recovered, their nerves on edge. Even the dependable Cheney seemed edgy. But within only minutes they heard the rumble of tires and the slosh of standing water disturbed, and the Lightning S-150 hove into view like a big metal beetle. The other Ghosts had heard the sound of Bear's flechette and had come to their rescue. Hawk exhaled sharply at the prospect of his family reunited, of everyone safe and together again. But at the same time, he thought anew of the monster that was still out there, waiting for another chance at them.

They piled into and on top of the Lightning, finding places where they could because no one was going to walk after what had just happened, and they drove on through the remainder of the night. They were out of the fog after less than an hour and within another two hours after that, out of the darkness, as well. By midday of the following day, they had found the camp with its children and caregivers and been welcomed back by Helen Rice and Angel Perez, who had arrived the day before, and were able to put the events of the previous night behind them.

All except Hawk, who could not stop thinking about the monster. He had looked into its eyes, and those eyes had told him everything. That their owner was heartless and implacable. That killing was its life's purpose. That he was powerless against it.

That at some point soon it would come for him again.

NINETEEN

The skrails flew south through the starlit night for several hours, winging their way along the eastern slopes of the Cintra Mountains with Kirisin Belloruus gripped firmly in their talons. Blood ran down his back from puncture wounds to his shoulders, and his body was racked with the pain. It did no good to try to struggle, because getting free of the skrails would mean falling to his death. It was bad enough that any sort of movement exacerbated his injuries, but the cold added measurably to his discomfort — enough so that his hands and feet quickly grew numb and there was nothing he could do about it. Stoically enduring, he hung limp and silent, listening to the steady beat of the great leathery wings and the occasional squawk from his captors that passed for communication.

At least he had managed to get rid of the Loden, he told himself. Whatever happened to him — and he had a pretty good idea what that would be — the Elfstone was safe.

It was a small victory given his present situation, but he took what comfort he could from it. Half a loaf was better than none at all. Even if the Loden had fallen to the ground undetected, if Praxia, running after him as he was carried away, had failed to glimpse it falling, it would still be safe from the demons. Someone would find it eventually. The Elves would be safe inside it until then, protected from whatever happened to the rest of their world and its inhabitants.

But his doubts persisted. He couldn't help wondering if his reasoning was skewed. How could he know if the Loden would withstand the destruction that was coming? How could he know how long the Elves could survive inside the Loden before needing to be released? How could he know that the Elfstone would ever be found?

He closed his eyes. The many boiled down to one: How could he be sure of anything?

Exhaustion overcame discomfort and pain, and the steady beating of skrail wings and the rush of the wind lulled him to sleep. The events of the previous day — the flight from the Cintra and now the battle with his captors — had drained him of his strength. He dozed on and off as they flew, always jerking awake in what seemed only moments. But finally he drifted away in a long, sweeping glide, and time stopped altogether.

The jarring impact of a hard surface brought him awake again. It was still night. He lay on a barren patch of earth, freed of his captors, who winged about him in watchful sweeps, cautious against any attempt at escape. He made no effort to challenge them, his body numb clear through, his senses still sleep-fogged and confused. He lay where he was, waiting for something to make sense, drawing in his arms and legs, hugging himself against the intrusions of the waking world.

"Get up, boy!" a voice snarled, and a heavy boot kicked him in the ribs.

He did not move immediately, the numbness from the cold making him immune to the pain of the blow. He rolled from his back onto his side and then onto his elbows and knees, trying to think what to do.

An impatient growl followed the kick, and strong arms hoisted Kirisin to his feet and a pair of skrails held him upright while the speaker began to search him, staying behind him and out of sight, fingers rummaging through his pockets and under his clothing, missing nothing in their efforts to unmask what might be hidden. Finding nothing, the speaker struck him a sharp blow to the head and ordered the skrails to drop him. He collapsed a second time, barely managing to cushion his fall, the feeling just beginning to come back into his limbs.

"Bind him," the speaker ordered, walking away.

Rolling onto his side, Kirisin caught just a glimpse of the other, a thin, gnarled figure, limbs and body all twisted, head hunched deep into shoulders so bony they were defined mostly by the blades that jutted against the fabric of an old tunic like ax heads.

Then the skrails were on him once more, bearing him to the ground, forcing his arms behind his back. He tried to create some slack in the cords that were wrapped about him, but the skrails just hissed and yanked his bonds tighter. They secured his ankles, as well, crossing them and wrapping them in another set of cords, leaving him thoroughly trussed. Their fingers were long and thin but very strong. Struggling was pointless.

When they were finished, they left him lying on the ground by himself in the dark, unable to do much more than wriggle, unable to stand or even to sit up. The minutes crawled past and no one came to check on him. He could sense the skrails watching him from the darkness. Maybe they were afraid of what he could do if they got too close. The idea came and went in the blink of an eye. If they had caught and bound him when he was still free, they weren't likely to be afraid of him now. It was more reasonable to assume that their minder was keeping them away.

He lay quietly for a time, miserable and

frightened. His wounds throbbed, but the bleeding had stopped. He tried to ignore the pain, but it was an insistent presence. He wished he could have a look at the punctures to see how bad they were. He wished he could have something to eat and drink. He wished he had dropped to the ground when Praxia shouted at him instead of trying to reach the AV. He wished he were smarter and stronger and quicker and a whole lot of other things that might have allowed him to escape.

In the end, he just wished he weren't so alone — that Simralin would come for him.

His wishes surfaced like ghosts and fled into the night.

He dozed for a time, lying on his side in the dark, hearing the skrails moving about nearby with a soft skittering and muted squawks. He woke often from his uneasy rest, and each time the pain from his wounds and his bindings felt worse than the time before. He tried to think of a way to escape, but with his hands and feet so securely bound there was little hope.

He had just fallen asleep when talons grasped his shoulders roughly and pulled him to his feet. A pair of skrails stood one on either side, and a third knelt to release his ankles. They shoved him ahead, and he tried to walk, but they had to hold him up for a dozen paces before the feeling returned to his feet. He stumbled ahead after that with the skrails guiding him, their leathery wings flapping softly as they walked, their reptilian faces bent close to his own. He could smell the swamp on them, fetid and raw, and he could feel the coldness of their talons where they gripped him.

Ahead, a fire was visible through gaps in a cluster of skeletal trees that were silhouetted against its glow like the bones of the dead. Shadowy forms moved through the firelight, winged and hunched. More skrails. Kirisin wondered what was happening. His stomach knotted and his throat tightened.

The minder was waiting, all bent and bony, looking like a smaller version of the trees. At the boy's appearance, he wheeled back from where he knelt before the fire, and then rose and walked over to greet him. Without a word, he struck Kirisin across the face with one callused hand, the blow sharp and hard and painful. Kirisin cried out and tried to pull away. The minder struck him again, harder.

"Now, then, boy," he hissed, "where is the Elfstone?"

Kirisin shook his head, tears running down his face. "I don't have it."

The minder struck him again. "Tell me something I don't know, you little fool! Where is it?"

Kirisin gritted his teeth in rage. "The Knight of the Word has it."

The gnarled creature hissed at him like a snake and struck him again. "You lie! Where is it?"

Kirisin thrashed in the grip of the skrails and almost succeeded in tearing free. He spat at the minder. "I told you!"

He met the other's gaze and held it, taking in the weathered face that was all collapsed hollows and jutting bones beneath wrinkled skin. The strange green eyes were lidded and bright, the nose flatted to little more than nostrils, and the mouth a sucking hole devoid of teeth. His stench was almost unbearable, but the boy refused to flinch from it.

"Well, maybe so, maybe not." The mouth twisted. "We'll ask another for advice on this."

He motioned, and the skrails holding Kirisin marched him to the edge of the fire and forced him to his knees. For a single terrifying instant, the boy thought they were going to throw him in. But then the minder stepped to the very edge of the fire and tossed something else into the flames. The fire exploded in a shower of sparks and changed to a wicked green color that spread to everything around it — the minder, the skrails, the boy, and the closest of the trees. Even the night itself seemed changed.

Then the minder began to gesture, chanting something in a language Kirisin had never heard. The skrails fell back, even the ones that had been holding his arms, and their squawking took on a new urgency. Kirisin was suddenly free, but he stayed where he was on his knees. He was surrounded by his captors, weakened to the point of collapse, wounded, and somewhere in the middle of country with which he was only marginally familiar. He might think of trying to flee, but such an attempt at this point seemed completely unrealistic.

He felt a presence at his shoulder. One of the skrails had moved closer again, perhaps sensing what he was thinking. His chance to escape, however slim, was gone.

His eyes shifted back to the fire. Something very strange was happening within its heart. A figure was taking shape, growing in size and rising out of the flames. At first it appeared to be a spirit formed of smoke and fire, peppered with ash and steaming from the heat. But then it began to take on definition, assuming the shape and visage of an old man cloaked in gray robes. Eyes as cold and implacable as a snake's peered out of the haze of smoke and flames, shifting from the minder to Kirisin and back again.

This is the one, the boy thought with a shiver that ran from his neck down to the base of his spine. *This is the demon that leads all the others, the one that hunts the Elves and the Loden.*

The demon in the flames hissed softly.

–Is this the boy–

"Yes, Master," the minder answered, inclining his head slightly in deference.

–Did you take the Elfstone from him–

The minder shuddered. "He didn't have it on him."

–Has he told you what he did with it–

"No, Master."

A long silence left the air stark and empty of life. The specter never moved as it regarded the minder carefully.

–Has he told you of the fate of our spies within the Elven city–

The minder shook his head.

–Of Delloreen and her hunt for the Knight of the Word–

The minder shook his head again, but less certainly this time.

–Of anything at all, you fool–

"Master, I tried to —"

The other cut him off with a wave of his arm. A fresh column of steam rose from his ethereal form, a white cloud against the darkness.

–Tried, did you? How very fortunate for me that you didn't try too hard. You do try too hard sometimes, Calyx! And it causes you to do too much of what you want so much to do. Doesn't it–

"Yes, Master," the minder answered meekly.

The wintry gaze shifted to Kirisin and settled on him like a great weight. There was the promise of suffering and death in that gaze, of agonizing hours of traveling from the first to the second, hours that would steal his sanity and leave him a mindless husk. The boy wanted badly to look away, but the other's eyes held him in shackles he could not break.

One cloaked arm gestured slightly, beckoning him.

–Rise–

Though Kirisin had no intention of doing so, though he wasn't even sure his legs would let him, he jerked to his feet obediently, a puppet dangling from invisible strings, trembling in the specter's presence.

–What of Culph, boy–

"Dead," Kirisin answered at once, unable to help himself.

–The Tracker, Tragen–

"Dead."

–Delloreen, too–

Kirisin hesitated.

–The one who tracked the female Knight of the Word–

"Dead," Kirisin replied.

There was a long silence as the old man studied him, a shadowy image that had something of the substance and presence of flesh and blood. Power radiated from the specter, power born of experience gained, skill acquired, battles survived, and enemies overcome. Power born of years of staying alive while others died.

The gaze shifted back to the minder. A smile twisted the old man's mouth, cold and frightening.

–That wasn't so hard, was it, Calyx? Simple answers to simple questions. An understanding reached by a meeting of eyes and minds. You should try it–

He turned back again to Kirisin, the smile still in place.

–You've done well, boy. Another few moments of your time and you may sit down again. You are the boy who retrieved the Elfstone that they call the Loden–

Kirisin fought back the urge to scream his frustration. "Yes."

–What have you done with it–

"I dropped it when the skrails took me."

Another long silence, and then all at once a terrible vise closed about the boy, a slow crushing force that threatened to break his bones and explode his flesh. He tried to scream out his pain and found he couldn't. He could only stand where he was; he could only endure.

Then the vise was released, and he crumpled to the ground in a quaking heap, gasping for air, fighting for consciousness.

The old man's voice was a whisper in the ensuing silence.

–You dropped it–

The question hung like a blade above Kirisin's neck. A wrong answer and it would fall and his head would be severed from his body. But he had answered truthfully, and giving another answer now would do him no good.

"I dropped it," he repeated, his voice dry and hoarse.

He waited for the end, but the old man turned away from him and looked once more at the minder.

–Keep him safe until I reach you. Do not question him further. Do not harm him in any way. But watch him carefully. I will speak with him again when I arrive–

The old man's image hung within the flames a moment longer, and then in a sharp burst of sparks it was gone. The fire fizzled and went out.

In the aftermath of its disappearance, Kirisin huddled by the cooling ashes and fought to stay calm.

They left him where he was, and he slept for a time, exhausted from his ordeal, happy to find any escape from his waking nightmare. But his nightmare followed him, a series of sharp images and frightening sequences that had him running and being caught and hiding and being found, always by things that were intent on his destruction.

He awoke in a sweat, curled into a ball on the hard earth, his hands and wrists aching and stiff from their binding. The heat from the leavings of the fire that had summoned the old man washed over him in suffocating waves. Using what strength he could muster, he rolled over so that he was facing out into the cooling darkness. He lay without moving for a time, letting his eyes adjust to the night, taking deep breaths of air to clear his lungs and mind. He was still traumatized by what the demon had done to him, how it had crushed him mercilessly with little more than a thought. He had been so helpless, unable to protect himself, a plaything for his enemy.

He closed his eyes as rage and shame washed through him. He would do anything to prevent a recurrence of such abject subjugation.

When his eyes reopened, he was thinking of only one thing. If he stayed where he was, that old man — that demon — would arrive and do much worse things to him in person than it had done through its avatar if it meant finding out exactly what he had done with the Loden. And Kirisin would tell because he wouldn't be able to help himself.

He knew he had to escape before that happened.

He tested his bonds. To his surprise, the skrails hadn't retied his ankles in the aftermath of the demon's appearance. Cautiously, he tried moving his legs. The feeling was back; he thought he could stand if he needed to, and if he could stand he could walk.

Maybe he could run.

He took a deep, steadying breath. If he could slip away now, if he could disappear before they realized he was gone, he might be able to elude them. He might have a chance after all.

A fresh wave of determination hardened into resolve. He tested the bonds that secured his wrists. They were still intact, but not quite so tight as before. Heat and sweat had dampened and stretched the leather. He twisted his wrists experimentally. He pulled hard against the tough cords in an effort to gain a little more space. The leather cut deep into his wrists, but gave slightly. He worked his hands back and forth, gritting his teeth with the effort.

Then he stopped and went still, peering out into the darkness, searching for movement, listening to the night. Had he heard something? He couldn't see anything of the skrails or their minder. But wouldn't someone be keeping watch over him? Didn't someone have to be on guard to prevent his escape?

It took him a long time, but eventually he found what he was looking for: a bulky shape settled back within the shadows, hunched over and unmoving. Kirisin studied the skrail carefully, waiting for it to do something. But it seemed chiseled from stone; it simply sat there, a motionless lump.

Then he heard it snore, a low, guttural, but

unmistakable sound. He waited, and it snored again.

He renewed his efforts to get free, twisting and turning his wrists, working the bonds to loosen them. The leather stretched a little more, and he redoubled his efforts, slowly working the leather bindings down over his wrists to his hands.

And then all at once the cords dropped away, and he was free.

He stayed where he was for a long time after that, resting himself, listening to the snoring of the guard, to the night, to the silence. He waited as he gathered his strength and his courage. He would have to move quickly and quietly to get clear of the camp and its inhabitants. He would have only one chance, and he would have to make the most of it. He thought again of the old man, and the dryness in his mouth intensified.

A careful scanning of the stars told him which direction was north. He would head back toward Logan Tom and the others, retracing his steps, following the path they were certain to take to reach Redonnelin Deep and Angel Perez. He would use his skill as an Elf to hide his passage, to remain hidden while he traveled, to prevent an almost certain pursuit from finding him. He could do this, he told himself. He was free, and he could do this.

Then, in a single smooth motion, he rolled

to his feet, crouching momentarily as he watched the dark shape of the skrail guard, and began creeping across the clearing, away from the ashes of the dead fire. He went quickly and silently, hardly daring to breathe, looking all around him as he went for any sign of other skrails, for any indication of danger. His wounds from the skrail talons ached, and his wrists were cut and bloodied from the cords, but he barely paid attention to them, his concentration centered on his escape.

He pictured the look in the eyes of the old man when he arrived and discovered Kirisin was gone. He imagined his rage. The image gave him immense satisfaction. He was sorry he wouldn't be there to witness it.

When he was clear of the camp, screened now by the skeletal trees that grew along its borders, he straightened and began walking toward the hills beyond. He was smiling with satisfaction and relief, the tension draining away, as he walked from the trees and into the shelter of a deep ravine. He had gone a dozen steps down its narrow passageway when a winged shadow fell across his path.

"Leaving us so soon, boy?" a familiar voice asked quietly.

Kirisin froze, his heart in his throat. He could not make himself look up at the speaker, knowing what he would find.

"Did you think escape would be so easy?"

the minder teased.

A second winged shadow appeared beside the first, and from the opposite side a third skrail dropped down into the ravine in front of him, effectively blocking any chance of flight. Kirisin looked up into the wizened countenance of the minder, unable to help himself.

"You wouldn't want to miss your meeting with Findo Gask, would you?" The other's voice was edged with expectation. "You won't believe how much pain he can cause you. It will be interesting to discover how much of it you can withstand."

Kirisin felt himself sag in defeat. There hadn't ever been any real chance of escape. "My sister will save me," he said softly. "Simralin will come for me."

"No one will come for you; no one will save you." The minder brushed the suggestion aside. "You are all alone in this, boy."

The skrails beat their wings softly, and the familiar squawking ensued, a sound Kirisin knew with terrible certainty could only be laughter.

TWENTY

In the aftermath of the battle with the skrails, Logan Tom wasn't sure what had become of Kirisin. At first he thought the boy had fled into the darkness to seek sanctuary from the attack, and that was why Praxia was chasing after him. He hadn't seen the skrails snatch the boy, his attention on the larger swarm circling overhead and the struggle taking place around the AV. But when Praxia came racing back clutching the small pouch with the Loden Elfstone, shouting at him that Kirisin was gone, he realized the truth of things.

Lost another one, he thought in frustration and dismay.

Praxia thrust the pouch at him like a weapon. "We can't use this without Kirisin!" she snapped. "All of our people are trapped inside unless he frees them!"

For a moment he just stood there, seething. First it was the gypsy morph and now the Elven boy. The Lady had given him responsibility for both, and he had failed them equally. It was a bitter realization, especially since he had thought that after so many years of ceaseless, debilitating effort at stemming the subversion of children in the demon camps, he had finally been given a charge for which there was an end.

Protect the gypsy morph — the street kid Hawk — long enough to permit him to lead an exodus to a safehold that would provide them all with shelter against the destruction that was coming.

Protect Kirisin Belloruus, the Chosen of the Ellcrys, into whose hands had been placed the fate of an entire race of people.

Straightforward charges. He should have been able to fulfill them. Yet he had lost Hawk to the madness of the inhabitants of a compound and now he had lost Kirisin to a flock of demon-summoned skrails. While he had been lucky enough to have Hawk returned by an intervening magic, he could not rely on that happening with Kirisin.

More to the point, he had endured enough of personal failure.

"What are we going to do?" Praxia demanded. "Those things flew off with him! There's no trail! We can't possibly find him now!"

"Yes, we can," he answered softly.

He told her to look after her companions, to bind their wounds and see to their needs.

Two were dead, and the other two injured. She hesitated a moment, and then turned away to do as he had asked, muttering something about how he better be telling the truth.

"Watch my back!" he snapped at her.

Without bothering to see if she had heard him, he walked over to the Ventra and went back to work on the solar connectors. The AV was supposed to be virtually indestructible, yet something as small and unexpected as this shut it down. He shook his head. You couldn't depend on machines to hold up, not anymore.

He had almost repaired the damage when the attack began, had been close enough to finishing that if he had been given just another half an hour, they would have escaped everything that had happened. He experienced a fresh wave of frustration thinking of this, but brushed it aside quickly so as not to disturb his concentration. Self-recrimination would not help. Anger would not help. Not yet. He would save all that for when he caught up to the skrails.

"Are you watching my back?" he called out again to Praxia.

She glanced at him from where she knelt by her injured companions, nodding her answer and saying nothing.

He should never have left Kirisin out in the open like that, he told himself. He should have kept him inside the Ventra where it would have been much more difficult for the skrails to get at him. He should have just locked the boy away. But would Kirisin have stood for it? He saw himself as a man, not a boy, and he would not have appreciated being treated as somehow less than the others. Besides, hindsight was twenty–twenty and all that. It was easy to second-guess himself now.

When he was finished with the repairs to the AV, he slipped behind the wheel, triggered the power key, and listened to the soft purr of the engine as it slowly revved up. Everything was working again. He gave it another minute, making sure, and then stepped back out and walked over to the Elves.

"When you're able, start walking. Stay on this road. Follow it north to the river and wait for me there. Stay out of sight. If I don't show by tomorrow, go in search of the camp where the children and their protectors are waiting. Find the boy Hawk. Tell him what has happened."

"Ruslan and Que'rue can go," Praxia replied. "I'm going with you."

He shook his head. "No, you're not. You're going to do what I told you to do."

Her face hardened. "I don't answer to you, no matter who or what you think you are."

He nodded. "No, you don't. But you do answer to Kirisin. He gave you the Loden Elfstone in trust. He gave it to you to hold and keep safe until his return. You can't give up that trust. And you can't come with me if you're holding the Elfstone."

She stared at him without saying anything for a moment. "You have to find him," she said finally. "You have to bring him back or everything we've done is for nothing."

He almost laughed. As if he needed reminding. "Stay on the road," he repeated. "I'll find him and then I'll find you."

He climbed into the Ventra, released the locking mechanisms on the wheels, and without looking back drove away into the night.

He was a dozen miles or so down the road, retracing the route they had taken after escaping the Cintra, before he allowed himself a moment to reflect on the hopelessness of what he was undertaking. He had perhaps another six hours of darkness before dawn broke, so he had some time to catch up to the skrails — which, while efficient and quick, were not built for endurance. Having flown all day to fight a difficult battle, they would have to land and rest before making the journey back to the demon that had dispatched them. In a best-case scenario, they would wait for the demon and its army to catch up to them.

That gave him a small window of time to track them down. But that was all he had going for him. He had little hope of finding much of anything hidden within the screen of gloom that cloaked the surrounding countryside. Unless the skrails were foolish enough to reveal their presence, he had no idea how he was going to find them. They would not be roosting on the roadway where he might stumble on them; they would be off in the heavy brush or up in the rocks in a place where they could protect themselves. They probably did not expect anyone to try to give chase, since they had left no trail to follow, but they were not stupid enough to chance discovery by being careless.

So what was he to do?

As if in response, a shadow swept down across the front windshield of the Ventra before soaring off again into the darkness. *Trim!* He hadn't seen the owl since he reached the Cintra. In truth, he had dismissed the bird from his mind completely.

The owl glided back across the road in front of him, as if marking his progress, and then disappeared into the darkness ahead. Trim was not there by accident or just to keep Logan company. He was taking him to Kirisin once more. He was showing him the way to where the skrails were holding the boy. If he could keep the bird in sight and if he were quick enough, he might have a chance at getting Kirisin back after all.

He accelerated the AV, one eye on the road

and one eye on the owl, a jolt of adrenaline rushing through him.

With Trim leading the way, he tracked onward through the night, back down the roadway south, the big Ventra throbbing and growling all around him. He did not stop to rest; he did not stop to consider where he was. He pushed ahead with single-mindedness, intent on getting back something of what he had lost — not just that night, but over the past few weeks. Whether it was pride or self-confidence or just a sense of self-worth, he couldn't say. Nor did it matter to him beyond the fact that he wanted to feel again that he could do what he had been given to do as a Knight of the Word.

It was still several hours until dawn when Trim took him off the road and into rougher country, high desert formed of mesquite and scrub and, in the distance, clusters of boulders and high bluffs. In between, ravines crisscrossed the landscape in a maze of deep rifts. Logan drove into this rolling, obstacle-riddled landscape almost recklessly, slowing only when the ravines or the boulders made it absolutely necessary. The Ventra was built for terrain like this and could take the shocks and jolts. Trim wheeled and soared in the sky ahead, giving Logan his direction, telling him where he should go. It almost seemed as if he were responding to what the Knight of the Word was thinking: *Hurry!*

The rough travel went on for what seemed an endless distance, and Logan began to feel that he might run out of time after all. Dawn could not be that far away, and once it was light there was a good chance that the skrails would move the boy again. At best, it would become more difficult to sneak up on them undetected. The danger in being caught out was not to himself, but to the boy. They might choose simply to kill him, or alternatively to move him again so that Logan could not follow. He had to reach Kirisin before it got light enough to see by.

Then all of a sudden Trim flew back at him from out of the night, wheeled about, and landed on the branch of a dead tree just ahead. Logan slowed the Ventra 5000 to a stop, shut it down, and climbed out. He walked over to the owl and stood looking up at him. Trim did not move, regarding him silently. Logan understood. The owl had taken him as far as possible with the AV. Now he must leave the vehicle and proceed on foot.

For just an instant, as he stood staring off into the night-shrouded distance, he considered casting off everything he had become as a Knight of the Word and reverting to how he had been when he was with Michael. It was an unexpected impulse, one born of his frustration with his present life and regrets for lost pieces of his last. His memories of his time with Michael — memories other than those of Michael's descent into madness — still resonated. Good memories. One was of times like this, when they would seek out enemy patrols come in search of them. They would strip down to almost nothing, paint themselves with camouflage, and go hunting their enemies with nothing but knives. They would stalk them and kill them and then disappear back into the night as if they had never been there. It was a game they played, a challenge they gave themselves, dangerous and seductive. Surviving it provided validation of who and what they were, of their ability to confront and defeat the death that was constantly stalking them.

Get in and get out. Leave no footprints. Those were Michael's words of caution to him each time they played the game. Leave no sign that you were ever there. That you even existed. Leave nothing but the bodies of the dead to show that death stalked their enemies, too.

Logan Tom thought about how it would feel to do that again, to turn back the clock, to strip away everything and go hunting. He thought about abandoning the staff of his office and taking up one of the big hunting knives instead. He would shed his identity as a Knight of the Word. He would become for just that night a nameless, faceless hunter — a predator, a warrior — confronting his enemies with nothing but his skill and strength and weapons that carried no magic upon which he could rely to defend himself.

It was a ridiculous idea, but there it was. He let it linger for just a moment, savoring the freedom it offered and the intense sense of satisfaction it would provide, and then he cast it aside. There was too much at stake for such madness, and he was no longer the boy he had been, no longer the student to Michael's teacher, no longer the willing follower of a man who would one day try to kill him.

He took a deep breath and exhaled, tightening his hands about his black staff. "Show me where they are, Trim," he said to the owl.

Trim seemed to understand. Lifting off the dead branch, he soared away into the distance. Logan Tom waited a moment, tracking the bird's flight, and then stripped off his jacket and followed after.

They passed through the darkness as silently as night's shadows, Trim flying ahead, Logan in pursuit. The Knight of the Word kept up a steady pace, running smoothly, eyes on the terrain he passed through, the black staff cradled beneath one arm. He was careful of the terrain, avoiding the rougher parts, the places he could be tripped up and injured, the deadwood and jagged rocks and deep crevices. He could feel the sweat form on his brow, and it mirrored the intense heat of his desire to track down the skrails. He had no illusions about what that meant; he understood the nature of who he was. He was trained to fight, and he looked forward to testing himself in combat. When he was going into battle, he was alive in a way that was both exciting and satisfying. He was complete. He was afraid, too, but that was to be expected. He was always afraid. He would have been a fool if he were not. But fear was something to be overcome, an enemy of a different sort, not something from which to run away but something to confront. He had done so many times in his life, and each time it made him a little stronger, a little more self-assured.

The minutes passed, and still he saw nothing of the skrails. Trim soared and dove, rose and fell, a fleet shadow against the sky, always wheeling back to find him, to make certain he was following. There was no sign of anything other than themselves in this desolate country, no movement amid the rocks and scrub, no sounds to break the silence. It felt as if they were alone in the world, the last two living things, running to escape the fate that had befallen all others.

And wasn't that, he wondered, pretty much the truth of what he was doing every day of his life?

Ahead, Trim wheeled back sharply and landed on a rock. Logan Tom slowed in response, sensed the hidden presence farther on, and stopped. He peered into the darkness, breathing heavily, his magic-enhanced senses registering the skrail keeping watch just out of sight.

He had found them.

He felt a fierce sense of satisfaction, knowing that they had not escaped him after all, that he had been right in supposing they must stop for the night, that they did not think they were in danger of being followed and thought themselves safe.

He stood where he was, unmoving. His breathing gradually slowed, but his mind was working rapidly as he considered his options. He would get Kirisin back from them; that much was settled. But how was he going to go about it? Should he annihilate them, so that he could be certain they would give no further pursuit? Or should he kill enough of them that they would think twice about coming after him? Or should he simply find and kill their leader?

Or should he do something else entirely?

The night was a soft, silky blanket of silence and darkness that enveloped him and rendered him invisible to those he had tracked and found. It whispered to him with words of encouragement. He could do whatever he wanted. He could make any choice and not be wrong in doing so. He could do anything. He was invincible.

Just like that, the choice was made.

■ ■ ■ ■

Kirisin was dozing, drifting in and out of a troubled sleep, his hands and feet bound once more and this time cinched together behind his back so that as he lay on the hard ground he was twisted backward almost double. He wouldn't have been able even to doze, so excruciating was his discomfort and pain, if he hadn't already been exhausted.

So it took a minute for him to come awake even after he felt the hands, one clamping over his mouth, the other pressing him back against the earth so that he could not move at all. His eyes opened in shock, and he found himself looking at a demon. Black and gray stripes painted the skin of its face and upper body, turning its human form into something animalistic and feral. Black cloth bound its hair back, and its eyes were bright with hunger. He tried to jerk away, but the hands held him fast.

"Lie still," Logan Tom whispered. "Don't talk."

Kirisin stared in disbelief.

"Do you know me now?" the other mouthed.

The boy nodded, though he could still scarcely believe who he was looking at.

The Knight of the Word — he was still that, Kirisin supposed — took his hands away. A finger went to his lips in further caution, and then Logan Tom was cutting him free, stripping off the bonds, rubbing his ankles and wrists. Again he mouthed, *Don't move.* Kirisin lay still, the circulation slowly returning. He glanced off into the night for his captors. One of them sat not a dozen feet away, propped up against the rocks. How it could not see them was beyond the boy's understanding. Logan Tom's disguise was good, blending him closely with the night-shrouded landscape, but he was crouched out there in the open as he worked over Kirisin, completely exposed.

"Lean on me," the other whispered in his ear.

Then he carefully pulled him to his feet and steadied him. After a moment, he began walking him out of the skrail camp. Kirisin glanced again at the guard, but the guard didn't move.

"It can't see you," Logan Tom whispered.

Kirisin didn't understand. Then he looked more closely. The skrail's head was cocked to one side at an unnatural angle. It was dead.

His rescuer put a finger to his lips once more. The strange mottled face and unnaturally bright eyes mirrored something the boy couldn't quite define. One rough hand reached up to grip his shoulder.

"Leave no footprints," the Knight of the

Word whispered, and his smile was bright and fierce.

TWENTY-ONE

Kirisin walked away from his captivity as if there were nothing to it, as free as the night air, although inwardly he was still grappling with how quickly things had turned around. He followed Logan Tom through the darkness, filled with a mix of relief and gratitude that exceeded anything he could remember. He had been certain of his fate when the skrails had caught him trying to escape, his hopes dashed, his courage gone. He had told himself that Simralin would come for him, but he'd had no real expectation that she would.

No real expectation that anyone would.

But here was Logan Tom, come out of nowhere, finding him when Kirisin knew in his heart that no one could. It was a genuine miracle, and he was so grateful for it that he almost cried.

Logan kept him moving, steadying him as they walked until at last he was able to continue unaided. Some distance farther on, just inside the screen of a grove of withered trees, the Knight of the Word turned aside to retrieve the clothing he had shed earlier. Kirisin stood silently nearby, watching him dress. He took his time, in no apparent hurry, using sleeves torn from his shirt to wipe himself clean of the camouflage paint before slipping back into his clothes. He said nothing to the boy the whole time. When he was finished dressing, he bent down to retrieve his black staff from where it was lying on the ground. It took a moment for Kirisin to realize what that meant, and when he did, he was stunned.

Logan Tom had gone into the skrail camp without his magic to protect him! He had left his staff behind!

The Knight of the Word caught him staring and turned away quickly. "Let's go, Kirisin."

They started out again. "Is Sim all right?" the boy asked him. "Has there been any sign of her? Of any of them?"

The other shrugged. "Can't tell yet. It's too early to know. Don't talk. Not until we're farther away."

They continued for perhaps another quarter mile before reaching the Ventra 5000, its bulky shape unmistakable even in the darkness. Logan Tom released the locks and alarms, and they climbed inside. Once settled, the Knight of the Word sat staring out into the darkness. Kirisin waited in silence for a moment before speaking.

"How did you find me?" he asked.

"A little bird told me." Logan looked at him. "You want to know why I didn't take my staff with me when I came to rescue you."

He made it a statement of fact. Kirisin started to say that it wasn't his business, but then simply nodded. Logan stared at him for a moment longer. The joy he had displayed earlier had leached away; all that remained was resignation and weariness. "Maybe later," he said.

He turned away, started the engine, retracted the wheel locks, put the AV in gear, and slowly pulled away into the night.

They drove for a long time in silence. Kirisin tried not to look at Logan, not to do anything that might upset him. He should have kept his curiosity to himself. Logan Tom had saved his life. He didn't deserve to be questioned about how he had done it. Certainly not by the boy he had saved. What sort of gratitude was that? Kirisin ground his teeth. He still had not learned when to keep things to himself.

"I'm sorry," he said finally, unable to stand it any longer. "I shouldn't have looked at you like that."

Logan Tom glanced over, then shrugged. "Did the skrails hurt you? Are you all right?" He seemed anxious to change the subject. "You look a little dazed."

"They knocked me around a bit at first," the boy answered. "But then the one who controls the skrails conjured up a specter or wraith out of the flames of a fire, and there was this old man. He had eyes . . ." He shook his head. "I've never seen eyes like that. So cold. He just stared at me, and I knew he could kill me just by looking at me, if he wanted."

Logan Tom was suddenly interested. "Did he wear a gray cloak and slouch hat?"

"That's right. Do you know him?"

Logan hesitated. "A little. What did he do?"

"Asked some questions. He wasn't happy that I didn't have the Loden with me." He paused. "Is it safe? Did Praxia find it?"

"She had it with her when she came to find me after the skrails had flown off with you. She wanted to come along to help rescue you, but I told her she couldn't do that. I told her that the Loden was her responsibility now, at least until you returned."

Kirisin pictured Praxia's reaction and smiled despite himself. "I'd guess she didn't like hearing that very much, did she?"

"She understood."

"That old man," Kirisin continued. "He did something to me. Without even being there, he was able to hurt me. He just looked at me from out of the flames and made me answer his questions about the Loden. I didn't tell him where it was, only that I lost it. But I think he knew I wasn't telling him everything. Then he hurt me so badly I thought I was going to scream from the pain. Just by looking at me, from somewhere else entirely, he could do that."

Logan looked off into the night, his eyes on the landscape ahead. "He's a very powerful demon. The leader of all of the demons, maybe. I saw him once, years ago, when I was still a boy. He led the attack that killed my family. He looked at me, too. In a different way. But I remember those eyes. I won't ever forget them."

"Will he come after us?" Kirisin asked.

"Like a wolf hunting sheep."

"Maybe we can outrun him."

Logan Tom didn't answer.

They drove on in silence for a time, putting miles between themselves and the skrails, watching the eastern sky lighten with dawn's approach as the stars faded. Kirisin was thinking of the old man, remembering how he had been made to do whatever the other wanted, how humiliated and helpless he had been made to feel. It was bad enough that he had almost lost the Loden to the skrails. But to know how easy it was for the demon to take it away from him if he should catch him with it another time was terrifying. He didn't think anyone could survive an encounter with such a creature — not even a Knight of the Word. He didn't think magic was enough —

354

not Elfstones and not a Knight's black staff. This demon was much more powerful than the ones he had encountered. If he caught up to them, it would take something special to escape.

It might take something that none of them had.

The new day began. It was midmorning when Logan finally pulled the AV over to the side of the road and let them get out to stretch their legs and eat something. Even then, he kept his eyes on the horizon of the country they had fled and his staff cradled in the crook of his arm. There was a fresh intensity to his look that Kirisin found scary — a concentration that was dark and private and suggested Logan Tom would not respond well to interruptions. The boy took it to heart and left him alone.

But as they were finishing, Kirisin already looking ahead to moving on, the Knight of the Word began to speak. "Do you know how old I am, Kirisin?" he asked. He didn't wait for a response. "Twenty-eight. Twice your age, but in my heart I don't feel that old. In my heart, I'm still a boy of fourteen or fifteen. Isn't that odd?"

He straightened his legs and rubbed his knees. "My body feels older, though. My body feels twice my age. Years of running and fighting after leaving the compound with Michael. Years of battles I just barely survived, injuries and sickness, wounds and poisons. You can't absorb all that and walk away unchanged. But it seems odd anyway, my body feeling so old, while my heart feels . . ."

He trailed off. His eyes fixed on the boy. "Here's what I want you to understand. The magic is dangerous. Even when it feels good using it, even when it makes you feel invincible, it's still dangerous. You're going to find that out. You're the keeper of those Elfstones, and their magic is yours to employ. You will use it again, probably soon. You might think you have a choice in the matter, that it was a onetime thing, using the magic to destroy that demon in the ice caves. But that's not the way it works. Once you've used the magic, you've committed yourself. It's a responsibility you can't give up."

Kirisin nodded. "I guess I know that."

Logan smiled. "Well, you might think you do, but you don't. Not yet. Not really. And you won't right away. You have to have the power in your care for more than a few weeks or even a few months. You have to have it in your care for years. You have to live with it awhile. Then you'll begin to see what I mean."

He gestured absently. "The danger comes from both using it and not using it. It comes just from having it, from possessing it, from being a part of it. It becomes the defining factor of your existence, the single most important truth you possess. It influences everything you do; it determines the nature of your character and it shapes your thinking."

He paused. "It's a two-edged sword, Kirisin. If you fail to use it at the right times in the right ways, people will die. Some of them might be people you know, but even if you don't, they are still people for whom you have become responsible simply because you possess the means of helping them and you have failed to do so. You've made a choice, and you have to live with that choice. Sometimes the choices you are given are bad ones, no matter which way you go. And therefore the consequences are bad ones, as well.

"But the consequences of using the magic in the very best way you can, in a way that helps people and saves lives, doesn't mean that things will work out any better. Using the magic in a way that works is just as dangerous. Not to them, you see, but to you. Because every time you use the magic, it eats away at you. It erodes the defenses you create to keep it from overwhelming you, from stealing away your soul. Do you think I exaggerate? Think again. Magic can do that. It *does* do that. By the very nature of what it is. It is an addictive, corrupting influence, and the more you use it, the more it makes you want to use it. Because it makes you feel so good when you do. It makes you feel invincible. It banishes all your insecurities and fears. It fills you up like liquid iron, hardening you against everything that might harm you. It dominates you in a way that nothing else can. It's a drug. An addiction, like I said. You find you want it, you need it, you have to have it. And the only way that can happen is if you allow yourself to find a use for it. Any use."

Kirisin was horrified. "It isn't that way with you. I don't see that with you, Logan."

The Knight of the Word smiled. "You don't see a lot of what I am. I keep it hidden pretty well. I keep my demons penned up. More to the point, I live my life alone. There's only me and this." He held out the black staff. "Me and my magic. We share a life that doesn't allow for intrusion or for sharing."

He shook his head. "I was like you when I first became a Knight of the Word. That's why I am telling you all this now. Not to frighten you, but to warn you. I had no one to warn me. I had to find it all out for myself. But I can pass it on to you, what I've learned, and maybe it will make a difference somewhere down the road. Maybe it will make your life a little easier to bear. Maybe you can do something more than I've done to keep yourself safe from what having the use of the magic will mean."

"But you said it yourself," Kirisin pointed out. "I have to use the Elfstones. So if I have to use them, maybe more than once, maybe a bunch of times, I'm at risk no matter what, aren't I? I can't avoid these consequences you're warning me about."

"You can't avoid your fate, no. None of us can. You've been given a responsibility, just as I was. You've been given the use of magic, and you can't take it back. But you can be aware of its dangers. You can appreciate that it has its darker side. Just knowing that that part of it exists and recognizing how it makes you feel might be enough to help you."

He looked down at his feet. "I've done some things . . ." He trailed off. "I've forgotten to remember the danger, sometimes. I haven't been careful enough. I've been reckless because either the situation called for it or I've allowed my emotions to rule my thinking. Bad choices, both. And don't be fooled. They were choices I made. I just wasn't controlled enough to avoid making them. I can't excuse what I've done. I can't excuse any of it. I have to live with my regrets."

He looked up again and gave Kirisin a quick smile. "But maybe you won't have to live with as many of those regrets as I do. Not if you're aware that they're out there."

They were silent for a moment, and then Kirisin said, "In a world like this one, where everything either has been destroyed or is in the process of being destroyed, maybe you have to be content with knowing that you're doing the best you can. Maybe you shouldn't spend too much time blaming yourself for what didn't work out. You do the best you can, don't you?"

Logan Tom nodded slowly. "Of course. And I'm sure you will, too. But that won't change things. It won't change the way the magic works or the effect it has on you. It won't change the bad choices. It won't absolve you of your guilt. In the end, you still have to live with yourself. But it might be easier to do so if you understand why sometimes you feel so terrible about who you are. I'm just telling you how it will be. I'm just doing what I can to pass along what I know."

Kirisin nodded. "I guess I understand."

"You make me remember what I was like at your age. I was a little older when I was given the magic, but I knew less about it than you do. I wasn't raised in a culture where magic existed. I was bitter and angry about what had been done to me. All I wanted was revenge. Especially against that old man. He took everything from me. My family. My life. I haven't forgiven or forgotten any of it. Every time I use the magic, I see his face. It's not a good thing. I know this. Rationally, I can say I know it. But it doesn't change how I feel. Even now."

He took a deep breath. "But your sister . . ."

"Sim?" Kirisin prodded, when he failed to continue.

Logan Tom nodded. "When I look at her, I can see what I've given up by being a Knight of the Word. It seemed the right thing until now. But she made me realize that my whole life is going by, and I don't have anything to show for it but the magic. And my promise to myself that I would hunt down and kill that demon."

The boy stared. "You're in love with her."

It sounded so naïve, so foolish, that he regretted the words the moment they left his mouth. But Logan Tom just shrugged. "I don't know anything about being in love. I just know she made me question what I wanted out of life, and I haven't done enough of that. I was burned out when I came to find the gypsy morph, but I thought it was just because I needed something new, a change from what I'd been doing." He hesitated, as if considering what that something was. "Now I'm not so sure. I think it's more complicated."

"I think she likes you," Kirisin said impulsively, wanting to do something to help. "In fact, I'm sure she does."

Logan shook his head. "Maybe she ought to think twice about it." He rose abruptly. "Well, I've said what I wanted to say. That's enough about it. Time to be going."

They climbed back into the AV and set out once more. Kirisin sat in silence, mulling over what Logan Tom had told him. He found that he believed almost all of it. He had known from the first moment he had used the blue

Elfstones and felt the power of the magic surging through him that nothing was ever going to be the same for him again. Nor did he dispute that use of the magic was dangerous — not just in a physical way, but in an emotional way, as well. He understood what the other was saying about the ways in which using power could subvert you. He understood that he would always be at risk, that he would always need to be cautious. That was the price you paid. And while he hadn't asked for that use, he had willingly embraced it. He had wanted to help the Ellcrys as a member of the Chosen, and had pledged on more than one occasion to do whatever was needed to see that she was protected.

So he couldn't very well complain now about the consequences of having made that commitment. He couldn't complain about not having fully understood what that meant.

On the other hand, he had somehow convinced himself that the commitment was only temporary; that once the Elves and their city were safely delivered to their destination and released back into the world, it would all be over. Things would go back to the way they had been with his life. He would continue as a Chosen in service to the tree until his time was up, and then he would enter the ranks of the Home Guard.

How naïve, he realized.

Because it wouldn't be so simple. What was

he going to do with the Elfstones? Not just the Loden, the use of which might be ended for his lifetime, at least, but the blue Elfstones, the seeking-Stones. What did he think he was going to do about them? Give them up? To whom? Who could he trust to see that they were used in the right way? He could give them to the King, but Arissen Belloruus wasn't the most dependable person with whom to entrust such a powerful magic. Changed or not, he was still a volatile personality. And if not to the King of the Elves, then to whom?

He couldn't give them to anyone.

Because Pancea Rolt Gotrin had given them to him and sworn him to the task of finding a way to convince the Elves that the magic that was their heritage must be recovered and put to use. In the rushed frenzy of everything that had happened since her shade had bestowed the blue Elfstones on him, he had forgotten his promise. But it recalled itself now in chilling detail, and he realized that nothing of this matter would ever be over for him. He had committed himself to a lifetime of service to a cause, an undertaking he must somehow resurrect from its thousand-year dormancy, that he must breathe fresh life into, that he must fully embrace.

If he did not . . .

He brushed the rest of that thought aside.

He did not care to speculate about what would happen if he did not. At best, he would be haunted for the remainder of his life by the breaking of the promise he had given. Some promises you could break and live with yourself after doing so, but not this one.

He was brooding on the consequences of having made that promise when Logan suddenly said, "You asked me why I didn't take the staff with me when I came to rescue you, Kirisin. Do you still want to know?"

It caught the boy off guard. He looked over at Logan, but the Knight of the Word had his eyes fixed on the road, maneuvering the AV through the obstacle course of debris and potholes.

"If you want to tell me," he said.

Logan nodded. "When I was living with Michael, after he saved me from the compound, we used to go hunting. We would strip down, paint ourselves with camouflage, arm ourselves with nothing but K-Bar Classics, and go after the militias that were always hunting us. Hunting the hunters, we called it. A game we played to scare them off. We'd go out, find a patrol, kill a few, and then disappear. Leave no footprints behind, no trace of who we were. Just the dead men. It was a warning to them. But it was something more to us."

He paused. "That all stopped a dozen years ago, when Michael stopped being Michael and became someone else."

He glanced over at Kirisin, and the boy found himself wondering — not for the first time — who Michael was. But Logan pressed on with no explanation. "Last night I found myself wanting to do that again. To strip down and go after those skrails with nothing but a hunting knife. It was a dangerous impulse, a foolish idea, and I knew it. It risked everything if I failed. It was selfish, too. I had been lucky enough to find you, to catch up to your captors, and now I was thinking about throwing it all away on a whim. I knew this. I recognized it right away."

He shook his head. "But I did it anyway." He went silent, eyes on the road. "I did it," he continued finally, "because I needed to do something to save myself."

His gaze shifted momentarily to Kirisin and then back again to the road. "Michael said once that automatic weapons were our best defense against the militias and the rogue armies and all the rest, but that you shouldn't let yourself rely on them too heavily. Sooner or later, one of them would fail. If that was all you had, you were dead. He said that we hunted to be sure we had more to work with than guns and armored vehicles. He said that sooner or later a time would come when you had only yourself, so you'd better be ready for when that time came around."

He gave a quick, hard laugh. "Even that

wasn't enough to save him in the end. He thought it would be, but it wasn't."

"Michael was your teacher?" Kirisin asked, wanting now to know something more about Michael, unwilling to let it slide further.

Logan Tom nodded. "That, and much more. My surrogate father. My best friend. My only family." He took a deep breath and exhaled sharply. "Everything, once."

His hands tightened on the steering wheel. "When I went into the skrail camp to rescue you, I was doing something for myself, too. I was proving to myself that there was more to me than the staff's magic, that I was more than a Knight of the Word. I had to reassure myself. Michael had warned about relying too heavily on automatic weapons. It's the same with magic. It's wrong to rely too much on anything."

"Like you were telling me earlier," Kirisin said. "The magic can be dangerous in more ways than you might think. It can undermine you in lots of unexpected ways."

"The magic hasn't been too reliable lately," the other continued. "I thought it was time to make sure I could still get along without it. I needed to test myself. Going in after you in the old way, the way I used to with Michael, was what I thought I needed to do."

"Well, if you thought it was important, then it probably was," the boy offered, at the same time wondering if that was really so.

"Maybe. I'm still not sure. You make a choice and it works out and you think it was the right one. But maybe you just got lucky. If you made that choice a second time, you might end up dead."

There was nothing Kirisin cared to say about that. He decided to leave the matter there, and he turned back to face down the road, looking off into space, seeing things that hadn't happened yet, but that one day would.

Neither said anything further.

Midday came and went, and in the lengthening shadows of the Cintra the afternoon crawled toward another lank, gray evening. Findo Gask stood at the edge of the skrail encampment and watched the sun slide toward the wall of the mountains west. Fifty of his once-men were engaged in cleaning up the mess behind him, diligent servants under the whip and blade of a pair of his newly promoted demon lieutenants. With Delloreen dead and the Klee still in search of the gypsy morph, he had need of new subordinates, of creatures anxious to move up in the pecking order, to take the place of those he had favored before. They lasted only a short while, for the most part, and then they were gone and there were others. They all had the same ambitions, the same central goal — to fawn for his favor while they schemed to replace him. They all wanted the same thing — his power, his status, his rule.

Except for the Klee — which wanted nothing but the opportunities he provided for it — they were all alike.

He thought momentarily of Delloreen. Unlike most of the others, he genuinely regretted losing her. Certainly, he would have had to kill her before much longer in any event, but he had admired her grit and determination. He had enjoyed their verbal sparring; staying alert to her endless machinations had helped keep him sharp. There was no one among the present crop who could scheme as she did and be prepared to back it up with savagery and cruelty, which even he had trouble matching.

The demon called Dariogue wandered over, slouching in that peculiar way it had developed, one leg shorter than the other, neck twice broken and reset, face all smashed in. Findo Gask didn't like Dariogue much and didn't trust him at all, but he was the most capable of the bunch.

"It's done, Master," his subordinate offered, gesturing vaguely.

"All of them?"

"All, Master."

"Do we know anything more than we did before about what happened to the boy?"

"No, Master, nothing."

Findo Gask was not pleased. Not that he

had expected Dariogue to be any more successful than himself at finding out how the Elf boy had escaped. Not that he didn't already have a pretty good idea.

"Let's have a look, then."

They started off toward the grove of skeletal trees north of the clearing. Findo Gask was already thinking ahead to his pursuit of the Elf boy. It didn't matter how he had escaped — or with whom. The end result would be the same. He would track the boy, find him, and extract from him the truth about the whereabouts of the Loden. The boy would have it near him or know where it was; he would have to if he expected to save his people. Culph had been quite clear about how the Elfstone worked. His ideas of manipulating the user remained valuable even though he himself was dead and gone.

Gask frowned on thinking of the deaths of his spies — the old man and the Tracker. How had the boy managed to kill not one, but two demons? He must have access to a magic Findo Gask did not yet know of; he would have to be cautious. The boy was capable of more than any of them had believed. The boy was dangerous.

"Here, Master," Dariogue advised, breaking into his musings.

He looked to where the other was pointing. The broken bodies of the minder and twenty-five skrails dangled from the limbs of the trees to which they had been nailed. They looked vaguely like bats. Or strange decorations for a pagan celebration.

The old man studied them with his cold, empty eyes, and was satisfied. Failure of the sort that had occurred here would not be tolerated.

"We're leaving," he said to Dariogue. "Send me something that can track the boy. Blood soaks or huntrys should do. Then bring up the rest of the army. March them by these trees so that they can see what happens when I am disappointed."

An object lesson, he thought as he brushed the other off with a wave of his hand. But it was nothing compared with the lesson he intended to teach the Elf boy.

TWENTY-TWO

Angel Perez stalked through the center of the refugee children's camp, radiating anger and dismay with every step. She walked purposefully, giving no sense that she had any doubt at all about where she was going. She had been in the camp for only three days, but that was enough time for her to find her way about. The camp sprawled, and its configuration changed continuously as its inhabitants were shifted from one care group and one location to the next. But Angel was a quick study. Besides, it didn't really matter where she was going. It only mattered that she was able to find the person she was looking for.

She heard Helen Rice before she saw her, and she saw her just about where she expected, down by the bridge where the work was going on, engaged in discussions with the demolition experts and the sappers. Helen was animated as she issued instructions and responded to questions, a small dynamo of energy. Nothing had changed since their time together at the Anaheim compound. Helen was still a take-charge kind of person, a born leader able to adjust to what the circumstances required. Even when she didn't possess knowledge specific enough to provide a solution, she knew how to find those who did and enlist them to her cause. Like she was doing now, as she set about preparing for the demon army that had pursued them all the way north from California.

Angel stopped a short distance away. She wanted to talk to Helen alone. The information she carried was not meant to be general knowledge. Not yet. It would happen soon enough, no matter what precautions they took. But there was no need to rush things.

She sighed inwardly. She was significantly improved since her injuries on Syrring Rise, if not yet entirely whole. She had healed well enough under the care of Larkin Quill, but it was not her physical health that had suffered the most damage. Emotionally, she was a wreck. Especially after Larkin's death at the hands of that monster, that demon-spawn. She might hide it from those around her, but she knew the truth of things. She could feel the upheaval working about inside. Doubts and fears roiled, and her mind was awash with growing uncertainties about her ability to carry on.

She was a Knight of the Word, but she was

human, too. The one didn't supplant the other. You carried your past life with you into the job; you didn't shed that life like an old skin. You remained the person you started out as, even if you wielded killing magic and projected an invincible aura. Your past was your heritage and the foundation on which you were built. You couldn't start over. You could only repair and move on.

What that meant in practical terms was that she wasn't sure of herself anymore. She had lost a significant piece of self-confidence.

"Helen!" she called out, suddenly impatient with the wait.

Helen turned, said something to the men and women with whom she was speaking, and walked over to Angel. "What is it?" she asked at once, seeing something of what was coming in Angel's eyes.

"We've lost another two children. A boy and his sister, ages seven and eight. They disappeared sometime during the night. No one is sure when. It wasn't noticed until they woke the other children in the group, counted heads, and came up short."

Helen shook her head vigorously. "They may have wandered off, Angel. We can't be sure. Can we?"

"We can be sure. You know so."

The other woman said nothing for a moment. "I suppose I do. How many does that make?"

"Eight. In a little more than forty-eight hours. It's taking them in pairs. I don't know how, but it's finding a way to get to them. We've doubled the guards, ringed the sleeping areas, the privies, the food storage, everywhere I can think of. Nothing seems to stop it. It comes in and goes out whenever and wherever it wants. No one sees it. Something that big, and no one even sees it."

She folded her arms and stepped close. "We know what it is. *I* know, anyway. It's that thing, Helen. That monster. It's tracked the boy Hawk and his bunch back to us, and now it's feeding on our children."

Helen winced. "I know. I know what it's doing."

"What's so maddening is that I don't know why!" Angel's voice was fierce and guttural. "I thought it was tracking me at first, that the old man had sent it to take the place of the one I killed on Syrring Rise. I thought it was trying to finish the job that it started at Larkin Quill's. But then it went after Hawk and the children traveling with him. So now I don't know what to think."

Helen nodded. "Hawk believes it's after him, that because he's been sent to lead the rest of us to safety this thing has been sent to kill him. He says he saw it in the creature's eyes when it found them in the mountains. But if that's so, why isn't it trying to get at him? Why is it killing these other children? It seems to be killing them just for sport! It's preying on them like some animal."

Angel looked away, troubled. Her hands gripped her black staff. "I saw it, Helen. Like Hawk. I was as close to it as I am to you. I looked into its eyes. I saw what was there. Doesn't matter that it stands on its hind legs and cloaks itself in human form — it *is* an animal. An animal like nothing I've ever seen. A black thing out of some pit . . ."

She couldn't finish. She wheeled back. "I have to go out there and find it and kill it," she said, her face twisted in fury.

Helen took hold of her arm and held on firmly. "I wish you wouldn't do that, Angel."

"You're afraid for me?"

"I'm afraid for the rest of us. If we lose you, who do we have to protect us? We need your magic, your experience and skill. We need your *heart.*" She brushed at her short-cropped blond hair and shook her head. "There aren't enough of us to do what is needed. We have weapons, we have transport, and we have food and water and maps. We have our determination, and that is not to be underestimated. But we are not Knights of the Word, and we are no match for the demon and his army if they catch up to us. We can't afford to risk losing you. Losing you would leave us terribly vulnerable."

"You won't lose me," Angel answered, slipping free her arm. "Besides, you have Hawk.

He has magic."

Helen nodded. "Very powerful magic, at that. But he's a boy, Angel. He's still a child himself. He lacks experience. His magic is an unknown, even to him. He can do things with it, but it isn't a weapon he can use to defend others in the same way your staff is. It's a whole unexplored country!" She paused. "Bottom line? He isn't you."

Angel saw the reason embedded in the other woman's words. It was more than just her magic. A Knight of the Word gave power to those she protected simply by virtue of her presence among them. There was belief in her. Her absence would leave a void that no one else could fill.

"Lo siento. Estoy cansada." She took Helen's hand in her own and squeezed gently. "I'm not thinking clearly. I know that."

"We're all under a terrible strain," Helen agreed. "We know we have to do something, but we can't afford to act out of haste, either."

"No tenemos mucho tiempo," Angel answered. "It's all slipping away from us, Helen. The longer we stay here, the worse things are likely to get. We need to start moving. We need this boy to take all of us to where we are supposed to go. If he can really do that."

Helen nodded. She hugged herself and exhaled sharply. The way her eyes fixed on Angel, it felt as if she were reaching deep inside for something to hold on to. "I think he can," she finally said. "I really do. Even if I can't explain it." She shook her head against whatever doubts she was experiencing. "But he says we can't leave yet. He says we have to wait. He won't say why."

Angel's lips tightened into a thin line of impatience. "I'll talk with him about it."

Helen looked uncertain. "Angel, I don't know . . ."

"I won't do anything but ask him for a reason. I just want to know that he has one, that he's sure about this."

Helen nodded. "Remember, he knows about the children, too."

"I'll remember." She hesitated. "Better send out search parties to look for those kids."

"I will, of course. You know that. Not that it will make any difference. We haven't found a single trace of any of the others. We won't find anything of these two, either."

She turned and started walking back to join the men and women with whom she had been speaking before Angel's interruption.

"It doesn't hurt to look," Angel called after her.

Helen glanced back over her shoulder. "Everything hurts," she said.

The white-hot orb of the midday sun was suspended overhead, the air so thick with its heat that the landscape shimmered as if formed of water. The countryside was burned brown and dry, and even the presence of the river flowing beneath the bluffs on which the refugee camp had been settled did nothing to temper its effect. Hawk stood at the top of the bluff and looked out across the broad expanse of the gorge to where the mountains south formed a black mass against the hazy blue sky.

He was waiting, and the waiting was painful. Not because he didn't know how to wait, but because he didn't know what he was waiting for.

Sometimes he wondered how he had come to this. He accepted that what he had believed to be true about himself for so many years was a lie. The King of the Silver River could call it anything he liked, but it was still a lie. His memories were layered with people and places that had never existed and events that had never happened. None of it was real. He accepted that he was a creature formed of magic, not of Faerie or humankind, but of some mix of the two. He even accepted that he was meant to be leader and guide to all these children and their caregivers and to others who would join them on their way to the place in which they would find safety from the end times.

Fine. But what was he to do about not knowing any of the particulars of his mission? How was he to come to terms with the fact that he must accept so much on faith?

What was it going to take for him to be at peace with the inexplicable and unknowable behavioral characteristics that were charting his decision making as surely as ocean currents would a rudderless ship's course?

And what of his uncertainty about himself? His surprising use of magic in the face of obstacles hindering their passage was a case in point. His ability to heal both Cheney and Logan Tom when death might have claimed them was another.

Now this. The waiting.

He was waiting for Logan Tom to return with the Elves, even though he had no way of knowing when that would happen or even if it would happen at all. He was acting on faith. Logan Tom would come, and he would bring what was needed. How did he know? He just did.

Even more troublesome was his reluctance to move the camp. Even though that creature the Ghosts had encountered in the mountains had followed them here and was preying on the children, he could not allow them to leave. *Would* not. Why? Because his instincts told him it wasn't time, that he must stay where he was until moving felt right.

It was difficult to explain. It was nothing more than a sense of what was needed, but the sense was very strong and very certain. He hadn't experienced it before going into the Gardens of Life and encountering the

King of the Silver River, but now it was such a dominant presence that he could not go against it. He had felt it surface within him the moment he had returned from the gardens and prepared to set out with Tessa to find the Ghosts. It hadn't left him since; it was a voice that whispered to him soundlessly and ruled his decision making with an iron hand. He wished it were otherwise, wished he could bargain with it or simply ignore it, but he knew . . .

"Hawk!"

The sound of his name snapped him out of his reverie and brought him about to face Angel Perez. She walked toward him purposefully, her face reflecting an unmistakable determination. He knew at once what she was going to say.

She stopped in front of him. "We lost two more children this morning. How much longer before we can leave this place?"

The question resonated with impatience and anger. It didn't ask for an answer; it demanded it.

"I don't know," he said truthfully. "Anyway, it doesn't matter. The monster will follow us wherever we go."

"That might be," she conceded. "But we have to do something anyway. We can't just wait around."

She was right, of course. They had to do something to stop the killings. He even knew what that something was. They had to hunt the monster down and find a way to destroy it. To do that, they had to use Hawk as bait because he was the one the monster wanted. Because the monster was a demon, and it had been sent to stop him. He knew that. But he also knew what he couldn't do. He couldn't put himself at risk. There was more at stake than his own life.

He wished momentarily that things could go back to the way they had been. He wished he could return to the city, to the abandoned building in Pioneer Square, that he could live there again with his family, and that the future could be nothing more than a dream that came every so often to remind him of what might one day be.

"Logan Tom will be here soon," he said. "When he gets here, we will go looking for the monster."

"I could do that myself," she said. Her eyes were dark with anger. "Just as well as he could. I might have to, if he doesn't return soon. We don't even know if he's still alive. There's nothing to say he is."

Which was true. "He's alive," Hawk said anyway, feeling inside the certainty that he was.

She studied him with a gaze that said everything about her feelings toward him. She didn't believe him. She didn't think that he could do the things he claimed. She hadn't

381

witnessed any of his magic firsthand, and she wasn't convinced by what she had been told. She was worried for the children he was going to lead and suspicious of where he was taking them. But he didn't know what to do about it.

"Maybe we can leave tomorrow," he told her. "I can tell you by tonight."

She shook her head. "I don't know what to make of you, *amigo.* I don't know if you're what you say you are or not. Maybe you don't know, either. Maybe you're doing what you think is right. Maybe. But if it turns out you don't know what you're doing, a lot of people are going to be very angry. Especially me."

"If I don't know what I'm doing, it won't matter," he replied. "Because we'll all be dead."

She stared at him for a long moment, as if undecided about whether to pursue the matter. Then she wheeled about wordlessly and walked away.

"You're sure about this?" Fixit pressed, hoping that maybe the other boy wasn't.

But Chalk gave a quick, firm nod. "I heard them talking. A couple of the caregivers. A boy and a girl disappeared sometime last night. Didn't come back. No one can find them. They sent out search parties, but there was no trace."

"Just like the others," Fixit said.

Chalk compressed his lips. "Just like the others."

It was late in the afternoon, another sultry, miserably hot day on the flats above the Columbia River, another day of sitting around and waiting for something to happen. They were crouched together in the partial shade of some tall brush off to one side of the main camp. Fixit was working on an explosives fuse he had picked up from the discards down by the bridge where the demolitions teams were wiring the bridge. If the demon army that they were expecting reached them before they could escape, they would blow the bridge. It would take time for the enemy to find another way across the river. It would gain them at least a day and maybe more.

He glanced at Chalk, who had begun drawing images in the dry earth with the end of a stick. Even using such rudimentary materials, he soon had the beginnings of a sketch of the mountains south, using dark and light earth and sand to shade and delineate. Fixit watched the picture take shape, struck once again by how talented his friend was. No one could create images with the precision and depth Chalk could.

"Do you think we might leave anytime soon?" he asked.

Chalk shrugged. "Hawk makes those kinds of decisions, not me. Even the lady who runs the camp listens to him. No one leaves until he says they should." He shook his head and looked up at Fixit. "The boy and his children. Can you believe it? We all thought it was a story. Oh, we thought it might really happen, someday. But we thought it was only meant for us, for the Ghosts, and not for all these others."

"I believed it," Fixit insisted.

"Sure. But think about it. We didn't believe it was going to happen *now*. Not right away. In the future, sure. But we're still just kids. We aren't ready for this."

Fixit looked at his friend's sunburned face, nodding. Chalk wasn't used to being out in the heat. He looked flushed and angry. "I know," he said, mostly to end the conversation. "You should get some water to drink. Aren't you hot?"

Chalk smirked. "Only all the time. Guys like me, pale-skinned guys, don't belong out in the sun. We belong inside. That's why it would be better if we were back in the city, in our home, away from all this." He paused. "What about the monster, Fixit? You think it's doing all this with the missing kids? You think it's taking them?"

Fixit didn't know, but he nodded anyway. "Hawk says so. He's convinced it's that demon that almost got him a couple of days back. Tracking him still, right to our doorstep."

Chalk shivered. "I wish it would just go away, go hunt someone else. I don't like having that thing out there. You heard how Panther described it."

Fixit nodded. He tried to picture the demon in his mind. It was hard because he hadn't seen it, only heard it described by the others. A big, shambling hulk formed of scales and hair and leathery hide, long arms with massive hands and claws, and a head that looked as if a boulder had fallen on it. He could see it, all right. Eyes that looked right through you, that cut you apart and left you helpless. He shook the image from his mind. He was glad he hadn't been there when it came after the others. If Hawk, Bear, Sparrow, and Cheney weren't enough, then he didn't know what was.

"Tell you what," Chalk said suddenly, breaking into his thoughts. "I'm not going anywhere until they kill that thing. I'm staying right here in camp."

"Those kids were in camp, too," Fixit pointed out. "It got to them anyway."

"I don't know about that." Chalk shook his head, his face flushed with more than the heat. "I think they must have wandered off, gone somewhere outside the perimeter. That's how it managed to get them. I mean, think about it. If they had stayed inside the camp, how could something that big take them and no one see or hear anything?"

"I don't want to think about it," Fixit said. He glanced past Chalk in the direction of the camp. "Hey, let's see what Owl has to say."

They turned to watch Owl approach, wheeling her chair carefully over the rocky ground, eyes fixed on them. River was walking with her, helping with the chair.

When she reached them, Owl took a moment to size them up. "Don't you think you're a little farther out than you should be?" she asked quietly.

Fixit and Chalk looked at each other. Neither one had given it a moment's thought. In fact, they had believed they were pretty close in.

"It's dangerous for you to be anywhere but in the center of the camp," River added. "You know why."

"You think that was what happened to those kids, Owl?" Fixit asked.

"I think you don't want to risk finding out," she replied. Then she smiled. "Let's just try to be very careful for a few days more, all right?"

Both boys nodded, feeling slightly foolish for not doing what their mother had expected of them. But the whole business didn't feel real somehow; it didn't feel as though it had anything to do with them. Fixit thought that if they had actually seen the monster, it might have helped convince them. On the other hand, he wasn't sure he ever wanted to see it.

"What does Hawk say about leaving this place?" Chalk asked. He made a face. "I'm tired of sitting around doing nothing."

"It's what you do most of the time anyway," a new voice declared, and Sparrow walked over to join them. She knelt next to him, blue eyes quizzical. "But I wouldn't argue with what you're suggesting. I'd like to get out of here, too. I don't like how being here makes me feel."

She was carrying the Parkhan Spray. She carried it constantly now, ever since their encounter with the monster. She seemed edgy all the time, too, Fixit thought. Not like the old Sparrow.

"Hawk says he hopes we can leave tomorrow," Owl offered. She squinted against the sun. "He's waiting for Logan Tom."

"Been waiting on him too long already," Panther declared, coming up to join the rest of them, Bear with him. He was armed, as well. "What's he doing, anyway? Does anyone know? He just left us and went off on his own. Not very responsible, frickin' Knight of Nothing."

"He doesn't answer to us," Sparrow snapped. "It's his business what he does."

"Okay, it's his business. But I don't see why we're waiting on him."

"Because if Hawk says to wait on him, that's good enough for me, Panther Puss!"

"If Bird-Man told you to jump off a cliff,

that would be good enough for you!" Panther snapped. "But I ain't like you, Sparrow. I don't stand around waiting for someone to tell me what to do."

"No, you just go do whatever you feel like, don't you?" Sparrow sneered. "Mister Who-Cares-About-Anyone-But-Me."

"Stop it!" Owl ordered sharply, silencing them both. "You sound like little children. You're not. You're big enough to know. We don't need this arguing. We need to be patient with each other and to look out for each other until we get to where we're going!"

"To get to where we're going, first we got to start walking," Panther grumbled. "Not sit around."

"We'll go," she insisted. "It won't be long now. Hawk will take us."

Panther rolled his eyes but didn't say anything further. After a few minutes, he muttered something about needing to find Cat and wandered off. Bear left with Sparrow shortly after that.

Owl and River sat with Fixit and Chalk for a while longer, not saying much, just keeping one another company. Fixit found himself thinking again of the old days in Pioneer Square, where their lives had been less complicated. He wished again that they could go back. He wished they could have their evenings together with stories after dinner from Owl. He felt rootless and disconnected from everything, and it bothered him more than he could say.

When the sun sank west toward the mountains, Owl told River they should go find Hawk and see if anything had changed. "Remember what I said," she admonished Fixit and Chalk before leaving. "Stay inside the camp and close to other people. Don't go off alone."

Both boys nodded. But after she was out of earshot, Chalk said, "She worries too much."

"That's her job," Fixit replied.

"Well, I think she's working overtime at it. She looks awfully tired. Did you see her face?"

Fixit nodded. "I saw."

He didn't like the way Owl looked, either. She hadn't looked good for some time now, ever since losing Squirrel, and none of them knew what to do about it. It wasn't the sort of thing you could address directly. You could suggest she get some more sleep and not try to do so much, but you couldn't just come out and tell her she wasn't looking well. At least, he couldn't. Maybe River could.

He would say something to River, he decided. Owl might listen to River.

They sat quietly for a time as the sun continued its slow journey toward the mountains behind them, the heat of the day pooling and settling like soup in a cauldron. The sounds of the camp changed as work was put aside in favor of dinner preparations. There wasn't much to eat these days, and everything was strictly rationed. The foraging groups were finding less and less from which to make a meal, which was another reason they needed to move somewhere else. This spot was used up, and the camp was in danger of becoming a breeding ground for bad things.

Fixit thought again of the monster, picturing it in his mind one more time before brushing it aside. It didn't help to think on it.

"Let's do what Owl says and stay inside the camp," he said finally. "You know, stick together."

"We're always together," Chalk pointed out.

Fixit shrugged. "I'm just saying."

They sat quietly for a few minutes more and then rose to go off and eat their dinner.

TWENTY-THREE

It was shortly after midday of the following day that Logan Tom pulled the Ventra 5000 onto the bridge that crossed north over the Columbia River to the refugee children's camp and was confronted by a cluster of barricades and armed guards. Suspicious looks greeted his appearance, cast first toward the rune-carved black staff he was carrying and then toward his passenger. While Kirisin had the basic appearance of a human, there was no mistaking that the strange pointed ears and slanted eyebrows marked him as something more. The commander of the bridge defenders was summoned, took a quick look at things, and politely but firmly asked Logan and Kirisin to wait where they were for just a few minutes more.

"Seeking to pass any decision as to what to do with us on to someone else," Logan said to the boy after the commander had departed.

"Don't they know who you are?" Kirisin asked him.

"They know *what* I am, but not *who* I am. Big difference. If Hawk and the Ghosts haven't made it here, no one will know anything at all about us." He sighed. "It's happened before. It'll happen again."

"Won't they let us cross? They won't turn us away, will they?" Kirisin paused. "Do you think that Praxia and the others are here?"

Now, that last was a good question, Logan thought. He shook his head at the boy, indicating his lack of a helpful answer. They should have caught up with Praxia and the other two Elves by now. Should have found them somewhere along the road coming up. But they had seen no sign of the Elves at all, and now Logan was starting to worry that something might have happened to them. And to the Loden Elfstone, which contained the bulk of the Elven nation, its talismanic tree, and its city. Logan didn't like to think what that would mean.

They were silent after that while they waited, surrounded by guards arrayed loosely about the Ventra, weapons not leveled but ready, eyes watchful. Logan didn't blame them. In their place, he would have assumed the same stance. He glanced past them to the barricades and then beyond to where a small cluster of men and women worked over what looked to be wires attached to detonators. He had done enough work with explosives while he was with Michael to know what he was looking at. The defenders of the camp were set to blow the bridge if they felt the barricades were in danger of being breached by an enemy.

He wondered if they had a specific enemy in mind. He wondered if they knew about the demon-led armies working their way inland from the coastal regions. Given that they had fled north from Los Angeles, it seemed likely they did.

"I'm worried about Angel Perez, too," Kirisin said suddenly. Logan looked over at him. "We left her just down the river with Larkin Quill, a former Tracker that Sim knows." He hesitated, as if he wanted to say something more. "He was looking after her until she was well enough to come join us. But we never heard anything more. She should be here, too. If she isn't, we need to find her."

Logan nodded without saying anything that would commit him. He couldn't make Kirisin any sort of promise at this point. He wasn't sure what he would and wouldn't be able to do. Obviously, it would help to have another Knight of the Word in their camp. But he couldn't be sure how fit she was or even if he could get to her. The demons under that old man would be coming as quickly as they could manage. Moving an army north through the mountains would take time, even if the demon drove them hard. But Logan could not depend on gaining more than a handful of days before the leading elements caught up to them and began efforts at forcing a crossing.

He couldn't even promise himself that he would go back and look for Simralin, something he wanted desperately to do.

He shook his head. Mostly, he needed to get everyone moving. The longer they delayed in getting to the haven that Hawk was supposed to lead them to, the greater the danger that they wouldn't reach it at all.

There was sudden movement from behind the barricades and guards. The commander of the bridge defense had returned in the company of two women. A small, intense woman with short-cropped blond hair and a determined step was in the lead. But it was the bronze-skinned woman walking next to her that caught his eye immediately.

Or, more particularly, the black staff she carried.

"Angel!" Kirisin shouted, scrambling out of the vehicle and rushing toward her.

A couple of the guards tried to stop him, but he was too quick for them, and the next thing anyone knew he had reached the second woman and flung his arms around her in an effusive hug. Logan watched in amusement, then extracted himself from the Ventra and walked over to join them.

The woman with the short blond hair

stepped forward to greet him. "I'm Helen Rice," she said, extending her hand. "I'm leader of this camp."

"Logan Tom," he replied, taking her hand in his own. Her grip was firm and reassuring. He liked how it felt. He shifted his gaze to Kirisin and the young woman he was hugging. "Angel Perez?"

The young woman gave him a quick smile. Then she whispered something to Kirisin, who immediately released her and stepped back, blushing as he did so. "Sorry," the boy mumbled.

Angel Perez reached out and ruffled his hair. "I'm glad to see you, too. We were worried about you." She extended her hand to Logan, who took it in his own. "I'm Angel," she affirmed. "It's good to have you here, Logan." She paused, looked past him, and then looked back again quickly. "Only the two of you? I was expecting quite a few more. What's happened to the rest of the Elves?"

"It's a long story," Logan said, shrugging.

"Let's go somewhere else for that," Helen Rice suggested. She glanced at the Ventra. "Someone will bring your AV along later."

She led them back through the barricades and guards and into the camp beyond. Logan took in the sprawl of tents and makeshift shelters, cooking fires, fenced-off areas of supplies and equipment, and armed guards who stood watch almost everywhere. Children were gathered in small groups within the perimeter of their cordon, working and playing, heads turning at his approach, eyes studying him briefly before shifting away. The children looked better than he thought they had a right to given the obvious lack of adequate food and shelter. Some even smiled.

Helen Rice took them into a large tent where they took seats around a folding table. "We can talk here," she told them.

She brought bottles of water for Logan and Kirisin, and then sat down next to Angel to listen while they related what had happened to the Elves. The Knight of the Word and the boy took turns explaining the parts they had played, the boy the more effusive, the Knight the more reticent. It took some time to cover it all, and both Angel and Helen stopped them often with questions along the way. But in the end they got through it, and it was their turn to ask questions.

Kirisin was first, unable to wait any longer. "Has Praxia reached you? Did she get here before us?"

Angel shook her head. "None of the Elves has gotten here yet, Kirisin. We've been wondering what happened to them. Now we know. I guess they're still trying to fight their way clear."

"But Praxia has the Loden!" The boy was beside himself. "We have to find her!"

Logan put a hand on his shoulder to calm

him. "Right after we're done here." He looked back at Helen and Angel. "What about a group of street kids called the Ghosts? Are they here?"

"For several days now," Helen Rice answered. "The boy Hawk said to look for you, that you would be coming."

Then she explained what Hawk had done some weeks earlier to gain a crossing for them over the bridge, how he had used some sort of magic, how astonishing it had been to witness. They had been convinced about him then, but now confidence was eroding. He claimed he was there to lead, but so far he hadn't taken them anywhere. What he had done was lead a monster to their camp, and the monster was killing the children.

"This monster is probably a demon," Angel added. "It killed Larkin Quill in his cottage, Kirisin. I was there when it happened. I couldn't stop it. I'm sorry about that."

Kirisin looked stricken, but didn't say anything. Logan guessed that everything he was hearing at this point was just another piece of bad news to add to what he was already dealing with. He hoped the subject of Simralin wouldn't come up.

"I can tell you about this boy," Logan said to Helen Rice. "He was born a gypsy morph, a thing of wild magic. But his past was hidden from him, and he only just found out the truth about himself. He was sent to lead these

397

children and their caregivers and some others who will join in the march to a place of safety."

He paused. "The end is coming for this world and its inhabitants. Most will be destroyed in a cataclysm more devastating than anything that's occurred yet. We have to get to where we are going before that happens."

"Hawk said just this morning — finally — that we can leave," Angel offered. "Whatever was holding him back isn't doing so anymore. We're preparing to set out tomorrow."

"Tell me about this monster that you think is a demon," Logan said. "You said you saw it?"

Angel nodded. "I saw it from as close as I am to you. Too close. Big and mutated — a human once, I think. It came through the floor to get to Larkin, and then it came after me. I used the staff's magic, but even that was barely enough."

"I've heard of a demon like that. It travels with the old man, the demon that's tracking you. But what does it want?"

"Hawk says it wants him. He says it was sent to kill him."

Logan sighed, folding himself forward about his staff, contemplative. "That's probably so. Kill him, and there's no escape for any of us." He looked at her. "We better find this thing before it manages to get to him."

She nodded, and for a moment no one said anything.

Then Logan stood up. "I need to speak with Hawk. Maybe you should all come with me."

All four went, wending their way through the controlled chaos of the camp. Everywhere, preparations for leaving were under way. Clothes and bedding, food stores, ammunition and weapons, tools, solar batteries and the machines they powered were being packed up. Children worked alongside adults, and only the very young and their caretakers were not involved. Logan took a moment to imagine what it was going to take for all these people to get to where they were going. Even without knowing where that was, he knew it was going to take a lot.

He was surprised, as they neared the perimeter of the camp, to spy a handful of Lizards. There were perhaps twenty of them, all ages and sizes, maybe a few families come together, but maybe just strays who had found their way and stayed. No one from the camp seemed to mind that they were there, and the Lizards were keeping carefully apart. The biggest of them carried weapons, but their attention was directed out toward the barren landscape.

Hawk said there would be others. He said the King of the Silver River had told him so.

Even the youngest of the camp's children

knew of Lizards and Croaks and Spiders and other mutants. They would have been taught early on in life to be wary of them, to avoid them whenever possible.

What must they think now, finding themselves banded together like this?

What will they think when they see the Elves?

He found Hawk and most of the other Ghosts clustered around a map that Owl had unfolded across her lap. The kids looked up as the newcomers approached, and immediate shouts of greeting were issued to Logan from one and all. Panther rushed forward and reached for his hand, gripping it firmly in his own.

" 'Bout time you got here. We got ourselves a mess! Gotta move all these people, gotta pack up all their stuff, gotta figure out where to go. On top of that, we got ourselves a stump head trying to kill anything it can get its hands on!"

"So I heard." Logan gave the boy's hand a firm squeeze. "Good thing we got you to handle it for us."

Panther made a rude noise. "Yeah, like that's gonna happen. Thing almost killed Bird-Man up there in the mountains. Along with Bear, Cheney, and even Kitty Cat. We need more claws to deal with that frickin' thing. If we even ever see it again. It's like a ghost. You know it almost got her, too, don't you?" He gestured toward Angel Perez.

"She's a Knight of the Word like you, so what does that say? Ain't nothing can stop it?"

He gave Panther a look. "We'll see."

He glanced at the others and greeted them by name. Only Fixit and Chalk were missing. He took a moment to lean down and give Owl a hug. It was an impulsive, totally out-of-character act for him, but something about her steadying presence made him want to do it. She laughed lightly and hugged him back.

"Hawk." He greeted the gypsy morph last, the boy with the magic. Hawk nodded without saying anything, waiting to see what this was about. "Is it finally time to start everyone moving?"

"Tomorrow morning," Hawk answered him.

Logan nodded. "Heard about the demon. You feel pretty certain that it's after you?"

He didn't need to explain any further what he was talking about. Hawk shrugged. "More than pretty certain. I looked into its eyes out there when it had me cornered. I could tell what it was thinking. I could see it. It's come for me. It almost had me, too. I don't think even Cheney could have stopped it."

Logan nodded. "Maybe not. But we're going to have to find something that can. It won't quit, even if we move the camp. Demons don't give up." He paused. "If it's after you, then taking all these children is a way to get at you. It probably hopes to lure you

401

outside the camp, maybe make you come looking for it."

"I don't think that's what it's doing," Angel interrupted suddenly. Logan turned. "I saw it, too. I looked into its eyes, and I think I know what it's doing. I think it's toying with us."

Logan took a moment to consider. "Could be. Some demons are like that. They play with humans when they have the chance. This one might feel so superior physically that it isn't worried about getting to Hawk. It might be showing off for us."

"For cat's sake!" Sparrow snapped. "Can't we just go out there and find it and kill it?"

Logan shook his head. "That job belongs to Angel and myself. The Ghosts have to stay inside the perimeter of the camp and watch out for each other." He looked at Hawk. "They have to look out for you, in particular."

"I have to look out for them," Hawk replied firmly.

Panther rolled his eyes and wheeled away. "Group hug," he muttered blackly.

Logan ignored him. Panther was just being Panther. "Just remember what I said. Stay together."

"So you gonna go out and hunt this thing been taking all the children, Mister Knight of the Word?" Panther demanded, wheeling back. "Want me to go with you? Look out for you?"

"What's your problem, Panther?" Sparrow snapped at him, blue eyes bright with anger. "Didn't you hear what he just said? We're supposed to stay out of this."

Panther glanced over. "I heard him. I just don't think he meant it. He needs someone he can depend on to back him up out there. Who's he got besides me?"

"Stop trying to get your way, Panther," Owl said quietly. "We need to stay out of this business. It will be enough if we can be of help to Hawk tomorrow. He's going to need all of us."

Bear muttered his agreement, and River added hers. Panther looked at them in turn and then shrugged. "Ain't no skin off my baby-smooth butt. Do what you want." He knelt next to Owl, feigning disinterest. "Let me see that map again."

Logan waited a moment, then said, "One more thing. I want you to keep Kirisin with you, as well. I want you to look after him the same way you look after each other."

The Ghosts waited, questioning looks on their faces. Kirisin had gone unnoticed up to this point, standing in the background while the others talked. Now Logan reached back and dragged him forward. "This is Kirisin. He's an Elf."

"Yeah, right," Panther sneered, turning his attention back to the map. "And I'm a dragon."

"No, look," said Sparrow quietly, eyes fixed on Kirisin. "Look at his ears. They're pointed."

"Like in Owl's stories," echoed Bear. "Pointed."

"Maybe he is an Elf," River said doubtfully.

Panther looked up again, took in Kirisin's face, and shook his head. "What's wrong with you, River? Ain't no such things as Elves. He's what he is — a kid with pointy ears. Ain't his fault. But he ain't no Elf, so let that one go. Frickin' hell."

"Can't do that," Logan replied. "Kirisin really is an Elf, one of an entire nation that's meant to join up with us. You need to know some things about him, so listen up."

Patiently, Logan explained Kirisin's background, including in his explanation a brief history of the Elves. Which, in fact, was all he could give, since he didn't know much anyway. Angel joined in, adding what she knew from her time spent within the Cintra and Arborlon. She insisted that everything Logan was telling them was true, that she had seen it, that she hadn't believed it, either, at first. The Ghosts listened attentively, all but Panther who kept poking at the map as if he had better things to do. But Logan could tell he was paying attention.

When the explanation was finished, the Ghosts looked at one another wordlessly. "Elves don't look like I thought they would,"

Bear said.

"Yeah, they don't look that much different from us," Sparrow added. She stepped forward and stuck out her hand. "I'm Sparrow," she said to Kirisin.

The others followed, one by one, until only Panther was left. The boy looked at Kirisin darkly, then at Logan. "Bad enough we got to watch out for Bird-Man. Now we got Pointy-Ears to look after, too. I don't know about this."

"I haven't got time to persuade you, Panther. You have to make up your own mind. But Kirisin is every bit as important to what's going to happen to us as Hawk. That thing out there that's hunting Hawk might be hunting Kirisin, as well. So I'm asking you to take care of him. Can you do that?"

Panther shrugged. "Might be." Then he caught the look on Owl's face. "Hey, sure. We know how to take care of each other. Took care of Cat when you asked, didn't we?"

"Just do the same here." Logan glanced at Kirisin. "I'm going out to look for Praxia. You stay here. Get to know these kids. They're a good bunch."

"He'll be fine with us," Owl said at once, wheeling over to Kirisin.

They were already deep in conversation, surrounded by the other Ghosts, when Logan beckoned Angel and Helen Rice away.

■ ■ ■ ■

Within thirty minutes, Logan was back inside the Ventra 5000 and driving south across the bridge. Angel went with him, and even though he thought about telling her she should stay behind to help protect the camp, he decided not to. She understood the consequences of her coming with him as well as he did, so if she was asking to go, it must be important to her. He thought that maybe she needed to be part of the search, that she was feeling what he had felt not more than two days earlier — marginalized by her failure to change events through use of her magic and questioning her effectiveness as a Knight of the Word. Lying injured and helpless in Larkin Quill's cottage while Kirisin and his sister returned to the Elves alone and then watching Larkin die right in front of her would have done that. Perhaps, like himself, she needed to reaffirm her worth in some small way before they set out. Coming with him to find the Loden gave her that chance.

They drove without speaking for a time, climbing slowly into the high desert he thought he had left behind him for good. The day was creeping toward midafternoon, the heat thick and damp, the air hazy, and the sky bright with sunlight. Around them, the countryside began to revert. Forests and grasslands, withered and grayish to begin with, thinned and disappeared, giving way to cactus and scrub that dotted acres of sandy flats bracketed by mountains distant and flat-surfaced against the emptiness of the horizon.

"How long have you been doing this?" he asked her finally, breaking the silence.

"About six years. You?"

"Ten. I was eighteen when I started."

"Sixteen," she said. "I had just lost my best friend — my mentor and protector from when I was a little girl."

"Lost mine just before I started, too. Michael. Same thing. He saved me in a compound raid, raised me, and trained me. He was the leader of a group of raiders that attacked enemy camps in the Midwest. A good man, like a father to me."

They drove on a bit more. Logan risked a quick glance at Angel Perez, taking in her features, her dark olive skin, her black eyes and hair, her young features. Just a girl, really. He looked back at the road.

"You think we're all that's left?" she asked him.

He nodded, knowing right away what she was asking. "Yeah, I think maybe so. If there's anybody else, I haven't heard of them."

"So this is it, huh? This . . . migration to wherever we're going, following Hawk to wherever he's taking us, this is what's left?"

He nodded. "This is what's left."

"What if he's wrong, Logan? Hawk, I mean."

"He isn't. He's what he says he is. He's a gypsy morph, a creature formed of the Word's magic and sent to save what's left of us." He looked over at her. "I believe that."

She studied him a moment, then nodded. "You don't look like someone who could be made to believe something that wasn't so. You don't seem like you could be fooled easily."

"Maybe. But in this case I've witnessed what he can do firsthand. He saved my life when I was dying just by touching me. The Ghosts say he saved their dog, too. Same way. But saving me? Well, I have to believe after that."

"Yeah, I guess so. You have to believe in something, don't you? Something more than what's in front of your eyes."

"Elves, for instance?"

She smiled, a good smile, warm and filled with mirth. "That was hard for me. Even after I found their city and was taken before their King and their High Council, I kept thinking, *How can this be? There are no such things as Elves.* But there they were, all around me." She glanced at him. "They don't much like us, Logan. They think we're responsible for all the damage that's been done, that we haven't been good caretakers of the earth."

He nodded, smiled back. "Can't do much

about that, can we? Not right now, anyway. Not until we set them free again. Then maybe we can learn something from them and do a better job next time around."

Her smile faded as she looked back toward the road. "Next time," she repeated softly. She shook her head. "I wouldn't let them pen me up like that. I don't care what the circumstances were. I wouldn't allow it." She sighed and looked over at him. "You saw it happen, didn't you?"

"I saw. It was painless, I guess. One minute they were there, the next they weren't. That boy — Kirisin — put them all inside the Loden Elfstone and took them away." He shook his head. "He's the one I feel for. He's the one who's responsible for them. He put them inside; he has to let them out. He has that power. But if we don't find Praxia and get that Elfstone back . . ." He trailed off. "Well, I wouldn't want to be him."

"Doesn't seem fair. Putting all this on his shoulders. He's just a boy." She compressed her lips in a tight line, frowning. "He didn't ask for any of this, did he?"

"None of them did, come to that," Logan responded. "But that's what life does to you. It gives you a whole lot of stuff you don't ask for and expects you to deal with it. No complaining, no excuses."

They crossed a dry wash where the asphalt road had given way and lay scattered all about in broken chunks. The Ventra skirted most of it and crawled over the rest, big and tough and able. There wasn't much short of a wall that could stop it. Logan loved how it handled. Maybe he liked it better than the Lightning, he thought.

"What happened to his sister?" Angel asked suddenly.

Logan felt his throat constrict. *Simralin.* An image of her face appeared in his mind, blond and smiling that crooked half smile. He shook his head. "I don't know. She stayed behind with the King and the army that was holding off the demons and once-men. She said she was the only one who could lead them to us once they had done all they could." He kept his eyes on the road. "We're still waiting."

"Kirisin is very close to her," Angel said. "He must be wild with worry."

Logan didn't answer. He was thinking about his own feelings, about his own sense of loss. If Simralin didn't make it, he wasn't sure what he would do. He'd tried hard not to think of her, but she was always in the forefront of his thoughts. He saw her all the time, watched her smile, heard her voice, smelled her scent when she leaned close . . .

"Maybe we need to look for her, too," Angel suggested.

He shook his head. "One thing at a time. The Loden is more important."

"How are we supposed to find it, anyway?"

He wasn't sure, of course. He could try using the vehicle's tracking system, but he knew it was unreliable. No way to differentiate between the things it would pick up on the screen. He had been hoping that he would have help from Trim. Without trying to be apparent about it, he had been searching the skies for the owl, thinking that since Trim had come to him before when he needed to find Kirisin and the Elven talismans, maybe he would come again.

"We'll find it," he insisted without offering any more.

Eventually, they did. But not until they had driven for several hours and the sun had begun to dip into the western horizon toward the Cascades. Then, all at once, Trim appeared, winging his way out of the skies, swooping down in front of the AV, and soaring away again.

"Look at that owl!" Angel exclaimed. "It almost hit us!"

"Not likely," Logan said, giving her a quick grin. "That's our guide to the Loden. He's called Trim. The Lady sent him to me when I came to find Kirisin. We just need to follow him."

They did so, working their way down the road as the shadows lengthened and the light faded. Logan began to worry that they might be getting too close to advance elements of the demon-led army. But they weren't yet back to where the skrails had attacked and seized Kirisin several days earlier, so he could assume that Praxia and the other two Elves had come farther than that, at least. His worst fear was that all three had been captured and taken back to the old man. If that had happened, he might never learn what had become of the Elfstone.

But within half an hour Trim took them off the road and down a dirt trail into a dry wash studded with scrub and cactus. They followed the wash for maybe five hundred yards, searching through layers of shadows and clumps of rocks and earth.

"Logan, over there!" Angel exclaimed suddenly.

He had already seen it. A pair of military jeeps sat abandoned in the center of the wash, a body hanging off the driver's seat of one, a second body sprawled on the hood of the other, and blood splashed everywhere. More bodies lay scattered on the ground nearby. Logan made a quick count. Four, five, six that he could see. He climbed out of the Ventra, Angel a step behind him. Both held their black staffs ready, eyes searching the wash and the high banks for any sign of life. But there was none, and the runes carved into the wood remained dark. The wash was a killing ground empty of life. Logan looked at the dead, the ground on which they lay, the jeeps and the tracks they had left, taking it all in, assessing it. Then he walked over to have a closer look at the bodies. He found the two male Elves lying together, riddled with bullets from automatic weapons. The men around them were wearing a patchwork collection of army surplus and makeshift insignia. Arrows and javelins had done for them.

He walked on, down the length of the wash and around a second bend, following a flurry of footprints. Someone running away, someone else chasing. He stopped. Ahead, draped in shadows, lay a second cluster of bodies. More would-be soldiers, their bodies heaped on top of one another. The fourth was Praxia.

He knew right away what had happened. A unit of rogue militia had found the Elves. Maybe just stumbled on them, maybe saw their tracks. They shot the male Elves in a firefight. Some of them died in the process. The three survivors went after Praxia. Caught up with her here. Big mistake. She killed them all, was killed herself. No one had survived. He knew this because a survivor would have taken one of the two jeeps, and all the tire tracks stopped where the two were parked.

He moved over to Praxia. She was propped against a large boulder, eyes closed. Patches of dried blood marked half a dozen wounds in her chest and stomach. She had been shot repeatedly. She looked frail and broken, all the toughness drained away. One hand clutched a Sig-Hauser twelve-shot automatic rapid fire, clip ejected on the ground next to her. It was a favorite weapon of militia commanders. How she had gotten hold of it or even known how to use it was a mystery.

He bent down and touched her cheek, and her eyes opened. He froze, staring at the blood-streaked face. "My hand," she whispered.

He looked down. The hand that wasn't holding the Sig-Hauser slowly opened. In the palm lay the pouch that contained the Loden Elfstone.

Her lips moved. "Tell Kirisin . . ."

Then she trailed off, and her eyes fixed. He felt her neck for a pulse, found none. He sat back on his heels, staring at her. What must it have taken for her to stay alive this long? The fight was clearly hours old.

He took the pouch from her hand, checked to make certain the Elfstone was still inside, and then slipped the pouch into his pocket.

Tell Kirisin . . .

He stood up wearily. "I'll tell him," he promised her.

Angel, standing next to him by now, didn't say anything, keeping her thoughts to herself. Logan searched Praxia's young face. Just a girl, he thought, but she had fought and died hard. He thought suddenly of Simralin. He tried to imagine how he would feel if something happened to her.

"We'd better bury them," Angel said to him.

He nodded. "And then get back to the camp."

Without waiting for her response, he started toward the Ventra to collect the shovels.

Twenty-Four

Another sweltering day, air thick with heat and steamy dampness, sky brilliant blue beneath a sun that burned white hot and implacable.

Angel Perez plodded ahead, her boots kicking up puffs of dust as she walked flats that stretched away for miles in all directions. Grasses were few and burned crisp and sapped of color, and what trees survived were withered scarecrows, their leaves in tatters. The Cascades were behind them and fading fast into the distant haze. If there were mountains ahead, they were not yet visible to the naked eye. Bluffs crested the horizon north, long stretches so distant they lacked clear definition.

No water was visible anywhere, and in the heat of the midday it felt as if there never would be.

The caravan stretched away for the better part of a mile, a collection of trucks and AVs, wagons and haulers, and people afoot. Supplies and equipment were loaded on the wagons and haulers along with the smaller children and the injured and sick. The AVs carried others, a select few who needed special attention or to whom had been assigned special tasks that required extra mobility: scouts, medics, machinists, and the like. One of the AVs just behind her, Logan Tom's Lightning S-150, carried Owl, River, Tessa, Candle, and a couple of smaller children from the camps. The older children and most of the caregivers walked, strung out through the line of vehicles in ragged clumps. Ahead, in the vanguard, Hawk led with Cheney, Panther, Bear, Sparrow, and several handfuls of armed men and women. Trailing everyone was a conglomeration of Lizards, Spiders, and other creatures, a couple of which she could not identify, even though she had thought she had seen everything there was to see by now.

It was the whole of the refugee camp save for those who had been left behind to defend the bridge. The caravan had been on the move since sunrise, traveling north and east away from the Columbia River and up into country that had once been farmland and was now dried-out hardpan. The caravan had started out as a cohesive whole, but over the course of the morning had begun to drift apart, to break into pieces that sprawled all over the flats and had taken on a segmented look.

Angel would have liked to keep everyone much closer together. Spread out as they were, they were impossible to protect. But she had realized early on that this was the best she could hope for. Any organization beyond what she was seeing was all but impossible. Too many children, too few adults, too little discipline. They were doing the best they could, and that would have to suffice. By nightfall, they would be back together, and by morning they would regroup to begin the march anew. In the meantime, she would just have to hope that an enemy force didn't catch them out in the open.

She glanced over at Kirisin, walking next to her, and felt her throat constrict. His face was so sad it made her heart break. She wished there were something she could do for him, something she could say. But she knew there wasn't. He would have to get through this on his own.

He caught her looking at him and gave her a quick smile. "I'm all right," he assured her. "Really, I am."

She nodded, said nothing. She glanced ahead to where Hawk was leading, moving at a steady pace, looking fit and ready. Cheney slouched at his side, shaggy and insolent, big head swaying as he walked, a mass of bristling hair and muscle. She didn't like the dog. She didn't trust him. But he seemed to belong with the Ghosts, as independent-minded and cocksure as they were. They seemed of a piece, and she was not the one who could pass judgment on that arrangement.

Kirisin, who up until now had barely spoken two words, suddenly said, "Do you think she might have gotten away if she hadn't been protecting the Loden?"

She shook her head. "No, Kirisin. Even without the Elfstone she wouldn't have escaped. Responsibility for the Elfstone wouldn't have slowed her down or changed her approach. Praxia was tough and smart, and she did the best she could. It just wasn't enough."

"But having responsibility for the Loden might have altered the way she was doing things." He glanced quickly at her. "I'm sorry. I know I shouldn't think like this."

Angel sighed. *Then stop doing so.* But she didn't say it, even though a part of her wanted to. She understood why he would be so insecure about Praxia. The boy had seen a lot of people die who had tried to help him, and the accumulation alone would breed substantial guilt. He was still very young, she reminded herself, and he wasn't all that well equipped to deal with any of this.

"She told you she envied you for what you were doing, didn't she?" she asked gently. "She said she wished it could have been her.

Well, in a way, she got her wish. She died knowing that she had done something that mattered. You have to let her have that, Kirisin, and not diminish her sacrifice by questioning whether you could have done something to avoid it."

She looked off into the distance, measuring the stretch that lay immediately ahead, wondering if they could cross it before sunset. "None of us could have changed what happened without knowing of it ahead of time. And even then . . ."

She trailed off, glanced over at him, waited. He mulled it over for a minute, then nodded. "I know it's so. But I can't help wondering anyway." He was silent a moment. "I guess I think about Praxia because I'm worried about Simralin."

This is what's really troubling him, she thought. His sister. She imagined that the boy had been thinking of little else ever since they had separated in the Cintra. That was almost a week ago now, and there had been no word of her. No word of any of the Elves who had remained behind with their King to slow the demon advance. It was hard not to think the worst.

"Simralin is experienced in staying alive," she said to him. "You said yourself that she is the best at what she does. I think she'll be all right. Maybe it's just taken longer to break off the fight than expected. Maybe they've just come a different way. A longer way, one that keeps them safer. There could be a lot of reasons why she isn't here yet, Kirisin."

"I just don't like it that we left her," he persisted. "I should have stayed with her."

"I know that's how you feel, but that would have been foolish. She stayed behind so that you could escape safely. Besides, you gave her the blue Elfstones. If she was in real danger, she could have used them."

"Maybe." He wasn't convinced. He scuffed at the dusty earth with the toe of his boot. "If she could figure out how to use them."

"She watched you, didn't she? I did, too. We both saw how it was done, what was required. We talked about it. I think she would find a way if it was needed."

She watched him lift a hand to his chest and finger the bulk of the Loden through the fabric of his tunic. "I wish this was over. I wish we were there, wherever *there* is." He looked at her. "Does Hawk have any idea how far we are going?"

She shook her head. "I don't think so. If he does, he isn't saying. He just seems to be following his nose. His instincts are telling him where he is supposed to take us. The girl, Tessa, says that's how it works. She insists that's enough." She shook her head. "I don't know if anyone much believes that, but it's all we've got to work with."

They were quiet for a few minutes, concen-

421

trating on walking, on the movement of their feet, placing one in front of the other, the repetition providing a strange sort of comfort. Angel glanced at the sky, at the white-hot ball of the sun, at the blue sweep surrounding it. She wished it would rain, but she knew it wouldn't.

"I guess we have to have faith in him," Kirisin said suddenly. "The same way we had faith in what we were doing when we went searching for the Loden and didn't know where it was or how we would find it. Sometimes faith in something is all you have."

"Sometimes," she agreed, giving him a smile.

She thought suddenly of Ailie, something she hadn't done for a while. Losing the tatterdemalion had tested her own faith, but she had gotten past it. In an odd way, it had even acted to focus her on what she must do for those she was trying to help. Ailie had told her she was there to be her conscience, to whisper in her ear when she needed to rethink something. But without Ailie to prod her, she had no one but herself to rely on, and it had made her more careful than ever about thinking things through before she acted. It wasn't that she was afraid of making a mistake so much as it was not wanting to disappoint Ailie. She owed her that much.

She glanced ahead again where Hawk walked side by side with Panther. How much pressure must he be feeling, she wondered, after what had happened last night?

"I'm telling you, Bird-Man, they'll be back!"

Panther was so insistent about it that Hawk almost felt sorry for him. The other was trying hard to make Hawk feel better when doing so was impossible, and it was painful to witness. Say anything, Panther apparently had decided, to make it seem as though somehow it would all work out.

But Hawk knew better.

"Look, it's just like I said," Panther went on. "Fixit wanders off and Chalk goes looking for his dim-brained friend 'cause Fixit never knows what's going on anyway. Chalk thinks he'll find him, like he's done before back in the city, but he gets himself lost because he isn't in the city anymore and can't find his way out of a closet. He wanders around all night, maybe sleeps, too, wakes up or whatever and starts back. He gets back, finds out Fixit didn't go anywhere and the only one missing is him. But by then, it's too late to let us know what's happened. We've left, so now the two of them are stuck at the bridge until the rest of the force can join us."

He paused, as if considering the reasonableness of his own argument, and then abruptly threw up his hands. "You know, it's not like there's any way they can tell us what's happened! It's not like there's cells or radios or anything to call us up on!"

"I know," Hawk said quietly. He glanced over at the other. "I hope you're right."

"But you don't think I am, is that it?"

Hawk shrugged, shook his head. "I don't know."

"That's right, you don't know!" Panther was scowling, his frustration getting the better of him. "You don't know a lot of stuff. Just because you're some sort of fairy creature all full up with magic and special powers doesn't mean you see things the right way all the time!"

"Okay, Panther."

"Doesn't mean that you got to be responsible for everyone, either. They're big boys and girls, all but maybe Candle. You can't be standing around keeping an eye on them every minute. You can't expect —"

Sparrow pushed up beside him, her face intense. "Give it a rest, Panther. This isn't helping."

Panther glanced over dismissively. "You got something to say, say it to him. He's the one needs it."

She shifted the weight of the Parkhan Spray from one shoulder to the other, a gesture that caused Hawk to glance over warily. "Just stop talking about it," she snapped, her eyes dark with anger and frustration. She was on the verge of tears. "We hate what's happened, and we all wish we'd kept better watch over those two. How many times have we warned them, all of us? But talking about it just makes everyone feel even worse. It doesn't do any good to shove it in Hawk's face and say, *I told you so.* We know all that, so let's give him a break, okay?"

"I'm saying he's not to blame, Sparrow, case you weren't listening to me." Panther was unwilling to back down. "I'm saying the same thing you are. But he's the one won't let it go, not me. He's the one thinks everything's his fault since he's leader and high mucky-muck and what have you. He's the one wants to take on everything that happens and make it personal."

He went silent, momentarily talked out. They plodded on for a few moments without saying anything more, flushed with the heat of the argument and its genesis. Hawk watched Cheney as he stalked ahead of them, his shaggy presence no longer as comforting as it had once been. In the city, Cheney would have warned them of unseen dangers. He would have guarded and protected them; he would have kept the bad things out. But out here, with no doors or windows or walls, what could he do? There was too much open space, too many ways the bad things could get at you.

He felt a sudden pang of regret, thinking of Cheney this way. He had saved them so many times, and still it wasn't enough. It was unfair to expect more. He expected it of himself, though. Even knowing it was taking on more than he could manage. Especially here. Panther was right; sometimes there was nothing you could do to save people; sometimes you just had to let go of them.

He broke away from Panther and Sparrow and sprinted up beside his dog. Cheney didn't so much as glance at him. He just kept walking, one paw in front of the other, big head swaying from side to side, heavy muscles rolling beneath his shaggy coat. Hawk walked next to him, keeping pace, his mind awash with unrealized expectations of how he had envisioned things would be and stark memories of other tragedies that had claimed the lives of other Ghosts. Mouse and Heron. Squirrel. Each time, he had felt like this — bereft, helpless, furious with himself, frustrated with his inability to act.

Behind him, he heard Sparrow and Panther whispering. They were all wondering the same thing: if he was as magical as he was supposed to be, then why couldn't he do more? Could he even do the one thing he had promised? Could he take them to a place where they would all be safe? He didn't know. He couldn't be sure of anything. All he could do was try to follow through and hope that somehow he would find a way.

But telling this to himself didn't make him feel any better. So much depended on him.

Even when he could stop thinking about Tessa and their unborn child, even when he could reduce the numbers of those he led to only those who were his immediate family, he was confounded by the enormity of his task.

His instincts guided him, just as the King of the Silver River had said they would, just as they had from the moment of his return. But his instincts were all he had. It didn't seem like enough.

Cheney veered suddenly and brushed against him with his big head. Hawk side-stepped, thinking he was the one who had veered out of his path, caught up in his musings. Then the big dog did it again, a deliberate act that conveyed an unmistakable meaning.

Tears filled Hawk's eyes, and he wiped them away quickly. He reached down and rubbed the grizzled head, smiling faintly. "Me, too," he whispered.

He is never a good fit for his family, he tells his best friend not long after they meet. He is an outsider almost from the beginning, for as far back as he can remember, seemingly forever. It isn't that anyone wants it that way. It's just how things work out. He isn't like them. He isn't a worker, a toiler, a committed survivor. He barely cares about the world around him. His mind is always somewhere else, never on the task at hand. He is unreliable, they say. He is a dreamer.

He knows this is so and that it isn't a good thing in the eyes of the others, but there is nothing he can do to change it.

His family is a large one, so the care and protection of the whole take precedence over worrying about the one. His mother spends time with him when he is little, fussing over him the way mothers do over small children. These are his fondest memories. She encourages his artistic pursuits, indulges his talent, his creativity. No harm in letting him be a child for just a little while. She thinks it will all drift away as he gets older, that he will move on to other things as he matures.

But he doesn't. He isn't like that. He isn't the sort of kid whose passions ebb and flow with the years. He is formed early on, shaped by his devotion to his artistic discoveries, by his need to explore things that no one but he can see. It is a useless talent in a world where everything is about being pragmatic, about staying alive and staying safe. He doesn't worry about such things; he worries about how he will make his drawings turn out the way he sees them in his mind. He does his work, and he fulfills his family obligations. Most of the time, at least. But he doesn't do anything more than that. He doesn't go the extra mile, as his older brothers keep telling him he must. He doesn't prepare himself against the unexpected. He doesn't live in preparation for what might happen. He lives in the moment.

When his mother and next oldest brother die after becoming afflicted by one of the endless plagues that scour their already ravaged community, their tinderbox fortress, a fresh siege mentality takes hold. The family must work harder, be more vigilant, and keep closer watch. He does not think this will help; in truth, he thinks nothing will help. They are victims of times and events that are overwhelming. They are trapped in their lives like rats in cages. They are dead men walking.

He doesn't let this thinking dominate him the way he thinks it probably dominates his brothers. He refuses. He is caught up in the magic of his art, and in art there is escape from the realities of life. There is peace and beauty and a sense of satisfaction. He cannot change the world around him, but he can make a stab at changing it in his drawings.

He becomes more and more of an oddity to his family. They are angry with and disappointed in him, and they no longer bother to hide it. They have come to view his behavior as a burden on the family — one that they increasingly see as unnecessary. If he is to be a part of the family, he must change. He must become like them — hardened to the future, focused on survival, willing to put aside childish pursuits in favor of mature commitments.

He is eleven years old.

He tries to live up to their expectations, but it

is impossible for him. He can carry out the tasks they give him, can fulfill the obligations he is assigned, but he cannot become what they are. Father, brothers, aunts, uncles, and cousins, they are all of a piece, and he does not fit.

A few of the younger cousins show interest in his drawings and his vision of things they cannot see. But their elders quickly discourage them and direct their attention elsewhere. They are told not to spend time with him, and are given work that will make certain that they can't. It is all done subtly and surreptitiously, but he sees what is happening. His isolation grows. His sense of disconnection increases.

One day, he is asked to accompany his father and two of his brothers on a foraging expedition that will take them down out of the foothills in which they reside to a nearby ghost town. It is an expedition that requires several nights away from home. He senses there is something odd in the way his father makes the request, but accepts that he must do as he is told.

When he returns, all of his drawings and art supplies are gone. He searches for them everywhere, but they are nowhere to be found. No one claims to know what has become of them. Several of his brothers suggest he has misplaced them. His father tells him to forget about them and think about more important things.

He is devastated. His art is all he has that he cares about, and now it has been taken away from him.

A week later, he leaves home in the middle of the night. He walks south and west toward the city of Seattle, a place where he knows he can find the supplies he needs. He has never been to Seattle. He has barely been anywhere and does not have experience or skill at finding his way. But he is lucky. Nothing bad happens to him in the five days it takes him to reach his goal. He is hungry and thirsty much of the time, having not thought to take much of anything with him to eat or drink. He reaches the city in one piece and begins his search.

Fortunately, his search puts him in a place where he encounters the Ghosts. He becomes a member of their family and finds a place where he is accepted for who and what he is. His passion for drawing is indulged. His eccentricities are tolerated and even admired. He is given a chance to become the person he knows he is meant to be. He is loved.

But finding you, he tells his best friend over and over again, is even more important than all of this. Finding you is the best thing that ever happened to me.

Fixit stared out across the abandoned campsite, the ground empty of tents, equipment, supplies, and vehicles, cleared of people. The wind was blowing dust in sharp gusts, sweeping across the hills and scooping out the gullies. Overhead, the midday sky was cloudless,

431

and the sun was a blazing white ball in an endless blue sweep.

Chalk would have admired a day like this one, if he had been there.

Fixit kept searching the landscape, thinking that he had overlooked something and might still find it or that he would miss something if he looked away. He already knew it was hopeless, that Chalk wasn't coming back. But he couldn't help himself; he still looked. A part of him refused to accept what the rest of him already had. A part of him still hoped.

How had it happened? How had he allowed it to happen?

He blamed himself, of course. He was Chalk's only real friend, and he knew that the thing hunting them was out there, stealing kids from the camp. He knew that they were supposed to look after each other, and he had resolved to do his part. But somehow he hadn't. Somehow, Chalk had slipped away when he wasn't looking, had stepped just out of view when he wasn't paying attention, and that was all it took. The other Ghosts had told him that Chalk would be back, that he had wandered off before — seemingly forgetting that Fixit was always the one who had wandered off, not Chalk. Or maybe hoping that he would forget the truth of things, and be encouraged.

Didn't matter. They were gone, following Hawk to their new refuge, wherever that was.

All of them save those who had remained behind to defend the bridge against the army coming up from the south. And himself, because he refused to leave his best friend. The others had wanted him to come, but he couldn't. He had to stay. As long as there was hope for Chalk, he had to wait. Maybe they were right. Maybe Chalk had wandered off and would be back. Maybe he needed Fixit.

Maybe.

He hugged himself against a chill that ran through him at the thought of what he knew was true and couldn't accept. He felt tears welling up, and he tightened his lips and eyes against them.

Then he heard footsteps behind him. Composing himself quickly, he turned. Logan Tom was there.

"We could use your help at the bridge, Fixit. They're finishing the wiring, and you know as much about it as any of the adults. More, even, than me. Will you help?"

Fixit shook his head. "I have to . . ."

"You have to keep an eye out for Chalk," Logan finished. "I know. But you can do it from there. It will help pass the time if you do something other than just stand around. And it will help us, as well."

Fixit stared at the other, at his hard face, at the grip he kept on the black staff. Nothing ever bothered him. He was as steady as the rising and setting of the sun. He wished he could be like that.

"All right," he said quietly. "I'll help."

"Fixit," Logan Tom called after him as he started to walk away. "Don't give up hope. We still don't know."

Fixit nodded, his thoughts dark and angry. *Maybe you don't,* he told the other silently, *but I do.*

He kept walking.

TWENTY-FIVE

Sometime during the night, Catalya disappeared.

She had insisted on staying behind when the remainder of the camp departed with Hawk and Angel, arguing that she could do more good by staying than leaving. When pressed for an explanation, she had shrugged the matter away by telling Logan it was obvious if you thought it through. Hadn't she saved him once already? What if he needed her to save him again? She was only half joking about this, and her determination to remain close to him was unshakable. What was really at work was her fear of losing him again, something she seemed terrified would happen. He had almost died once already and then disappeared for days afterward in search of the Elves and their talismans and been seriously threatened a second time. Apparently, she had decided that enough was enough; she would take her chances sticking close to him rather than seeking safety by leaving.

He had chosen not to press the matter. When Panther's attempts at talking her out of it failed, including a futile effort at insisting that if she stayed, so would he, he saw the handwriting on the wall. Some things you had to back away from. She was sufficiently grown that she could make her own choice in the matter. He did not feel that she really belonged back with him or that her staying made him any safer, but if she felt so then it was better to let her have her way.

That was what he had thought the previous day. Now he was sorry he had not insisted she go. Early that afternoon, when his attention was focused on other things, she had suggested almost casually that she should go out in search of Chalk and the other children. She had a better chance of finding them than anyone else, she insisted; she was more experienced in these sorts of things. He had no idea why she thought that this was so, but it didn't matter because he wasn't about to agree. He told her no, pointing out that the creature stalking the children of the camp was far too dangerous to take chances with.

"Why would a monster stalking human children want anything to do with me?" she asked at once. "I'm a bigger freak than it is."

He stuck to his refusal, and when she shrugged and walked away without saying anything more, he thought that was the end of it. Obviously, he had been mistaken.

Sometimes he wondered what good he was doing. He was supposed to serve and protect those weaker and more vulnerable than himself. He was supposed to keep them safe. But when no one would listen to him, when they did whatever they chose despite his warnings — which was true of almost everyone, it sometimes seemed — what was he supposed to do? Even Simralin had refused to listen to him when he told her she should come with Kirisin and himself and flee the Cintra, that it was too dangerous to remain behind, that she would not be safe.

He hadn't allowed himself to think of her during the past few days, keeping his concerns carefully locked away and separate from his responsibilities for the inhabitants of the camp. But with the disappearance of Chalk and now Catalya, all his doubts and fears resurfaced in a rush. It was like a dam breaking, its walls giving way all at once under the crushing weight of his emotions.

He could tell himself whatever he wanted to about her, but it didn't change the truth of things. He was in love with her, and he couldn't come to terms with the idea that something might have happened to her, too.

By midday, though, two things happened that diverted his attention once more. The first was that Catalya returned, sauntering into camp with Rabbit hopping along beside her, seemingly unaware that she had done anything either unexpected or wrong. Her search had been unsuccessful, but she hadn't looked everywhere yet. There were still places she needed to search. She hadn't seen any sign of the creature or anything else, and she had never been in any danger.

It took everything Logan had not to tell her what he was really thinking, but instead to let it all pass unmentioned. He did suggest that if she was going out again, maybe he should go with her. At least they should discuss it.

Then a short while later, as he was still weighing the advisability of his suggestion, an alarm rose from the defenders on the bridge. He hurried down to see what was happening and found the men and women on watch gathered together at the bridge center pointing and gesturing toward the other side.

Skrails were landing in small groups of two and three, perhaps a dozen with as many as fifty that were still airborne. They clustered safely back from the bridge defenses, hunched over like ghouls as they stared across at the humans, eyes baleful and calculating. Beyond them, the slopes of the Cascades were blanketed with dark shapes flowing down toward the banks of the Columbia. Thousands of misshapen, nightmarish forms, they stretched away into the hazy distance for as far as the eye could see.

Logan Tom took a deep breath and exhaled slowly.

The army of demons and once-men had caught up to them.

With Helen Rice directing traffic, Logan Tom reset their defenses. It was something that had been discussed at length in the time they had been waiting for the enemy to arrive, so it didn't require much discussion now. Mostly it was a matter of making the best use of limited resources and a superior defensive position.

Logan had no idea how many of the enemy there might be, but from the look of things they numbered well over ten thousand. His own force of men and women was less than two hundred, a small contingent even against an enemy a quarter of the size of the one approaching. They would be fighting a battle they already knew they could not win. At best, they could delay the assault, could tie up the attackers long enough to allow the children and caregivers already in flight to put even more distance between them. When it became clear that the enemy was going to break through, they would blow the bridge and retreat, effectively stopping any pursuit until a second bridge or shallows could be found. Helen Rice had sent scouting parties up- and downriver for thirty miles in both directions days earlier, and neither was in evidence.

The forward defenses were situated about halfway across the bridge and consisted of steel buttresses and overturned trucks scavenged from the prior defenders and repositioned to suit Logan's needs. Heavy-caliber sprays and cannons filled the gaps. In addition, the arched bridgework formed a heavy metal canopy over the heads of the defenders. The dense foliage that Hawk had summoned to secure the bridge several weeks earlier was still flourishing, and it covered the whole of the bridge spans and trusses, forming a thick screen behind and under which the defenders could hide. From an enemy's viewpoint on the far bank, it would be difficult to tell exactly where their targets were positioned or what sort of weapons they had at their disposal.

In any case, the attackers would be forced to rely on small arms and light-caliber field weapons in making an assault. Anything heavier would chance compromising the stability of the bridge, and losing the bridge would defeat their purpose in attacking in the first place. The enemy needed it in one piece to cross.

The defenders had no such problem. Their only purpose in defending the bridge was to delay the enemy advance. If they were forced to blow the bridge earlier than planned, it wouldn't matter. Blowing the bridge was a given. But the enemy didn't know this. It didn't know that they had the necessary explosives. It would have to attack to find out. It would have to strike as hard and fast as it could in the hope of overrunning the defenders before they had a chance to do anything.

But Logan had a few surprises planned. Midway between the far bank and the forward defenses were trip wires that would trigger dozens of cluster mines designed to shatter any assault. A line of flamethrowers secured to the bridge trusses just in back of the mines could be ignited from behind the defenses. Snap spikes — wicked spring teeth secured to the bridge planking — were layered all across the two dozen or so yards right in front of the forward defenses.

If all that failed, banks of weapons were mounted three-deep behind the forward defenses in small redoubts where the defenders would make their last stand. When the defenders were overrun at last, the charges that would blow the bridge, packed in place beneath the steel spans and all along the cross-ties, could be detonated from a command station situated just at the edge of the north bank. When the bridge went up, it would take everyone with it and stop any advance in its tracks.

Logan shook his head, thinking it all through. It wasn't the greatest plan, but it was the best he could come up with. Maybe Michael, if he were there, could have come up with something better. He was always smarter than Logan when it came to battle tactics. But like so much else, that was all in the past.

The defenders finished their preparations and took their positions, watching the demonled army advance out of the mountains. Attackers continued to flood down out of the broad slopes all afternoon and into the night, gathering on the south riverbank, where their leaders began forming them up for the attack. Logan watched impassively. The attack wouldn't come until dawn; this sort of full frontal assault required a reasonable amount of light to coordinate and maneuver, and the glare from the rising sun would be in the eyes of the defenders. A flat-out strike relying on strength of numbers alone would work, too, but it would sacrifice an awful lot of men and risk mistakes that could cost the demons possession of the bridge. So they would wait.

At one point, with the sun already sinking behind the mountains, Logan went looking for Catalya, thinking to speak with her again about searching for the missing children. But no one had seen her, and his efforts to ferret her out failed. After a long, frustrating hour searching, he was forced to admit the obvious. She had ignored his advice and once again gone out alone.

Darkness settled in, and watch fires burned all across the far bank, their glow visible for miles in all directions. There were so many attackers by now that the defenders were growing disheartened. These were tough-minded men and women, guerrilla fighters from outside the compounds, experienced fighters. But even these could be intimidated by what they were seeing. Logan went out with Helen Rice to reassure them, to point out that only so many of the enemy could crowd onto the bridge at any one time and there was reason to hope that they would get in one another's way when they did so.

Afterward, he spoke alone with Helen about what to expect. She was not battle-tested, had never faced an adversary of this size, did not have the training in tactical combat that he had. Fortunately, some of her lieutenants did. They would take command of various units when the attack came. But even though Helen would cede authority on the battlefield, she would still be the one nominally responsible for deciding when it was time to give way. Logan would advise her, of course, would do his best to prepare her, but as leader of the camp the decision would be hers.

He stood down by the bridgehead after that, thinking through how the battle would be fought, searching for loopholes in his defensive plan, for possibilities he might have overlooked. Mostly, he decided, it didn't much matter. He had so few men and women fighting to hold the bridge that if they could hold the demon army off even for a single day, it would be a miracle.

He thought, too, about that old man in the gray cloak and the slouch hat. The demon Kirisin had seen in his vision. The one Angel had fought against in Anaheim. The one that kept sending its minions to kill them. The one to which Logan had lost his family twenty years earlier. He could still see the old man's face, smiling at him approvingly as he fired the Tyson Flechette into a horde of once-men attackers.

He had been promised a chance to right things with that demon if he fulfilled his mission to find and protect the gypsy morph. He thought he had done that. He had kept his bargain, and now he was beginning to wonder if the Lady intended to keep hers.

"Logan."

His thoughts scattered as he heard his name called. He turned around to find Catalya standing behind him, holding Rabbit in her arms. She was a mess. Her clothes were torn and filthy, her face streaked with dirt and sweat, and her eyes haunted. Her cat was hunched down in the cradle of her arms, eyes wide with a mix of fear and readiness. Something had scared them both badly.

"We found them," she said.

444

He knew at once. "The children?"

She nodded. "Rabbit and me. Rabbit, really. He led me to them. They were hidden behind some rocks and earth, half buried in a ravine. I might have walked right by them yesterday, but it was dark by then so I can't be sure."

"All of them?" He didn't want to ask, but he couldn't help himself. "All those that were missing?"

She took a deep breath, held it a moment, and then exhaled slowly. "I think so. They were in pieces, so it was hard to be sure."

She waited for his reaction, her face expressionless. No, he decided suddenly, changing his mind, she wasn't waiting for anything. She was in shock. She had seen something so terrible that she had been forced to lock down her emotions and retreat inside herself. It was taking everything she had just to stand there and talk to him in a composed way about what she had discovered.

"I'm sorry it had to be you," he said, wishing she had listened to him about not going out alone. He gestured at her. "Did anything happen to you? Are you all right?"

She stared at him a moment, and then looked down at herself. "Oh, this. It's nothing, Logan. I'm not hurt or anything. I just stayed long enough to bury them, to give them someplace to rest that wasn't out in the open where they might be . . ."

She shuddered, shaking her head. "I didn't have any real digging tools, and the ground was hard. It took me a while to get it done."

"You did the right thing. It was brave of you to go out like that and then stay out."

She shrugged. "I wasn't in any danger. Not really. See?" She lifted her mottled face as if to demonstrate.

"Better go get cleaned up and get some sleep," he told her. "Wash off, change your clothes, have something to eat. The demon army is here, across the river. They'll attack at sunrise."

She didn't move; she just stood there. "I'm tired of all this," she said finally.

"We all are. We all want it to end."

She bent down and set Rabbit on his feet next to her. The cat moved over at once and rubbed up against her legs, a small cry escaping. "You're all right, toughie," she said.

"Let's not say anything to Fixit right away," he told her. "Let's give it a day, get past whatever's going to happen tomorrow. He doesn't need to hear about this until then."

She smiled bleakly. "He doesn't need to hear about this ever," she said as she walked away. "I wish none of us did."

She disappeared back into the darkness, Rabbit hopping at her heels.

The once-men attacked just after sunrise, just as Logan had known they would. They dispensed with preliminaries, eschewing any sort of effort at softening up the defenses with light-weapons fire or small cluster shells, and just threw themselves into the fray. They swept out of the fading shadow of the mountain range and through the glare of the morning sun in wave after wave of screaming, howling insanity. Some carried automatic weapons, but many had nothing more than rudimentary blades and lengths of pipe and wood. Weapons seemed of little consequence to them. Rational behavior was swept away by undisguised bloodlust. There was no coordination to the attack, no semblance of order or sophistication of battle tactics in evidence. It was primal and raw and bereft of anything but maddened determination.

Feeders followed in their wake, thousands strong, bounding across the terrain like wild animals.

The defenders did what Logan had ordered them to do. They crouched behind their protective barricades and watched. The first waves of attackers triggered the cluster mines and were blown apart. The second and third waves triggered the flamethrowers and were burned to ash. The next wave, struggling now just to get past the carnage that the first several had created, triggered the snap spikes. At the unmistakable sound of the spring traps releasing, the defenders opened fire on the attackers. Hundreds died in the five minutes or so that followed, bodies mounding up on the bridge floor in blood-soaked heaps, the whole of the bridge itself wreathed in smoke, the air rank with the smells of weapons fire and death.

The last of the attackers expended their lives under the withering crossfire of the entrenched defenders, and then as suddenly as the attack had begun it stopped. A deep silence settled over the bridge and the flats leading up to it from the south bluff, as if somehow all the attackers had been killed and the battle was over.

Logan knew better. Crouched down, moving quickly from position to position, he warned the defenders to be ready. "They'll come again right away," he told them. "When they do, trigger the flamethrowers first. That won't stop them, but it will slow them. Fire into those who get past for as long as it takes them to reach the last of the snap spikes, then fall back to the redoubts."

He could have ordered them to hold their positions, to keep the enemy from breaching the forward defenses. But he already knew that this would be impossible, that they wouldn't last the day no matter what they did. He didn't want them all killed when they were only delaying the inevitable. They would have to blow the bridge if they were to escape.

Helen Rice came up to him, crouched low, face stricken. She gestured at the carnage.

448

"How much more of this can they take?"

"More than we can. These are once-men, Helen. They don't feel anything the way we do. Dying isn't a deterrent. They'll keep coming at us until they break through." He put his hand on her shoulder, steadying her. "I'm sorry, but we aren't going to be able to hold them for long. Go back and tell them at the command post to stand ready to blow the bridge. When we fall back from the redoubts, I'll give you the signal. When you see it, trigger the detonator."

She fled back off the bridge at once, happy to be away from the killing field. Logan took up a fresh position at the center of the barricades. He peered out across the carpet of dead and wondered what the enemy would try next. He was already worrying that the bridge defenders weren't sufficiently prepared to deal with it.

He was right. When the attack came, it took an entirely different form. While they were searching the far shore for signs of movement, dozens of skrails swept down out of the skies in long, looping lines and dropped canisters of flammables that exploded on contact. In seconds, defenders and defenses alike were engulfed in flames, and everything at the center of the bridge became clouded with roiling black smoke. As soon as that happened, the once-men attacked again, charging out of the flats and onto the bridge, clambering over the remains of their fallen comrades, rushing through the invisible, porous bodies of the ravening feeders.

The bridge would have been lost and most of the defenders with it except that the prevailing winds blowing down the canyon from the ocean cleared the smoke away in seconds. The fires continued to burn, and a handful of the defenders died in the conflagration, but the rest stood their ground, heeding Logan Tom's orders and triggering the flamethrowers and firing their automatic weapons as their attackers closed. For the first time since the attack began, Logan used his staff, shattering the center of the enemy rush, leaving the wings to more conventional weapons.

Everywhere, the feeders leapt and dove among the dead and dying, joyful scavengers of the dark, terrible emotions expended.

Again, the attack was broken, leaving hundreds more of the once-men dead and dying on the bridge span.

But Logan had seen enough. The damage to the forward defenses was extensive, and the central portion of the bridge was a shambles. On the next attack, either the defenses or the defenders or both would collapse, and they would all be swept away.

"Everyone back!" he ordered them. "Take cover in the redoubts!"

They retreated at once, crouched low as

they backed toward the half dozen redoubts, carrying their weapons with them. Logan went last, still watching the smoke-clouded south bank and the movement he could see taking place within. Another attack was coming, and it was coming sooner than he would have liked.

He took a quick head count of those missing, and then pulled out those too badly injured to do much good and sent them back to Helen and the command post. He redistributed the others so that the redoubts were as evenly defended as was possible. But they were down to less than fifty able-bodied men and women, counting those getting ready for the flight north, so he could count on no more than five or six for each redoubt.

It wasn't enough. But then, what number would be in the face of this enemy?

He scanned the far bank once more, searching for something that would tell him what was happening. They wouldn't use the skrails again; they knew the defenders would be looking for that. Something else, he thought. But what?

Then a dark mass pushed through the smoke and crowded onto the bridge. Dozens of Elves, chained together like slaves, their hands bound behind them, their ankles shackled so they could do no more than shuffle, were being marched in front of a fresh body of once-men. The Elves had a desperate, helpless look to them, faces stricken, eyes rolling wildly. He could hear them crying out, begging for help. He could see their terrible injuries and their blood-streaked limbs.

In the very center was Simralin.

Logan Tom experienced a moment of heart-stopping shock. *Simralin!* The once-men were using her — using all of the Elven prisoners — as a living shield. *If you want to kill us,* they were saying, *first you have to kill them.*

For a second he was so stricken that he couldn't think straight. They must have captured her in the Cintra. They must have forced her to talk, forced her to reveal that he was a Knight of the Word and in love with her. Otherwise, how would they know to place her right at the center of things like this? How would they know that this, of all possible tactics, would undo him? The choice he was being given was both horrific and impossible to make. The defenders surrounding him were yelling wildly, demanding orders, unsure themselves of what to do. He felt frozen by what had happened, unable to act.

How could he kill Simralin?

Then, eyes still scanning the faces of the Elves being marched toward them, he saw Praxia, too. For just a second, he thought he must be imagining it. But no, there she was — Praxia — her small, dark pixie-face unmistakable amid the other, lighter-complexioned faces.

But Praxia was . . .

He had buried her . . .

Then he noticed that there were no feeders among the prisoners, not one dark shape in all that hapless mass of potential victims.

He caught his breath. It was a trick.

"Fire!" he ordered at once. He levered his black staff and roared in fury and fresh shock. "Now! Fire!"

The defenders pulled the triggers on their automatic weapons and the Elven wall collapsed and then disappeared in smoke, gone in an instant, vanished completely. An illusion, as Logan had realized just in time — a trick to make the defenders think the Elves were hostages when in fact they were not. It had almost worked. Logan had almost been taken in by it. His feelings for Simralin had very nearly persuaded him.

That old man, he thought suddenly. That old man had found him out and used what he had learned — maybe from his spies, maybe from Kirisin — against him. He could still see the other's cunning face, the knowing smile, the certainty that he owned an eight-year-old boy whose parents and brother and sister he had just killed.

Or maybe this wasn't about him at all, but about Kirisin. Maybe the use of Simralin was an effort to flush him out and cause him to expose himself while at the same time over-running the defenders of the bridge. The old man would still covet the boy's power over the Elves, and would not hesitate to use his sister against him.

Logan felt a rush of hatred so intense that for a moment it threatened to overwhelm him completely.

The foremost ranks of once-men had reached the barricades and taken cover behind them. More were surging out of the flats, hundreds of them, thousands, scream-ing and brandishing their weapons, swarms of feeders rushing after. Logan's defenders were firing into them, but the effect was negligible. The once-men had secured a foothold, and they wouldn't stop now until they had it all, no matter how many were killed.

The bridge was lost.

Logan steadied, his hatred for the demon put aside. "Everyone get off!" he called out, and motioned for the defenders to fall back.

He stood his ground as they did so, using the black staff's magic to create a wall of bright flames between themselves and the once-men, holding their attackers at bay. The bridge was cleared in seconds, and when it was, he wheeled away, as well, racing for the far bank. As he leapt onto solid ground once more, he gave Helen the signal she was wait-ing for.

"Blow the bridge!" she shouted, just as he reached the command station.

The man designated to do so threw the detonator switch.

Nothing happened.

Fixit had been crouched down behind the command station through the entirety of the enemy attack, cringing at every assault, barely able to look at what was happening. It wasn't until he saw the defenders streaming back off the bridge and heard Logan Tom give the order to ignite the explosives that he lifted his head for a look. He saw Cranston, who was the senior explosives expert, throw the switch, stare at it in disbelief when it failed to function, and then throw it again and again in a desperate attempt to get it to work.

But Fixit already knew the problem. He had warned them about it when he had watched them wiring the charges the day before, sent to see if there was something he could do to help by Logan. Nobody wanted his help; nobody cared to listen. He was a fourteen-year-old boy; what did he know?

In fact, he did know something. The detonator was wired to a central relay, and the relay sent a signal to the various charges. If the relay failed to function, the charges would not ignite. No one thought that would happen. The relay was solar-powered and had a backup battery. But it still relied on the wires from the detonator to trigger its internal mechanisms, and the wires, though carefully protected, were still suspect. Too many things could happen to break their connection to the relay. Use Redline wireless, he had argued. Use Bluetooth Extreme. Use something that wasn't hardwired. It was more dependable, less subject to malfunctions than the more rudimentary system they were using might invite.

So now, kneeling several yards behind them as they struggled to correct the problem from the command station, he knew at once that they were going to fail. There wasn't enough time for them to do anything from there. Not now. The once-men were coming out from behind the barricades, challenging the cover fire laid down by the retreating defenders, seeing an opportunity to cross the bridge and seize it intact. Even Logan Tom, turning to face this new assault, seemed at a loss.

But Fixit knew what to do. Without stopping to think about the wisdom of it, he came to his feet and charged onto the bridge. Shouts and cries trailed after him, and Logan's outstretched arm barely missed him. The relay was strapped to a bridge truss fifteen yards away, protected by steel girders and a makeshift steel frame. He raced straight for it, ignoring the ranks of approaching once-men and the stray bullets that whizzed by his head. He threw himself down as the weapons fire increased, crawling and rolling the last several yards until he was behind the steel frame and pressed up against the girders. He raised himself up on his elbows, keeping his head safely behind the steel supports, and snapped open the relay box.

Inside, he found the wires still connected.

He had been wrong.

Furious with himself, he began searching the relay mechanism for other possible failures, convinced that the problem was here, not somewhere else. The weapons fire had grown heavier, and he could sense the steady approach of the once-men. Logan was using his staff to keep them back, aided by the bridge defenders, but the once-men were pressing forward anyway. Even without risking a glance to see how close they were, he knew it wouldn't be long until they were on top of him.

Then he found it. A tiny bit of debris had wedged itself between the contacts, breaking the circuit and preventing the signal from activating. He blew hard into the mechanism, cleared the contact, jammed the relay box back into place within its protective frame, and was on his feet once more, racing back the way he had come.

His heart was pounding. How long did he have? Didn't matter. If he was quick, he should still be able to rea

Twenty-Six

The third day of their march dawned very much the same as the previous two, the sky bright and cloudless, the sun a white-hot ball in the eastern horizon, and the air already heavy and sweltering. All around them, the land spread away in an unchanging landscape of barren earth, wintry scrub, and open plains dotted with clumps of dead grass. Now and then they would cross through a shallow depression or climb a low rise, but most of what they saw was endlessly flat and empty.

Tessa walked with Hawk as he led the way, the caravan still moving north and east, headed for distant mountains that were no more than a faint tracing against the skyline. She had chosen not to ride this day, at least for the first part of it, but to stay by him. He knew she missed their time alone, which had eroded to almost nothing, the demands placed on him as leader taking away what little privacy they might have enjoyed. They talked when they could, they slept together

458

when Hawk slept at all, but mostly they were apart.

Today Panther drove the Lightning AV with Owl and a handful of smaller children as passengers. Panther grumbled at the assignment, mostly because he grumbled at almost everything, but it got him out of Hawk's hair for a few hours, which was the best he could hope for. Sparrow, River, and even Candle had decided to walk, and they formed a small group with Bear not too far back from Hawk and Tessa, but far enough to give them their privacy.

Strung out behind them, the children from the compounds followed with their caregivers, and farther back still Lizards, Spiders, and a growing handful of others.

Where those other creatures, humans mutating into something new, had come from was something of a mystery. Hawk was aware of them right from the start. Some of them were already in camp when they had departed the bridge and begun the march, but others had joined them since. There was no way of telling how they had found their way to him or knew that it was all right to stay. Perhaps word had gotten around in the camp that he was taking anyone who chose to come along. Perhaps they were just hoping for something better in their lives.

There were even a few children and adults who had arrived from as far away as Portland

and Seattle. Strays, they had made their way overland in an effort to escape from places where they were no longer safe. Last night, a skinny girl with lank brown hair and haunted eyes, traveling in the company of several other kids, all just a little younger than she was, had caught up to the caravan. She had been asking about a man carrying a black staff, saying she had done what he had told her and come north along the roads he said to follow and now she was looking for him. Hawk asked her name, but she refused to give it. He left her with Tessa, who spent a long time with her. She didn't seem to want to talk to him. She just wanted to know what had happened to Logan.

"Are you still thinking about Chalk?" Tessa asked him suddenly.

He shook his head. "I was just wondering about that girl, the one I asked you to talk with. Did you ever find out anything about her?"

Tessa's brow furrowed. "I found out more than I wanted to. She's had a hard time of it. Her parents are dead, her family gone, and she's been out on her own for weeks. She's had a lot done to her, none of it good. She said she found Logan while he was traveling south toward the mountains in Oregon. He shared his food with her and told her to come north across the Columbia and then east to find us. She managed it somehow. Found

460

some other kids along the way and brought them with her."

"So she's got a new family now, I guess."

"Like all of us." Tessa looked away. "I miss my mother. I know I don't have any reason to, not after what she did to me. But I do. I wish I could have done something to help her."

"Everyone wishes that about someone," he said, thinking suddenly of Chalk. "But regrets don't help. We have to forget about what we couldn't do and concentrate on what we can."

She gave him a sideways glance. "I just wish I could do more to help you. I don't like not being able to do anything more than this."

"Than this?"

"This. Walking with you. Keeping you company. Giving you a chance to talk with someone who won't judge or criticize or demand anything."

He smiled. "Because you love me."

She smiled back. "Because I do. Very much."

"I liked it when you had to sneak out of the compound to meet me. Not putting you in danger like that, but the adventure of it. It was exciting."

"Everything we did was exciting," she said. "I liked it, too."

They walked in silence for a time, their boots scuffing up clouds of dust on the dry flats, their faces streaked with dirt and sweat.

Hawk felt the heat of the day bearing down on him, a great weight that reflected accurately the weight of his self-doubt. In the distance, gusts of wind blew up dust devils, their funnels churning through the hazy air in wild bursts. The sun had crested the mountains and flooded the sky with a panoramic wash of blinding white light.

"Is it a long way to where we have to go?" she asked him after a while.

He shrugged. "Couldn't say. I don't know yet."

She grinned. "Do you even know where we are?"

"Not really. Do you?"

She brushed at her curly dark hair and frowned. "I think so. I was talking about it with Owl. We both remember this country as being a part of an Indian reservation in the old days. Long time ago, when there was a government. Not much to look at now, is it?"

He shook his head. "I wonder if they're still holding the bridge against that army. I wonder if they've been able to keep them from crossing."

Tessa didn't say anything. They walked on, and he found himself listening to the soft drone of the Lightning following several dozen yards behind. He glanced over his shoulder at the caravan, stretched out behind him for almost a mile, a jumble of vehicles and figures, shrouded in dust and sweltering heat. Behind them, the Cascade Mountains were a strange gray-blue smudge against the horizon, jagged peaks stretching north and south for as far as the eye could see.

"I don't think they can hold that bridge for long," he said, dark eyes intense as he studied the land ahead again. "I don't think anyone could. Not against what's coming." He shook his head. "It's odd, but I can see the shape of it, can sense its power, even without knowing what it is exactly. I can make out just enough, in my mind's eye, to know that it's too much for anyone." He paused, looked at her again. "I really can, Tessa."

"I believe you," she said.

"I wish things could go back to the way they were," he said softly.

She reached over for his hand and placed it against her stomach. "Everything?"

He smiled. "Okay, maybe not everything."

She hooked her arm through his and pressed against him.

At midday, when they stopped to eat, Owl joined them. She wheeled herself over from the AV to where Hawk and Tessa sat apart from the other Ghosts in the dappled shadow of a skeletal tree stripped of leaves and life alike. She handed each a small hunk of cheese she had been saving, her face lined with worry.

"Are you all right?" she asked them. "You

look tired."

They were, of course. Everyone was. But Owl wasn't looking for an answer; she was trying to give them a chance to talk about it.

"We're okay," Tessa assured her, a smile brightening her dark face. She patted the soft swell of her belly. "Baby says to tell you not to worry."

"Maybe you should ride with us after we eat," Owl suggested.

"She should." Hawk pounced on the suggestion. When Tessa started to object, he shook his head. "You should, Tessa."

They ate in silence, concentrating on the food and trying to ignore the heat. The rest of the caravan had stopped as well, strung out for more than a mile behind them, the vehicles halted, the children and their caregivers and the others who had come with them taking a small rest before continuing on. Hawk was thinking that Helen Rice was right, that if this heat continued they would have to think about traveling at night. It was too hard on the children to keep going like this during the day.

"Do you think we have much farther to go?" Owl asked him after she had finished her meal.

He hesitated before answering. She was trying to hide it, but he could hear the concern in her voice, a ragged, furtive thing. Normally, Owl was the steady, optimistic one. She was the center of their family; she held them all together. He didn't like what he was thinking.

"I'm not sure," he admitted finally.

No one said anything. The midday heat beat down on them, baking their bodies within the oven of clothes long since gone stiff with sweat and dirt, their minds as tired as their expectations. Hawk couldn't remember his last real bath. None of them had done more than wash off a little dirt and cool down their faces at the end of each day's trek since they had set out. Before that, things hadn't been much better. Food was growing scarce, too.

Time was as thin as hope.

"Will the King of the Silver River help you?" she pressed.

He shook his head and shrugged.

"Has he spoken to you since we set out?"

He shook his head again.

"Then how do you . . . ?"

"Owl, I don't know!" he snapped, silencing her. He regretted his anger at once. He gave her an apologetic smile. "I wish I did know. I wish I knew everything about what we are doing instead of nothing. I think about it every day, all day, and then at night I lie awake and I think about it some more. I hate it that so much depends on me. But I don't know what else to do other than what I'm doing — to just keep going."

"Faith has gotten us this far," Tessa offered quietly.

"Faith is pretty much all we have," Owl agreed.

He took a deep breath and exhaled. "I'll tell you something. The truth? Faith isn't what keeps me going. It isn't what drives me. Fear does. I have faith, but it's the fear that won't let me give up. Fear that if I fail, everyone will die. I can't deal with it. I'm running all the time. Not *to* the King of the Silver River so much as *away* from the fear."

Owl reached over and touched his cheek. "I shouldn't be asking you questions," she told him. "I know better. I know you are doing the best you can. I can't help myself. I'm afraid, too. I want our family to be safe. I want all of them to be safe."

"We just have to keep going," Tessa declared firmly. "We just have to remind ourselves not to lose hope." She took Hawk's hand and squeezed. "The King of the Silver River said you would find him, didn't he? He said you would reach him if you followed your instincts, if you did what they told you. And that's what you've done."

"But I can't help wondering how all this will end," he replied, squeezing her hand in response. "Even if we find him, how will he protect us? If the world really is about to be destroyed, how can we be safe anywhere? Besides, what's the point? The world's destroyed — what's left for us?"

"A new world," Owl said at once. "Even if the old is gone, there will be a new one born of it. That's the lesson of life. New replaces old. It will be like that here, too, don't you think? We are staying alive so that new generations can be born. Like your baby."

"Owl is right," Tessa agreed. "Like our baby."

Hawk nodded, pretended he was in accord, but inside he found himself fighting doubt and confusion. *New worlds born of old* sounded good. So how did that happen exactly? What did it take for people to survive a cataclysm of the sort that had been promised? Their world was already ravaged beyond repair. Even back in Pioneer Square in the city, they had been doing little more than surviving, living hand-to-mouth, day-to-day. How could it be any better when things got worse?

There were no answers to such questions, of course. Wouldn't be until they got to where they were going — wherever that was — so that they could discover what was waiting.

A leap of faith was required. A huge leap.

Sure, he thought. Tell that to Squirrel. Tell it to Chalk. Tell it to the other children they had lost. Tell it to all those who would be taken from them before this was over. He felt his throat tighten. How many more lives, he wondered, would his leap of faith cost?

He found himself thinking anew of the vision of the boy who would lead his children to the Promised Land, of the boy who would find a safehold where all could survive the coming destruction. A vision rooted in dreams, but not necessarily in reality. He had believed in that vision so strongly when he was waiting for it to come to pass. He had never doubted it, never questioned that he would be the one to do what it had shown.

For the first time ever, he was wondering if it had played him false.

Logan Tom parked the AV at the lee of a long, low rise that snaked through the barren, empty land. When he was satisfied that it was safe, he climbed out to look around. The sun boiled down out of the cloudless sky, a ball of fire that had baked the surface of the drought-starved terrain until it was riven with cracks. From where he stood, gazing out across the flats, he might have been alone in the world.

Using the directions Cat had given him, he stood by the outcropping amid the wilted sage and measured off the twenty-nine yards north-northwest on his compass that led to the burial site down inside the shallow ravine. Then he walked it off, black staff held ready. On reaching the final steps, he saw where she had dug, the earth already beginning to harden anew in the heat. Chalk and the other children, all jammed together, less than three feet down. He felt renewed rage for the thing that had done this. A demon of the worst sort, a killer that enjoyed playing games with the helpless and unprotected.

But just another demon, as well, he told himself. One he intended to hunt down and destroy before it could take any other lives.

He thought suddenly of Fixit, another casualty of the madness that had enveloped them. Dead without knowing what had happened to his best friend. Gone in the blink of an eye.

He had sent Cat on ahead with the surviving bridge defenders, telling her to let Hawk and the others know what had happened, asking her to warn them to stay close together and inside the camp perimeter until this was over. She had refused at first, unwilling to leave him. But this was something he knew he must do alone, and he had told her so in no uncertain terms. She had been hurt by his insistence, but she would be safe. There was no room for argument.

They had stood looking at each other in the aftermath of his insistence, the silence between them uncomfortable, and then she had walked right up to him, put her arms around him, and buried her face in his shoulder.

"Don't make me go," she had pleaded again. "Let me stay with you."

He relented enough to hug her back, to put his hand on her hair as he held her. "We've had this discussion," he replied. "It won't help to have it again."

"There was no discussion. You told me what I had to do, nothing more. But you're wrong. You shouldn't make me go."

"The others need to be warned. Right away."

"You will be alone," she insisted. "It's too dangerous."

He almost laughed, but instead he simply patted her head. "I've been alone for a long time, Catalya. I've been alone for more than ten years. I know how to take care of myself."

She shook her head in denial. "Not with this thing. This thing is different. Worse than Krilka Koos or anything else we've come across. You almost died the last time. Do you remember who saved you?"

He backed her away. "I remember. Now go. Do what you have to do, and I'll do the same."

He turned then and walked away, ignoring her calls to turn around, to come back and stop being foolish. Before he was far enough away to miss it, he heard her crying.

He remembered it now. She was so strong, so confident in what she could do, but she was still emotionally vulnerable, whether she cared to admit it or not. It was in the nature of who and what she was. It was a part of being human.

He should know. When the bridge went up and the world exploded in fire and smoke, he had cried for Fixit.

He broke away from his reverie and began circling the burial site, searching for tracks. He found them easily enough; others would have missed the telltale scrapes entirely. There were several sets of tracks, all identical, but it was the ones that led off to the northeast in the direction of the caravan that determined his path. These were the ones that mattered. He had already decided that the demon would follow the caravan and its children, would continue to pursue its culling of those unwary enough to get within reach, always hoping its efforts would eventually bring Hawk out to face it.

There was real danger in that happening, of course. Both Angel Perez and he had warned the boy that under no circumstances must he attempt to settle this business on his own. If he were lost, the entire caravan and perhaps the future, as well, were lost. He might want to stop the killings, might desire revenge, might even think that there was something he could do to change things, but he must not act on those impulses.

Hawk was a gypsy morph, though, and in the end he would do whatever he decided needed doing, no matter what anyone said. He was formed of wild magic and was unpredictable. He would only listen to them for so long.

Which was why Logan had to find the demon first.

Which was why he would track it until he caught up with it.

It was a calculated risk, but nothing else had worked. This demon was skilled at hiding its presence and staying all but invisible. Guards and search parties did not seem to trouble it. There was an obsessive quality to its hunting of the children; it would not quit until it got what it wanted. It had come for the gypsy morph, and it meant to have him.

Logan walked back to the Ventra and stood beside it for a moment. He would catch up to the caravan by nightfall tomorrow if he traveled steadily. He might even catch up to the demon by then, as well. He would have preferred to travel afoot, but the Ventra would allow him to cover ground faster. The risk in driving was that it didn't allow him to read the demon's signs of passage as carefully as he would have preferred, which meant he might miss something. Still, he would have to make the best of things.

He drank from his water bottle and thought about how skewed things had gotten. What had begun as a simple enough task — to find and guide the gypsy morph and those it led to a safehold the morph would find — had evolved into a complex struggle for survival involving thousands of children, an entire nation of Elves, and various other species of mutated humans. His original charge had been altered so often that he was no longer certain exactly what it was. He supposed it was still the same, only grown larger.

He started to climb back into the AV when something in the distance caught his eye. He froze, one foot already inside the vehicle, and stared at the sky.

A hot-air balloon hung silhouetted against the western horizon, floating slowly on the sluggish air. He blinked in disbelief, watching its progress.

It was coming his way.

No, he thought, *it isn't possible.*

Praying at the same time that it was. Praying with every last shred of faith he could muster that he wasn't mistaken. Watching the balloon grow larger, settling lower in the sky as it neared him, the details growing sharper, more certain.

Until at last there could no longer be any doubt.

It was Simralin.

TWENTY-SEVEN

After he had held her for long minutes, needing the feel of her body pressing against his own to make her presence real enough that he could accept it, grateful beyond anything words could express, he asked her to tell him everything. She did so as he drove the Ventra in pursuit of the demon, eyes on the rough terrain as he listened, searching for tracks, for sign of his quarry's passing, his hands steadied by their grip on the wheel in a way they might not have been if they were only resting in his lap.

He had been so afraid of losing her, of having to live without her, of the consequences of his decision not to insist that she come with him. He had been terrified, and now he could breathe again in a way he hadn't been able to in many days.

She seemed aware of this, and she touched him frequently, smiled often, and reassured him that she was really there. She was feeling the same way he was, he told himself, as much in love with him as he was with her. He couldn't have explained how he knew this beyond what his instincts and his heart told him. It was in things that would have been barely noticeable to others — the small gestures, quick asides, and momentary glances. It was in the changes in her tone of voice when she spoke and in the silences in between. In these little things, seemingly unimportant and fleeting, everything was made known. It was cemented by her physical closeness to him, by the fact that she had come back from the precipice on which he had left her standing, alive and well, a whole person still despite the terrible struggle she had been through.

Almost no one else, he thought, could have done what she had done and lived to tell about it.

Even so, she had not survived unscathed. There was blood and dirt on her ripped clothing. Save for her adzl, her weapons were gone. She had been wounded several times, although she had cleaned her injuries and bound them up. She had not eaten in more than a week save for what she had managed to forage. Her face was gaunt, her cheeks hollow, and her eyes haunted.

Even in this condition he found her the most beautiful woman he had ever known.

After he leaves her days earlier in the mountains

475

of the Cintra, she goes back in search of Arissen Belloruus and the others who remain behind to defend against the demon army. She is with another dozen or so Trackers and scouts, all of them mindful of the need to find routes of escape for those who fight to provide cover for Kirisin's escape.

They encounter resistance almost at once, the once-men under demon command flooding through the trees and rocks in an unstoppable torrent. The Elves under her command take cover and fight back with bow and arrow and javelin, slowing but not stopping the attack. Gradually, they are forced to give ground, unable to get through or stem the tide. They back their way clear of the forests and up into the rocks, counterattacking the entire way. The once-men try to get at them, but fail. They lack automatic weapons or even blades in most cases and are forced to rely on pieces of pipe and lengths of wood. These poor weapons are useless against the experienced and well-trained Elves.

Still, Simralin and her companions cannot reach the main body. They cannot even determine where it is. The shouts and cries of battle seem to come from all sides, and the trees hide the truth of what is happening.

"Chenowyn!" she calls finally to one of her scouts. "Climb higher into the rocks and try to see what is happening!"

The other woman is gone at once, and Simralin moves the rest into a position where the rocks narrow down into a space barely wide enough for two abreast to pass, and she chooses to defend there. Their attackers may find a way around them, may even cut them off, but for now it is the best they can do. The once-men are still streaming out of the trees, seemingly without order or leadership, consumed by their efforts to find their quarry, scattering this way and that like wild things.

Then, before Chenowyn can report back, a large body of Elves bursts clear of the trees into open ground below, colliding with the once-men that have gotten around behind them. Other once-men erupt from the forests, a massive force of attackers. The Elves try to stand and fight them off, but there are too many. They give ground quickly, retreating toward the rocks and the high ground that Simralin and her companions occupy.

She makes a quick head count and doesn't get past a hundred.

Where are the rest?

She doesn't like to think about the answer. Instead, in an effort to make a difference, she takes her own small force down out of the rocks in a counterattack that catches the nearest of the once-men by surprise and opens a path for the beleaguered Elves. She sees the King then, trying to rally his soldiers. He is bloodied and disheveled, and he fights with short swords in both hands. The once-men recognize that he is the leader and try to get at him. But Home Guards surround the King protectively and fight them off. Sporadic gunfire erupts from the trees, but it doesn't seem to have any effect on the combatants.

"Home Guard!" the big Tracker Eliasson roars from just below her, throwing back the creatures that come at him. "To me, Elven! To the rocks!"

The Elves hear and see, and in a tangled body they begin to fight their way toward him. Simralin pulls her diminished force — now down to eight — into the shelter of the rocks, where they use longbows on the once-men in an effort to help. But it makes scant difference. The forest below is alive with others, masses of them pouring out of the trees, too many to count or stand against.

Arissen Belloruus is still trying to pull back, to fight his way free with his Home Guards.

Hurry, Arissen, Simralin pleads silently.

Chenowyn is back beside her, as white as a wraith at the new moon. "What have you seen?" Simralin demands of her.

"There are thousands more." Chenowyn has to shout to make herself heard. "So many they fill the forest at every turn. We cannot hope to stop them all."

"Stay here." Simralin is already moving. "Keep the way open."

She is down out of the rocks in seconds and charging across the open spaces toward the Elves below. Dozens have gone down, their numbers diminished as if by magic. The trees continue to bleed once-men, an endless stream of bodies exploding out of the shadows in a cacophony of screams and waves of wild-eyed madness. More Elves go down, fighting to the end, dying on their feet. The Home Guard surrounding the King is reduced to less than a dozen, separated from the main body of Elves fleeing for the path she has opened for them.

Get out, Arrisen, she wants to scream at him, but knows she will not be heard.

An instant later a burst of automatic weapons fire erupts from the edge of the trees and a creature only vaguely human pushes out of the woods with a huge double-barreled killing machine that spits fire and death everywhere. Most of the Home Guards collapse. The King goes down as well, dropping to one knee, head lowered. He is spitting blood.

"Arissen!" She screams his name aloud.

The creature has raised its arms in triumph and is howling with glee when the first arrow pierces it through its right eye and knocks it backward a step. It tears the arrow free, heedless of the pain, but a second arrow splits its throat and a third buries itself deep in the hairy chest. Eliasson is fitting another arrow to his bow when the creature staggers and sinks to the earth and does not move again.

Simralin is fighting to reach the King, but she is already too late. The last of the Home Guards are cut down, and the once-men fall on Arissen

Belloruus like wolves. The King disappears beneath the swarm and does not reappear.

There is nothing Simralin can do. She backs away, calling the rest of the Elves to her, those she can still see amid the carnage, those who are still standing. Maybe half are able to reach her, breaking clear of their attackers. The rest are lost in seconds, buried in the monstrous swarm of bodies that converge on them and bear them to the earth.

She retreats into the rocks with those who remain alive, and they turn their weapons on their attackers. There are so many of them by now that it is virtually impossible not to hit something, and dozens collapse as they surge toward the defenders.

"What do we do?" Chenowyn shouts in her ear.

Indeed. What is there to do? The King is dead and with him almost the whole of his command. Kirisin is safely away, and there is nothing left for the Elves who remain but to fight to save their own lives. A reasonable choice, but flight seems the better option.

"Fall back!" she shouts.

She leads them up into the rocks, through the narrow defiles and rugged terrain, knowing the best ways to go to keep the enemy from massing in pursuit. They may come after the Elves — indeed, they almost certainly will — but they will have to do it in ones and twos. That gives the Elves a chance. There are fewer than fifty of them now, and once they manage to put some distance between themselves and their pursuers, they can go to ground, can find places to hide where they will never be found.

But first they must get clear of the fighting.

For a time, it appears they will. The passage they follow is riddled with dead ends and side trails that go back the way they have come, and if you didn't know the way, as she did, you would become quickly lost. Their pursuit falls away and then disappears entirely. They continue to climb into the mountains, and she knows that when they reach the high desert beyond, they will be able to use the ravines and ridgelines to hide themselves as they make their way eastward. They will not turn south until they are safely clear of the roads that Kirisin and Logan will have taken. Those roads are too easily discovered, and they would be run down before they reached Redonnelin Deep. Better to fade into the barren landscape beyond, where trails are much harder to find and tracks may be more easily disguised.

"We've lost them," Chenowyn declares with a grin after they have crested the mountains and can see the eastern slopes and the desert beyond.

Indeed, they have. But the demons that control the army have thought ahead to this and sent winged creatures to track them. The creatures swoop down in attack not a mile beyond the rim, when they are still descending

the exposed rocky slopes of the higher elevations. They rip and tear at the Elves, who try in
vain to protect themselves. The winged creatures are swift and their strikes precise. Several
of the Elves are wounded and one is killed
before their attackers fly back the way they
have come.

Simralin knows what will happen next, and
there is no defense against it if they stay
together.

"We must separate into smaller groups," she
tells them. "No more than half a dozen each.
Then we must fan out and go to ground. The
winged things will guide the once-men to where
we are, if we give them the chance. We do better by separating. Stay hidden until nightfall,
then make your way north to the river. Track it
east until you find the camp or signs of its passage. Track it from there to those who will be
helping Kirisin."

They embrace, all of them, before setting out.
They do not know which of them will survive
this. Some will not. Some will never be seen
again.

Eliasson takes one group and is gone. Chenowyn chooses to stay with Simralin. She is not
a leader and has no desire to start learning to
be one now. With another three in tow, they
head directly east into the badlands of the high
desert, working their way quickly across a long
stretch of flats to where fissures and upheavals
have changed the terrain into a jumble of ridges

and ravines. They travel through midday, and then Simralin takes them several miles down a dry wash strewn with small rocks. Before the wash ends, they climb out again and turn down a slide that leads to a carapace; here they find an overhang and take shelter.

They stay all night, peering into the darkness, listening to the silence. At one point, they hear screams, but the screams come from a long way off and it is impossible to determine their direction. They take turns standing watch. They wait to be discovered.

When morning dawns, though, they are still safe. Simralin goes out for a quick look and comes back right away. Smoke rises from several places west, closer to the mountains. The smell is of burning flesh. The winged creatures patrol the skies in ones and twos, visible in all directions, even east. They must stay where they are until it is dark again.

They pass the day in misery. The sun beats down on the empty terrain and turns it into a furnace. The air is so stiflingly hot and dust-filled that they choke on it when they breathe. They have almost nothing to eat or drink, but they share what they have. Simralin knows where to find water farther north, but it is a long journey. She knows, as well, where they can find another of the hot-air balloons the Trackers have stashed across the Cintra and north. But the balloon is slow and cumbersome, and it is no match for the winged creatures if they spy it.

She tells the others she has made a decision. When night comes, they must leave their hiding place. If they stay, they risk discovery. Hiding is no longer an option. The once-men are actively hunting them, using the flying creatures to ferret them out. Worse, they have almost no food or water left, and the circle of predators is tightening. They cannot risk staying where they are. Their choice is simple: they can try to reach water, or they can try to reach the hot-air balloon.

Her companions choose the balloon. Anything that will get them away from the Cintra quickly.

When it grows dark, she leads the others out from their hiding place and onto the flats. The sky is clear and filled with stars, but the moon hangs low and distant against the horizon, reduced to a tiny sliver. The balloon is perhaps three days off, if they travel steadily. She chooses a route that takes them east through the high desert and away from the larger body of their hunters. The flying creatures, if they sight them, will not be able to bring the once-men right away. But she knows, as well, that any sighting is probably the end of them. Once seen, they can be tracked from the air until help arrives, no matter how long it takes.

They travel single-file through the night. She stops them frequently to check for the flying creatures, but sees no sign of them. In the darkened sky, nothing moves. On the landscape about them, nothing moves. They are alone with their thoughts and one another.

Still, she is not comfortable that they are safely clear.

And she wonders about their companions, the ones from whom they separated, gone other ways, to other places.

They find new shelter as the dawn nears and go to ground for another day. They have nothing to eat or drink. The heat is unbearable, and their thirst acute. They sit waiting for the day to pass, miserable and despairing. The journey to reach the balloon will take another two days, and they are already weak and exhausted. It is questionable if they will be able to finish the trek.

At midday, Simralin goes out to look around. The sky is clear, the land empty of life. There is no sign of the winged hunters. She settles on a fresh course of action. This is country she knows. She decides to leave the others long enough to hunt for water. If she is lucky, she will come upon food, as well. The greatest danger lies in not being able to find her way back. But she is a skilled Tracker, and she is certain she will be able to do so.

"Stay hidden through the day," she tells them. "I will be back before dark with whatever I can find."

She sets out determined not to return without at least finding water for them to drink. She slogs through the heat alone, a solitary figure in an unchanging landscape. She scans land and sky frequently for signs of pursuit, but sees nothing. She has a compass to chart her passage, and she measures the distances between changes of course. It is an endless, tiresome process, but she is careful to keep track of everything, knowing that if she gets lost, she will never find her way back to them.

She finds the water she seeks around mid-afternoon in a deep ravine walled away by steep banks formed of bedrock that feels entirely out of place with the desert. But the water is good, and she fills the containers she carries after drinking her fill, and starts back the way she has come.

It takes her the rest of the day to make the return. It is dusk by the time she arrives back, the shadows deep and layered. She has hurried, but she needn't have. Her companions are dead. They lie scattered about the space in which they were hiding, torn apart by whatever found them. The tracks of something huge are visible in a patch of soft earth. Neither demon nor once-men made these tracks. This is something else entirely, a desert hunter come in search of food, in all probability a mutant beast born of the changes wrought by humans. Pieces of the Elves killed are missing; parts of them have been eaten.

Almost nothing of Chenowyn's body remains. It appears from the marks on the rocks that the larger part of it was dragged away.

She feels the heart go out of her then, and for a moment she considers just sitting down and waiting for the inevitable. She is going to die, and she knows it. All of the Elves are going to die. But the moment passes, and her despair recedes. She will not give in. She will find a way to stay alive.

She slips from the rocks where the lifeless bodies of her companions lie and begins to walk. She travels all night through the scrub and the rocks, and by morning, when she has seen nothing more of the winged creatures, she knows she will be all right.

He waited until he was sure she had finished, his eyes on the land ahead, and then he said, "Skrails."

She looked over at him. "What?"

"That's what they're called. The winged creatures. Skrails."

She nodded without comment. They drove in silence for a while, and he kept thinking she would say more about what had happened. Because something important was missing from her explanation, and it troubled him.

At last, he could leave it alone no longer. "Why didn't you use the Elfstones?" he asked.

Her face was stony. "I couldn't."

"You couldn't?"

Suddenly there were tears in her eyes. She gestured absently. "I couldn't make them respond. I don't know why. I watched Kirisin do it. I saw what he did. We spoke of it afterward, and I understood what was needed. It wasn't as if I didn't know what to do."

She exhaled sharply. "But I couldn't call up the magic. I tried, did everything I knew to do to summon it. I held the Elfstones in my hand and I begged for the magic to help me. I was fighting to stay alive, to keep the others alive, and I begged for the Stones to do something. But there was no response at all. And then there was no time, either. I shoved the Elfstones back in my pocket and fell back on what I knew best without even thinking about it."

She wiped at her eyes, but it didn't seem to help. He had never seen her cry. She was always so composed, so in control. It seemed as if all her defenses had simply collapsed. He didn't know what to do.

"It's not your fault," he said.

"Of course it is."

"I would have done the same thing you did," he said finally.

Her laugh was sharp and bitter. "Not you. You would have found a way. You would have made the magic obey you. You know you would have. I should have found a way."

"You can't know that. It was the first time you tried. Maybe trying to use them in the heat of battle was asking too much. Even

488

Kirisin wasn't asked to do that."

She stopped crying finally, wiped again at her face, and looked at him. "I keep trying to forgive myself. I tell myself that using the magic would have just attracted the demons. That's what happened to Kirisin when he used the Stones: it brought the demons hunting us. They could sense it." She shook her head. "But it's just an excuse. I don't know how it would have worked out. I think I'm just looking for a way to get myself off the hook."

"It doesn't seem to be working," he said. He gave her a quick smile. "You can't second-guess yourself about things like this, Sim. You do the best you can and you walk away. If you try to rethink what you should have done or could have done, you'll drive yourself crazy."

She nodded, looking off into the distance again. "I can't help it. They're all dead, Logan. All of them. No one made it out but me." She looked over quickly. "Did they?"

"No. You're the only one. Maybe, later, there will be some others." He smiled again. "I'm just glad to see you."

This time she smiled back. "I really didn't think I would find you."

Her face was battered and dirt-streaked, and he reached out to touch her cheek. "You say that as if you were looking for me." He studied her blue eyes, surprised at what he saw there. "You were, weren't you?"

She touched him back. "What do you think?"

It wasn't a question that required an answer.

Miles distant from Logan and Simralin, Catalya hunkered down in the bed of a truck hauling tents and cooking supplies, cradling Rabbit in her arms. The truck jounced and swayed over the uneven terrain, causing metal fittings and tools to clank noisily as they rolled about in their wooden containers. The day was hot and windless, but she had found some small shade in the lee of the piles of canvas where the sun did not penetrate, and what air was stirred by their passing helped cool her heated face.

She was two hours gone from Logan Tom and still thinking about him. He'd been so quick to dismiss her, she thought angrily, as if having her with him was a hindrance rather than a help. She supposed she understood his thinking. He was trying to protect her, doing so in the best way he knew, by sending her away. But his thinking was flawed, and she couldn't help wishing he could have seen so. She was better equipped to survive this country than the Ghosts — perhaps as well equipped, in her own way, as he was. She had been doing so for several years now, and under less-than-ideal conditions. She had been outcast to all but the Senator, and he had protected her so that he could use her. She had been able to survive that; how could Logan doubt that she could survive this demon that was hunting the children?

She hadn't been joking when she had told him she wasn't in danger. A demon hunting human children would not bother with her. Not with another Freak. She might have been in danger once, but her transformation was sufficiently progressed that she was as much Lizard as human, and the mix made her something more than either.

Or something less.

She didn't like thinking about it, and until now she had thought about it less and less since Logan had taken her away from the Senator. The Ghosts had embraced her, too. Even Panther, who had disparaged her so openly at first, had now become her newly appointed protector. As if Panther could protect her better than she could protect him! Her smile came and went. At least Panther didn't want anything from her. He was just being a friend. He might have been something more, in other circumstances. She thought maybe he even wanted that. But she knew it could never happen.

Not just with him, but with anyone.

She pushed back the loose sleeve of her shirt and looked at her arm where the fresh Lizard patch had appeared two days before.

It was already bigger.

Like the one on her leg and the one on her back.

Rabbit lifted his fuzzy face to nuzzle her nose, and she nuzzled him back. Rabbit was her best friend — her only real friend. Rabbit wouldn't care that she was mutating again, the inevitability of what she was becoming so overwhelming she could barely stand to think of it.

No, Rabbit wouldn't care.

But the rest of them would.

Twenty-Eight

The wind appeared shortly after mid-afternoon in the worst heat of the day. Hawk noticed it first as a series of small gusts that touched down just long enough to stir the loose earth. The larger blow was distant still, too far away for its full force to be felt, an invisible presence kicking at the barren flats. He was walking point with Cheney, his eyes sweeping the horizon when he could make himself stop looking at the steady, monotonous movement of his feet. One foot in front of the other, second foot in front of the first, over and over. He was bone-weary and disheartened, but he was keeping it to himself.

Wind, he thought in surprise, and then glanced at the cloudless sky. Was a change in the weather coming?

Within minutes, the first breezes blew across his face, hot and dry and empty of any promise of rain. The blown air was thick with dirt, and it stung the skin of his face as it swept past, died away, and started up again. He searched the horizon more carefully. Any clouds he could spy were clustered atop either the mountains they had left or the ones they were heading toward, the former seemingly no farther away and the latter seemingly no closer than when they had set out. He fought down the sensation of having gotten nowhere, of having not moved at all. He understood that distances were deceiving, but the perception was disconcerting nevertheless.

Ahead several paces, Cheney lowered his head against the bursts of wind and plodded on, ruff flattened.

As if he knew where he was going even if Hawk didn't. The boy smiled despite himself. Good old Cheney.

As the force of the wind increased, he glanced over his shoulder at the caravan, a winding snake trailing away behind him in a ragged collection of vehicles, wagons, and people, a pall of dust hanging over everything. The muttering that had begun the night before seeming to trail after it, small whispers of discontent and doubt that circulated through the camp like bothersome flies. They had no specific source, only a specific target. He didn't hear it himself; the speakers were careful not to say anything in his presence. But word got back to him nevertheless, the way word always does.

"You got to do something about these compound kids flapping their lips, Bird-Man," Panther had told him as they'd set out earlier. "All they do is talk, talk, talk about how you don't know nothing, you just wandering about like some fool. They say you brought them out here to die. This ain't the little ones; this is the bigger kids, ones who ought to know better. I told a couple of them if I hear that kind of talk again, I'm gonna hit them so hard it'll kill their whole family. Frickin' fools."

Panther, never one to hold anything back. Hawk told him to let it be, that there was bound to be some of that sort of talk. What mattered was that the Ghosts still believed in him.

But did they? Though openly supportive, they, too, must be harboring doubts by now. Some of them, at least. Owl would never doubt him. River probably wouldn't, either. But the others were struggling, he imagined. They couldn't help it, whether they admitted to it or not. He didn't blame them. After all, he was struggling, too.

Not too much farther ahead, he believed, they would find the north–south branch of the Columbia River. Owl had told him so, had shown him the river on one of her maps, tracing their route from where they had left the bridge and its defenders. A little town called Vantage marked the crossing point, a

495

bridge that he hoped was still intact. That was where they were heading. Once across, the landscape would change again, becoming rolling hill country for a time. Maybe they would find water in those hills. Maybe the sun wouldn't be so intense.

Yet he still had no idea where it was they were going or how far yet they must travel. His sense of where they were meant to go, his instincts, kept him on this path, moving forward. But his instincts were blind, the path invisible, and time short. Everyone knew that the demon-led army would be hunting them. Perhaps Logan Tom and the men and women left behind at the bridge had stopped it momentarily, had turned it aside. But sooner or later it would find a way across the gorge and come after them anew.

Nothing would change for them until they reached the safehold promised in his dream. Nothing would change until he could find the King of the Silver River.

He felt a presence at his side, and a small hand reached over to take his own. Candle, her mop of red hair tangled and wild, her clothes disheveled and dusty, and her face intense, stared up at him, the look in her blue eyes uncertain.

"Can I walk with you?" she asked.

"Of course you can walk with me, peanut," he told her.

He squeezed her small hand reassuringly

and shortened his longer stride to match her own. They walked without speaking for a time, and Hawk found an unexpected measure of comfort in the warm touch of her little girl's grip.

Ahead, the dust clouded the horizon in widening sweeps, and the wind gathered force.

"Tell me a story, Hawk?" Candle asked suddenly.

He glanced over. "What kind of story?"

"A story about the King of the Silver River. You saw him, didn't you?"

"I did, but only for a little bit. And I don't know any stories about him."

"Tell me what he looks like."

Hawk thought about it for a moment. "He is very old. An old man with white hair and a beard. But he has a nice voice."

"What color are his eyes?"

"Blue, I think. He can appear and disappear just like that." He snapped his fingers. "He did it to me once. It was so quick. First he was there and then he was gone and then a little later he was back again."

"Was it magic?"

"I think probably it was."

She didn't say anything for a moment, her eyes on the ground as she walked, thinking. He let her be. He knew she was going through a difficult period, that the loss of her ability to detect potential danger had left her feeling

497

diminished and perhaps even useless to the family. Her talent had defined her for so long that it was hard for him to think of her in any other way, even knowing that she was different now. He could only imagine how it had affected her.

"Are the gardens beautiful, Hawk?" she asked finally.

"As beautiful as anything I have ever seen."

"Can you tell me about them, too?"

He did so, taking time to describe all of the beds and bushes and vines, the colors and types of flowers and the way they formed patterns and shapes against their lush green backdrop. He talked about the skies and the sweep of the land. He sketched pictures of the fountains and the pools that dotted the countryside. He told her how the gardens stretched away farther than the eye could see, as if they might run on forever. He had walked and walked, and he had never seen their end.

She smiled when he was done, squinting against the glare of the sun and the gusts of wind. "I would like to see them," she said.

"You will," he answered.

She shook her head, as if uncertain of that. "I wish I could do more to help you. I'm just another kid like all those compound kids. I can't do anything anymore."

"That's not true. You help Owl every day. She depends on you. She told me so."

"River and Sparrow can help her better than I can."

He took a deep breath. "Look, Candle. I want you to stop thinking about what you can't do. I know you miss it. We all do. But things change. People change. I'm not the same, either. I worried about it all the time, at first. But I've learned to stop. You have to do that, too. Besides, I think you should give yourself some time before you decide that you've changed for good."

"What if we don't have time? Look at what's happened to us in just a few weeks." Her gaze was steady, her face calm. She looked so grown-up. "If something happens that I should have known about, it will be my fault."

"Nothing that happens will be your fault," he said, squeezing her hand to emphasize the point.

"What happened to Chalk was my fault."

He felt his reply catch in his throat. "No, it wasn't. Not any more than it was with Squirrel or Mouse. Even if you could have sensed things the way you used to, you couldn't have done anything. None of us could. We all look out for each other the best way we can. But sometimes even that isn't enough. You know that."

She nodded, but didn't look as if she believed it.

"Like I said," he followed up quickly, "your

ability to sense danger might be on vacation for a time. Maybe it will come back. You need to give it a chance."

She nodded again, still looking doubtful. He gave her a moment, and then he said, "Maybe you're trying too hard. Maybe you can still sense danger just like you used to. Maybe you've just forgotten how to let it happen." He paused. "When that boy who killed Squirrel took you away from us, you had a pretty bad time of it. Maybe that was part of it."

She still didn't say anything, her forehead furrowed in thought, her mouth pursed. "Maybe."

The wind gusted sharply and particles of dust flew through the air like tiny needles, stinging the flesh. Hawk ducked his head and covered his mouth and nose with his collar. Candle's lowered face was completely hidden by the mop of her hair. Hawk wanted to talk to her some more, but it had become impossible to do anything but slog on through the screen of grit and debris whirling around them. Moments later, Helen Rice, riding one of the AVs, caught up to them and announced that the caravan was becoming too strung out and they were going to have to close the gaps before they got separated altogether. What had started as a normal wind stirring up the loose earth of the flats was turning into a full-blown dust storm, and she was stopping the caravan until it passed.

Reluctantly, Hawk agreed. "You better get back with Owl," he told Candle. "She might need your help. We'll talk some more later. I promise."

The little girl turned away, heading back toward the Lightning, her head still lowered, her face hidden. He wasn't happy with leaving things this way, but there wasn't any choice.

"Take Cheney with you!" he called after her. "Go on, Cheney," he urged the big dog, gesturing.

With a rueful glance over his shoulder, Cheney slouched over to join Candle. As the pair headed back toward the Lightning, Hawk stood where he was for a while, waiting for the rest of the caravan to catch up. In bits and pieces, it did so. The children were shepherded into the center of the camp by their caregivers while the drivers and guards worked quickly to construct makeshift facilities. The intensity of the storm continued to increase. By now the flats east were roiling with clouds of dust so high, the distant mountains were blocked from view. Hawk walked back through the camp, helping where he could, speaking to everyone, making it a point to let those he led know he was still there and still actively involved in what was happening. He did what he could to reassure them. It took almost an hour for the last of the stragglers to wander in, and by then everyone was in the process of covering up as best they could. There was little protection to be had for those outside the vehicles and the wagons; most simply hunkered down behind whatever shelter they could find. The wind howled, and the dust spattered against metal and canvas with a strange hissing sound. The storm was all around now, closing the members of the caravan away in a whispery, whirling shroud, and the world beyond disappeared as if blown away.

Hawk finished walking the camp from end to end, taking time to check that there were guards posted everywhere, and that no gaps in the defenses would allow an unnoticed breach. On his way back to the point, he stopped to speak with the caregivers who had gathered the bulk of the children inside a trio of broad, squat tents where they could be kept close together and carefully watched. He had not forgotten what was out there in the invisible nothing, what was waiting to steal away more victims if it could. Their predator was still hunting them. He did not pretend to understand its reasoning. But he had looked into its strange eyes and he understood well enough what sort of monster it was.

Once outside, he started toward the Lightning AV where Owl and the other Ghosts would have gathered. He had almost reached it when he caught sight of Tessa moving at the perimeter of the camp. She was between an old truck and a wagon, weaving her way through a series of small tents toward the waiting storm. At first he could not believe that he was seeing correctly, but then he saw her lift her head momentarily as if searching for something.

A second later, she was through the gap between the vehicles and outside the camp.

He stared in disbelief. *Tessa!*

He paused only a second to wonder what she was doing, and then he was running after her, hurrying to catch up.

In the wild rush of the wind and dust, with everyone trying to get under cover, only one member of the caravan saw him go.

Farther west, still many miles away, Logan Tom and Simralin Belloruus rode the Ventra 5000 toward the roiling gray wall of the dust storm. They had watched it grow in intensity during the past hour, and now they knew with certainty how severe it was going to be. They also knew that there was no time to get out of its path.

"We have to take shelter," Logan said, giving voice to what they were both thinking.

He drove on for a short distance, then turned the big AV down into a ravine and parked it in the lee of a rocky outcropping that formed a barrier between themselves and the approaching storm. Glancing doubtfully at their meager protection, he shut down the engine and turned off the power. Outside, the wind howled across the barren landscape with such force that the entire vehicle shuddered.

"Guess this will have to do," he said.

Simralin made no reply. They sat in silence, listening to the wind. The storm rolled over them, thick with dirt particles, and the sky and the earth disappeared within its roiling shroud. The light died and left them shadows cloaked in a gray-brown haze. The sound of the sand striking the hard surfaces of the outcropping and the AV was like the buzzing of angry bees. Outside the shell of the vehicle, the world slowly disappeared behind the wall of the storm.

"Tell me the rest of what happened to you," she urged him.

He had begun relating the details of his own experience in escaping from the Cintra shortly after they had set out yesterday, then lost the thread somewhere along the way and hadn't gotten back to it. He had gotten as far as Kirisin's ordeal as a prisoner of the skrails, assuring her first that her brother was safe and well, but he hadn't gone on from there. She knew of Praxia's role in retrieving the Loden after Kirisin had dropped it, but not anything of the aftermath.

So he finished up now with Praxia's death

and the deaths of her companions, Que'rue and Ruslan, as they defended the Elfstone against the rogue militia that had stumbled on them while they tried to reach the Columbia River and safety. Simralin listened without comment, her eyes on his face, her gaze so intense that it almost hurt to bear its weight.

"I wish I could have gotten back to them," he confessed. "But saving Kirisin was more important. I almost didn't manage that."

"You managed just fine," she said. "If Kirisin had been lost, everything would have been lost. An entire people, Logan. Anyway, you did the best you could with the others. You have nothing to apologize for."

"It doesn't feel that way."

She was silent a moment. "I'm surprised about Praxia. She never demonstrated that level of selflessness before. She was always so self-involved. But not this time."

He shrugged. "Sometimes we rise above ourselves."

"Sometimes." She shook her head. "I just can't believe it. They're all gone, the whole squad I worked with all these years. Just like that. I've known some of them all my life, Logan."

"Almost everything is hard to believe. I've stopped being surprised." He gave her a half smile. "Except by you."

"I'm not so surprising."

"You don't think so? I don't know anyone

who could have made it back here alone the way you did. Not in the face of what was chasing you. Not through land as dangerous as this. You talk about what I can manage, but I don't think I am anywhere near as capable as you are."

"Then maybe it's a good thing we found each other. What do you think? An Elf and a human? Do you think there's any kind of chance?"

"I think there's always a chance."

He kissed her, and she laid her head against his shoulder. They stayed like that as the storm raged, and he found himself thinking of something he hadn't told her. When the once-men had stormed the bridge and it had seemed as if they were using Simralin and the other Elves as shields, he'd had to make a choice, one based almost solely on instinct. He had believed that what he was seeing was an illusion, that Simralin and the others weren't real. But he hadn't known for certain. Even so, he had ordered them fired upon, a death sentence if he was wrong.

And if he had been wrong, he would have been forced to live with the knowledge that he had killed the woman he loved.

It was a stark reality, even in a world where reality was never anything but hard-edged and brutal. He had chosen the lives of the many over the lives of the few. But the truth he was forced to confront in retrospect was darker still. If he had it to do over again, even knowing that what he was seeing wasn't an illusion, he would make the same choice.

He thought suddenly that he should tell her this, that she deserved to know. But he couldn't make himself. Besides, didn't she already know how it was with him? Didn't she understand him well enough by now to realize how it was always likely to be? He considered several explanations and rejected them all. He didn't want to talk about such things with her. The world was a dark enough place; he didn't need to speak of the particulars of that darkness.

He stayed silent instead, holding her, taking advantage of moments that might not come again.

Candle had gone back with Cheney to join the others, hunkering down in the AV as the fury of the wind increased, thinking through what Hawk had told her. Maybe he was right. Maybe her instincts were just taking a rest, and she needed to give them time to recover. She knew she hadn't been the same since that boy with the ruined face had kidnapped her. Though she hadn't told anyone, she was still haunted by nightmares of being taken, of being forcibly separated from her family. She still dreamed of what it had been like. She still dreamed, as well, of his screams as whatever it was that had been stalking them had caught up to him.

She didn't want to hear screaming like that ever again.

Glancing out the window, she saw Hawk walk by, head down, shoulders hunched, heading for the rear of the column as the caravan closed ranks and prepared to wait out the storm. Something about him bothered her, but she couldn't decide what it was. A little while later, Angel Perez stopped to look in on them. Candle huddled against Owl, a silent presence, as the Knight of the Word spoke a few words of encouragement and departed. The little girl was still thinking about Hawk when she saw him coming back again, appearing unexpectedly out of the haze. She hesitated, and then for reasons she didn't fully understand, she bolted from the vehicle and went after him. She wasn't sure what she intended to do, only that she needed to reach him. It was an impulsive and mysterious act, tied to what she was feeling, though not in any way she could have explained.

Owl's protestations trailed after her, but she didn't slow. The wind gusted in stinging swipes, blowing clouds of dirt into her face. She squinted, lowered her head, and ran as best she could. But Hawk was striding ahead determinedly, and her calls to him were swallowed up in the wind's booming howl.

She had almost lost him when he stopped and stared between the encircling vehicles and wagons at something moving in the haze. She caught sight of a familiar figure slipping through a gap between the wagons, there one moment and gone the next, moving out into the empty landscape. Was that really Tessa? She watched Hawk hesitate and then rush after the other girl. She called to him once more, but he didn't hear. A second later, he had disappeared.

Almost instantly, she knew that something was wrong. She could feel it the way she used to. Just like that, she could tell. Her heart began to pound, her nerves caught fire, and in the blink of an eye her instincts kicked back into life, returned from wherever they had been hiding. She didn't need to be told what was happening. She didn't need to second-guess what she was feeling. She recognized it for what it was.

She knew, too, with a certainty that was frightening, that Hawk was in trouble.

Come back, Hawk! Don't go!

She thought to follow him, to go after him and help. But she was only a little girl. What could she do? Instead, she turned and raced back toward the AV and her family. She was almost there when she ran right into Panther, who had been sent by Owl to bring her back.

"Whoa, wild thing, what do you think you're doing?" he shouted at her through the wail of the wind, grasping her shoulders and holding her fast. He knelt in front of her, his dark face bent close, his eyes blinking against the swirl of dust. "You want to get blown away?"

"Hawk's in trouble!" she gasped, clutching him back. "He went outside the camp! He's following Tessa, but something's wrong, Panther! I know it! I can tell!"

She was sobbing now, overcome with the intensity of her feelings, of the dark whispers in her head. He didn't question her, didn't even pause to ask for details. He straightened at once, picked her up, and trotted back to the Lightning, saying, "Okay, okay, you did good, did the right thing, don't worry, we'll get the Bird-Man back."

He literally tossed her inside the AV, shouting for Bear to grab the Tyson Flechette and come with him. Sparrow was out of the Lightning, as well, Parkhan Spray leveled. "What's happened?"

"Don't know. But Candle ain't never wrong, and if she says Bird-Man's in trouble, that's what it is. You coming? Bear, get me my weapon! Where's Cheney?"

In moments, the three were gathered together, huddled around Cheney, who had been sleeping under the AV. The others had crowded into the open doorway, watching anxiously. "Panther, I don't think you should do this!" Owl shouted at him through the rush of wind. "Don't go out there alone! Wait for help!"

510

"Can't do that!" the boy shouted back, racking the slide on the spray. "Might not be time! Not if it's that . . ." He didn't finish, bending down to Cheney, whispering to him, holding Hawk's leather gloves under the big dog's nose and then leading him over to where Hawk had walked past earlier.

"Track, Cheney!" he ordered.

Cheney seemed to know what was needed, setting off at once into the haze. "Send help if you can find it!" Panther called back over his shoulder, and disappeared with Bear and Sparrow after the dog.

Owl shut the AV's door and sat back. Candle huddled down in the seat next to her, staring, her instincts still as sharp and jagged as broken glass. Nothing felt right. Panther and the others weren't going to be enough. She could sense it already. They weren't strong enough, even with their weapons.

Seconds later she leapt up, threw open the door, and jumped from the vehicle once more, shouting to Owl that she would be back, that she was going for help.

She already knew where she would find it.

TWENTY-NINE

The world was a seething cauldron of heat, wind, and dust, the whole of the visible landscape enveloped in an impenetrable haze. Hawk pushed through it as if it were quicksand threatening to suck him down and swallow him, fighting to keep Tessa in view. For the most part, he could not do so, only catching sudden glimpses of her as she appeared and then faded ahead of him. Each time he thought he was closing the gap between them she would disappear once more, and when he found her again she would still be far ahead.

Tessa!

He called to her silently, knowing that it was pointless to call aloud in this wind. For a second it seemed she had heard, half turning back. Then she was gone again into the haze. He could not understand what she was doing, why she had left the safety of the caravan to come out into the flats. Tessa did not take chances without a reason, and it was inconceivable that she would do so now, carrying the baby. He could not think of anything that would have persuaded her to put herself and their child at risk this way; it made him both uncertain and afraid for her. That there was something very wrong was undeniable, and his fear of what that might be drove him on even when his common sense warned him that he was being reckless.

Just ahead of him, Tessa reappeared suddenly, turned all the way back, saw him, and stopped. Then she waved to him and started back to where he stood, smiling in a confused sort of way. She glanced back momentarily in the direction she had been going, as if looking for something.

He desperately tried to figure out what was wrong. Everything she was doing was completely out of character. He glanced back over his shoulder for the caravan, but it had disappeared in the storm. There was no sign of the vehicles or their occupants. There was only the emptiness of the plains, a vast roiling sweep in the grip of the wind and dust. He felt a moment of panic. Even his tracks had been blown away. His sense of direction was so skewed that he wasn't sure he could find his way back even if he wanted to. In fact, he was quite sure he couldn't.

As she came up to him, she said, "I thought you were still ahead of me. I must have gotten turned around."

He stared. "Ahead of you?"

"Well, you were ahead when you motioned for me to follow you out of the camp. Why did you bring me out here, anyway?"

He looked around quickly, dark suspicion sweeping through him. A huge bulky form materialized from the haze, one he recognized instantly. The monster that had been tracking him for days. The monster that had taken all the other children. The demon. It stood not a dozen yards away, and he realized with sudden clarity what had happened.

The demon was a shape-shifter. It had lured them away from the others by pretending to be something it wasn't, isolating them out on these flats in the midst of a concealing dust storm. It had deceived them as it must have deceived the other children — by assuming the form of someone they cared for. That was how it had gotten to Chalk, even though he had been warned of the danger, even though he knew what was out there. It had taken the shape of his best friend, Fixit, and drawn him out to be destroyed.

This time it had taken Hawk's form, tricking Tessa into following it. It must have been its intention to kill her and leave her for him to discover. But having him follow Tessa, in turn, was an unexpected bonus. Now it could kill them both.

He was suddenly enraged all over again. All of those children had been lured to their deaths by false images of loved ones, of friends, of family. It was so hateful to him that for a moment he forgot his own peril and thought only of how much he would like to see the monster destroyed.

But he was carrying no weapons, and he knew already that even with his magic he was no match for this creature.

He took Tessa's arm, pulling her to him, thinking they must run, must escape any way they could. Then he remembered. In his pocket was a pair of viper-pricks, each with enough lethal poison to kill a dozen Lizards. Would they do what was needed?

He would have to find out. He didn't have any other choice. The creature was already advancing on him, taking a more solid shape as it came, the outline of its huge shoulders and arms, its massive chest, its great clawed hands solidifying against the wispy curtain of the blown dust. He could see the glint of its eyes from beneath the heavy bone of its flattened brow. It was staring at him with undisguised anticipation, eager for what it was about to do.

He backed away slowly, pulling Tessa with him, one hand groping in his pocket for the viper-pricks. He found them right away, and his fingers closed about one plastic sheath and began to draw it out. Then, impulsively, he let go and instead reached down hurriedly to touch the earth. If he could make himself blend with the land, could disappear into it as he had before, he could gain a small advantage. His magic had let him do this once; perhaps he could do so again. If the monster couldn't see him, it couldn't hurt him.

But he realized the flaw in his thinking almost immediately. Even if he could disguise himself, he could not disguise Tessa. The demon might not be able to find him, but it would still be able to find her. He saw the demon watching him, measuring his efforts with interest. He could tell what it was thinking. Unlike the last time, the demon was not confused. It had learned from that encounter. It knew he would not abandon the girl.

He straightened and continued backing away, his hand returning to his pocket and gripping the viper-prick anew. The demon continued to watch him, ambling ahead slowly, not bothering to try to close the gap between them just yet. It was playing with him, Hawk realized. It was enjoying this. It knew he was trapped and could not escape. It knew he could be killed at leisure and without interruption.

And Hawk knew, in turn, with a certainty that was chilling, that the viper-prick was useless.

The memory of his boyhood dream of the dark and malevolent presence he could not escape resurfaced, a wraith from a past that was all too uncertain, but felt real nevertheless. This creature, this monster was the embodiment of that dream; he had known as much at their first encounter. He had known, as well, that he had no defense against it. There were things in this world that were too much for you, no matter who or what you were. This creature was one. Hawk was born of magic, and he had magic at his command, but he was helpless here. He could feel it in a way that defied explanation, but was no less real. This demon was anathema, a force of nature he could not withstand, could not escape, and could not survive. He had a moment of regret that it was so, that all those who were depending on him would be let down, that his efforts to find the King of the Silver River had come to nothing. Disappointment washed through him.

I should have been smarter than this, he thought.

He stared into the eyes of the predator that had brought him to this end. By the time he decided that flight was his only option, fear generated by the creature's terrible eyes had locked his legs in place and he could not move.

The Klee had waited for several days for its chance at the gypsy morph, tracking the caravan without ever letting itself be seen, patiently biding its time, occupying itself with taking other victims to sate its need. Because it could shape-shift for short periods of time, taking on the appearance of other creatures, it could lure its victims from the safety of the camp. All of them had believed they were following someone they could trust. All of them had believed they were safe right up until the end.

The taking of the children was just a way to let the morph know it could do as it wished whenever it wished and there was nothing to be done about it. It was a game the Klee enjoyed, playing with its prey before killing it. There was no need to hurry, after all. The end result was always the same.

When the dust storm arrived, the Klee recognized its chance. Taking on the appearance of the morph to lure away the female the morph cared about was not difficult. It had watched the morph interact with her from the darkness beyond the camp and intuited easily enough how the morph felt about her. Luring the female away at the height of the storm, knowing she would follow if she thought the morph wished her to come, required little planning and no special skill.

Looking at the morph now, trapped and helpless, it felt a fierce satisfaction. The game was over. The old man had sent it to kill this creature of magic, and it always did what the old man told him. But there would be other victims, it knew — others to track and kill. The old man would see to it. Hunting this one, though, had been especially difficult. It would be hard to find another that would provide such a challenge. But there would be another, of course. There would always be another.

It was still musing on this when a dark shape hurtled out of the wind and dust, and 180 pounds of muscle and bone slammed into it, teeth slashing.

Cheney had begun tracking Hawk in typical fashion, big head lowered, nose to the ground, working his way through the camp and out into the teeth of the storm. Panther, Bear, and Sparrow had been able to follow without much difficulty, the heavy screen of dust and debris notwithstanding. Even outside the camp, the big dog had kept up his slow, steady pace. He was moving so slowly, in fact, that Panther was just beginning to worry that they were going to be too late to do anything to help, when Cheney bolted ahead with a snarl and disappeared into the haze.

Panther shouted in frustration and charged after him, Bear and Sparrow right behind.

The three ran as fast as they could, trying to catch up to the dog, but Cheney was already far ahead. If he changed course, Panther knew, they would lose him completely and probably become lost themselves in the bargain. He spit out a mouthful of grit, and his hands tightened on the flechette.

Shoulda leashed that stump-head animal!

Then, from somewhere distant, Cheney's growls tore through the howl of the storm and gave them fresh direction. All three quickened their pace, weapons leveled as they closed on the sounds of a ferocious struggle. They broke through the screen so suddenly that they almost ran into the huge creature fighting to throw off Cheney, who had locked his jaws on one huge thigh. Panther caught a glimpse of Hawk standing off to one side, frozen in place, looking lost and helpless, with Tessa pulling at him futilely.

Ain't like the Bird-Man, Panther thought. *What's wrong with him?*

Then he was firing the Parkhan Spray, the bullets ripping into the monster's huge body. "Shoot it!" he screamed at his companions.

Bear took a moment to respond. He recognized the thing in front of him as the monster that had brushed him aside so easily during their last encounter. He hesitated despite himself, suddenly afraid all over again of what this creature might do. Then, shaking off his fear, he brought up the Tyson Flechette and fired three quick loads, the charges ripping huge pieces off the arms and shoulders and chest of his target. The monster staggered back, clearly wounded. It made no sound at all as it absorbed the hits; it suffered its punishment silently, backing away.

Got you! Panther thought gleefully as he saw the effect their weapons were having. He continued firing, advancing on the beast. Cheney had dropped away, crouching and snarling to one side as the three Ghosts fired round after round into their target, the loads tearing into it. Panther heard Hawk cry out, saying something now, but the words were lost in the blast of the weapons and the scream of the wind.

Then all of a sudden the monster was gone, disappeared into the haze of the storm. For an instant Panther and Bear kept firing, even after Sparrow screamed at them to stop. Neither could believe that the creature wasn't there, that somehow it had vanished. But when the wind rippled the curtain of the haze and it was still not visible, the pair held up again, swinging the muzzles of their weapons this way and that, searching frantically.

"Panther!" Sparrow screamed, and opened fire to his left.

He swung about, but by then the Klee was on top of him, attacking with terrifying speed. One huge arm knocked him flying, his weapon lost, his head spinning. He crashed to the earth and rolled hard, heard Bear roar in response, heard the boom of the flechette, heard Cheney's deep snarl. Then everything seemed to jumble together, and he couldn't make sense of what was happening. He hauled himself to his feet, swaying drunkenly. Blood was running down into his eyes. He looked around, saw that Bear lay sprawled on the ground, a motionless lump. Sparrow was yelling at Cheney, who was attacking the monster once more.

Feebly, Panther cast about for Bear's flechette, caught sight of it a short distance away, and staggered toward it, wiping the blood from his eyes. Cheney's shaggy body flew past him, nearly taking his head off, thrown like a paper doll by the monster. Sparrow was firing again, standing all alone in front of their attacker, her warrior mother reborn. She wasn't enough by herself, Panther thought, reaching down for the flechette. None of them was.

He snatched up the flechette and faced the monster, bracing himself for another attack. It registered then, a sudden frightening realization, that all the damage their weapons had inflicted had been for nothing. The creature looked as if it hadn't been touched; its wounds had healed over.

How could that be?

He started forward, intent on helping Sparrow before it was too late, and heard Hawk calling his name. The Bird-Man was beside him, grasping his shoulder, holding him back and calling off Sparrow, too. Tessa was still clinging to him, eyes wide with fear. In the span of no more than a handful of seconds, Hawk had brought them together with a dazed and bloodied Bear, all of them watching as the monster turned for another attack.

"You see what that thing can do?" Panther hissed in rage. "Weapons don't mean nuthin' to it! What are we supposed to —"

"I want you to stay back," Hawk told him, his voice steady, his gaze fixed on their attacker. "Keep Cheney back, too."

"As if!" Panther snorted, dropping into a crouch.

"Do what I say!" Hawk gave him a quick, angry glance. "Sparrow, you too!" He snatched the spray from her hands. "It's me it wants. I'll try to draw it off. You go for help."

Panther came right up against him. "You crazy! You'll be dead before you get a dozen steps! We're a family, remember? A family! We stick together!"

"He's right!" Sparrow snapped. "Give me that!" She snatched back the Parkhan Spray. "You don't even know what to do with that!"

They shoved Hawk and Tessa behind them and turned to face the monster's slow advance. It looked huge, unstoppable. But they held their ground.

"Try to take out its legs," Panther muttered.

"Or its eyes." Sparrow was breathing hard.

They began firing their weapons, the Parkhan Spray's steady burp contrasting with the boom of the Tyson Flechette, all of it backdropped by the howl of the wind. Panther knew they were going to die, but at least they wouldn't die of some stupid plague and they wouldn't die alone. If it had to happen, better that it be like this.

His dark face tightened. The monster was still coming, brushing aside the damage the weapons were causing, unfazed by the damage, lumbering through the smoke and fire and explosions to reach them.

Frickin' hell, he thought in despair and rage.

The Klee saw the trapped look in the eyes of its quarry and was pleased. They belonged to it now, all of them. It would kill them one by one. It would take its time.

But an instant later, a little girl appeared from out of the gloom. She rushed toward the others, a tiny figure pinned against the wall of the storm, red hair flying, arms waving, shouting something indecipherable. Her friends screamed at her to get back, to run away, but she kept coming.

The Klee turned, its flat head swiveling, its huge body following, blocking the little girl's way. She seemed to have no sense of what she was doing, charging into the fray with such wild determination that she might have thought herself invulnerable to harm. The Klee reached for her, but the fierce dog knocked the little girl down, and wheeled back to stand over her protectively.

Then a second figure appeared, this one more substantial and measured in its approach. A rune-carved black staff levered downward, pointing at the Klee's midsection, and the demon felt a chill run up its spine. White fire exploded from the black staff, fire so bright and pure that it was blinding. The force of the strike staggered the Klee, burning into it. A second strike followed close on the first, hammering into the low, flat head before enveloping it in fire.

This new attacker was someone the Klee knew. She had escaped it at the cottage home of the blind man. A mistake, it thought, leaving her alive. She was shouting at the other humans to run, keeping up her attack as she did so, advancing one slow step at a time.

"Run, yourself!" the dark-skinned one shouted back, firing his weapon anew.

The skinny girl who stood beside him was quick to join in. All three produced a steady barrage, weapons fire and bright magic catching the Klee from two sides. The demon was infuriated. It stood its ground a moment, and then advanced on the female Knight of the Word. But the force of her magic was too intense, and it had to give way. The woman was screaming, words that caused the others to press forward. The Klee swung its great arms furiously, turning this way and that. Then it tried to turn away altogether, to use its shape-shifting skills to disappear back into the haze. But its strength was sapped and its concentration fragmented. It could not seem to make anything work.

Now the dog had moved to block its way, too, and suddenly it had nowhere to go. It chose to attack the boy and the girl firing the automatic weapons, seemingly the weakest of its attackers. The girl dropped back quickly, but the boy held his ground. When the Klee was right on top of him, he jammed the barrel of his weapon under its chin. The Klee's great claws were ripping at the barrel as the weapon discharged and blew away the lower half of its face. One arm caught the boy a glancing blow as he tried to duck aside and sent him sprawling.

But the damage was done. The Klee's head was in ruins, and it could no longer see. It could heal, but only slowly now, very slowly. It could hardly believe what had been done to it. It staggered about blindly, trying to escape, to gain time. Too late. The Knight of the Word's white fire was burning into it once more, scorching it in a dozen places, setting its body afire, turning flesh and bone to ash. The Klee lurched badly and dropped to one knee.

It could feel its life draining away. It could feel death's cold approach. It heaved upward and fell back again. Realization of what was happening took hold. It had one final mo-

ment of frustration and rage, and then it was
dead.

THIRTY

Twilight arrived, and the storm departed. The winds died away into breezes and then into stillness, the dust and grit settled, and the air freshened. Three of the four horizons returned for a short time in the form of stark outlines against the deep blue of the sky — mountains east, hills north, and plains south. Then darkness descended and swallowed everything but the moon and the stars.

The weary members of the caravan dug themselves out, brushed themselves off, ate a much-needed dinner, and settled in for the night. Groups formed and dispersed, one after the other, exchanging stories and encouragements, rehashing what had happened and speculating on what lay ahead.

In the distance, west of where they were encamped, visible until the darkness cloaked it and audible even after that, the dust storm raged undiminished, a blinding wall of swirling debris and raging winds.

Somewhere in that haze was the army of

the demons and once-men. Somewhere, too, was a missing Knight of the Word.

Owl sat with Sparrow, River, and Candle, and all four spoke of him in hushed, worried tones.

"I think he's done what we've done," Owl said, steadfast in her optimism, the one who always adopted the most positive outlook. "He's found shelter to wait out the storm. It's just taking him longer to get free of it."

Sparrow frowned. "I don't know. He should have been here by now. He has that big AV to drive. He could drive through a dust storm."

"I don't know . . . ," River said, trailing off.

"I hope the demons didn't find him," Candle said quietly. "I don't want anybody else to get hurt."

No one spoke for a moment, thinking as one of Fixit. The survivors of the bridge defenders had arrived just as the storm was closing in, but their news of what had happened two days earlier in the battle with the demon army had only just begun to circulate. It was Cat, come back with the defenders, who had told Owl of the death of Fixit and the disappearance of Logan Tom. Then she'd gone off by herself, and they hadn't seen her since.

"Fixit was so brave," River said. "I couldn't have done what he did."

"It won't seem like a family without him and Chalk," Sparrow added. "Not like we're a whole family anymore."

"We're a whole family," Owl insisted. "We just have to start over. We just have to go on with our lives. This has been very hard and very sad. None of us thought we wouldn't all get to where we are going. But three of us are gone, and we can't change that. If we want to make losing them matter, we must tell ourselves that giving up is not the answer. Going on is how we can heal."

"I'm not saying we should give up," Sparrow said defensively. "I would never suggest that."

Owl nodded. "I know that. I'm only giving voice to what I'm thinking. I feel emptied out by this, and I need all of you to fill me up again. Do you feel something of that, too?"

They nodded, no one saying anything. In the darkness beyond where they sat, a baby began crying. They could hear its caregiver hushing it softly, and then the crying stopped.

Sparrow brushed at her spiky blond hair. "At least we got rid of that demon," she said. "At least we don't have to worry about it lurking out there in the darkness anymore."

Angel had told the Ghosts what it was they had faced and how brave they had been to stand against it and see it destroyed. It made Owl wonder, thinking of it anew, how evil the world had become in the aftermath of civilization's destruction. Or perhaps the evil had always been there and just taken different forms. Weren't there probably always demons in their midst, taking whatever forms suited them? She thought maybe so. Creatures like the demons and once-men didn't just spring up out of nowhere. If they weren't there already, the potential to create them certainly was.

"You know, it was Candle who saved us," Sparrow said suddenly. "She was the one who warned us about Hawk going out alone. She was the one who found Angel and brought her to help us." She gave the little girl a broad smile. "You've got your instincts back again, don't you? Just like they used to be."

Candle blushed and nodded. "I don't know what happened."

"It doesn't matter what happened," Sparrow pressed on. "You're back to how you were and you can warn us now when we are in danger. That's a very big thing, little girl."

Candle suddenly looked uncomfortable.

"Sparrow," Owl said softly. "Don't make Candle feel she has to do anything different from what she's been doing. She's always tried to warn us. It just didn't happen for a time. And if it happens again, that's all right, too."

"It won't happen," Candle declared, determination mirrored in her blue eyes. "I won't let it."

"Of course you won't," Sparrow agreed. "Everything's fine now."

River exchanged a quick glance with Owl, both of them thinking the same thing. Everything wasn't right and wouldn't be right again for some time. Certainly not until they reached the promised safehold, a place where they might at last be able to stop thinking about demons and once-men and monsters out of nightmares stalking them across the devastated landscape of their former home. Certainly not until then.

"Has Hawk said anything more about how close we are to where we're supposed to be going?" River asked.

No one spoke. Then Owl said, "I don't think he knows yet."

"He isn't even himself," Sparrow offered suddenly. "You didn't see him out in that storm, when we were fighting that demon. He looked as if he didn't even know what was happening. I've never seen him like that. He just stood there, almost like he was unable to move."

"I think he was afraid," Candle said.

"Well, that's not like Hawk." Sparrow looked around for confirmation, but the others were quiet. "I mean, he's always been strong for the rest of us." She seemed to want to say more, but then just shrugged. "I just think something might be wrong."

"What's wrong is that he's supposed to save several thousand people by finding a safe place for them and he doesn't even know for sure where it is and there's demons and once-men chasing him and trying to kill him and we're all saying there's something wrong with him when maybe we ought to just stop saying these things!" Candle clenched her fists for emphasis. "I'm just saying, Sparrow," she finished, mimicking Panther.

Sparrow stared at her for a moment in surprise, then nodded. "You're right. I'm not helping, am I?"

"Maybe it's our turn to be strong for Hawk," Owl suggested. "Maybe we need to let him know we still believe in him. He's carrying a lot of weight on his shoulders."

Sparrow stood up abruptly. "Let's go find him right now. Let's tell him how we feel."

River, sitting next to her, took hold of her hand. "Let's not. He's with Tessa. Maybe they need to be alone. We can tell him tomorrow."

Sparrow hesitated and then sat down again. "Okay. Tomorrow for sure, though."

Their talk quickly turned to other things.

Panther walked through the mostly sleeping inhabitants of the camp, searching for Catalya. It took a long time before he found her. She was sitting alone on the bumper of an old truck near the front of the caravan, wrapped in her gray cloak and staring out at the night. She didn't see him approach — he was sure of it — but she seemed to sense his presence anyway.

"Go to sleep, Panther," she said without looking at him, her face concealed by the hood of her cloak.

He sat down next to her. "How'd you know it was me?"

"I could smell you."

"Ha, ha. That's funny. You make me laugh, being so funny."

She looked at him now, and he was surprised at how haggard her face was and how sad her eyes. "Go to bed," she repeated.

He looked away self-consciously. "Can't. Too wound up from this afternoon. You come that close to dying, you don't want to sleep for a while. The two seem too much alike, I guess."

She nodded. "You were lucky."

"Huh. Staying alive is always about luck. You didn't know that?" He flashed her a quick grin. "You taught me, remember? Back when we went looking to rescue Logan Tom from that other out-of-control Knight of Whatever-He-Thought-He-Was?"

"That was a long time ago," she said, looking away again.

"Not so long. Hey, I missed you. Got no one else I can rag on like I can on you. I might have been jealous, too, you know. You choosing to stay with Logan instead of coming with me, I mean. 'Cept I'm not like that."

She kept her gaze averted. "You don't need to be jealous of me. There's no reason for it.

Now go to bed."

"You think we're getting any closer to where we're supposed to go?" he asked, ignoring her.

"If I had any idea where it was we were going, I might be able to answer that. Go ask your friend Hawk."

"Ah, Bird-Man won't say anything. He's not over our fight with the demon yet. Something happened to him out there. He won't say what, but something. You could see it. He was all froze up when we found him. He couldn't move, even to defend himself. Like he lost his nerve, something I didn't think he would ever do. He was just standing there, waiting to die." He paused. "I don't know about him. Might be he can't even find his way anymore. He's got that look, as if everything's a mystery and nothing he does will make it clearer."

"Maybe you should try to help him out then. You and the other Ghosts. You're his family, aren't you?"

"Naw, he won't listen to me. Never has. Never will."

She glanced at him, irritation mirrored on her face. "Better that you go try to change the situation there than continue sitting around here annoying me. Okay?"

"Hey, I'm just trying to —"

"Panther, are you listening to me? Do you understand what I'm saying to you? I'm telling you I want to be alone. Got it?"

He went silent then, staring at her in confusion. His anger surfaced in a hot wave, but he tamped it down quickly. "Sure, I got it." He gave her a nonchalant salute. "No problem, Kitty Cat. See you later."

He got up and stalked off, stung by the rebuke. He hadn't quite gotten to where he couldn't look back and still see her when the last vestiges of his anger gave way to concern. Something was wrong. He almost turned back, wanting to know what it was and if he could help her deal with it.

But he knew what her response would be, how she would treat him, and he didn't feel like he wanted to risk that. So he continued on.

He would try again tomorrow, he told himself.

When sunrise broke and the camp began to stir, Panther went looking for Catalya once more, determined to get to the bottom of things. If there were something wrong, he would find out what it was and what he could do to make it better. He wasn't entirely sure what motivated his thinking except that it bothered him when she was like this. He knew things had changed since she had first come into the camp and he had called her a Freak. He knew all that was behind him, and that he genuinely cared about her. What he didn't know was why. It wasn't as if they were all that much alike or anything. Really, they were about as different as you could get. But there was something between them. Sometimes he ached with knowing it, with wanting to be friends, needing her to realize that he cared and to respond to what he was offering. Maybe it was the admiration he felt for her, a girl with skills like that, with courage and composure and determination.

Any way you looked at it, she made him feel things that no one else did.

He took his time searching for her, not eager to rush this, but intent on doing it all the same. He didn't like how they had left things last night. He didn't like how it had made him feel. He hadn't slept well, thinking about it, and he wasn't going to spend the whole of the day brooding over the details. He would find her and work out what the problem was and things would go back to being the way they had been.

He walked the length of the caravan and back again and still didn't find her. She was obviously hiding out somewhere, nursing her anger or frustration or whatever it was that was eating at her. It irritated him that she was making it so hard on him, and his face reflected this as he strode on, increasingly out of sorts. Those who encountered him saw the look on his face and moved quickly out of the way, and he found it hard to get anyone even to talk to him.

Finally, he went to find Owl. She would know where Cat was, if anyone did.

He found her sitting by the AV watching Sparrow and River packing up the last of the supplies and equipment in the bins and on the roof. Candle stood next to her, holding her hand.

"Hey, Mother Owl," he greeted, walking up quickly, trying to sound nonchalant. "I need your help."

Owl looked at him, saw his face, and turned to Candle. "I need to speak with Panther alone. Why don't you help Sparrow and River, sweetie?"

Candle moved away, giving Panther a curious look as she did so. Panther didn't like that look, wasn't sure what it meant. Owl waited until the little girl was out of sight, and then she motioned for Panther to come close.

"I already know what you're going to ask me," she said.

"You do?"

"You're going to ask me about Cat."

Panther knelt beside her, his lean face intense. "Yeah, that's right. Where is she?"

"She's gone."

Panther stared at her. "What do you mean, *She's gone?* She's gone where? Where would she go?" He gestured angrily. "What are you talking about?"

Owl put a hand on his shoulder. "Calm down. She left during the night, not long after she talked to you. She came to me first and told me what she was going to do. I tried to talk her out of it, but she had her mind made up. I couldn't change it."

"She left? Just like that?" Panther was stunned. He gripped the arms of Owl's wheelchair in frustration and dismay. "No reason for it? She just left?"

Owl furrowed her brow, and by doing so Panther could tell that he wasn't going to like whatever she was about to say next. "She had a reason, Panther. A reason she felt strongly about, which is why I couldn't change her mind."

She glanced over at the three girls, who were still working, but who were trying hard, as well, to listen in on what she and Panther were saying. "She's begun to mutate again. She's changing into a Lizard."

Panther shook his head. "What? That's not true! Is it? She's changing? When did this start to happen? Why didn't she say anything to me about it?"

"She didn't say anything to anyone. She could barely bring herself to tell me, but she didn't want to leave without anyone knowing the reason. She was so unhappy, Panther. She just couldn't face what it would mean once you found out."

"Once *I* found out?"

"Once *anyone* found out. She was convinced it would change everything. That none of us would feel the same way about her. She believed we wouldn't want to be with her anymore. Or if not that, that we would simply tolerate her because we wouldn't want to tell her the truth. We would pretend to care, but really we would want her to go away."

She held up her hands to stop him from saying what he was about to say. "Let me finish. I told her that was nonsense, that we loved her for who she was on the inside, not for what she looked like. I told her she was making a mistake, leaving like this without talking it out. I even asked her to wait until Logan Tom returned. But she refused. She said she had made up her mind, and there was nothing I could say or do to change it. She asked me to tell the rest of you, to tell you she was sorry but she couldn't stay. Then she left."

Panther was beside himself. "This is frickin' bull! What is wrong with that girl! She don't think much of us, does she? Doesn't trust us enough to believe we care —"

"She's afraid, Panther!" Owl cut him short. "She's terrified! She's discovered that the one thing she didn't want to happen is happening, and she can't do anything about it! Think about how life has been for her. Trapped with the Senator, a slave and maybe something much worse. Getting Logan to take her away was the first real freedom she's known, and the Ghosts were her first real family. Now she thinks she's going to lose all that, and she doesn't want to stay around and watch it happen. So she's doing the one thing she thinks will avoid that."

"Well, she's wrong!" He spat angrily. "She's all wrong!"

"I know. I told her so."

"You should have come and told me right then!"

She gave him a sad look. "I said I wouldn't. I gave my word."

They stared at each other for a moment. Behind them, Sparrow, River, and Candle were staring, too. No one moved.

Panther stood up. "I'm going after her."

Owl shook her head. "She doesn't want that. She specifically said that you were to let this be her decision."

"Well, it ain't!" He was so angry he could barely think straight, shouting now, fists clenched. "It ain't just hers!" He didn't know where to go from there. He glared at all of them, tried to say something more, found he couldn't, and just wheeled away.

"Panther, wait!" Owl called after him.

He kept going, but then all at once Sparrow was right in front of him. "You sure about this?" Her face was right up against his, her features calm but determined, too. "Really sure?"

He nodded. "Yeah, I am. I got to do this."

"She went north." Sparrow tightened her lips, glanced quickly at Owl. "I overheard. I told the others earlier. We all know." She kept her blue eyes fixed on him. "Will you bring her back?"

"I'll try."

She put her arms around him and hugged him close. "You do what you have to do, Panther Puss."

One by one, they came up to him and hugged him. He relented enough then to hug them back, to whisper a few words of apology, to hear a few words whispered back. Even Owl wheeled over and gave him a long embrace from the chair.

"We love you," she told him. "We always will."

He nodded into her shoulder. "Yeah, I know that." He broke free. "Got to get some stuff together. You know."

He was practically crying when he left them, but he did not look back. Looking back would destroy him.

He stuffed his backpack with food and water, tied on a blanket, pocketed a compass and a pack of viper-pricks, and strapped on his knife. He shouldered a Parkhan Spray, picked up a prod, and set out. He took a route through the camp that bypassed Owl and the girls and walked out into the flats beyond, heading north. He had gotten to where the caravan was just beginning to fade from view when he heard his name called.

He turned and found Hawk and Cheney approaching. "Wait, Panther." Hawk trotted up to him, and they stood looking at each other for a moment. "I heard you were leaving. And why. I just wanted to say good-bye."

Panther nodded. "You and me, we don't need that. We're brothers, Bird-Man. We don't never need to say good-bye."

Hawk nodded. "I suppose not. But still."

"You got to be careful without me around to protect you. Can't be worrying that you'll do something stupid once I'm not here. Okay?"

"Okay. Anyway, you'll be back."

Panther nodded. "I'll be back."

"Take Cheney with you." Hawk glanced down at the shaggy dog. "Keep him for as long as you need him." He handed Panther a piece of clothing. "That belongs to Cat. Cheney can track her from the scent."

Panther took the offering, a blouse, and held it woodenly. "Yeah, this is good. But I don't know. Cheney belongs to you. He don't even like me all that much."

"He'll stick with you long enough." Hawk bent down to the big dog and whispered to him. Then he stood up again. "You come back."

Panther nodded. Then, impulsively, he embraced the other boy, gripping him tightly.

"You get them all to where they'll be safe, Bird-Man. You can do it. Ain't nuthin' can stop you."

Hawk hugged him back wordlessly.

"Frickin' hell," Panther muttered.

Then they broke the embrace, turned away from each other, and began walking. Neither looked back.

THIRTY-ONE

At daybreak, the caravan set out anew, continuing east toward the mountains. Most of the vehicles were still running, although several of the older ones had to be left behind because sand and grit had clogged their motors, and there wasn't time to fix them. Those who needed to ride simply doubled up. Conditions were perfect for travel. The day was clear and bright, the storm a thing of the past. Even west, where it had raged on through much of the night, all traces had vanished. Angel Perez, knowing the weather would favor the demons and the once-men as much as it did them, asked Helen Rice to send scouts back the way they had come to see if there was any sign of pursuit. She didn't have any illusions about the possibility of preventing their enemies from crossing the Columbia. Destroying the bridge would not stop them. Once-men lives were expendable. Whatever it took, the army would come after the caravan. If Angel and the other defenders were going to face another battle before reaching the promised safehold, they had better be ready.

She spoke briefly with Hawk, who was back in the lead, walking with a handful of his family members. She tried talking to him about their destination, to find out once again if he had any idea of how much farther they had to go. But the boy simply shook his head and said he didn't know, and the other Ghosts closed about him protectively. When it was apparent that no one wanted her there, she let the matter drop and moved away.

She traveled alone for a time after that, lost in thoughts of expectations, good and bad. She had been plagued by a sense of foreboding since rising and setting out. She should not have felt that way; in fact, she should have felt renewed confidence following the destruction of the demon. The children were safe again, and the caravan was moving forward. But for reasons she could not explain, her mood was dark and uneasy.

Eventually, Kirisin Belloruus joined her and reiterated his growing concern over his missing sister. Even though a handful of Elves who had escaped the massacre in the Cintra had found their way to the caravan, his sister was not among them. Angel understood. She was worried about Simralin, as well, not to mention the absent and long-overdue Logan Tom. Like the Elven Tracker, he should have been back before this. It was a difficult situation, having both of them missing at the same time and not knowing where to look for either. Nevertheless, Angel promised the boy that a new set of scouts would be dispatched to see if any sign could be found.

"Do you have any idea what's wrong with Hawk and the Ghosts?" she asked him after a while. "When I tried to talk to them earlier this morning, they made it clear they wanted me to go somewhere else."

"The halfling, Catalya, disappeared during the night, and Panther went after her," he said. "The others didn't want him to go. They tried to talk him out of it, but he went anyway. I think they are afraid they won't see him again."

She sighed wearily. *"Ay Dios mío."* Her mood darkened further. "Well, I'll ask the scouts to look out for them, too."

"I wish we could just get to wherever it is we're going," the boy muttered.

Angel nodded but didn't say anything more.

The morning slipped away, and it was nearing midday when they sighted the dam.

They saw it first as what appeared to be a cluster of dilapidated buildings and collapsed power lines settled within a depression. But as they drew nearer, they saw the smooth curve of a massive concrete wall spanning a deep gorge, and recognized it for what it was: an enormous structure built to hold in check the waters of what was, if the maps could be trusted, the north–south branch of the Columbia River. It appeared that the gates had been locked in place for a long time. Even a cursory glance revealed that the waters above the dam were perhaps two hundred feet higher than those below.

The caravan slowed as it came up on the banks of the gorge, and Angel found Helen Rice and had the bulk of the vehicles and all of the children kept well back while they went forward to decide what to do next. Then she gathered with Helen and the Ghosts on a high embankment and peered down at the dam and the gorge. This close, Angel could see cracks in the dam's smooth wall, spiderwebs across the whole of its curved surface. Water was leaking through some of the larger splits. The leakage appeared to be steady and had dozens of sources, all of them feeding the waters below the dam wall. Mounds of debris lay clustered along the banks of the gorge, including abandoned cars, pieces of sheet metal, and old appliances, all of it turned to rust.

"Doesn't look like anyone's come this way in a while," Helen said quietly. She glanced at Hawk. "Do we have to cross this?"

Hawk nodded without hesitating. "Yes."

Helen rolled her eyes at Angel. "I'm sending AVs in both directions to see if there's a bridge somewhere."

She turned and walked away. Angel stayed where she was, already considering alternatives. The top of the dam wall was clustered with housings for machinery and controls and iron railings, not all of them still in one piece. As well, the flat surface tilted at odd intervals, forming ramps and chutes. While the members of the caravan could probably make their way across, if they were careful and passed in single file, it was too narrow for vehicles. Even so, she was doubtful. She didn't like the look of the cracks in the concrete wall. The dam looked weathered and old and unsafe, even if it was still holding back all that water.

"Maybe we could build rafts and float the caravan across," said Helen, coming up beside her once more.

Angel looked around at the barren sweep of the hills and cocked one eyebrow at her. "Out of what? Trash and deadwood?"

They were silent then for a few minutes, all of them staring at the broad span of the gorge, mulling over the problem of crossing. Angel brushed at her short-cropped hair and thought how long it had been since she had washed it. Washed any part of the rest of her, for that matter. Days. She didn't like how it made her feel, thinking of it. She didn't care that the others were every bit as ragged and dirty as she was. She wanted to feel clean again.

She shook her head. Well, there was no help

for it. She glanced at the gorge and the dam once more. Maybe there was no help for anything.

"Let's give everyone something to eat," Helen suggested.

Angel nodded her agreement. "Go ahead. I want to have a closer look at that dam."

She left the others and walked along the embankment to where steps led down to a catwalk that opened out onto the top of the wall and the buildings beyond. She stood at the top of the steps and studied the structure. She didn't know anything about dams, so she didn't have any idea what she should be looking for, but she looked anyway.

Waste of time, she thought.

She looked beyond the dam wall to the waters trapped behind it. The river was thick with deadwood, and an ugly slick covered its surface where it brushed against the concrete. She wrinkled her nose. She wouldn't want to wash herself in that. She was still studying the morass when Kirisin appeared unexpectedly at her elbow. Wordlessly, he pointed skyward. When she looked, she saw a pair of winged creatures circling the caravan.

"Skrails," she said at once, a dark sense of inevitability sweeping through her.

"Candle sensed their presence even before we saw them," the boy said. "There were more in the beginning, but some flew away south."

"To warn the others. They must be close." She tightened her grip on the black staff. "They'll be coming for us."

"Helen Rice said to tell you she's getting the children and their protectors ready to cross the dam if the scouts don't find a bridge. She said we'll pack what we can carry on our backs and leave the rest. Even the vehicles."

It was an unpleasant prospect for more reasons than Angel cared to consider, but she kept her thoughts to herself.

"What are you doing?" he asked.

She gave him a brief smile. "I'm not sure. Come along. We'll find out together."

They descended the steps, stepped onto the dam wall, and walked out to the cluster of machinery housings. The doors were locked, but she was able to use her staff to burn away the locks. Inside, it was dark and close and thick with cobwebs and dust. The machinery consisted of banks of consoles that had long ago ceased to function, even with the aid of solar panels. The turbines that had fed water-generated electricity to the cities were silent, as dead as the cities themselves. Stairs led down into rooms embedded in the dam wall where it adjoined the gorge embankment, and here they found a series of huge wheels and connecting gears that probably allowed for the gates of the dam to be opened. But the wheels were locked in place by rust and time and perhaps by mechanical means that neither could comprehend.

Nothing here that will help, she thought.

With Kirisin in tow, she walked back out into the sunshine. Hawk was still meandering along the upper embankment, stopping every so often to kneel and feel the ground. His concentration was so intense that he didn't even notice them. She watched him for a moment, Kirisin beside her.

"What is he doing?" the boy asked.

She shook her head. "I don't know."

"He seems to be searching for something. What would he be looking for up there?"

Hawk dropped suddenly to his knees, both hands on the ground, head bent forward, eyes closed as if he were stricken physically. He stayed where he was for long moments, unmoving. Then he straightened, climbed slowly to his feet, and stood gazing south.

"Let's go find something to eat," Angel said, turning away.

She had rejoined Helen Rice and the others, collected a plate of food, taken her first bites, and was just thinking that things might work out despite the odds when the scouts Helen had sent north and south along the Columbia drove in, one right after the other. Those who had driven north reported that the only bridge they had found was collapsed into the river. The southern patrol had gotten less than ten miles before encountering the forward elements of the demon army, moving toward them at a rapid pace.

Helen was on her feet at once. "Get the children together. We're crossing the river right now."

Farther to the west, deep in foothills swept clean of all but the hardiest scrub by the dust storm of the previous day, Logan Tom was nursing the Ventra 5000 along with a mother's gentle touch. The big AV, having survived the dust storm with its moving parts intact, was on its last legs. Logan and Simralin had started out the day with the expectation of catching up to the caravan by nightfall. Buried under almost three feet of sand and dust, they had dug their way clear at sunrise, with the storm gone past and the air clear once more, and set out. At first, everything had seemed fine, but then Logan had noticed that the indicator lights on the dash were showing no power flowing from the solar panels to the cells, and the cells were almost empty. He stopped long enough to confirm that the panels were both cracked — either by windblown debris or heat — neither panel repairable, and used the spares to replace them. But the indicator lights still showed no exchange between the fresh panels and solar receptors, and he was forced to admit that the problem was more complicated.

Electing to go on rather than waste any

more time, leaving to chance the actual amount of time the residual power stored in the cells would give them, he concentrated on conserving what was there by running the engine on low and choosing the flattest route available. If the engine died, he would have to make a choice about what to do next. He was hoping he would not have to face that choice.

"Any idea where we are?" Simralin asked after a long silence between them.

"Some. We're not too far from the north–south branch of the Columbia River. The caravan has to cross there, probably at one of the dams or a bridge, if there's still one in place."

"Unless they've changed direction," she pointed out.

"I don't think that's going to happen. I think they're headed for the mountains." He pointed east across the flats. "You can't see them from here, but they're out there, over the horizon. I crossed them coming west weeks ago."

"I know those mountains," she said.

He nodded. "Well, somewhere in there is where we'll find this safehold Hawk is searching for. That's my opinion, anyway."

As if in response, the Ventra engine coughed and died, the vehicle lurched, and they rolled to a stop. Logan sat staring at the controls, as if an answer might present itself amid the vast array of colored lights and blinking switches.

"What's your opinion about that?" Simralin asked archly.

Without answering, he adjusted a few of the switches and dials, made several concerted efforts to restart the engine, and finally sat back. "My opinion is she's finished. Either I go to work on the wiring or we walk."

"Which will take longer?"

He glanced over. "Hard to say."

"Then let's walk."

He nodded. "At least we'll be moving."

They loaded up on food and water, sleeping gear and weapons, and set out. The day was warm and still, but not unreasonably so, and travel even at midday was pleasant enough. Logan hated leaving the big AV, a machine that up until now had provided both reliable transportation and protection. But he had known all along that he would probably have to abandon it at some point. What mattered just now was catching up to the caravan and reuniting with Hawk, the boy he was supposed to be protecting.

He grimaced inwardly. Not that he had done much of a job of it so far. He had failed to prevent Hawk from being thrown from the walls of the compound in Seattle, and it was the boy who had saved his life while he lay unconscious following his battle with the rogue Knight of the Word. Immediately afterward, Logan had been dispatched by the Lady to find the Elves and bring Kirisin Belloruus to safety, which once again had separated him from Hawk. Reaching the caravan and finding the boy anew, he had elected to stay behind to help defend the bridge against the demon army, and again they had become separated.

After all the emphasis placed by Two Bears and the Lady on the importance of finding and protecting the gypsy morph, he had expected to expend considerable effort doing so. But when you took the measure of the thing, he had done hardly anything at all. It disturbed him to admit this more than he cared to think about. He did not like it that the charge he had accepted had come to so little. Finding the boy had not been difficult; protecting him had been all but impossible.

It wasn't his place to question the things he was asked to do as a Knight of the Word. It wasn't given to him to judge. But he did so anyway. He always had. It was what had led him to this place and time. When offered the chance to do so, he had abandoned his life as a destroyer of the slave camps and their demon masters, worn down by the struggle, weary of the fight, eager to travel a new road. Searching out the gypsy morph was the price of the bargain. Find the morph and protect it, O'olish Amaneh had asked of him. Do this, and you will have your chance to face that old man who killed your family, the Lady had promised.

He had agreed in a heartbeat.

But why had they even bothered asking him? What was it that they expected him to do when for virtually the entire time since he had found the morph they had been separated?

There were no answers to be found, and no point in thinking on it further. He kicked at the earth with one boot, a pointed response to his frustration, and let the matter drop. One day, somewhere down the road, he might better understand what he was doing in this business, what his role was really supposed to be. For now, he would have to accept on faith that he had a purpose to fulfill, whether he saw it clearly or not.

They had walked less than ten miles when Simralin said, "Do you hear something?"

He stopped and listened. "Weapons fire, shouting. There's a battle being fought, just ahead."

They continued walking, faster now, their efforts more directed. Logan felt a clutch of fear in his chest at the prospect of what they would find. He had been afraid for some time that he might catch up to the caravan too late, that he might return only to bear witness to its destruction. He had lived in silence with that fear, refusing to admit to it. But now it was full-blown and pressing down on him on like a great weight.

Clouds of dust began to fill the air ahead of them, billowing up from the parched earth to form a broad haze across the horizon. The battle was intense and covered a broad span of ground from north to south. Logan was practically running now, Simralin keeping close.

"Look," she said, pointing.

Winged forms swept in and out of the haze ahead. Skrails, Logan realized at once. If there were skrails, there were likely once-men and demons close at hand.

Then they crested a long, low rise, and the whole of what was happening ahead was revealed.

The littlest of the children were already being led across the narrow span of the dam, hands linked together, a long winding chain of tiny forms, when Angel told Helen to move the vehicles into position in front of the crossing point to form a protective barrier. They would have to make a stand here if there were still children who had not gotten safely over by the time the lead elements of the demon army reached them. Helen selected from among the adults those who would act as defenders and began passing out what weapons they had. The engineers and explosives experts went to work laying charges along the perimeter of the battlefield to help defend against the enemy approach. Everything was pandemonium, a barely controlled chaos that Angel and Helen kept in check with close supervision and repeated reassurances.

When the Lizards and Elves and some of the other creatures who had been traveling with them came down to the dam head and offered to help, Angel made a quick decision.

"Helen, give everyone who volunteers weapons to use, and I'll put them at the barrier with the others. We need as many defenders as we can manage. No time to get choosy about who we're using."

Helen Rice didn't question her, but handed out what weapons remained, and when those were gone sent the rest of the newcomers down to the dam to help with the children. Angel watched for a few minutes more and then walked up to the barricade of wagons and vehicles and made some last-minute adjustments. Even Logan Tom's Lightning was pulled into line, its weapons pointed outward, one of the better defenders who'd come up from Los Angeles at the wheel. She wished more than she could say that the other Knight of the Word was there to help. She missed his steady resolve and fierce determination. She found herself wondering anew if she would ever see him again.

Kirisin was there briefly, ashen-faced and edgy amid all the activity, asking finally what they were going to do about Simralin. She had no answer for him. She told him to join the Ghosts and cross to the other side. He was carrying the fate of a nation in the Elfstone tucked in his shirt, and he had to remember that. His sister would tell him the same thing, if she were there. He left with tears in his eyes, unable to look at her.

Helen Rice reappeared. "How are we going to defend when they get here?" she asked.

Angel shook her head. "Send the explosives people down to the dam when they've finished with the perimeter. Wire it to explode. Tell them to do the best they can. We'll slow the attack down, hold the once-men for as long as we can." She gripped the other woman's arm. "The truth is, Helen, we're running out of choices."

"I know that. I've known it for some time." Helen gave her a brave smile. "But we're not giving up, Angel. No matter what."

"No, *amiga,* we're not giving up."

Helen folded her arms and hugged herself. "I'm so afraid."

Todos tenemos el derecho de sentir miedo, Angel thought. We all have a right to be afraid. She gave the other woman a hug. "Let's keep working."

She returned to positioning the armed vehicles and defenders among the haulers and wagons. Some of the latter she ordered overturned to provide better cover. She had the wheels removed from the rest, hoping to prevent the enemy from being able to pull them aside. She was not entirely sure of what else she should do. They relied on her, all of them, Helen included. But she was not the skilled and experienced warrior that Logan Tom was.

She thought momentarily of Johnny, the first time she had done so in days. If he were there, he would know what to do. He would sense instinctively what was needed and see to it that it was done. But her own sense of things paled by comparison and left her feeling inadequate.

The crossing over of the children to the far side of the gorge was almost finished when dust clouds appeared on the horizon and the lead elements of the demon army came into view. Once-men, wild and unkempt, ragged figures numbering first in the hundreds and then in the thousands, crowded forward. They came running across the flats — running! Their makeshift weapons were raised over their heads, and their voices were shrill and frenzied. They made no effort at an organized attack. They simply threw themselves into the fray like animals, their blood-lust driving them.

Thousands of feeders bounded through their midst, gimlet-eyed and hungry for what was about to happen.

"Keep coming," Angel whispered to herself, ignoring the feeders, concentrating on the once-men, her teeth clenched, the black staff gripped tightly. *But there are so many! Too many for us to stop!*

The front ranks reached the perimeter of the defensive lines, and the hidden explosives detonated, shredding hundreds of once-men. Screams mingled with clouds of smoke, and body parts flew everywhere. But the assault continued, fresh waves of attackers replacing those that had been decimated. A second set of charges went off, and again the attackers vanished in smoke and screams. This time the assault slowed, and the once-men, fragmented and scattered, struggled to mass anew.

Angel glanced over her shoulder at the dam. The last of the children were crossing, and now the adults who had helped them were beginning to file over as well.

"Fall back!" she shouted to the closest of the defenders, and then started down the line, drawing the attention of the rest. "Get back! Get across the dam!"

They began to withdraw in ones and twos, a too-slow response to her order. Frustrated, she stepped out into the open as the now fully regrouped once-men threw themselves at the defensive lines, and she sent the Word's fire exploding out of her black staff into the attackers. The front ranks collapsed, but more kept coming. Skrails were diving at her from out of the sky, tearing at her with their claws, trying to distract or disable her. She ignored them, sweeping the fire across the flats and into the enemy hordes that filled them.

But there were too many to hold, even for her, and she screamed at the last of the defenders to run for the dam. Some did not make it. Some were caught from behind and dragged down. She tried to cover the retreat, but the once-men were coming at her from all sides, the feeders on their heels, invisible shadows. A pair of defenders wheeled back and cleared out those closest to her with their Parkhan Sprays, bravely standing their ground even as they were overrun. She raced for the dam, engulfed by the screams of those who sought to reach her, fighting through smoke and ash from the explosives and fires.

She had just reached the gorge embankment and was scrambling for the relative safety of the far side when a makeshift arrow drove deep into her shoulder and spun her about. She righted herself and kept going, but another caught her in the leg. Then a third buried itself deep in her side, and she felt a wave of shock and nausea wash through her. Her strength failing, she scrambled forward, bleeding heavily now, and then she was on the embankment crest, the dam wall just below her, and she saw someone standing not a dozen feet away, fully exposed as he faced the rush of the oncoming hordes . . .

Hawk!

She could hardly believe what she was seeing. The boy somehow had managed to stay behind instead of crossing over as he should have, and now he was just standing there, alone and unprotected.

Then suddenly the boy knelt and placed both palms against the earth, and she realized this was exactly where she had seen him kneeling earlier, when she had come up from examining the dam with Kirisin. His head was bent as before, and his eyes were closed. He might have been alone in the world for all the difference the ranks of attackers coming at him made. Steel-tipped arrows and spears and automatic weapons fire flew all around him, but he never moved.

Angel, crouching not twenty feet from him, wheeled back and sprayed the closest of the attackers with the black staff's deadly fire. It wasn't enough. The rush barely slowed. The feeders had outpaced the once-men and were almost on top of Angel and Hawk. They were both going to die. Why hadn't the boy run, as he was supposed to? Why hadn't he saved himself, when so much depended on it?

As if in answer, a massive tremor shook the earth, followed by a series of shudders that rippled outward from the embankment into the plains beyond, throwing the once-men to their knees. The attack stalled as bodies tumbled everywhere. The feeders broke off their rush to reach her, suddenly confused.

The tremors continued, rough-edged and powerful, generated from somewhere deep underground.

But it wasn't an earthquake that was causing them, Angel realized. It was Hawk.

A sharp cracking sound rose above the rumble of the tremors and the screams and cries of the attackers, and a spiderweb of jagged fissures split the barren ground, spreading out from where Hawk knelt and running on for as far as the eye could see, across the flats and under the feet of the once-men. The cracking sound deepened, and the splits widened into huge gaps, and then into dark, bottomless chasms. Everywhere, frantic attackers tumbled from view and were swallowed. They tried to run, but the cracks, angling this way and that, growing in number, chased them down as if they were food to be eaten. By the handfuls, by the dozens, and finally by the hundreds, the once-men dropped away into the chasms.

The feeders threw themselves after them, caught hold of them as they fell, and tumbled from view.

In moments the flats were swept clean of all but a handful of the thousands that had composed the demon army, and those few cowered in small clusters here and there, swaying and moaning like ragged trees left standing in the wake of a terrible storm. Then the earth began to rumble anew, and the myriad chasms closed like great mouths, the cracks sealed over, and a deep silence settled over everything, a shroud thrown over the bodies of the dead.

THIRTY-TWO

Standing apart from the other demons, Findo Gask considered his options in the wake of the destruction of his army. He had watched it all happen from high ground far enough removed from the carnage that he had never been in danger. Until now, of course, when his subordinates began to look at him as something less than infallible. A demon that could lose an entire army of once-men to a mere boy was not as all-powerful as they might have thought. A demon that could sacrifice that many followers without accomplishing anything, no matter the reason, was demonstrably less able than what they had believed.

Which meant, of course, that they were already considering which of them should replace him.

He glanced at them accusingly, and some, but not all, looked away. It enraged him that they should be so bold. Fools, he thought. Not a one of them could do what he had done. Not a one could command his power. They were children in the presence of a master, and he needed none of them.

Still, he would have to watch them closely.

He turned back to the plains, empty now save for clusters of survivors who cowered together like frightened sheep. The loss of his army mattered little to him. It was but a single arm of a much larger force, and replacing once-men had never been a problem. Whatever his needs, there would always be fresh bodies — at least until no more were needed and he could dispose of them all. He would simply send for another supply. The caravan might have escaped him for the moment, but it was a temporary escape at best.

What mattered just now was the boy, the gypsy morph, wielding all that magic.

The fact that he was still alive was proof positive that the Klee had failed. Findo Gask had suspected as much for days, knowing that the Klee must have found the boy by now and yet had not returned. That the Klee had failed was inconceivable. Delloreen, yes. But not the Klee. That anything or anyone was strong enough to destroy it — for it must be dead — was an impossibility he could not fathom. Only he had power enough to destroy a demon as powerful as the Klee. He could not imagine how any of these humans — even a Knight of the Word — could have managed such a feat. A shape-shifter, a trickster, a creature of great cunning and strength, it had proven itself invincible time after time.

But now it was gone. There was no doubting that.

And here was that boy, the gypsy morph, still alive.

The boy lay sprawled on the ground, unmoving. How badly was he hurt? Not all that badly, Findo Gask judged. He had barely been touched in the assault. No, he was merely exhausted from the exercise of his magic. Which was hardly a surprise, given the power it must have required to open up the earth like that. The demon watched as the female Knight of the Word, lying nearby, began hauling herself to her feet, using her staff to provide leverage. But exhaustion had overtaken her, as well, and she fell back again. Then, as if consumed with desperation, she began to crawl.

Findo Gask had seen enough. He needed to put an end to this business once and for all. The gypsy morph had to be destroyed, and this was the perfect chance to do so. Weakened, depleted of magic, it would provide little resistance. Not only would he kill the morph, but he would kill the Knight, as well. It was not a task he would delegate; others would welcome the chance to take credit for such an accomplishment, but he would not allow them to do so. He would handle this himself because it would serve as an object lesson to his treacherous subordinates and enhance his somewhat diminished stature as leader.

Then he could reassemble his army and continue to hunt down those still alive in the ragtag band of misfits the morph had been leading, humans and Elves and others.

He signaled to the pair of skrails hunkered down nearby, beckoning them to him. They came at once, seized him by his shoulders, and lifted off. In seconds they were airborne, flying toward the boy and the Knight of the Word. He glanced across the gorge to where the members of the caravan were gathered on the embankment edge, watching his approach. Some were already yelling in warning. None, he noticed, had made any effort to try to come back. He would give them no chance to rethink that decision. He would make quick work of their precious leaders, of this boy and his protector. He was already relishing what it would feel like when the morph died beneath the crushing weight of his magic. They believed this boy so powerful, but they had no concept of what real power entailed. They had no idea what he could do.

The Knight of the Word was turned about now, facing him as he flew closer, somehow back on her feet, leaning heavily on her black staff. She would die hard, this one. She had found a way to elude him for years, fighting for the compounds in Southern California, salvaging scores of children from the ruins, keeping them from the camps and his experiments. He assumed she had found a way to put an end to Delloreen, no easy task. No, she would not die easily. But she would be dead, all the same.

Angel Perez watched the old man's descent through a film of pain and weariness. She was no match for him like this, but there was little choice. Behind her, Hawk lay unconscious on the ground, unable to defend himself. She was all he had, and she had sworn to protect him. Even if she knew that she would fail, she had to try.

She had mustered strength enough to get back to her feet when she saw the skrails flying the old man toward her. She had known at once who he was and why he was coming. His army destroyed, he must salvage something from his defeat. Killing her would be a start. Destroying the gypsy morph would put an end to everything. He might not know why this was so, but he must sense the truth of it. He would not be hunting the morph otherwise, would not have expended demons like the female creature that had tracked her or the monstrous thing that had come for Hawk.

She felt a great despair fill her at the prospect of failure. Dying was a given in the lives of the Knights of the Word. She had always known that. Johnny had died for a similar cause, trying to save others, trying to make a difference in a savage world. She understood and accepted this, just as she believed he had. But failure of the sort that would befall the human race with the loss of the gypsy morph was unthinkable.

"I must find a way," she whispered to herself.

The skrails lowered the old man to the ground, leaving him perhaps thirty feet from where she waited, and then backed away, knowing better than to become involved in this, sensing perhaps that he did not want or need their help. He would face her alone. He was intent on making this personal.

He stood where he was for a moment. Even in the sunlight that filtered down through the lingering haze, he was a wispy figure that had the look of something born out of smoke and ash. His body was hunched slightly, perhaps with age, perhaps with the weight of something less measurable, but equally debilitating. His face was seamed and worn, but even at this distance she could see the bright and compelling light of his strange eyes.

A distraction from across the river drew his attention. A handful of youngsters, including several of the Ghosts and Kirisin, were charging back toward the dam, finally come to their senses, determined now to try to help. The old man watched them for a moment, and there was a mix of curiosity and contempt mirrored on his face. Then he glanced at her for just a moment, turned back almost casually, lifted one arm, and pointed. Fire exploded from his fingertips and tracked across the top of the dam wall. Flames rose dozens of feet into the air, burning from end to end, finding fuel where they was seemingly none to be found.

The flames blocked any passage across, and those trying to reach Hawk and herself fell back. The rescue attempt collapsed.

The old man turned back to her and started to walk forward. "Let me have the boy, and you may go!" he told her.

He made a slight motion as if to go around her, and she moved immediately to block his way. "I don't think so, *diablo*. Back away."

He slowed to a halt. "You don't seriously think you can stop me from taking him, do you?" he asked her.

"I don't know what I can do," she said. She was aware suddenly of fresh pain radiating through her, the consequence of even those few simple steps. She looked down at the ends of the darts protruding from her body like spikes. "Why don't you find out?"

"I'm going to kill you, you know. I could do it even if you were fresh and uninjured. I could do it even if you had help." He gave her a searching look. "I'm not like those others you dispatched. Do you understand that?

573

Do you know who I am?"

She nodded. "You are the one."

She said it without rancor, but it conveyed a good deal more than its tone revealed. She summoned the magic and watched the runes glow dimly beneath her fingers. *Too little,* she thought. *I haven't magic enough left to do this. I won't be able to stop him.*

"I am the one," he agreed. He continued to study her, as if seeing something he hadn't recognized before. "Why not consider the advantages of what accepting that means."

"Join with you, you mean?"

He shrugged. "Why not? If you live, you would have much to contribute. Others have done so; you would not be the first."

She had blood soaking through her clothing, and her face was streaked with sweat and dirt. She was aware of how vulnerable she looked to him. Had there been any reason at all to do so, she would have given the matter thought. But there was no reason, of course.

"I would sooner rut with wild dogs," she answered.

He laughed softly. "No need for that. No need for anything more from you. I asked out of false hope that reason would transcend pride. I should have known. It never does with your kind."

"Better pride transcending reason than contempt for the sanctity of life transcending a sense of right and wrong."

She was fighting for time now, for a chance to gain a small advantage, for anything that would work in her favor. She would keep him talking for as long as she could.

He came forward a few more steps and stopped again. "You are all alike, you Knights of the Word. Passionate in your beliefs, dedicated to your causes, blind to everything but your righteous commitment to a faith in something that has doomed you from the beginning. Humans can't sustain what is needed for such faith, woman, even if you can. Humans lack the iron necessary to see it through. They are so fallible and so easily subverted. You've seen it for yourself, time and again. We are where we are, you and I, standing on this empty plain, because of that."

"Some of us might see it differently. Humans are not perfect; I wouldn't argue otherwise. But their faith is what sets them apart from creatures like you. They believe in the impossible, in what they cannot see and touch. They think that if you don't seek to be better than what you are, you live to no purpose. What is the point of life if not to improve it for yourself and others?"

He laughed anew. "Life's sole purpose is in staying alive for as long as you can. Power facilitates that end. I saw that centuries ago when I shed my human skin to become my demon self. I gained control over magic that you can only dream about. I gained power over my life and the lives of others. Faith in anything other than that is a waste. What can you hope for but disappointment?"

"You can hope for a world in which living things flourish, not one in which they are systematically destroyed. You can hope for a world where power for its own sake is disdained. You can hope for a common ground that fosters compassion and understanding provides space for all living things."

"A very pretty image."

"You wouldn't understand."

"What I understand is that a world of living things is overrated."

She sensed a change in his stance, in the expression on his face. She held herself steady, using her magic to buttress her failing strength, a little here, a little there.

"You struggle so hard in the service of the Word," the old man said quietly. "But in the end, you die anyway."

She had summoned what magic she could to defend herself, but it wasn't enough. The old man's bright fire exploded into her with pile-driver force, knocking her off her feet and sending her sprawling. She felt all the strength leave her, felt pain rip through her body. Smoke rose from her clothing in wispy trailers. She lay helpless on the ground, the black staff clutched against her body.

Help me, Johnny, she prayed.

"Such a waste," the old man said, shaking his head as he approached across the flats.

Sudden movement caught her eye. Feeders, thousands of them, were oozing from the ground like the ghosts of the dead come back to life. They emerged like strange, twisted trees, their black shapes liquid and sinuous, their eyes bright with hunger. They were there to feed on her.

The old man saw them, too, and he smiled approvingly, until a sudden explosion of fire generated by a magic that was not hers caught him squarely in the back and threw him to the ground.

Simralin and Logan Tom watched in disbelief as the boy Hawk used his gypsy morph powers to open the earth and swallow the demon army whole. They stood atop the embankment until the shaking of the ground forced them to their knees, and then they remained kneeling as the shock of what they had witnessed left them momentarily frozen. How could any creature possess power enough to do what they had seen this boy do?

But then the skrails flew the old man over the empty flats to confront Angel Perez, and Logan Tom was back on his feet instantly. He could hardly believe what he was seeing. It was the enemy he had searched for all these years. He knew him instantly, as if he were eight years old once more and standing amid the bodies of his family and the destruction of his home, as if seeing that sly smile and those cold, hard eyes, as if feeling anew the other's tacit approval of his killing of the once-men with the Tyson Flechette.

He turned at once to Simralin, and she saw everything he had told her about the old man reflected on his face. "Is that him?" she asked.

"It's him. I have to go down and face him. I want you to wait until he is engaged with me, and then I want you to slip around behind us and get Angel and Hawk on their feet and across the bridge. Can you do that?"

She nodded. "But I want to go with you."

He shook his head, backing away. "I can't be worried for you when I do this. I can't bear thinking of him hurting you, too. Don't ask it of me."

She let him go then, not because she had no other choice, but because she understood the kind of determination that ruled him in this matter and knew there was no point in questioning it. They were close enough by now that he didn't need her to tell him so to know that it was true. There was something in her eyes at the last, just before he turned away, but there was no time left to consider what it meant. He did not look back, hurrying down the embankment and onto the flats, intent on reaching the old man, who had already been set down by the skrails and was walking toward Angel. He felt the adrenaline

578

pump through him; he was almost light-headed with expectation. This was the reward the Lady had promised him all those weeks ago. By finding and protecting the gypsy morph, he would have his chance at avenging his family. He had wondered all along if the promise had meaning, if it would be kept. Now he found himself wondering if he could make it count.

He was a long way out yet when the demon set fire to the dam to stop the futile rescue attempt from the eastern bank of the gorge. He was still too far away to be effective when the demon tried to go around Angel, and even though she was clearly wounded and sapped of her strength, she blocked his way. He wasn't much closer when the two began talk to each other, and the feeders began to appear. He saw all this in glimpses as he passed through curtains of residual smoke and floating ash. The tableau played itself out in small snapshots, as if an album of pictures taken of a single event. He kept thinking that he was going to be too late to save either Angel or the boy, that the old man would kill them both before he could get close enough to prevent it.

But suddenly he was through the last of the haze, and the confrontation between the old man and Angel Perez was taking place right in front of him. Neither saw him, and he did not wait for them to do so. Levering the black staff, he summoned the magic of his order, letting it build until it was so thickly gathered within him that he could no longer contain it. Then he released it in a blinding explosion that ripped through the still afternoon air with a sound like metal tearing.

The demon was unprepared for the attack, its attention focused on Angel. It had no defenses in place, save the ones that its preternatural instincts allowed it to summon at the last minute. The Word's fire slammed into it, lifted it off its feet, and threw it to the ground, singed and smoking. Logan did not slow. He came on, walking toward the slumped form, catching a quick glimpse of the hard old face as it turned to him, feeling the sting of those terrible eyes.

He sent the Word's cleansing fire burning into it a second time, a long, sustained stream that engulfed the gray-cloaked demon and set it aflame. Logan watched it burn as he closed on it, fighting his way through fresh waves of smoke and ash. He was filled with a fierce, terrible joy. *For my mother and father,* he thought. *For Tyler and Megan.* He kept the magic of his staff burning into the demon until he felt his strength begin to sap. Then, and only then, did he pause his attack to measure the results.

He was very close by then, but flames and smoke hid much of what he needed to see. He moved closer still, wary now, his instincts warning him that this might not be over, that he might not be seeing things as clearly as he should.

His instincts were correct. Just as he realized that the smoking, flaming lump in front of him was only empty robes, he was struck a terrific blow from behind and sent sprawling. He managed to hang on to his staff, but only barely. As he tumbled to the ground, he caught a quick glimpse of the skeletal form that had been standing at his back, stick-thin and hunched over, the demon in its old man form.

Then its killing fire was burning into him, and all of his concentration was on mustering sufficient magic to ward it off. He did so at terrible cost to his own reserves and only barely managed to keep the flames at bay. The demon had tricked him, giving the impression that it lay helpless on the ground when in fact it had slipped away after that first strike. He had been too ready to accept what his eyes told him. His eagerness had blinded him to the truth.

The demon fire ceased, and Logan rolled away from a scorched patch of earth so hot that it made him cry out. He tried to rise and couldn't. Feeders hovered at the periphery of his vision, crouched and waiting. With his black staff shielding him, he faced the demon from a prone position, looking for a way to fend it off. Again, he had misjudged. This demon was so much stronger than any other, and he had not been sufficiently prepared to defend against it.

The demon was approaching him now, a strange look on its face. It moved a step closer to Logan, as if needing to see him more clearly.

"I know you," it hissed, its voice a whisper that spoke from the depths of a bottomless well. Surprise reflected in its wicked green eyes. "You're the boy from the compound, all those years ago . . ."

Logan screamed in fury and counterattacked. Only his rage at the knowledge that the other recognized him gave him the strength to do so. It felt as if the demon had claimed a kind of ownership over him, and he could not bear that. But the effort was futile; the other's power responded instantly, eroding his own, beating back his defenses, collapsing his shield. Even when he was close to being consumed by demon flames, his skin beginning to sear, he fought to regain his feet, lurching to his knees, struggling to rise.

It was not enough. He could not save himself. The feeders were all around him now and closing. He felt his magic giving way. Despite everything, he was going to die.

Then a wave of blue fire struck the demon from behind, a fire so bright and pure that Logan was almost blinded by its intense glow. He watched it envelop his attacker and saw the look of shocked surprise that crossed the hateful face. His first thought was that Angel had regained her feet and was trying to help him. But this was not Word fire, and Angel still lay where she had fallen, barely risen on one elbow.

He shifted his gaze, and through billowing clouds of dust and smoke he found Simralin.

She was standing not a dozen feet away, the Elfstones gripped in both hands, her face a mask of concentration. Blue fire erupted from between her fingers, burning into the old man. Logan was stunned. She must have disobeyed him and followed him down. She must have decided she would help. And against all odds, she had found a way to master the power of the Stones.

Fighting through pain and rage, the demon began to turn toward her, shifting his own magic to defend himself. The Elven fire illuminated his bones as if he were transparent, and his head was thrown back in concentration. The moment he began to turn, Logan lurched to his feet. He threw off his weariness and his fear of failure, recovered his shattered determination, and walked toward the demon. When he was right on top of him, he jammed one end of his black staff into the other's back, penetrating skin and muscle and bone, and summoned the magic.

Instantly the Word's fire responded, ripping into the demon, an explosion of power released from a place inside himself that he did not know existed.

In a flood of dark shapes, the feeders were all over Findo Gask.

The demon half turned, pinned between the killing fires, eyes bright with madness and hatred. Lips skinned back from pointed teeth, and its gaze conveyed to Logan Tom its terrible loathing. But Logan did not relent; he pressed his attack even harder. He pressed it until it was all there was left of him, until the entire world disappeared beneath the weight of his resolve to see the demon destroyed.

There was a moment in which Logan could feel a shift in the tides that marked the battle's momentum. The demon twisted and thrashed, changing as it did so into something unspeakable, a creature from an older time come at last to the end of its life. The feeders clung to it, ripping and tearing, driven into a frenzy.

Then it exploded into flames and smoke and ash, and Findo Gask was gone forever.

THIRTY-THREE

In the aftermath of the struggle, the skrails lifted off and flew south, and the remnants of the once-men drifted away. Even the lesser demons, perhaps not appreciating that had they chosen to do so, they might have combined forces and overwhelmed the pair that had destroyed their leader — perhaps too stunned even to think such thoughts — turned away. Atop the wall of the dam, the demon fires died out, leaving blackened stone and scorched air. East, the members of the caravan stood grouped along the banks of the gorge, and in the sweep of the land west, the plains lay abandoned and empty.

Logan Tom lowered his black staff and looked down at the remains of the old man, the enemy he had hunted for so long, and realized that he didn't feel any of the things he should have been feeling. He should have felt elation or relief or satisfaction, shouldn't he? Something? But all he felt was emptiness, as if the fulfillment of the Lady's promise had done nothing more than hollow him out. *All those years,* he kept repeating in his mind, over and over. *All those years.*

Then Simralin's arms were about him, and she was holding him, and he could feel something breaking inside, and the emotions flooded through him with such intensity that he began to shake. Forgotten memories surfaced like the ghosts of the dead, memories of his parents and his siblings, of his life after they were gone, of his loneliness and resolve, of so much he hadn't allowed himself to think about for twenty years.

Her arms tightened, and he said softly, "I'm all right."

But she held on to him anyway, and it was not until the shaking finally stopped that she whispered, "Now you are."

She released him then, and they hurried over to Angel Perez. When they knelt next to her and tried to help her to her feet, she shook her head quickly and said, "*No puedo. Me duele todo el cuerpo.* I can't. I hurt everywhere. Leave me, and see about the boy." She looked at them each in turn. "*Son muy valientes, mis amigos.* Very brave."

They moved to Hawk and found him awake, breathing regularly and unharmed. Simralin knelt and lifted the boy's head into her lap, and when he opened his eyes and tried to speak, she put a finger to his lips and said, "Shhh, just rest. Everyone is safe."

A stream of adults and children came charging back across the bridge to help them, ignoring the fresh network of cracks and fissures that had developed in the concrete. Soon the Ghosts were clustered around Hawk, hugging him and telling him they believed in him and would never leave him, and Tessa was kissing him and telling him she loved him more than ever.

Kirisin appeared suddenly from the throng, came running up to Simralin, and threw his arms around her. He was crying, even though he kept trying to hide it, and he couldn't speak at first. She hugged him back, and simply said, "I missed you, too, Little K."

With Helen Rice directing traffic, they carried Angel across the dam to the far side of the gorge, and a woman with medical skills set about removing the darts, cleaning out the wounds, and binding her up. No bones had been broken, and these injuries, like those she had received before, would heal with time. All that was needed was rest, and the woman gave Angel a medication that put her to sleep in moments. Helen had a makeshift stretcher built using a pair of slender trees and an old canvas greatcoat, placed the sleeping Knight of the Word atop it, and assigned two strong men the task of attending to her.

When the caravan set out again, its members were filled with a fresh sense of hope and confidence. From the youngest to the oldest, everyone's spirits had been lifted. People talked and joked and related memories of the battle they had witnessed and the near disaster they had escaped. In softer tones they spoke of Hawk, of a boy who could open the earth and make it swallow their enemies, and they told themselves that as long as he led them they would come to no harm.

Hawk walked apart with Tessa and the Ghosts, choosing their path and not saying much to anyone. If he heard what people were saying about him, he didn't let on. When Sparrow tried to speak of what he had done, daring, as usual, what no other would in the absence of Panther, he only shook his head and said he didn't want to talk about it.

They walked through the remainder of the day, the sun drifting slowly west behind them, the light dimming, and finally, after far too long, Logan Tom found himself alone with Simralin.

"Your little brother doesn't want to let you out of his sight," he said, having just sent the boy to the rear of the caravan, ostensibly to make certain that everyone was keeping up.

"Little brothers are like that," she replied, moving close to him and linking her arm in his.

They walked on for a time without speaking further, content just to be close, their eyes shifting from the ground to the land ahead, where night was creeping into view.

"What you did back there . . . ," he said finally.

"Was necessary."

"Was incredibly brave. You couldn't have known you could make the Elfstones work. You took a terrible risk."

"Some risks you have to take. I had to take this one. I had to try to help you."

He shook his head. "You didn't listen to anything I said about waiting, did you? You were right behind me the whole time."

She was silent a moment. "I kept thinking of all those I left behind in the Cintra, all those who died and I will never see again. Friends and family, people I cared about." She shrugged without looking at him. "You know how important you are to me, Logan. I wasn't going to lose you, too. I am bound to you in so many ways. Not by words or writing, but by how I feel. If I lose you, I lose myself."

"You won't lose me," he said.

"At the time, I wasn't so sure."

He gave her a small, weary smile. "I told you that you might be able to use the Elfstones, even if it didn't seem so when you tried before. Didn't I? Didn't I say you just had to give yourself a chance?"

"You did. It seemed so easy this time. Perhaps it was because I was so determined that it would work; because I wanted it so badly. I just called the magic up the way I'd seen Kirisin do it, and there it was. You were right."

"But I could have been wrong. You could have been killed."

"You could have been killed, too."

"I love you," he said impulsively.

She squeezed his arm. "I love you, too."

"I didn't think this would ever happen to me." He was feeling giddy, light-headed. "Meeting someone like you. Falling in love like this."

"But it did. Despite everything."

"I can hardly believe it. Even now. It feels so strange. Like I don't deserve it. Like it isn't real."

She laughed. "You'll get used to it."

He exhaled sharply, filled with wonder. "Good thing you didn't listen to me when I told you not to come after me. If you'd listened, we wouldn't be having this conversation."

She didn't say anything, her face suddenly serious. He touched her dirt-streaked cheek. "You saved my life."

She shook her head slowly. "No, Logan." She leaned into him, kissing his cheek once more. "I saved my own."

It was late in the afternoon, the sun sinking toward the horizon, when Panther finally caught up to her. With Cheney's help, he had been tracking her since sunrise, the shaggy wolf dog setting a steady pace, big head swinging from side to side, muzzle lowered to the ground. At times, Panther wasn't so sure that he had the scent. But he knew better than to doubt the dog's ability, and besides, Cheney was all he had. Without him, he wouldn't have stood a chance of finding her.

"There she is," he whispered, almost to himself.

Catalya was walking just far enough ahead that until a few moments ago, she had been lost in the deepening shadows of a rapidly descending twilight. But he could see her clearly enough now to be certain of who she was, a small, cloaked figure outlined against the graying sky.

"C'mon, Cheney," Panther urged, and picked up the pace.

He caught up to her quickly, pressing hard to close the gap, determined not to lose her to the darkness. She didn't hear his approach until he was almost on top of her, when the sound of his footsteps or his breathing caught her attention and brought her about. She stood where she was, staring at him with Rabbit crouched guardedly at her feet. The look on her face told him right away that she was not happy he was there.

"So the going got too rough for you back there?" he snapped, deciding to be aggressive about this.

She stood her ground. "Go back, Panther. I don't want you here."

"You got a serious attitude problem, little Kitty Cat, you know that?"

"You're the one with the serious problem. Your ears aren't working. Didn't Owl tell you not to come after me?"

"She said." He gave her a shrug. "I decided maybe you didn't really mean it. Maybe you was confused about who your real friends were."

She waved him off, turned around, and started walking again. Panther fell into step beside her with Cheney following. Rabbit hopped along to one side, indifferent to all of them.

"See, Owl told me what was wrong. She told me everything. She laid it right out there, no beating around. You ain't got to be alone in this, Cat. Some of us want to be there with you. We don't abandon our friends just because they got a problem."

He waited for her response, but she stayed silent, moving steadily forward, as if by doing so she might somehow leave him behind. It made him all the more determined.

"Why don't you want to talk to me about this?" he snapped. "I come all this way to find you, you won't even talk to me? Bird-Man, he even let me bring Cheney to help find you. That wasn't something he had to do, but he did it anyway. Shows you something, don't you think?"

"I don't think you get it, Panther," she said wearily.

"Well, why don't you explain it to me then. I got nothing better to do than listen to you."

She stopped and stared at him. "Well, you maybe ought to *find* something better to do and go somewhere else while you're doing it. How much clearer do I have to be about this?"

"I don't know. You tell me."

She glared at him, but he didn't move. In frustration she pulled up one sleeve of her shirt. Her arm, once mostly clear of the infection that was apparent elsewhere, was a mass of scaly patches, rough and gray-hued. She thrust it at him as if by doing so he might change his mind about staying, but he refused to move.

"So?" he said.

She dropped her sleeve over her arm. "So, Panther, it's happening all over my body. Just like that, it started up again. I thought it had stopped. I thought that it might be in remission. No such luck. It's come back, and it's changing me faster than it did earlier. You know what that means, don't you? You and your street smarts, your vast knowledge of *Freaks*."

He almost said something sharp in return, especially when she used the word *Freaks* as if it were an accusation. But he held his tongue and nodded. "Guess I had that coming. But it doesn't change things."

She laughed, bitter and sharp. "Of course it changes things. It changes *everything!* Within weeks, maybe less, I'll be one of *them.* One of the *Freaks!* I'll be a Lizard, and when that happens no one who's still human is going to want to have anything to do with me! Especially you!" She was shaking with rage. "So don't pretend that what's happening doesn't change things! You know it does! I've seen what it does, over and over while living with the Senator. If you aren't *human,* you aren't fit to be with humans! That's just the way it is with people."

She snatched up Rabbit, turned, and stalked away, but he quickly caught up. "Maybe where you used to live, people was like that. Ain't so with the Ghosts. You can tell yourself it's no different, but that don't make it so. You know that."

She shook her head. "Where do you come up with this stuff, Panther? You think nothing will change when I'm all scales and Lizard looks? Think again. The Ghosts will quit on me, quick as that. So will you. You might not think so now, but you will. You have to accept that. I'm a Lizard!"

He grabbed her by the shoulders and wheeled her about to face him. "You might be a Lizard on the outside, but you're still who you always was on the inside. You're the bravest girl I ever knew, even including Sparrow. You're smart and strong and ain't afraid of nuthin' 'cept things you make up to be afraid about. But you ain't making me one of them, you hear me? I didn't come all this way to be told I don't know how I feel about you. I came because I made up my mind on that subject a long time ago."

"That right? You made up your mind how you feel about me?" She brushed him aside and began walking again. "What a load."

"I came to bring you back to your family!" he shouted in rage. "You left your family, Cat! You know that? You walked out on them! They didn't walk out on you. You walked out on them!"

She didn't answer, just kept walking. So he kept walking with her, waiting to see how long it would take for her to speak to him again. It took a long time, and when she did, all she said was, "Go home."

"Can't do that."

"Sure you can. Go home."

"Nope. I'm staying."

They walked on until it was dark, and neither said another word. Finally, Cat turned into a copse of graying fir and made a place for herself to sit and eat her supper. Panther joined her, pulling out food and water of his own. Rabbit curled up at their feet and began to purr. Cheney lay down nearby and closed his eyes.

The meal was consumed without conversation. Afterward, the pair sat across from each other and exchanged surreptitious glances while the night air grew chilly, the darkness deepened, and the stars came out by the thousands, sprinkling the blackness with bright bits of silvery light. The moon rose above the eastern horizon, orange initially and then white. *Be the same moon back at the caravan,* Panther thought, and wondered if anyone was missing him yet.

They unrolled blankets and wrapped themselves up, still sitting across from each other, still not speaking. The minutes slipped away, and Panther felt his eyes growing heavy. Maybe her plan was to wait him out, let him fall asleep, and then slip away. Well, it wouldn't work. He wouldn't sleep until she did. Even if he had to stay up all night, he wouldn't sleep. Besides, it didn't matter if he did. Cheney would just track her down again if she tried to lose him.

But her stubbornness was frustrating. It made him wonder anew what he was doing out here. If she didn't want to come back, why was he going to all this trouble to change her mind? Oh, sure, he liked her. He thought she was special, all right. But what was he planning to do if he couldn't get her to go back? Tell her *good luck* and give it up? Stick it out? For how long? Days? How long could he afford to stay out here?

"You are so stubborn!" she said suddenly.

Like you ain't, he thought. But he didn't say anything.

"I shouldn't be mad at you," she continued after a moment. "Maybe I'm not. Maybe I'm just mad at how things have worked out. Disappointed, I guess. I wanted it all to be over, and now I find out that it won't ever be over, that I'm not going to be what I was, not ever. That's hard."

He nodded again. "Yeah."

"I just don't know what you expect me to do."

"I don't know what I expect you to do, either," he admitted. "I was just thinking I'm not really sure what I'm doing out here. I came because I couldn't let you leave thinking it didn't make a difference to me. Or to the others, 'cause they care, too. I thought I might persuade you to come back with me, try it out, see how it works. It might not be like you think."

She studied him a moment, and then she got up, her blanket draped over her shoulders, and sat down beside him, close enough that they were touching shoulders.

"Here's the thing of it, Panther," she said. Her mottled face turned toward him, the scales glinting in the moonlight. "When I discovered I was changing again, I didn't decide right away that I was leaving. I thought

597

about it first. I looked for a way to do just the opposite. I knew how you and the other Ghosts felt about me. I loved being a part of your family. It was what I had wanted for a long time."

She rubbed her hands together to warm them before tucking them back under the blanket, hugging herself. "But then I realized something. Hawk is taking us to a safe place, sure. But that's where we're going to be for a long time. Maybe years, maybe longer. Chances are, there won't be any going out in the meantime. Not for any reason. 'Cause the world outside's going to be destroyed."

His face darkened as he thought of it. "Yeah, guess that's so."

"Well, I don't want to be shut away. I've been shut away in one place or another for my entire life. I've never been free to travel where I wanted, not until Logan took me away. I don't think I can give that up. Not under any circumstances. It would be like living in a compound. I don't want that. And what happens if after I've changed and become a Lizard, no one wants me around except maybe you and the other Ghosts and maybe Logan? What if all the Lizards are made to live in one place because everyone else is afraid of them? Because that's how it's been in the world before, hasn't it? Why should it be any different this time? Humans are already afraid of Lizards, aren't they? So how is this going to work once I'm a full-blown Lizard girl?"

He shook his head. "Don't know. But at least you'll be alive."

"Yeah, that's what I said, at first. If the world is going to be destroyed, maybe this place we're going to is all that will be left. But maybe not. Maybe there will be something else, too. I mean, ask yourself this. Is there really something that can destroy everything? That's never happened. The world goes on, no matter how bad things get. Life changes? That's a constant. Species die out, species are born, like that. You know. Owl must have read something about this to you."

"Well, yeah, but . . ."

"I have to consider what life will be worth if the safe place we're going to becomes like a prison. Or a place that feels like a prison, anyway. To me, the little Lizard girl. I don't want to live like that. That's not living, that's dying by inches. I would rather have it all end at once than go into a place I couldn't get out of and ended up hating. I would rather be free for whatever time I have left."

She took a deep breath. "So that's why I left. I made a choice, but it wasn't made for the reasons I've been saying. Not really. Not if I'm honest with myself. I told you stuff that I wanted you to believe. I thought that it would make it easier for you to let me go. I know you'd stand by me. All of you. I know it doesn't matter to you what I become or how I look."

"Good," he said. "Better. That's better. At least, it makes me *feel* better." He hunched forward. "But you really think that it won't work, going back? You really think it might be like a prison?"

"It's going to end up being a confined space. There will be boundaries and rules. There will be limits on where you can go and what you can do. I don't want that. I can't live with it. Even with the possibility of it."

"So where are you going?"

"North. Fewer people, more open space, less likelihood of disease, pollution, militia, all the rest. Space enough to get lost in, to find a new life."

"Cold up there."

She stared at him. "I know what's up there. I know what I'm facing. You choose your poison in this world, Panther. You don't get a guarantee of safe passage anywhere."

They sat together in silence again after that, lost in separate thoughts. After a while, Panther reached over and put his arm around her, and she leaned into him. "You mind if I stay with you for tonight?" he asked her.

"I wish you would."

A little while later, they nestled down together with the blankets wrapped close about them. They lay spoon-fashion for warmth, with Panther pressed up against her from behind. When he reached up and gently touched the scales on her cheek, she did not move his hand away.

They rose with the dawn, ate their breakfast, and packed their gear. When everything was ready, they shouldered their packs and stood looking at each other awkwardly. The sun was a bright glow across the eastern mountains, and the air was bright and clear and sharp with the cold wind blowing down from the north. Cheney stood nearby, watching them.

Panther shivered. "So you really gonna do this, huh?"

She nodded. Rabbit romped past, chasing a moth. She reached down and picked up the cat and cradled him to her. "Good-bye, Panther. Tell the others . . . tell them whatever you think is best."

"Well, let's you and me talk about that."

She shook her head, holding out one hand in warning. "Don't start. I told you. I'm not going back."

"Okay, I got that."

"What, then?"

He shrugged. "Been thinking. Last night, while you slept, I was awake awhile, going over everything you said. It made me look at things different than I did before. See, you and me, we're more alike than you know. I don't like being closed away, either. I'm used to doing what I want, going where I want, not having any rules that I don't like. Makes me different from Hawk and the others. They like having rules. They like having walls and doors and feeling safe. I wasn't raised like that. I've always been free. Thinking about what I'm doing, maybe committing to living in a place that's like a compound, makes me uneasy. More than uneasy, really."

Her brow furrowed. "What are you saying?"

"That I don't think I'm going back, either. I'm going with you."

She stared at him without speaking. She clasped her hands and twisted the fingers together.

"Maybe this sounds crazy," he continued, "but it's not. It makes sense. Anyway, it's more than that. I was wondering why I came after you, remember? Told you that last night. Well, I think it's because I knew somewhere deep inside that I wanted to be with you. Only way to make that happen is to go where you go."

"No." She shook her head firmly. "You don't want to go with me. You want to go back to the others. They need you. I don't."

He smiled. "Thought you'd say something like that. But I don't think it's true. I think you do need me."

She sighed and turned away. "Good-bye, Panther."

She started walking, but he caught up with

her in seconds. "We got to find some warmer clothes along the way. Forage for some food and water, too. I brought a map. Took it from the caravan stores, thinking I might find use for it. It can help us locate a city somewhere along the way, someplace large enough for stores and stuff."

"You're not coming with me," she repeated.

"Probably not right away. Probably I'm just going in the same direction."

"This is crazy."

"No, it ain't. Not when you care about someone like I care about you."

They walked for a while with neither of them speaking further. Catalya was huddled down inside her cloak and hood, and Panther could barely catch a glimpse of her face. He let her be. *Better to wait on this,* he thought.

Then all of a sudden she stopped where she was, set Rabbit on the ground, and turned to face him. He could see the tear tracks on her cheeks. "You understand, we can't ever have a normal . . . not ever be like other . . ." She couldn't finish. She just shook her head in frustration. "It can't ever be more than what it is right now. For us. For you and me."

He shrugged. "Guess we'll have to wait and see. I don't need to know about that right now anyway." He reached out and wiped away one damp track from her cheek. "But if that's how it turns out, that will be enough. I

603

ain't asking for anything else."

She studied him again, as if trying to see past whatever was visible, and then she nodded slowly. "I see you brought your Parkhan Spray. The barrel's sticking out of your backpack. You must have broken it down to carry it like that."

"Yeah, I did," he admitted.

"You have to promise you won't use it unless I tell you to."

"Hey, this is your journey, Kitty Cat. You the one in charge. I'm just along for company."

"What about the other Ghosts? What about your family? They're going to wonder what's happened to you, aren't they?"

He shook his head. "They're smarter than they look. They'll know."

"Speaking of which." She pointed at Cheney, still sitting a few yards off, watching.

"Well, he's got to go back by his own self." Panther gestured at the dog. "Go home, Cheney. Go back to the Bird-Man."

Cheney stared at him and didn't move.

"Go on, get out of here!" Panther yelled.

But the big dog just sat there. Panther thought about rushing at him, trying to scare him, but decided that might not be the thing to do.

"Forget him," he said, shrugging. "He'll go back when he's ready."

They started walking again. Panther forced

himself not to look back, to keep his eyes directed ahead. But then out of the corner of his eye he caught Cat smiling. "What?"

She pointed at Cheney, who was sauntering along right behind him. "Guess he's not ready yet," she said, arching one eyebrow.

Panther nodded and shrugged. "Who cares? Stump-head dog."

In the distance, far out on the horizon, mountain peaks rose against the skyline, stark and jagged in relief. There was, to Panther's way of thinking, fresh promise in a country you had never visited before. There were mysteries to be uncovered and wonders to be explored.

He was looking forward to doing both.

THIRTY-FOUR

For weeks, Hawk led the caravan eastward from the Columbia, pressing on toward the mountains. Children, their caregivers and protectors, Elves, Lizards, Spiders, and others trailed behind him in an exodus that would for years afterward be recounted by the descendants of those who survived it. They crossed first through flatlands and gently rolling hills ravaged by drought and dust storms, the landscape barren and empty of everything but scrub and clusters of farm buildings long since abandoned and collapsing back into the earth until that, in turn, gave way to pine forests, whole stretches of which were dead or dying, but some of which still thrived on water and nutrients somehow left free of the poisons that had infected the rest. Finally, they found themselves approaching what a battered green sign announced to have once been the city of Spokane.

They were more than two weeks into their journey by then, their food and water almost gone and their strength failing. They had been following a freeway they had come across on the second day of their march. Without vehicles for transport and reduced to walking, the ribbon of concrete offered the path of least resistance. Logan, Angel, and Helen Rice all agreed that following the highway was the best option for making their way and probably the safest. They also hoped that one or more of the small towns that normally bracketed major roadways like this one would yield the supplies they needed. But while the former proved out, the latter did not, and by the time of their arrival in Spokane the situation was desperate.

Then things turned around.

First Logan and a handful of others, searching through an industrial complex on the outskirts of the city, discovered a warehouse filled with haulers and tractors. They were all meant for farm use and not for the purpose of carrying people, but there was nothing to say that they couldn't be adapted to the uses the caravan required. Their solar engines were in working order, and once they were pulled out into the sunlight, their cells began to charge immediately. The tractors would be slow — not much faster than walking, once the wagons were attached — but they would allow most of the children to ride.

Later that same day, prowling deeper into buildings in the same complex, they found a handful of working AVs. The AVs were not on the same order as the Lightning or the Ventra; they were not armed or armored or meant for fighting use of any sort. Even so, they would provide the caravan with swift, mobile vehicles for scouting and foraging. Five were still working.

The following day, while the caravan was passing down the freeway through the city itself, another foraging party found an outlet filled with bottled water and dried foods that could still be eaten. Helen had one of the tractors and a slat-sided wagon taken off the road and brought down to be loaded with the supplies. They might still have some distance to go, but at least they would have something to eat and drink along the way.

While all this was going on, Hawk stayed with the main body of the caravan, knowing that his job was to keep its members moving toward their destination. He still didn't know where that was or how far they had to go, and he could sense the restlessness growing in those he led. At times, he could sense hostility, as well. But when he spoke of it to Logan, the Knight of the Word told him to ignore it. Those who traveled with him did so of their own volition. They did so at his sufferance. If they didn't want to go with him, they could leave at any time. Hawk refrained from pointing out how many of these were children who didn't really have a choice because he knew Logan meant well.

But his own uneasiness persisted, and the restlessness and even the hostility were reflections of what he was feeling toward himself.

Spokane seemed virtually deserted, an oddity given the nature of most cities, which served as havens for refugees of all sorts. But no one appeared to challenge them, and there were only glimpses of brief, furtive movements in the shadows of the buildings they passed. Hawk asked Logan and Angel to keep an eye out for others who might want to come with them, but no one appeared to do so. Perhaps they were frightened of the size of the caravan, or perhaps they simply didn't want to go. Whatever the case, the residents of the city, human or otherwise, remained in the shadows.

At one point Hawk saw a sign by the side of the freeway that read CHENEY. He was so surprised that he stopped to stare at it momentarily, and Candle, walking with him, stopped, too.

After they began walking again, she said, "Do you think they will ever come back?"

He put his hand on her head and stroked her hair. "I don't know, Candle."

But he did know, though he wouldn't admit it. He had known from the look in Panther's eyes when they had said good-bye. He had known when he had sent Cheney with him, a protector for the boy and for Cat, once he found her. None of them would be coming back.

It was instinctive by now. It was a part of his transformation since leaving the gardens of the King of the Silver River. He knew a lot of things he should not have been able to know, knew them with increasing regularity and with unshakable certainty. More and more, he sensed the truths that were hidden from the others. Without that sense he would have faltered long ago, he believed. Without that mystic reassurance that told him how things were he would have despaired.

So it was that he knew Panther would find Cat and stay with her, and Cheney would stay to watch over them both. Their lives would take them in a different direction from the other Ghosts, and the family would shrink accordingly.

Now and then, he wished he had been able to keep Cheney with him for a little while longer. It was hard to think of going on without the big dog.

But what was the point of hanging on to something you weren't going to need?

The caravan traveled east for another three weeks, the speed of its already slow passage further diminished by changes in the land-scape. Flatlands gave way to steeply rolling hills that were rocky and forested, and then to miles of foothills leading into the mountains they had been heading for all along. Hawk began to gain a fresh sense of perspective on their destination, and at last felt comfortable enough to tell Owl and Tessa, if no one else, that he believed they were getting close to where they were meant to go.

They had passed through the city of Spokane without finding anyone who wished to join their pilgrimage, but all that changed when they neared the mountains. Other families drifted in from the wilderness, some bringing what remained of their livestock, some bringing household pets. There was only a scattering of each, but enough so that it began to feel as if a full-blown community was forming. They might be starting over, wherever they were going, but they were bringing with them vestiges of the old world, and it felt comforting to be able to do so.

Then one evening a band of men and women rode in on horseback, the first horses anyone had seen in years. They had been living up in the hills, isolated and protected by the natural terrain, veterans of living off the land, and they had seen the caravan passing from afar. Anxious to learn what they could of the world, they stayed to eat dinner and talk, and then chose to stay for good and travel to wherever the caravan was going. Hawk was never certain what decided them, although they spent a long time talking with Logan and Simralin. They had never seen an

Elf or a Knight of the Word, but whatever the two conveyed was persuasive enough to convince them that hiding out in the hills was not what they should do.

In the morning, they rode back for the rest of their community, and by nightfall another fifty had joined the march.

The three weeks following Spokane passed quickly and without incident. Once, a militia rolled up to them in armed vehicles and confronted them near the passes leading into the mountains. But Simralin had marked their approach long before they arrived, and the defenders were waiting to greet them. A brief exchange resulted in a few threats and some bitter words, and Logan gave the raiders some of their water to appease them. It was just enough to avoid bloodshed, and the raiders, sensing the probable outcome, took the water and left.

Then, on a bright sunlit morning, they crossed through a high pass in the mountains and looked out over a broad valley dotted with lakes and trees that were still fresh and green to a horizon clustered with even bigger mountains that stretched away for as far as they could see, blue-black and jagged shadows backlit by the sunrise.

"This is it," Hawk said softly, standing alone at the forefront of the march, and he went to tell the others.

■ ■ ■ ■

Simralin completed her measurements and stood at the very center of the forested bluff, looking around. "I think this is the place, Kirisin."

The boy nodded. "It feels right. The Elves will want height and distance when they emerge, a sense of being apart from the rest of the world. They won't be able to change their feelings about that right away. It will be hard enough for them to accept that they can no longer hide."

He's growing up, Logan thought approvingly. He was standing next to the boy watching Simralin pace off the distance atop the bluff, measuring the available space for the Elven city. His black staff was strapped across his back, out of his hands for the first time that he could remember. He'd tied it there for the journey across the valley. There hadn't been any need for it since they had arrived. For reasons he couldn't explain, he didn't think there would be any need for it again.

He smiled despite himself at the idea.

"The others from the caravan will have to get used to the Elves, too," he interrupted the siblings. "They all have to share this valley together."

"It will help that most of them are children," Simralin added.

It will help mostly that they have to make it work because this is all there is, Logan amended. But he kept that to himself, too.

In the company of the remainder of the Elves, the handful who had found their way clear of the Cintra, they had traveled all day to reach this spot. Simralin had explored it two days earlier and come back with her report. By then, they had been inside the valley — this safehold to which Hawk had taken them — for three weeks. The caravan was already beginning to split apart and its members to take their leave and go out to make their homes in this new world. The Lizards and Spiders and the other mutants had been the first, gone the very night of their arrival. No one had suggested that they needed to live apart; it was mostly an individual choice that each species had made. Some distance between the different groups wasn't necessarily a bad thing, Logan thought. They would need time to adjust to this new life. They would need space to grow accustomed to what that required.

But the distance felt odd to him. He had made his decision, too. In choosing to be Simralin's partner, he had stepped across a line. He must go with the Elves because those were her people and she had told him from the first that she would always live among them. Because he had no people, it felt right that he should live with hers. But it was hard

614

leaving the Ghosts. Hawk, Tessa, Owl, Sparrow, little Candle, River, and Bear — they had become a kind of family for him over the past weeks, children he had taken under his wing, the first children he had really gotten to know in all the years he had been saving them from the slave camps.

Still, Angel Perez had stayed behind, and they would all be a part of the community of children and caregivers living under the leadership of Helen Rice. Already, they had begun work on permanent homes, building with the tools they had managed to carry with them in their flight. It was probably best for them to be together there and for him to be with Simralin here.

A part of him ached nevertheless.

"What do you think I need to do now?" Kirisin asked, glancing from Logan to his sister and back again.

"I think you need to do what your heart tells you, Little K," Simralin said.

"We better back off a ways," Logan advised. "We're standing right in the middle of where you plan to put the city."

They did as he advised, taking the other Elves with them, moving to one side of the open space on which they intended to locate the city and its Elves when they were released from the Loden. When they were safely clear, Kirisin took out the Loden and held it in his hand, looking down at it dubiously.

"I wish I knew more about what I was doing," he said, glancing at Logan.

Logan understood. He had wished for that more than once on this journey. But much of life didn't allow for knowing things in advance, and you had to trust to your instincts and common sense. Kirisin knew as much about Elven magic as anyone alive, including all those trapped inside the Elfstone. So there was nothing much anyone else could do to help him through this.

"Go on," he said gently. "You used it before to put them inside. Do the same thing now to bring them back out."

The boy nodded, finding some measure of sense in this advice. He took a deep breath, exhaled, and closed his eyes. He stood without moving while the others watched. *Don't rush this,* Logan said silently. Westward, the sun was dropping toward the horizon, and the daylight was fading from the sky. Even so, there was light enough for whatever was required to complete the transition. Logan glanced at Simralin, but she had her eyes fixed on Kirisin. Willing him to do what he must do. Willing him to be strong and sure-handed enough not to make a mistake.

Abruptly the Loden flared within the boy's clenched fist, a blinding glow that spread outward and built in intensity. Logan shielded his eyes. As the glow rose and spread outward, covering the whole of the bluff from end to end and even into the trees beyond, a wind rose with it, come out of nowhere. So powerful was the wind that it nearly knocked the Knight of the Word and the Elves sprawling. As it was, they had to crouch protectively, bracing themselves against its force. Only Kirisin was unaffected, standing at its center as if untouched.

The wind howled like a living thing. It whipped at the light, scattering it in four directions, a giant hand pushing bright water in a pond. Within the light, Logan could see movement. Something was coming alive. He could see the hazy images of buildings and people; he could see the bright scarlet-and-silver canopy of the Ellcrys. The city of the Elves and its inhabitants were reemerging, coming back from their confinement.

Then there was a wrenching of earth and rock, and the entire bluff shuddered with the weight of Arborlon settling into place. Like mist, the light swirled about the Elven city and its people, a hazy curtain slowly being lifted. The wind built to a fever pitch, and the light assumed a liquid appearance. Within the soup, buildings and roadways, gardens and trees, and people and animals assumed a sharper definition. There was an odd sense of two worlds coming together, a blending of the one with the other.

Then the wind diminished, the light faded, and it was finished. Arborlon stood before them, sprawled across the whole of the bluff running back into the trees beyond, looking just as it had when Kirisin had used the Loden to close it away.

A crowd was already starting to gather, Elves coming out from their homes and along the pathways, filling up that piece of the bluff closest to where Kirisin and his companions stood. They were looking around, as if not quite sure where they were or what had happened. Reasonable enough, Logan thought. He stayed in the background, letting Kirisin and his sister step forward to meet those they had left behind. A few hands waved and a few voices called. There was shock on the faces of many and tears in more than a few eyes. Daylight mingled with shadows to streak the whole of the bluff in gold and black layers that gave those assembled the look of exotic creatures.

Then a single figure broke from the crowd, a pinch-faced boy about Kirisin's age who approached with a wide grin.

"Kirisin!" he greeted, embracing him.

"Biat!" Kirisin replied, and hugged him back.

When they broke apart, the other boy glanced down at the Loden, which his friend was still clutching in a death grip, and declared with a bright laugh, "You have a lot of explaining to do."

■ ■ ■ ■

On that same day, at the other end of the valley, Hawk looked out at the setting sun and prepared to say good-bye. He wasn't at all sure how to go about it. He guessed that when you came right down to it, there wasn't any good way. But his dream of the King of the Silver River had been sharp and clear, so there wasn't any point in trying to avoid what was coming. Perhaps he had always known this moment would arrive, even after they had reached their destination and he had hoped his work finished.

The dream only confirmed what he already knew was true.

"It is time, young one."

The old man speaks the words gently, but they cut him like a knife. He doesn't want to hear them, hasn't wanted even to think of them. The old man stands before him, his seamed and bearded countenance unexpectedly kind, and waits for his response.

"I am ready," he says. "But I am afraid."

Tessa came up beside him and took his arm, squeezing it. "What are you thinking about?"

"You and me. The baby." He put his arm around her and pulled her against him. "About how lucky we are."

She took his hand and put it on her belly, where the first faint swelling had begun. "It won't be long. I think it will be a boy."

He started to say something in reply, but his voice caught in his throat. "I have something to do," he said finally. "Back up in the pass."

"Right now?"

"It would be better."

"But it's almost dark."

"That won't matter."

She looked at him carefully. "Wait until morning. Please?"

He hesitated. "All right," he agreed.

He waited until it was fully dark and she was asleep, then he rose from their bed and slipped from their shelter. He walked steadily from there, not looking back, trying not to think of what he was leaving. The air was cool and still, and the sky was filled with stars. The way was brightly lit, the path easy to follow. He took time to recall memories of his days with the Ghosts, of their life in the city and then on the road, of each of them in turn, calling up their faces and holding them before him in his mind like pictures from a camera. He wished he could have said good-bye to them, could have told them how much they meant to him, could have tried to convey what he was feeling.

But that would have been so difficult. There was no easy way to say what needed saying.

He would have to trust that they would be able to imagine the words he would have said simply by knowing him.

"There is no need to be frightened, Hawk," the King of the Silver River says, smiling. "Your magic will protect you. There will be no pain. There will only be peace."

"What am I to do?"

"You are to go to the head of the pass that brought you into the valley. You will know what to do when you get there."

He already knows, although he doesn't say so. He thinks, again, that perhaps he has always known. He has brought his followers to this place of safety, brought them through the wilderness and out of the path of the destruction that is coming. Only one thing remains in order for them to be made secure. Only he can provide it.

"It is because of who you are," says the old man. "A gypsy morph, a creature of wild magic, a giver of special gifts. To those you lead, you give the gift of life."

Thinking of it now, he hoped that it was true. He needed to believe that it was why he was making this journey. He needed to feel that it mattered in the way he wanted it to.

As he climbed into the mountains from the valley floor, he paused to look back. The starlight was bright enough that he could see to the far horizons. Bits and pieces of the valley floor were visible, as well. From the camp he had departed, a few lights glowed in the darkness. Not everyone was sleeping. He experienced a sudden urge to turn back, to return to what he so badly wanted to hold on to. But the urge came and went, and he began to climb once more.

When he reached the head of the pass, he stopped to collect himself. He was visibly shaking by now, and his fear of what was going to happen was almost overwhelming. He replayed in his mind the words of the King of the Silver River, reassuring himself that the old man would not have lied. He reminded himself of his origins, of the power that was given him at birth, of the magic that had served him so well. It would not fail him now, he told himself. Nor would he fail in his duty.

It *was* a duty, after all. It sounded strange to say so, but it was what he had been given to do. To keep them protected. To keep them safe. Those he had brought to this place, friends and family and strangers alike. They were his responsibility, and he must embrace that responsibility as a soldier would his duty.

Still.

He squeezed his eyes shut and whispered Tessa's name.

"How can I just leave them?" he asks the old man. "My wife and child, my friends, all those who care about me?"

The King of the Silver River places a hand on his shoulder. "You won't be leaving them forever. Only for a little while."

Hawk does not know what he means, but he is not reassured. Leaving them at all seems wrong. He thinks that this is unfair, to require him to do this after he has already done so much. He did not ask for this responsibility. He did not ask to have his life directed so. All he has ever wanted is a family, and now it is to be taken away from him. How can anyone make such a sacrifice?

"I don't know if I can do this," he says.

"I don't know that, either," the old man agrees. "Yet you must."

He looked westward then across the vast reaches of the empty, barren land the caravan crossed in coming here, and was reminded anew what the rest of the world was like. In that moment he was reminded, as well, of the dark and twisted place the world would become in the aftermath of the approaching destruction. He could not allow this valley, this newly found haven, and all those he had brought here to live, to fall under that shadow. He could not permit such a monstrous subversion.

But he would be doing so if he failed to act now, as the King of the Silver River had told him he must.

There was no point in waiting any longer.

He took a moment to calm himself, breathing in the night air and staring upward at the stars. He was standing at the highest point of the pass, directly at its center. From this vista, he could see the mountains that ringed the valley, the valley itself, and everything that lay within its vast cradle. Even though the details were hidden by the darkness, he could see them in his mind.

He knelt and placed his hands against the earth.

Slowly, ever so slowly, the magic began to build within him as the familiar sensations began to surface. He took his time letting it do so, giving it space and freedom to find the necessary level of intensity. He knew what was needed, but not what it would take. He could only assume that the magic he wielded was sufficient and the price it would demand bearable. He knelt with his eyes closed and his head bent, with his arms braced in rigid support, his back bowed, a supplicant seeking relief.

It took a long time for the magic within to fuse with the magic without. When it did, he felt himself begin to join with the earth; felt the elements that composed its body and the life that it sustained to find a home in him. In the smells and tastes and sounds and feel of the world, he found himself made whole, all his separate parts become one. He was the world, and the world was in him.

It was the strangest feeling.

It made him smile.

Then the ground heaved beneath him, and dozens of tiny vents opened from deep underground. A fine gray mist rose into the night, layering the cool air. An opaque curtain rose and spread, winding outward in a vast spiral, filling up the open space with layered shrouds that draped the darkness, one on top of the other. From the place where Hawk knelt, the mist began to infiltrate the trees and rocks and then the mountains themselves. It gained speed and height and thickness, a silent storm front wrapping about, running north and south for miles before bending east and closing the haven that sheltered his followers like a giant's hands about a cup.

The mountains and the valley they cradled disappeared. Rocks, trees, cliffs, grasses, streams, and rivers — all that encompassed the perimeter of the peaks and their protected valley — slowly faded away.

Hawk's strength was drained from him as his gypsy morph magic was steadily, implacably leached away.

I am so tired, he thought near the end.

Then the mist swallowed him.

When the residents of the camp that housed the children and their protectors woke the

625

following morning, they noticed the difference in their world right away. The light was altered, although no one was able to agree in what way. The sky was clear and cloudless, a day like any other except that it wasn't. There were changes in the texture of the air, in the slant of the sunlight, in the way that shadows fell and sounds reverberated.

There was a wall of mist that had settled into the mountains on all sides, thick and impenetrable, miles of it, encircling the whole of the valley.

Tessa stood beside Owl in the company of Sparrow, River, and Candle, staring at the mountains and waiting for Angel to return. It was nearing midday, and the Knight of the Word had been gone since early morning. She had left as soon as she had discovered the strange transformations, gone out into the mountains to discover its source. Others had wanted to go with her, but she had insisted that it would be safer for everyone if she went alone. So there had been nothing left for any of them to do but to wait for her return.

Tessa had waited with the others, although she already knew what had happened. Hawk had left during the night and climbed back up into the mountain pass as he had told her he must. He had done something with the magic, used it in the way that was meant to make them all safe.

Just as he had done when he had driven the rogue militia from the bridge and the demon army from the plains.

With one important difference. He had used the magic for the last time. He was gone, and he wasn't coming back.

She could barely keep her tears in check when Angel finally reappeared and walked toward them. She was prepared for what she was going to hear but unable to imagine living with what it meant. She had struggled all day to keep from breaking down completely, and several times had gone off alone to cry. Owl must have known, perhaps the others, as well, but no one had said anything.

Angel trudged up to them, her face reflecting frustration. "I couldn't find anything of the source," she said. "But something's certainly happened. That mist is impenetrable. No matter how often you go in, you come out again right where you started. As far as I can tell, it wraps around the entire valley. I tried everything to get through it. I even used the Word's magic. Nothing worked."

She looked from face to face, stopping finally with Owl. "It was Hawk who did this, wasn't it?"

Owl nodded. "Tessa told me that he said yesterday he was going back up into the pass to do something. She made him promise to wait until morning, but he went up sometime

627

during the night."

"I didn't see him," Angel said. "Are you sure he isn't here? He didn't come back?"

Heads shook slowly. Candle was crying soundlessly. Sparrow stood with her hands on Owl's shoulders, and River was hugging herself.

They tried not to look at Tessa, but they couldn't help themselves. She bore the weight of their shifting gazes for as long as she could and then walked away before they could see her break down.

THIRTY-FIVE

Wills walked the empty corridors of Hell, talking with the ghosts of the dead. A quarter mile underground, buried in his coffin of concrete and steel, he carried on his one-sided conversation with Abramson, Perlo, and Anderson — or was it Andrews? He could never remember her name. They had begun appearing to him a while back — he wasn't sure exactly how long — come to keep him company. They were only faint presences at first, shadowy and elusive, enough so that he wasn't sure if he was seeing things or not. It wasn't until they began to be there all the time that he knew they were real.

He hadn't understood what they were doing there, why they had returned, what mission they were on. Soldiers come back from the grave to haunt him — why? But after a time, he had come to realize their purpose. It wasn't so difficult to understand. Deep Rock was their home, the final resting place of their corporeal remains, which were still locked away in one of the storage rooms . . . although their bodies were beginning to rot now, he had noticed, even with the refrigeration units operating on high.

In any event, it made sense that they should return. Deep Rock was their home, just as it was his.

Until he joined them, of course. Which wouldn't be all that long. Which was why they had come back for him.

When you were a soldier, you never left your buddies behind. You always took them with you.

It touched him deeply that they would care that much about him, and he told them so repeatedly. Well, he told Perlo and Abramson, anyway. He didn't talk that much with the woman, and she didn't seem much interested in him, in any case. She only seemed interested in poking about through the complex, as if searching for something she had mislaid. He thought it might be the code that would have allowed them all access to the surface and freedom. But he couldn't be sure. He would have welcomed a chance at escape, even at this point. He would have taken it gladly, gone back to the surface, gone out into what remained of the world, even if it was just long enough to breathe the air and feel the sunlight on his skin.

He cried about it sometimes. He missed it so.

Most of it, he had long since forgotten. Time's passing had erased the particulars from his memory bank, and all he had left was a dimly remembered happiness at how it had made him feel. He asked Abramson and Perlo if it was like that with them, too, but they only shrugged. That was pretty much all they ever did when he asked them questions. But at least they were paying attention. Anderson never even did that.

"Got to make the rounds," he told them as he walked down the corridors of the missile complex, moving from room to room, checking the computers, the monitors, the screens, the windows to what remained of his connection to the outside world. Routine was important, he reminded them. Routine was what kept you busy and engaged. Routine was what kept you from going insane.

But he was having increasing difficulty understanding why any of this mattered. Routine did all the things he said it did, but to what end? He wasn't ever leaving this place; he had accepted that some time back. He wasn't ever going to get out, and no one besides his friends was ever going to get in. Time was going to pass, he was going to age, and sooner or later he was going to die. The inevitability of it was the eight-hundred-pound gorilla sitting on his lap. In the face of such an overwhelming truth, what did anything else matter?

His buddies had nothing to offer. They listened to his thoughts as he voiced them, considered his questions and shrugged.

The truth was, they had known all along something he was just beginning to realize. Even routine wasn't enough to keep your mental trolley on the tracks. Even routine could drive you crazy.

He paused at the reflective window of the door opening into the sick bay — as if the entire place wasn't one big sick bay, ha, ha, joke — and looked at himself in the glass. He didn't recognize the stranger looking back. Bearded, disheveled, hollow-eyed, and gaunt, the other man stared at him. A man who had let himself go, who had ceased to do anything to keep up his appearance, who had given up eating regularly, who seldom slept, who prowled the complex like the ghosts who kept him company.

A man who had become a ghost himself.

I know this man, he thought, but couldn't put a name to the face.

He shrugged his indifference, taking a page from the book of Abramson and Perlo. Didn't matter.

"Over here, we have the command center," he continued, his narration of his daily routine, a smooth and practiced recitation by now. "You may remember its purpose. The missiles are monitored from here. All of them, all over the United States. All those that haven't already been dispatched to their intended targets." He grinned knowingly. "The launch switches are kept under lock and key, even if there's no one but me left to launch them. Kind of silly at this point, when you think about it. I mean, why monitor all this when there's really no reason. You know, before we had a world to be concerned about. When we had people and animals and cities and towns and hope. When we had a working civilization. All gone now. All you have to do is look at the monitoring screens and you can tell. There's nothing out there. Nothing that matters, anyway. A few people, sure. A few monsters, too. But nothing of importance. Nothing that is going to change what's happened. We let it go too far for that. We let it decay like a set of bad teeth. We didn't brush. We didn't floss or rinse."

His grin widened. Excellent analogy, he told himself. He had gone away from his usual narration, but he didn't care. It felt good.

"You think about it a moment, you'll see I'm right. We just ignored what was right in front of our eyes. We didn't take care of business. Not the business that really mattered. We were too busy living our lives to do that. So now what do we have?"

He paused, considering. "I'll tell you what we have. We have what we deserve."

He saw both Abramson and Perlo nod in agreement and was encouraged. They understood. They knew he was right. That was a part of why they stayed with him. They liked listening to what he had to say. It helped pass the time for them, too.

Impulsively, he walked over to the command console and seated himself at the launch board. A faint memory surfaced of that time, now long past, when the last general strike had been called in from the National Command Authority, and he and the other key holder, Graves or whatever — now, *that* was an appropriate name — had activated the triggers to missiles housed in launch silos all over the country.

How long ago had that been, anyway?

He could do that again right now, if he chose. It was a thought that crossed his mind at least several times a day. His retinal scan and the keys slung around his neck were all that was needed. Once, he would have needed authority from farther up the chain of command, a direct order come down from the general. But there wasn't any chain of command left. There wasn't anyone left but himself. He had to accept that. All his efforts at communication with the outside world had failed. He still tried, now and then. He still kept an open channel on the broadband. He still scanned the surrounding countryside through the monitors. He still hoped.

But he knew it was pointless.

Why don't you just do it?

He jumped at the sound of the voice. It was Perlo who had spoken. But Perlo never spoke! None of his buddies did. He wheeled his chair around and stared at the other's face, shocked.

Really, I mean it. Why don't you just do it?

He knew what Perlo was talking about, and he was vaguely resentful that the other man thought he had a right to make such a suggestion. It wasn't up to him. He was dead, a ghost. What did he know?

But then he saw Abramson nodding in agreement. Abramson, for whom he had more respect, thought Perlo was right!

Wills stared at them for a moment and then turned back to the console, studying the blinking lights and the bright empty screens as if they had something to tell him. He thought about it for a long time, and the prospect became a faint buzzing in his brain that teased at him with feathery touches, causing him to itch all over.

Why not? He could launch just one, see what happened. Just one.

What difference could it possibly make?

Once, not that long ago, such an act would have been unthinkable. But he had become increasingly convinced that no one deserved to live once he was gone. After all, what had they done to help look after things? He had seen what was out there, and it wasn't human. Or not human enough to matter.

635

Even so, he still required a better reason than that. He had that much discipline left in him.

You launch one, you might attract attention. Someone might come for you, get you out.

Perlo again. He glared over his shoulder at the other man, wanting him to mind his own business. The command center was his responsibility. The missiles were in his care. No one had the right to tell him what to do with them. Certainly not a ghost.

But Perlo did have a point. If there were still someone out there with the right training, they might be able to come for him. It was possible, after all. He couldn't see everywhere. There might be someone left.

The faces of his wife and boys stared out at him from the framed picture on the shelf in front of him. He had abandoned them. He had left them to die. He could see it in their eyes. They knew.

He sat there for a long time, staring at nothing. He forgot about Perlo and Abramson. He forgot about everything but his dead family and his lost life. He began to cry softly.

"What the hell?" he whispered.

Impulsively he pulled out the red keys and inserted them into the locks. He leaned forward to allow for the retinal scan, waited for the clearance authorization to kick in, and turned the keys. The panel concealing the launch switches slid back. He heard the locks to the switches releasing, one after the other. And then the lights above the switches turned amber and everything was activated.

Just one.

He studied the switches intently, trying to decide which. There was a book with codes designating targets and launch sites, but he didn't know where that was anymore. He wasn't entirely sure he remembered the codes, in any case. Five years was a long time to remember something you didn't ever use.

Abramson and Perlo were standing at his back, watching him. Anderson was there, too, come to join them. Maybe it was time, he thought. Maybe they knew. He studied the switches some more.

Finally, he flipped one.

The amber light turned green, blinking furiously. The missile was launched.

He waited for a response — any response — but there was none forthcoming. Not from the console, not from the screens, not from those watching, not even from his own emotional center. It was as if nothing had happened.

Because, he thought, nothing had. A missile was launched, a target was obliterated, and nothing was changed. Nothing would ever change again because there was nothing left.

He shook his head in despair. He was just so tired of it all, so sick and tired. None of it made any difference, did it? What was the point of anything that he did or didn't do? He was just passing time until it ran out and he died.

He was just waiting for the inevitable.

Perlo's soft whisper brushed his ear. *Try another.*

He was surprised to discover that he liked the idea. He liked it a lot.

Why not? Matter of fact, why just one?

He flipped them all.

The boy who was the gypsy morph slept within the mists, encapsulated and sheltered in the way of the storybook princesses of old. He had no need of food or drink, and the passing of time meant nothing to him. Still, he was neither comatose nor unaware. Though he slept, he was hard at work fulfilling his destiny.

In a dream-like existence, that part of him that had always been a thing of wild magic was reaching beyond his human form and its limited abilities to complete the task of strengthening the barrier he had created to protect those who depended on him for their safety. The wild magic flew through the mists, an invisible presence, and everywhere it touched it left a part of itself in reserve. The mists must last a long time, it knew, and so they must have durability and resilience. No stress or strain, no matter how massive, must be allowed to break them down.

When the bombs exploded and the shock

waves struck, the wall was ready. When the winds blew and the fallout began, the walls held firm. When the nuclear winter settled down across cities and plains, engulfing entire countries and in some cases whole continents, the wall kept it out. It was made of the same wild magic that creates a gypsy morph, magic rare and unfathomable, magic that comes along only now and then to do something that has never been seen before.

The King of the Silver River had understood its potential, had housed it when it had taken the boy's form, had cared for and nurtured it, had released it back into the world when there was no other choice, and then waited to see what would happen. No one could ever know for sure how it would respond, not even him. Not even the Word could shape wild magic. It took its own form, as it had done since the beginning of time. It served its own purpose.

Time after time it circled the mountains that cradled the valley, infusing itself within the guardian mists, bleeding out of the boy who slept, and becoming what it must. The wild magic would endure until its time was finished, and then it would go back into the ether and wait until one day it would be born again into the world. The mists thickened and strengthened, and the madness and destruction of civilization's collapse were locked outside the valley in which the survivors of the caravan were beginning their new lives.

When it was all used up, drained away entirely, and all that remained of the boy was flesh and blood and bone, the boy awoke. No longer a gypsy morph, the wild magic no longer a part of him, he stood within the mists and remembered that his life was something more than what the wild magic had demanded of him. There was a residue, a leaving. That part of him that was human had loved a girl and fathered a child. That part of him had lived among other children, who had been his friends and been left behind when he had come into the mountains and created the wall of mist.

He wanted to go back to them. He wanted to go home.

So the boy Hawk, who was a man now, a man whose mortal coil was no different from that of any other, walked out of the mists into the valley, alive and well and whole, and went in search of his life.

ABOUT THE AUTHOR

Terry Brooks is the *New York Times* bestselling author of more than twenty-five books, including the Genesis of Shannara novels *Armageddon's Children* and *The Elves of Cintra; The Sword of Shannara;* the Voyage of the Jerle Shannara trilogy: *Ilse Witch, Antrax,* and *Morgawr;* the High Druid of Shannara trilogy: *Jarka Ruus, Tanequil,* and *Straken;* the nonfiction book *Sometimes the Magic Works: Lessons from a Writing Life;* and the novel based upon the screenplay and story by George Lucas, *Star Wars®: Episode I The Phantom Menace.*™ His novels *Running with the Demon* and *A Knight of the Word* were selected by the *Rocky Mountain News* as two of the best science fiction/fantasy novels of the twentieth century. The author was a practicing attorney for many years but now writes full-time. He lives with his wife, Judine, in the Pacific Northwest.

www.shannara.com
Terrybrooks.net